Eighteenth-Century Novels by Women

Isobel Grundy, Editor

The Injur'd Husband: or, The Mistaken Resentment

and

Lasselia: or, The Self-Abandon'd

Eliza Haywood

~

Jerry C. Beasley, Editor

THE UNIVERSITY PRESS OF KENTUCKY

Publication of this volume was made possible in part
by a grant from the National Endowment for the Humanities.

Scholarly publisher for the Commonwealth,
serving Bellarmine College, Berea College, Centre College of Kentucky,
Eastern Kentucky University, The Filson Club Historical Society,
Georgetown College, Kentucky Historical Society,
Kentucky State University, Morehead State University,
Murray State University, Northern Kentucky University,
Transylvania University, University of Kentucky,
University of Louisville, and Western Kentucky University.

Editorial and Sales Offices: The University Press of Kentucky
663 South Limestone Street, Lexington, Kentucky 40508-4008

03 02 01 00 99 5 4 3 2 1

Frontispiece: Eliza Haywood, by George Vertue (1684-1756),
engraved from the original by Jacques Parmentier (1658-1730)
and first published as the frontispiece to her *Secret Histories,
Novels and Poems,* 1724 (dated 1725). By permission of the Rare Book
and Special Collections Library, University of Illinois at Urbana-Champaign.

Library of Congress Cataloging-in-Publication Data

Haywood, Eliza Fowler, 1693?-1756
The injur'd husband, or, The mistaken resentment ; Lasselia, or, The self-abandon'd /
Eliza Haywood ; Jerry C. Beasley, editor.
p. cm. — (Eighteenth-century novels by women)
Includes bibliographical references (p.)
ISBN 0-8131-2104-3 (cloth : alk. paper).—ISBN 0-8131-0961-2 (pbk. : alk. paper)
1. Man-woman relationships—France—Fiction. 2. Women—France—Fiction. I.
Haywood, Eliza Fowler, 1693?-1756. Lasselia, or, The self-abandon'd. II. Beasley, Jerry C.
III. Title. IV. Title: Lasselia, or, The self-abandon'd. V. Title: Lasselia. VI. Title: Self-
abandon'd. VII. Series.
PR3506.H94I5 1999
823'.5—dc21 98-30252

This book is printed on acid-free recycled paper meeting
the requirements of the American National Standard
for Permanence of Paper for Printed Library Materials.

Manufactured in the United States of America

Contents

Illustrations

Preface

The Injur'd Husband and *Lasselia* have never before been edited, and they are only rarely even mentioned in studies of early English fiction. Their obscurity requires that they be placed in context for the modern reader. The introduction to this edition seeks to provide the necessary context, with special emphasis upon the biographical background of Eliza Haywood's life and career; it concludes with a discussion calling attention to the main centers of interest to be found in the two novels. Annotation of the texts is relatively light, as Haywood was not an allusive writer; the explanatory notes are generally confined to the identification of historical persons and places, to definitions of obscure or archaic words (if not clear from context), to clarification of obsolete usages, and, for *The Injur'd Husband,* to commentary on the French names assigned to most of the characters. The *Oxford English Dictionary* has been consulted for definitions of English words; the source for French words has been the *Larousse French-English / English-French Dictionary,* edited by Marguerite-Marie Dubois et al. (Paris: Librairie Larousse, 1960).

No edition like this one could ever be prepared without the generous assistance of friends and colleagues. I have a number of such people to thank, for kindnesses too numerous and varied to mention; I shall trust each of those I name here to remember for what favor or favors my gratitude is due: Phyllis J. Guskin, John Harwood, Matthew Kinservik, Donald C. Mell, Lois Potter, Cedric Reverand, and James A. Winn. For their patient and always prompt assistance I wish also to thank the many helpful staff members at the Boston Public Library, the Newberry Library, and the libraries of Yale University, the University of Pennsylvania, the University of Delaware, the University of Michigan, the University of Illinois, and the University of Chicago. Christine Blouch has kindly shared her work--and her enthusiasm for Haywood--with me; I am especially grateful to her. My graduate assistants, Sue Anne Beyer and Greg Weight, suffered long over the texts of *The Injur'd Husband* and *Lasselia,* helping me to get them right; their labors were invaluable in this and many other ways, and I thank them heartily. In the last phase of my work, David Oakleaf provided a very careful reading of the entire manuscript, and Isobel Grundy proved her worth as a wise and dedicated series editor; I am indebted to them both for saving me from a number of embarrassing errors, omissions, and lapses in style. Finally, I wish to express my appreciation to the University of Delaware for granting me a sabbatical leave so that I might devote full time to the edition at a crucial stage of its progress toward completion.

Introduction

The Life and Career

The facts of Eliza Haywood's life, and to some extent those of her career, have always been frustratingly elusive for a writer so prolific and so popular as she was, and their elusiveness has caused nearly everyone who has attempted to chronicle them to fall into numerous errors—a situation that has begun to change only during the last few years.[1] Haywood herself bears a primary responsibility for the general failure of those who have tried to tell her story to get it right. According to her very first biographer, David Erskine Baker, she deliberately suppressed much of what a person like himself would have wished to know. In his entry on Haywood for a biographical dictionary of the English theater titled *The Companion to the Play-House* (1764), Baker wrote that she feared the mangling of her character after her death "by the Intermixture of Truth and Falshood with her History," and so she "laid a solemn Injunction on a particular Person, who was well acquainted with all the Particulars of it, not to communicate to any one the least Circumstance relating to her." The "particular Person," whoever she or he may have been, seems to have carried out Haywood's injunction most faithfully, and with great success, obscuring not only the juicy details of her youthful love affairs and other regrettable frivolities (as she herself characterized them in a later phase of her life[2]) but also the essential facts of her birth and marriage along with the full truth about her professional activities during the extended period beginning in the early 1730s when she departed from her earlier practice to write anonymously and, it appears, without seeking the kind of public recognition enjoyed by others—such as Samuel Richardson—who did not sign their names to their works.

Specifically, the major errors of Haywood's biographers have been these: that she was most certainly born to Robert and Elizabeth Fowler of London, a family of shopkeepers, probably in January 1692/93 but possibly as early as

January 1689/90;[3] that she married the clergyman Valentine Haywood in 1711 and then eloped from him ten years later, presumably because her conduct as actress and author met with his disapproval; and that Alexander Pope's blast at her in Book 2 of the 1728 *Dunciad* (lines 149-58) all but destroyed both her reputation and her career, causing her virtual disappearance from the public scene for more than a decade.[4] Christine Blouch's very welcome correction of these errors has opened the way for new understanding of Haywood's personal life and literary career—the two are closely intertwined—so that we may now see her "History" with a more accurate and appreciative eye. A summary of that "History" follows, in some detail, but it may be well before beginning it to set the record straight regarding the errors just cited.

The facts about Haywood's birth and parentage are still in some doubt, but Blouch has made an interesting case for the Fowlers of Harnage Grange, Shropshire, as the family into which she was born, citing a manuscript source in which she actually claims to be "nearly related to Sir Richard of the Grange"; a daughter of these Fowlers, Sir Richard's sister Elizabeth, was christened at the family parish church in Shropshire on 12 January 1692/3.[5] While there is as yet no absolute proof that this Elizabeth Fowler was the same person as the later Eliza Fowler Haywood, the circumstantial evidence for the identification is stronger than that for any other. All early biographical sources, including David Erskine Baker, give 1693 as the date of Haywood's birth, but there is no record whatsoever of a daughter born in that year to the London Fowlers preferred by her first modern biographer, George Frisbie Whicher—their Elizabeth made her appearance in the world three years earlier, and Whicher speculates (2) that when she grew up to be Eliza Haywood she simply lied about her age. This seems unlikely, though admittedly it is possible, given Haywood's known desire to blur the facts of her life. Whicher strains determinedly at his preferred identification of Haywood's parents, but there are very good reasons, besides the verified date of birth, to favor the Shropshire over the London Fowlers. Among the most crucial is that her membership in a baronet's family would help to explain how it was that Haywood had access to an education "more liberal," as she described it herself, than that usually available to women in her day.[6] Such status was not a necessary condition for this kind of opportunity, but the Shropshire Fowlers were cultivated and well connected (one in-law was Sir Hans Sloane, whose vast library and collections of artifacts formed the nucleus of the British Museum); and Haywood certainly was, by comparison with most of her female contemporaries, a learned woman: she possessed at least some command of the classics, though not in their original languages, and her work displays a broad and deep understanding of history both ancient and modern, of English and Continental literature, of playwrights and theatrical tradition. Finally, there is a most intriguing hint of her family connection in *The Injur'd Husband,* when the brother of the heroine Montamour (a fictionalized representation of Haywood herself) is characterized by the narrator in a gratuitous aside as a person of "great Employments," and these are of just the sort (he is a magistrate engaged both with the law and with politics) that might occupy an important provincial baronet like Sir Richard Fowler.[7]

If some uncertainty remains about Haywood's birth and parentage, none lingers over the question of her supposed marriage to the Rev. Valentine Haywood. Blouch has established once and for all that this marriage did not happen, that the Rev. Haywood married Elizabeth Foord, and that this marriage occurred in 1706, five years before he was supposed by Whicher to have married Elizabeth Fowler.[8] Neither Blouch nor anyone else has been able to determine just whom our Eliza Fowler did marry, or when; but by 1715, when she appeared on the Dublin stage in Thomas Shadwell's adaptation of *Timon of Athens,* she was Eliza Haywood. Nothing more is known of her marriage, except that Haywood herself, in two letters written late in the 1720s, characterized it as "unfortunate" and claimed that she was left a widow at a young age, two circumstances that helped to turn her inclination for writing into a necessity.[9]

And write she did. Beginning with *Love in Excess* in 1719-20, she published more than thirty novels (some of which we would call novellas), a biography, and four translations within a brief frenzied period of ten years; she also wrote poems, a series of pamphlets, and three plays (all produced in London theaters); and her works were twice gathered into popular collected editions.[10] In the midst of all this activity she found time and energy for occasional appearances on the stage as an actress. How she was able to maintain such a pace is almost beyond imagining; no doubt she found necessity an exacting taskmaster. But success itself may also have been an equally strong encouragement. Her stories of strong women, their men and their amorous intrigues, found a receptive audience that was always eager for more. It was the popularity of her tales of passion and intrigue, sometimes based on the characters of real people, that so distressed contemporaries like Swift and Pope, who clearly believed that Haywood was contributing mightily to a cultural degeneracy, and who also felt strongly that such performances from a woman were disgraceful. For a woman to break from her proper role of silence into the public realm of authorship was bad enough in its own right; for her to write so openly of sexual experience, or to engage in personal satire (as Haywood often did in her stories), was an outrage. Her predecessor Delarivière Manley, in *The Secret History of Queen Zarah* (1705) and *The New Atalantis* (1709-10), had sensationalized court life and satirically reduced politics to an exercise in sexual adventuring. Haywood, following Manley's lead, sought to turn an equally skeptical female eye upon the conduct of public people and, in the interest of "exposing" their real characters, to reinvent them for her audience as frauds, dangerously driven by twin desires for sex and power.

Pope was especially incensed by Haywood's *Secret History of the Present Intrigues of the Court of Caramania* (1726), a chronicle of scandal in high places in which she savaged the poet's neighbor and friend, Mrs. Henrietta Howard, as the licentious Ismonda, mistress to Prince Theodore (a portrait of the Prince of Wales, soon to be George II) and, as such, the destroyer both of the prince's family and of the stability of the court itself.[11] Swift was equally incensed, but confined himself to a letter in which he described Haywood as "a stupid, infamous, scribbling woman."[12] He was not alone in his assessment, private though it was, and indeed his very terms of opprobrium were all too often repeated by others throughout Haywood's career and after. Pope was still more blunt than his crony Swift, and brutally public. By enshrining Haywood in the *Dunciad* he tried to shame her, picturing her as the quintessential licentious woman, two illegitimate babies at her "cow-like" breasts and adorned with "flowers and pearls," her private person and her public character as an author united in a scathing representation that exceeded—at least in its intensity—anything Haywood herself had ever been guilty of.[13] In retrospect one is tempted to say that the shame here is all Pope's.

The *Dunciad* portrait was devastating. But it did not, as was once thought, succeed in its real object, which was to ruin Haywood professionally—and here we may proceed at last to correction of the third major error committed by most of her biographers. Haywood hardly slowed her pace at all for the remainder of the 1720s, and when she finally did so it was probably more because of a shift in taste away from her forte, the tale of amorous intrigue, than a result of Pope's maliciousness. For that matter, her level of activity did not decline by much; she simply diverted her energies. Throughout the 1730s she was heavily engaged in theatrical work as playwright and performer, most conspicuously with Henry Fielding's company at the Little Theater in the Haymarket. During this same period she produced a major work of literary history titled *The Dramatic Historiographer; or, The British Theatre Delineated* (1735), the first thing of its kind ever to be written by a woman;[14] and she published a substantial political romance, *The Adventures of Eovaai, Princess of Ijaveo* (1736), which treats the character of the prime minister, Sir Robert

Walpole, with energetic severity and which no doubt helped the Opposition in its campaign against Walpole's corrupt administration.[15] In the 1740s Haywood resumed her career as a novelist full steam, producing about a dozen separate works in fifteen years, including one of the first important parodies of Richardson's *Pamela* (*Anti-Pamela; or, Feign'd Innocence Detected,* 1741) and, ten years later, the narrative for which she is now perhaps best known, *The History of Miss Betsy Thoughtless* (1751). Meanwhile she renewed her interest in translation (three works), launched a Covent Garden publishing business in 1741 that she kept going for eight years or perhaps longer, wrote a vade mecum for girls in service (*A Present for a Servant-Maid,* 1743), and conducted three separate periodicals. The best known of her periodicals, *The Female Spectator* (1744-46), was the first monthly magazine written by a woman specifically for women. Thus Haywood finished her career as she had begun it, in a relentless flurry of varied and very public activity, in the process reaffirming her presence as a literary professional of exceptional gifts, amazing energy, and astonishing versatility.

The key word here is *professional.* As a writerly presence in the first half of the eighteenth century, Haywood bears comparison with such professional *men* of letters as Daniel Defoe, Tobias Smollett, and Samuel Johnson. Like all of them she practiced in a variety of genres and, always at lower pay than her efforts were worth, made her living with her pen. She was not the first woman in England to live by writing; that distinction belongs to Aphra Behn, whose mantle passed first to Delarivière Manley and then to Haywood. These three—Behn, Manley, and Haywood—came to be known as the "fair Triumvirate of Wit";[16] and together, against the great odds posed by male domination in the world of writing, they proclaimed both the woman's ability and her right to practice the profession of letters. Their achievements helped to create a legacy without which later generations of female authors might well have needed to find something else to do. Haywood deserves particular recognition for her part in creating that legacy, since her career lasted so many years (almost forty) and since it ranged over so many forms—fiction, translation, poetry, the drama, journalism, literary history.

Haywood was, of course (and still is), best known as a novelist, and there can be no arguing the importance of her example throughout all of the early formative years—from the 1720s into the 1750s—when the novel as we know it first began to define itself as a "new" form. Altogether she published more than four dozen works of fiction, the sheer volume of her output as a storyteller far exceeding the achievement of all of her contemporaries, male and female alike. The kinds of stories she told, as Ros Ballaster has observed, succeeded in "constructing the modern female reader of romance fiction" because they projected erotic fantasies while making them safe for their audience by routinely taming or punishing sexually aggressive behavior.[17] In other words, Haywood boldly represented the power of female desire, while shrewdly grasping and articulating the paradox that such desire always involved for women of her generation. What she understood was that, however real and palpable, it could not be acted out, but only indulged in an act of the imagination by participation in a fantasy; and it finally had to be restrained (fantasy itself had to come to an end) if the woman was to live without imperiling herself.

Sexual desire in Haywood's narratives is exactly that, and her dramatizations of it frequently titillate; their appeal is direct and immediate. But female sexual desire is also a metaphor for a larger, more comprehensive desire—for freedom from constraint, for entry into the forbidden world of masculine adventurousness, for an unfettered expressiveness. Haywood herself perilously lived out the desire of which she wrote, daring to express herself and, most scandalously, to describe female sexuality in action—drawing, no doubt, upon her personal experience as an unconventional woman. The restraints of punishment or transformation she imposed upon her aberrant female characters—Mary Anne Schofield has called them rebels[18]—she did not impose upon herself; for she wrote without ceasing, always doing the unwomanly thing and thus achieving on behalf of her female readers what (with few exceptions) they could not achieve for themselves: an actively independent, successful life in a public world upon which she dared to intrude and which no other woman could enter without an equivalent sacrifice of her own safety from reproach. Haywood, continually reproached, was a brave as well as a talented woman, and her determined professionalism must have provided a great many members of her audience with vicarious pleasures actually exceeding those provided by her bold heroines.

Her very first novel, *Love in Excess; or, The Fatal Enquiry,* at once defined the appeal of the kind of amatory fiction she would continue to write for almost a dozen years and launched her career as a professional author with a measure of commercial success that was surely beyond anything she could have dreamed of. The elaborate plot of the work's three parts centers upon the libertine Count D'Elmont, who, finally transformed by the example of the matchless Melliora, marries her as the narrative comes to an end; but the most compelling figure among the large cast of characters is the conniving Alovisa, who pursues D'Elmont until he is persuaded to marry her but who gets her comeuppance when she is accidentally killed by his hand. Alovisa is a sexual and emotional predator, and it is through her that Haywood first exemplifies the fascinations and the dangers of the woman who refuses to be bound by conventions of silence and passivity. If social reality in the early eighteenth required that Alovisa be punished and then displaced for her transgressions, Haywood nonetheless—without approving her conduct any more than she approved D'Elmont's—made her the novel's absolute center of primal energy and a striking instance of the urgency of female passion. Surely it was the disruptiveness of her presence and her scheming, much more than the steady progress of the story's assorted adventurers and virgins toward the calm stasis of the several marriages with which it concludes, that captivated Haywood's audience. At any rate *Love in Excess* was a bona fide bestseller; as many as seven editions of the work appeared between 1719-20 and 1732, and indeed during this period only Defoe's *Robinson Crusoe* among native works of contemporary novelistic fiction proved more popular with readers.

It would be inaccurate and unfair to say that, having discovered a successful formula in her first novel, Haywood merely rushed to repeat and embellish it—like some drugstore romance writer of the twentieth century—so as to ensure her continued popularity. Her work for the next several years was much too varied to permit such an assessment. But she certainly seems to have been aware of the nerve she had touched in her readers; and, no less alert to the marketplace than her contemporary Defoe, she cultivated the field of amatory fiction with a determined vigor. Her great subject throughout the years of the 1720s was female passion in a context of forbidding, powerful, and inevitable constraints. Her explorations of this subject all betray a real ambivalence, paralleling the ambivalence that must also have been in the minds of her readers. In the end her stories routinely represent the constraints, as if somehow their author knew they must if they were to be read. Perhaps Haywood even approved submission to them—grudgingly—because, in her personal life, she knew firsthand the consequences of failure to do so. The point here is that the young writer Eliza Haywood was not some zealous revolutionary, an early hero on the ramparts of feminism, as modern commentators have occasionally made her out to be—in the process reducing her complexity of character and sensibility to an ideologically convenient simplicity. She was, instead, a thoughtful—if also opportunistic—interpreter of the gender politics of her time, when patriarchal principles of authority still determined what was what in the world of real experience and when women were only just beginning to awaken into a modern consciousness of themselves as potentially powerful sexual and social beings.

Haywood wrote so much during the decade of the 1720s that only the highlights can be mentioned here. In story after story she gave her readers the fantasy experience she knew they wanted. Her women are sometimes monsters of aggression and ruthless exploiters of the power politics of sexuality—*The Injur'd Husband's* Baroness de Tortillée, for example, or the aptly named Gigantilla of *The Perplex'd Dutchess; or, Treachery Rewarded* (1727). Alantha, in *The Force of Nature; or, The Lucky Disappointment* (1724), is another such woman, though somewhat less outrageous in her schemes for personal gratification and more moderate in her sensual appetites. The appeal of these aberrant women and others like them is obvious. They are almost transvestites, duplicating in their behavior the vile excesses of the male libertines who also figure in almost every Haywood narrative and over whom her women often triumph; through such characters as the baroness, Gigantilla, and Alantha, Haywood daringly imagines a kind of female liberation, and by finally rejecting their conduct as morally repugnant, she simultaneously condemns the patterns of male sexual predation they have copied. The freedom to use and to violate the objects of one's desire is no freedom at all, for female or male, Haywood seems to suggest; at least it is not a freedom worth having, for unbridled passion is destructive to the world beyond the self and is disastrously binding and confining in its effects upon the individual moral life. In Haywood's view, desire without regulation sets a trap, constructs a prison, for the desiring as well as the desired.

Confinement of another sort is a frequent theme in these narratives, as a good many of Haywood's imaginary people are quite literally confined by the actions of others; they are usually virginal young girls who have displeased their fathers or guardians by wishing for lovers or husbands they are not allowed to have. In *The Force of Nature,* the heroine Felisinda is sent to a convent for daring to yearn after someone her father cannot approve, and is then further victimized by her supposed friend Alantha, whose help she enlists in carrying on a correspondence with the forbidden one. Haywood complicates the plot by revealing that the man Felisinda loves is actually her half-brother, thus introducing a theme of incest (she does this in several other tales as well) that raises disturbing questions about the thrill of filial disobedience. The titular heroine of *Idalia; or, The Unfortunate Mistress* (1723) provides a different version of the virtuous girl, one whose life is distressed and even ruined by the effects of passion. No predatory aggressor, Idalia foolishly dallies with a man who ruins her by awakening her into awareness of her previously suppressed sexual nature, whereupon she flees and is thereafter repeatedly beset by rapacious men until at last, attempting to murder her original destroyer, she instead accidentally kills the one man she has ever loved and then, despairing, takes her own life.

Idalia's resemblances to *Lasselia*, published later in the same year, suggest that when writing the latter work Haywood felt she had not yet explored the full range of possibilities presented by the heroine of the former. Idalia—obedient, pious, chaste—falls into misery and disaster because she breaks from the mold of the dutiful daughter when her father forbids his house to the man who has teased her into desire so that he might seduce her. As in *The Force of Nature,* disobedience precedes the acting out of desire, but the consequences of both are much worse for the heroine. *Lasselia* tells a story that is at once simpler and more disturbing. An orphan at the court of Louis XIV and thus deprived of meaningful parental guidance, the heroine successfully resists the advances of the king but is then helpless before the attractions of the married man to whom she later loses her virginity, losing herself as well and at last disappearing altogether into a nunnery when her lover, de l'Amye, returns to his wife.[19] Haywood widens still further the range of her concern with the virtuous maiden when, in *Philidore and Placentia; or, L'Amour trop Delicat* (1727), she makes her heroine (named second in the title) an admirable exemplar of chastity, constancy, and generosity, rewarding her (after a succession of scarifying adventures, including slavery to a Moslem merchant in Persia) with the hand of her equally constant and virtuous lover, Philidore. This novel is, purely and simply, a romance of virtue triumphant, and as such it serves to counter the effects of Haywood's other narratives of the same period. Thematically it looks directly ahead to Richardson's *Pamela; or, Virtue Rewarded* while echoing the appeal of the pious Penelope Aubin's adventurous stories (most importantly *The Life of Madam de Beaumont,* 1721, and *The Life of Charlotta Du Pont,* 1723), which were themselves apparently written in part as alternatives to Haywood's *Love in Excess* and the numerous other amatory novels that so quickly followed it from her pen.

Structurally, *Philidore and Placentia* anticipates the complex dual plotting of *The Fortunate Foundlings* (1744), the most technically ambitious novel Haywood ever wrote. Tame though it may be by comparison with other early tales such as *The Perplex'd Dutchess* and *Idalia,* it is still an interesting experiment with the more circumspect subject matter and the more sophisticated formal designs that would characterize Haywood's later fiction. Neither *Philidore and Placentia,* however, nor any of her other youthful performances has interested recent critics so much as a novel that seems to have been hardly noticed at all when it first appeared, the "masquerade" story titled *Fantomina; or, Love in a Maze* (1724).[20] *Fantomina,* only one of several works in which Haywood used the theme of the masquerade as a way of projecting her heroines into the world,[21] is among the most skillfully conducted of her early narratives, but the extensive notice it has lately received may be owing just as much to its unhesitating (at least until the end) celebration of female perseverance in pursuit of the pleasures of conquest. It very easily satisfies the desire of some modern readers to see Haywood as a feminist ideologue, a position the full range of her work does not support, while it neatly fits the schematics of others who are more interested in the "masquerade" as a cultural topic than in Haywood. Still, *Fantomina* is worthy of the attention it has been getting, and some of the commentary on it has certainly helped to further a broader interest in its author's larger achievement.[22]

The novel plays cleverly upon the device of female disguise, as the heroine smoothly alternates between her true identity as an innocent (but, significantly, nameless) country girl just up to London and the adopted roles of courtesan (Fantomina), chambermaid (Celia), bereaved lady (the Widow Bloomer), and masked domino (the fair Incognita)—all in an attempt, not very successful, to win and then keep the affections of the rakish Beauplaisir. It is the ingenuity of Haywood's strategy, along with the ambiguity of its effects, that makes *Fantomina* such an intriguing performance. On the one hand the story is a demonstration of female intelligence and wiliness, an exhilarating portrait of a woman as accomplished at the male game of deception as any libertine. On the other, it is the dramatization of a series of severe losses. With every new disguise Haywood's heroine inevitably loses her true identity; she loses her virginity when Beauplaisir rapes her on the occasion of their first private assignation, and in the end, left pregnant by him, she loses all access to the public world in which she has so determinedly sought a meaningful place as she is obliged to retreat into the silent confinement of a convent. *Fantomina* thus provides the same fantasy of rebellion and liberation as so many others among Haywood's early amatory narratives, and likewise the same withdrawal into a recognition of the real truth about the limitations upon female ambition and desire. But it also provides an unusual and sobering emphasis upon the costs in denial of the self exacted by the exercise of imagination in the quest for an alternative life, a life of freedom and power—for a different version of the woman's story, as it were. One wonders whether, as she wrote, Haywood may have had in mind her personal experience as a maverick female author whose profession it was to construct the very fantasies she then felt it necessary to deny. In any case she knew that the trajectory defined by such fantasies could only leave the woman who followed it at the extreme outer margins of society, far more alone and unprotected than the most docile and submissive paragon of conventional virtue.

The most controversial works of Haywood's early period, and the ones that did most to put her at risk of complete marginalization, were her two chronicles of scandal in public places, the *Memoirs of a Certain Island Adjacent to the Kingdom of Utopia* (1724-25) and *The Secret History of the Present Intrigues of the Court of Caramania.* We have already noted that the latter of these works immediately precipitated Pope's attack on Haywood in the *Dunciad.* The former extends its range far beyond the confines of the Georgian court to include assaults against such personages as the unscrupulous publisher Edmund Curll, the dowager duchess of Marlborough (Sarah Churchill), the poet Richard Savage, and, of greatest personal importance to Haywood herself, the literary lady Martha Fowke Sansom. Haywood had earlier incorporated devices of the scandal chronicle in some of her novels—in *Fantomina,* for example, which purports to be (as its title page declares) "a Secret History of an Amour between two Persons of Condition," and, as we shall see, in *The Injur'd Husband.* But in *The Court of Caramania* and *Memoirs of a Certain Island* she tried her hand at full-blown imitations of that most famous of all previous works of its kind, Manley's *New Atalantis.* Both imitations were commercial successes, but from them Haywood no doubt earned more notoriety than cash. In any event they left her exposed to the most vicious attacks she had ever endured—from Pope, of course, but also from Savage, her former friend and lover, in a poem titled "The Authors of the Town" (1725) and, later, in a satire called *An Author to Be Lett* (1729).[23]

With *Memoirs of a Certain Island* Haywood indulged in an extensive interplay between her personal life and her public role as a writer, more extensive even than in the earlier *Injur'd Husband,* which glances significantly at some of the same people. Savage, the author of a laudatory prefatory poem affixed to her novel *The Rash Resolve,* was almost certainly the father of one of her illegitimate children (the father of the other was the playwright William Hatchett, her friend, lover, and sometime collaborator for more than twenty years[24]). The reason for their falling out remains unclear, but it may have arisen somehow from their mutual connection with Martha Fowke—so Haywood implies in *Memoirs of a Certain Island,* where she accuses Gloatitia (Fowke) of defaming her reputation to Riverius (Savage). With Savage and Fowke, and with the poet John Dyer, the playwright David Mallet, and the actress Susanna Centlivre, Haywood was a member of the London literary circle surrounding Aaron Hill (who was later to be Samuel Richardson's friend and frequent correspondent) in the early 1720s. Haywood and Fowke (herself a writer who dabbled in poetry and in 1723 completed a long autobiographical work) were rivals for Hill's admiration and affection; their relations with him appear to have been only platonic, but potent enough to make eventual enemies of the onetime friends.[25] By the time Haywood came to write *The Injur'd Husband* sometime during the year 1722, their rivalry had already turned nasty. In anticipation of her characterization of Fowke as Gloatitia—an exceedingly brash and licentious female—in *Memoirs of a Certain Island*, Haywood took her as the model for the rapacious, sexually voracious Baroness de Tortillée. Hill provided at least the inspiration for Beauclair, the wandering male momentarily enchanted by the baroness but at last tamed by the love of the virtuous Montamour (the name means "lover of Hill"), who seems intended to suggest Haywood herself. *The Injur'd Husband* is thus not only the story of an aberrant female whose career in aggression and sexual adventurousness comes to a necessary and inevitable end, but it is also—like *Memoirs of a Certain Island*—an exercise in personal vengeance. It is, in addition, an interesting experiment with the relations between fiction and contemporary history.

Haywood was by no means the first to conduct such an experiment. The blending of fact and fiction was a hallmark of seventeenth-century French romances like Madeleine de Scudéry's *Artamène, ou le Grand Cyrus* (1649-53) and *Clélie, histoire romaine* (1654-60). These works and others of the same kind enjoyed a long popularity in England, significantly influencing such writers as Manley and the more circumspect Jane Barker, whose *Love Intrigues; or, The History of the Amours of Bosvil and Galesia* (1713) and *A Patch-Work Screen for the Ladies* (1723)—among other works—mix explorations of the theme of unrequited female desire with glancing references to contemporary politics and social conditions. Haywood was influenced by the French romancers too. Like Manley and Barker, but with an ingenuity that only sometimes relied on identifiable correspondences, she made the intersections between the actual and the imagined a principal distinguishing feature of her fiction—in *The Injur'd Husband,* and in *Memoirs of a Certain Island* and the *Court of Caramania,* but also in *Fantomina, The Force of Nature, Philidore and Placentia, Love in Excess,* and many other narratives, amatory or scandalous, including *Lasselia.* For all their varied dependence upon remote or even exotic settings, romance plots, and grandiose names, such works seek to record—even more to interpret—the facts of real experience in the opening decades of the eighteenth century, especially as those facts were felt by women. In these early narratives Haywood is rarely realistic in the later sense of the term; she shows little interest in the devices of verisimilitude that so preoccupied Defoe and later powerfully informed the novels of Richardson. But she knew what it was like to be a woman in a man's world, full of desire for more independence of action and expression than was considered proper to her own sex and always confronted by the demand that such desire should yield before the expectations imposed by the other. Her ambivalence over these issues gave her stories an air of authenticity that is as important a source of their contemporary appeal and their renewed interest to readers of our own generation as her considerable narrative skills or the genuine fertility of her imagination.

This introduction has lingered so long over the early years of Haywood's life and career because, obviously, they provide the most immediate and relevant context for *The Injur'd Husband* and *Lasselia.* The remaining years, up to her death in 1756, may be treated with more dispatch. The 1730s were a quieter time for her than the 1720s. She ceased signing her works, though without taking extraordinary steps to conceal her authorship, as they were sometimes advertised as written by her. She did less narrative writing—*The Adventures of Eovaai* is her only important work of fiction in the decade—and was perhaps for this reason a less controversial figure than she had been just a few years previously, when her novels had commanded so much attention and stirred up such animus against her. The lack of controversy may also explain why we have few details of her personal life in this period. What we do know, as suggested many pages ago, is that she by no means disappeared from the public scene. Nor did her reputation as a novelist fade away. Indeed, she may have acted the role of "Mrs. Novel"—the character was based on her career—in Fielding's *Author's Farce,* one of the most popular plays of the theatrical season of 1729-30. Three years later, in collaboration with William Hatchett, she wrote a very successful musical parody of Fielding's *Tragedy of Tragedies; or, The Life and Death of Tom Thumb the Great* (1731) titled *The Opera of Operas; or, Tom Thumb the Great.* The play was a genuine hit both on the stage and in published form. Haywood's engagement with the theater actually figured more largely than anything else in her life through several more years. Her ambitious *Dramatic Historiographer* first appeared in 1735, and meanwhile she improved upon her connection with Fielding, appearing at the Little Haymarket in 1736 as Mrs. Arden in George Lillo's tragedy, *Arden of Feversham.*[26] A few months later, at a benefit night staged for her on Monday, 23 May 1737, she was on the same stage in both *The Historical Register for the Year 1736* and the afterpiece *Eurydice Hiss'd,* Fielding's popular twin bill attacking the Walpole government. These were her last performances anywhere as an actress. On the preceding Friday, Walpole presented to the House of Commons a Licensing Act intended to silence Fielding; the bill's passage was inevitable and swift, and so Fielding and Haywood ended their days in the theater together.[27]

Like Fielding, Haywood may have had to turn—in her case it would have been a *re*turn—to writing fiction in order to salvage her literary career. Like him, also, she did so by responding to Richardson's blockbuster *Pamela* with a devastating satire; her *Anti-Pamela* followed Fielding's *Shamela* (April 1741) by only a few months. Over the next fifteen years of continual activity she would produce ten new novels, beginning with *The Fortunate Foundlings* in 1744 and concluding with *The History of Leonora Meadowson,* finished just weeks before her death and published posthumously in 1788, more than thirty years later. Among these new novels are her most famous works of all, *The History of Miss Betsy Thoughtless,* published in 1751, and *The History of Jemmy and Jenny Jessamy,* which appeared in the following year (dated 1753).[28] The critical commonplace about the novels of Haywood's later career is that they are not only longer but more sober than the amatory tales of the 1720s, as she accommodated herself to the impact of the pious, prolix Richardson. This is true enough, but her subject matter is often nearly the same. Betsy Thoughtless, for example, is a headstrong girl who at first refuses to give in to the demand of her brother and guardian that she marry where she cannot love and then, when she does yield, is brutalized by her husband's cruelty. She survives his treatment of her only because he dies and frees her, now chastened, to marry for a second time. Her new husband is Mr. Trueworth, the good man who has always loved her and who would gladly have married her earlier, saving her much misery, if she had not been so determined to assert her independence.

During this same period, besides her novels, Haywood produced a very considerable body of other work. She wrote three conduct books: *A Present for a Servant-Maid,* published in 1743, was followed by *The Wife* in 1755, and by its companion piece *The Husband* in 1756. She carried on *The Female Spectator* for two years (1744-46) and then *The Parrot* for eight weeks (early August to early October 1746).[29] In addition, she prepared three new translations from the French (*The Busy-Body* and *The Virtuous Villager,* both published in 1741, and *Memoirs of a Man of Honour,* published in 1747); and she issued a controversial pamphlet (*A Letter from H—— G——g, Esq.,* 1750), supposedly written by the Gentleman of the Bedchamber to the Young Pretender, that led to her arrest by a government still nervous in the aftermath of the Jacobite uprising of 1745-46. Through many of these years Haywood also carried on her publishing business, which may have come to an end partly as a result of her arrest. As she approached the end of her astonishingly active life and her even more astonishingly productive career, she was once more controversial, and still a prominent figure in a public domain that did not often welcome her presence but could not ignore her. No other female writer of her generation was so visible or so vocal as she remained until, just a few months before her death, she was forced into retreat and quietude by poor health.

Haywood died 25 February 1756. For many years her gravesite remained in as complete an obscurity as that into which her reputation later sank. We now know that she was buried in Saint Margaret's parish churchyard next to Westminster Abbey.[30] But a century after her death no one, it appears, knew where her body lay, and almost no one knew her writings. Those few who did read her seem to have done so only to revile her. The first critic to consider her seriously—not long after the patronizing dismissals of two influential late-Victorians, the anecdotal literary historians Edmund Gosse and Austin Dobson—was George Frisbie Whicher, whose *Life and Romances* of 1915 undertook an exhaustive review and evaluation of her entire body of work. Whicher was himself often patronizing and dismissive, but for more than sixty years his book remained the only available full-length treatment of its subject.[31] In the 1980s, beginning with the pioneering work of Mary Anne Schofield, Haywood's fortunes improved significantly, and she is now undergoing a revival that has already led to a reassessment of her overall achievement and is advancing quickly toward proper recognition of her important place in the tradition of English letters—and particularly in the tradition of English fiction. Just a few short years ago a "Select Bibliography" like the one concluding this volume would hardly have needed to be "select" at all; it could have been relatively brief and still more or less exhaustive. Now the compiler's task has become a difficult one, for there is more worthy commentary from the last two decades than from all the preceding years, and much of it must be excluded in the interest of conserving space. This is a happy circumstance. It is a circumstance that seems unlikely to change, as there is now every reason to believe that the remarkable Mrs. Haywood, so long scorned when she was not neglected altogether, will continue for many years to enjoy the kind of respectful attention she has always deserved.

The Injur'd Husband and *Lasselia*

Late in the year 1720 William Chetwood, the publisher of Haywood's *Love in Excess,* announced the imminent appearance of a book by the same author titled *The Danger of Giving Way to Passion, in Five Exemplary Novels.*[32] The novels to be included were *The British Recluse; or, The Secret History of Cleomira, The Injur'd Husband, Lasselia, The Rash Resolve,* and *Idalia.* For reasons that are not clear, this collection never was printed. Possibly Chetwood decided that he could make a greater profit by issuing the novels separately; in any event, beginning in the spring of 1722 he did exactly that, with the assistance of the booksellers Daniel Browne, Jr., and Samuel Chapman.[33] The delay preceding publication suggests that the works may not have been written when they were first announced. But that is only speculation; we know nothing of their composition, though it seems certain that Haywood was very busy with them for a period of some months, for the intervals between them were brief. *The British Recluse* was the first to appear, in April 1722, followed by *The Injur'd Husband* in December, *Idalia* in April 1723, and *Lasselia* and *The Rash Resolve* in October and December of the same year, respectively.[34] Together, these works accurately represent what Haywood sought to do with her amatory fiction in the early years of her career, and they show us how she meant to do it; her object, clearly, was to capture completely and then to keep the audience for fast-paced, provocative, and passionate stories that *Love in Excess* had already shown her was out there and ready to be enthralled. *The Injur'd Husband* and *Lasselia* are not the most skillful and polished among this early group of five "exemplary" novels (*Lasselia,* especially, seems rushed and at times technically crude), but they are of unusual interest because they are especially striking examples of Haywood's youthful experiments with the character of the aberrant female as figure of monstrous evil and with the more sympathetic figure of the good girl ruined by an overpowering passion.

The Injur'd Husband's Baroness de Tortillée, a sex-crazed wife who mistreats and betrays her trusting husband and even indirectly causes his eventual death, is by far the more compelling of the two characters, largely because her voracious appetites and relentlessly energetic scheming make her dangerous and thus irresistibly fascinating. With the conniving assistance of her Iago-like lackey Du Lache, and under the cover of her titled position, she sets out to possess as many men as she can, collecting them—the Marquis de Sonville, the Chevalier St. Aumar, the aged La Sourbe, and a host of others—like trophies and then, but without casting them off, tiring of them and moving on to other conquests. Ros Ballaster has remarked that the baroness actually takes on the attributes of a male sexual predator whose desire is insatiable, waning only with enjoyment.[35] The reversal of gender roles is, ironically, part of this woman's perverse appeal, as the reader is expected to respond to her with a mixture of horror and glee. The baroness does what no woman should do, achieving again and again a kind of ecstatic triumph, but she is nonetheless by any standard—male or female—an evil villain who must be restrained and stripped of her power, which is exactly what happens before her story ends.

Her primary victim in the novel is the gallant Beauclair, a man of basic decency whose devotion to the beautiful and virtuous Montamour is genuine and deep but who is no match for the wiles of the talented seductress. The baroness wants him because he seems unattainable; indeed, she seems more driven—her desire is a kind of compulsion—as her prey is more difficult to capture and devour. Beauclair is an early example of the type of the sentimental man of feeling, but with a remaining touch of the Restoration rake, and he becomes susceptible as soon as he is persuaded by Du Lache—rather too easily, the reader may judge—that Montamour has been unfaithful and has renounced her submission to him. He falls helplessly before the rapacious Tortillée, weakened by his own lack of resolve and drawn by her desire. Once he has done so, the remainder of the story has nothing to do but show how, in a process of clarification furthered by a disguised Montamour (she becomes Vrayment, a faithful friend who, as a man, has the authority to affirm Beauclair's merit and the strength to rescue him from infamy), he recovers himself and is able to deserve a life of happiness with his original beloved. The baroness, undone by exposure of her duplicity, is completely displaced, leaving the world she has dominated by her wickedness in a condition of stasis and quietude.

Very early in the story Haywood firmly establishes that the baroness's power to disrupt the world actually derives from more than just her sexuality, though that is certainly the source of her need to exercise it. She is so dangerous to moral order because, in order to satisfy her passion, she has perfected the transformative art of controlling both the way she herself is perceived and the way others—particularly the virtuous Montamour—are seen as well. In the baroness's hands, truth is not even relative, open to interpretation; it—or, rather, its appearance—is purely a product of invention. This woman is a maker of fictions who perverts the storyteller's art by using it to lie, and because she is so skillful her version of the truth threatens to supplant all other possible versions. As a self-created (but false) exemplar of female purity, she seduces the foolish baron into marrying her and her many lovers into her bed; as the purveyor of a scandal she has created to serve the ends of her desire, she destroys Montamour's reputation in the eyes of Beauclair, re-creating this virtuous girl in a way that ironically mirrors her own real character. This contrived image of Montamour prevails because, unlike the baroness with her accomplices and agents, Haywood's heroine remains nobly and proudly alone, seeking no assistance and indeed appearing unwilling—and, because she is silent, unable—to project an authentic version of herself. Meanwhile Beauclair, equally proud, cannot act to redeem his own reputation, tarnished by his association with the baroness, and he is unable to discover the truth about

Montamour because he does not aggressively seek it. When the two former lovers meet accidentally at what is perhaps the moment of their greatest mutual misunderstanding, neither is willing to trust the other, so completely have the villainous Tortillée's manipulations transformed them in each other's eyes: "both believing themselves injur'd," says Haywood's narrator, "each disdain'd to do any thing which might appear like a Desire of Reconciliation: and this little Pride, fatal alike to the Repose of both, gave the common Deceivers all the Opportunity they cou'd wish to compass their pernicious Ends, of separating two Hearts which by all the Ties of Gratitude and Tenderness were thought to be cemented" (48).

Montamour and Beauclair seem to behave as they do toward each other out of fidelity to some aristocratic code of self-regard and social propriety. Certainly they have both adopted a model of reserved conduct that compels them to be inert. But if virtue as they practice it is necessarily a passive attribute, Haywood seems to suggest, then it is in greatest peril when challenged by its opposite in an active, vocal, manipulating agent of villainy. The baroness is such an agent, all the more menacing because she is female. The power she possesses to transform or reinvent the characters of other persons is much greater and much more fundamentally destructive than the power to violate a body by an act of sexual aggression, which is the male libertine's usual crime. Because the baroness's power is so threatening and so all-encompassing, it can be defeated only by an agency as active as her own. Among the characters in the novel only the Marquis de Sonville, one of her discarded lovers, is able to enact such agency when he reads aloud from her letters to a new lover in the presence of Beauclair and others who have shared his unhappy fate. On a larger scale and in a more comprehensive way, the novel itself provides similar agency. Early on, Haywood's narrator points directly to the disjunction between the baroness's posturing and the deviousness of her language, which masks the truth about her: "one had need to be perfectly acquainted with her *Actions,*" she says, "before one cou'd distrust her *Words*"; only "her History" can furnish the necessary acquaintance and give the reader a "just Notion of her Character" (8). From this moment forward it is clear that the entire narrative is intended to be "historical," in the nearly literal sense Haywood hints at here. Its purpose, in other words, is to tell the truth. Such is indeed the proper purpose of all narrative art, Haywood suggests as she counterposes her own fictionmaking to the baroness's lies.

Montamour, of course, is in her own way as devious as the baroness, though her deviousness is in the cause of what she understands to be the demands of proper female conduct. Far from wishing to acknowledge how deeply she has been wounded by Beauclair's rejection of her faithful love, she consistently dissembles in her dealings with him. Her response to his initial accusing letter refers emphatically to the "*Tranquility of Mind*" with which she bears the "*eternal Loss*" of his love (29). Throughout the story, though we are shown that she suffers keenly in private, often weeping and sometimes even swooning from the weakness her pain causes her, she keeps a brave face before the world, preserving a "Presence of Mind, which very few, if any Woman, beside herself, cou'd boast of" (39), and never forgetting the "Decorum, and Mildness of Behaviour, which ought to be the distinguishing Character of Womanhood" (41). Others, Beauclair among them, wonder whether her indifference to his loss might be feigned; she is able to persuade her brother that she no longer loves the man she had once hoped to marry, but to many of her acquaintance it is obvious that in this matter she is "not free from Dissimulation" (36). Perhaps Haywood is in an ironic way echoing the old idea, familiar especially from early satires against women, that fine ladies were trained to be devious. The same possibility is further raised by Montamour's later appearance in male disguise as Vrayment (the name translates from the French as "Truly"); only in such a disguise, it appears, can she break from the female practice of deceit she has earlier followed. But Montamour's conduct by no means partakes of the wickedness of the baroness's deceptions; her motive of self-preservation is just, and it is not at all surprising that she should refuse to acknowledge either the pain of being displaced by a woman of vicious character or the shame of having her own character maligned. What is remarkable about Montamour is her capacity to rise above feelings she never denies to herself; in this she is manifestly superior to the baroness, whose passions dictate her every thought and action. Montamour's stoicism in the face of all her trials unmistakably echoes the doctrines of Mary Astell, whose sober views of the disciplined female life remained very much in the air during the early 1720s, when *The Injur'd Husband* was written. Astell's ascetic principles must have been rather uncongenial to Haywood personally, but they were perfectly serviceable for her portrait of a heroine who, through much of the story in which she figures so importantly, finds it necessary to hide "all that she had of Woman" (43) from the rest of the world.[36]

The Injur'd Husband actually develops dual plots deriving from Haywood's conception of her two women, though the relations between the plots are not especially complex. With Beauclair standing at the center as the object of the baroness's craving and of Montamour's long-suffering love, we see first the successful progress of the former's schemes and then, during a long interlude following her exposure, the triumph of the latter's patient devotion. Montamour is a presence in the early part of the story, but for the most part only distantly, except when she follows Beauclair and his temptress into the gardens of the Tuileries, a sensual bower of bliss, where the two are to meet in an illicit assignation. Overcome by her surroundings almost as much as by the event she has come to witness, she faints away and shortly thereafter disappears altogether into the confines of a convent. Haywood's language on the occasion of Montamour's venture into the gardens is significant, as it is a language of weakness and submission: "when she was about to shew herself" to Beauclair and the baroness, "to speak, and to upbraid, she lost the Power, her Voice forsook her, and her every Sense flew frighted at the Tempest, and left her Body motionless on the Earth" (45). She finds her voice again when an enlightened Beauclair comes to the convent to plead for a renewal of her love and, surrounded and protected by the sacred walls (the contrast with the gardens is purposeful and striking), she is able to renounce him—or to appear to do so. She finds yet a different voice in the public world outside the convent when she appears as Vrayment, and in that guise she is able to precipitate the happy resolution of the entire narrative.

The Tortillée and Montamour stories are, obviously, balanced against one another, but structurally they intersect only through Beauclair; in the drama of the developing narrative they are sequential. In the end, Montamour's story supersedes and displaces the baroness's, just as Montamour herself has the joy of superseding and displacing her rival in Beauclair's affections. The meaning of this sequence is unmistakable: in an echo of a familiar myth pattern (here the pattern is essentially Christian and redemptive), good rises above evil, chaste female virtue wins out over vile sexual perversion, and all is finally as it should be in the moral universe and in the immediate world of romantic love and gender politics.[37] Haywood has everything both ways, of course; the conventional exemplary ending justifies all of the pages given to erotic tension and sexual plotting; the success of the pious girl makes the portrait of the sexy female predator quite safe.

Haywood clearly knew exactly what she was doing in devising the story of *The Injur'd Husband* for maximum appeal to its audience. No doubt some readers felt their interest heighten as they recognized the real people behind the fictional characters—Martha Fowke Sansom, Aaron Hill, Haywood herself; but the fundamental appeal of the work is through its carefully resolved fantasy of deviant female conduct. The frequently intensive language of the novel could only have reinforced the attractions of its dual plotting and conventional conclusion. Montamour, the very emblem of female propriety, is nearly voiceless except when she speaks in the assumed character of Vrayment;

in the words of the gossipy Sansfoy, she is all "Silence, Meekness, Obedience and Humility" (14). But the baroness is aggressively vocal and full of the language of passion; indeed, the strength and decibel level of her voice constitute important evidence of her perversion. Her instructions to Du Lache as she sends him out to ensnare Beauclair are urgent and even shrill in their expressions of her desire, while her words to the hero himself are often such as these: "Ah then" she cries (deviously) upon the occasion of their first assignation, adopting the appearance of virtuous vulnerability, "there is no Power in Heaven or Earth can save me—Fame, Duty, Virtue, are too weak Defence—against those conquering Eyes, that Shape, that Air, that Mein, that Wit, that Voice, those thousand, thousand Worlds of Charms: Death only is a Refuge for *Tortillée*" (27).

Interestingly, it is the baroness's language that undoes her at the gathering in her home during which the Marquis de Sonville reads aloud from her letters to her latest conquest, the foppish La Branche. "What shall I do?" she had written of her new lover's failure to keep an appointment with her. "I am wild with Apprehension——the Memory of *past Delights* but heightens *present Woes*——O, *La Branche!* . . . make haste my Love, my Life! my Angel, make haste to give and take such Joys as but in *Idea* to the vulgar World are known" (59). The cadences of such language, which find exact parallels in the voice of the narrator as it fills out the novel's account of the baroness's passionate urges, are those of a frenzied sensibility, driven to excess. In all respects, then, including her manner of expression, the baroness is an outrage against received morality and, more important, against accepted standards of female thought and conduct. She may be appealing, but she must be repudiated and punished. Lascivious and vile, fiendish and even murderous, she dies a fittingly gruesome death, poisoned by her own hand, "hopeless of Mercy here or hereafter" (100). The ending leaves no doubt as to where the narrative and its author stand on the character of this extraordinary woman. Yet the thrill of the reader's encounter with her is real, and it lingers long after the storm she has created has subsided.

Lasselia is a milder work, less concerned with deliberate female deviance than with the failure of a character too weak to resist powerful inner urges to passionate indulgence. It is also a much shorter novel than *The Injur'd Husband,* and there are signs of hasty composition; in particular, the interpolated history of the hero de l'Amye's entanglement with the Douxmourie daughters is awkwardly managed, and the reader may even have minor difficulty—at least initially—in grasping the relation between this history and the main story line. Probably Haywood, rushing to complete the work so she could turn to *The Rash Resolve,* which appeared only two months after it, had no time to revise so as to eliminate such clumsiness. Still, the novel tells an engaging story of a virtuous young girl who, brought up amidst the glitter of the French court as the niece of Madame de Montespan, one of Louis XIV's most powerful mistresses, finds the resources to preserve her honor against the king's desire for her and to escape from his reach into the country. The story may be a slight one by comparison to *The Injur'd Husband* and other works from the same early period, but at the very outset Haywood makes clear the import of its moral and social message. In the decadent world it depicts, the threat to innocence begins in the highest places; the king's promiscuous seductions—"this amorous Monarch," he is called (109)—are as much above moral judgment as they are above the law.

It is in the country that Lasselia discovers her true nature as a sensual being when she falls into the company of the handsome de l'Amye, a decent man but also a sexual wanderer whose wife is a friend of the family with whom Lasselia has taken refuge. If de l'Amye, since his marriage, has had no previous affairs of the kind he launches into with Lasselia, it is only because he has never been attracted by a girl of such delicacy, beauty, and vulnerable innocence. Heroine and hero alike, then, are the victims of strong feelings that they do not, actually cannot, control. Haywood makes the purpose of her story plain in its dedication, where she remarks that it is—like "*those I have formerly publish'd*"—intended "*only to remind the unthinking Part of the World, how dangerous it is to give way to Passion*"; this purpose, she hopes, will "*excuse the too great Warmth, which may perhaps, appear in some particular Pages*" (105). *Lasselia,* then, like *The British Recluse, The Force of Nature, Idalia,* and the other amatory novels published almost simultaneously with it, is to be read as a cautionary tale. But the vicarious pleasure of sensual experience is to be enjoyed as the caution is absorbed. The work is indeed characterized by "warmth" of feeling and, frequently, by an equal and insistent warmth of expression. Haywood was no doubt wise to anticipate objections from at least some members of her audience, but she certainly knew that the very qualities for which she apologized were the surest guarantee of her readers' satisfaction with what she had written.

Lasselia does have its own wicked female, a lesser figure than the Baroness de Tortillée but still a formidable one. She is the elder Douxmourie daughter, the original intended bride of de l'Amye, who is rejected by him and thereafter pursues him with a shrewish vengeance. The hero's past unhappy involvement with this young woman's family led him nearly to disaster; smitten by the younger daughter, but denied to her in marriage by her tyrant father, he had gotten her with child and then, in a duel, killed a well-meaning rival suitor who wanted only to avenge her honor. Having fled the country to avoid punishment, de l'Amye learns that the girl has given up her newborn baby and withdrawn into a convent. He returns home after being granted a pardon and, chastened, he soon marries, vowing eternal faithfulness to his wife. But he had not anticipated the appearance of a Lasselia, whose catastrophic relationship with him all but duplicates that of Mlle Douxmourie. Haywood did not succeed in arranging the details of all these complications very well, as she placed the account of de l'Amye's early history too late in the novel for it to be dramatically or rhetorically effective. Yet she managed to create an interesting parallel between the two young girls, one that strongly illustrates the perils to which virginal innocence is vulnerable, even from a man of some real moral character, in a corrupt and perverse world.

Lasselia and de l'Amye, and the younger Douxmourie sister as well, are helplessly subject to the unbidden power of their passions—to what, in Haywood's imagined world, might appropriately be called the sovereignty of love. But they are also subject to the rule of Chance—"my Deity," as de l'Amye interestingly names that ungovernable force (129). It is Chance, or Fortune, that causes him to fall in love with the Douxmourie daughter who was not intended for him, flinging him into a whirlwind of desire, difficulty, and error. Disappointed in love as a youth, he is destined to repeat his sufferings and failures of conduct and character later, after he has seemingly redeemed himself in a faithful marriage only to have his life disrupted again upon his encounter with Lasselia. That Chance governs Lasselia's life also is made plain when, having escaped the grasp of the king, she falls into the company of de l'Amye; her certain fate, and his, are announced by the mysterious nosebleed he suffers at their first meeting—it is the "Omen of a future Union" between them (114), but a grimly ironic one because they can be united only illicitly, and therefore disastrously.

In this novel love and Chance wield their joint sovereignty with an inexorable power. Both Mlle Douxmourie and Lasselia, when they meet de l'Amye, experience love at first sight, a sudden and uncontrollable rush of emotional turbulence and sensual awakening that puts reason to flight. This is the immediate and lasting cause of their failure to maintain themselves in a poised, safe, stable condition of distance from the forces that might threaten them. Haywood may appear to judge them, but she is compassionate toward them too, as she makes it clear that their fall is almost helpless. We see only Lasselia's fall, but as a result we also know later just how the same thing had happened to de l'Amye's past victim. The crucial and very dramatic moment of the heroine's seduction comes in a garden setting, where "the amorous *Lasselia*" lies "extended at her length on a fine grassy Bank, canopy'd o'er with shading Jessamins, and spreading Vines" (117)—Haywood does not hold back in setting the voluptuousness of her scene.[38] When the messenger who delivers to her an impassioned letter from de l'Amye turns out to be no other than the lover himself, she is instantly lost: "her Eyes confess'd the unwilling Transport of her Soul, and told him all he wish'd to ask: . . . and now *Love!* transported, raptur'd *Love!*" overcame her. "Trembling and panting, 'twixt Desire and Fear, at last she lay resistless in his Arms" (119). The consummation of their sudden passion is postponed only by their fear of discovery, but soon accomplished. And Lasselia, no longer an innocent, becomes the increasingly desperate mistress of a married man, losing her new home, all other companions, and, of course, herself. Her yielding, however helpless, threatens disruption of the proper social order as represented in de l'Amye's family, while it thrusts her into a prison created by her own desire. Cut off from all but de l'Amye, she is literally sequestered in a room at the inn where their love is at last consummated and where he then keeps and visits her, allowing no one else to know of her presence except the landlord and landlady. Forbidden passion, Haywood seems to say while reveling in the display of it, is forbidden for good reason.

The highly colored language of *Lasselia*—and we may find similar language in others of Haywood's novels from this same period in her career—generates much of the story's energy, and it represents an attempt to capture feeling and passion directly. If the language seems stylized, that is because it is deliberately extravagant and antirational; if it becomes repetitious (and it does), bound by its own eccentric conventions, that is because Haywood was working within strict limitations of linguistic propriety that circumscribed both vocabulary and range of subject matter. Some things could not be written, but only suggested. The rhythms of *Lasselia*'s emotive language, with the proliferation of dashes and exclamation points and with the frequent irruptions of certain high-powered words—*transports, raptures, pantings, tremors, swoons,* and so on—serve as a kind of code to mark impulsive erotic or other urgently felt inner experience. The resemblances to the language associated with the baroness's sexual compulsions in *The Injur'd Husband* are real. But there is a significant difference, too, for the baroness is too vile to be capable of the feelings of a Lasselia; her outbreaks of passionate action or expression are all false and calculated, the devices of her desire for power and conquest, whereas Lasselia's arise from some primal female depth, unbidden, their effects depriving her of all self-control and causing her to lose all desire except to be in the arms of the man she truly loves. One might say that in novels like *Lasselia,* Haywood sought for a way to express the inexpressible, to bring to light the repressed sexual feeling that women really do have and to render the depth of female emotional life accessible not by analyzing it but by simply reflecting its urgencies. John J. Richetti has observed that the language with which Haywood achieved such expression is not a literary language, but the product of a "spontaneous, uncultivated ability to imagine passion and its effects."[39] It is obviously true that Haywood avoided a conventional literary language; on this point there is no arguing with Richetti's influential assessment. But the language in which she did write can hardly be called "spontaneous" or "uncultivated." Clearly, Haywood worked very hard to invent a distinctive style that would seem authentic within the contexts of her narratives. The evidence of her popularity suggests that many of her early readers thought she had succeeded in doing so.

The Injur'd Husband and *Lasselia,* while they do not possess all of the attractions of the earlier *Love in Excess* or the later *Betsy Thoughtless,* are certainly accomplished enough to reward the attention of the modern reader. They have a great deal to tell us about their author's understanding of the tastes and obsessions of her audience, an understanding that would shape her entire career; and they are lively stories of two very interesting women. Controversial in their time, these novels may seem tame now. But they are not, for they raise fundamental issues of female language, female sexuality, and the woman's desire for power and love that remain as compelling as ever. If Haywood was unable to arrive at perfectly stable positions on all of these issues, she was among the first to open them to public contemplation, and in the process she helped to stimulate the consciousness of an entire generation of women. *The Injur'd Husband* and *Lasselia* show us how she did so, and they are, besides, among the many worthy achievements of a busy career that did perhaps as much as any other in its time to establish the novel as the dominant mode of literary expression in the modern English-speaking world. For many years, since a time not long after their first appearance, these stories could not be read except by scholars with access to rare surviving copies in research libraries. That situation, fortunately, will now change with this new edition.

Notes

1. The change is owing principally to the detective work of Christine Blouch. See her doctoral dissertation, "Eliza Haywood: Questions in the Life and Works" (University of Michigan, 1991); and see also her essay, "Eliza Haywood and the Romance of Obscurity," *Studies in English Literature* 31 (1991): 535-51.

2. "I have run through as many Scenes of Vanity and Folly as the greatest Coquet of them all," Haywood wrote in opening the first number of *The Female Spectator* (April 1744). "Dress, Equipage, and Flattery, were the Idols of my Heart. . . . My Life, for some Years, was a continued Round of what I then called Pleasure, and my whole Time engrossed by a Hurry of promiscuous Diversions." It is possible that Haywood is exaggerating or even to some extent fictionalizing her life in these remarks, but what little we know of her early years suggests that they contain at least some elements of truth.

3. Until the calendar reform of 1751, the new year began on 25 March. Thus the dates given here would have been 1692 and 1689 Old Style, 1693 and 1690 New Style.

4. In the twentieth century the most influential purveyor of these errors has been George Frisbie Whicher, whose professedly authoritative *Life and Romances of Mrs. Eliza Haywood* (New York: Columbia University Press, 1915) became the source followed unquestioningly by almost all subsequent students of his subject. Even Mary Anne Schofield, the most active and enthusiastic Haywood scholar of the last two decades, has perpetuated Whicher's errors in two important critical and biographical studies: *Quiet Rebellion: The Fictional Heroines of Eliza Fowler Haywood* (Washington, D.C.: University Press of America, 1982), and *Eliza Haywood* (Boston: Twayne, 1985). I have done the same thing in my entry on Haywood in *The Dictionary of Literary Biography: British Novelists, 1660-1800,* ed. Martin C. Battestin (Detroit: Gale, 1985), vol. 39, pt. 1.

5. See Blouch, "Eliza Haywood and the Romance of Obscurity," 537.

6. *The Female Spectator* 1 (April 1744): 3.

7. See below, *The Injur'd Husband*, 36 and n. 39.

8. See Blouch, "Eliza Haywood: Questions in the Life and Works," 15-20, and "Eliza Haywood and the Romance of Obscurity," 538-40.

9. See Blouch, "Eliza Haywood and the Romance of Obscurity," 539-40 and n. 26.

10. These were *The Works of Mrs. Eliza Haywood: Consisting of Novels, Letters, Poems, and Plays,* 4 vols. (London, 1723-24), and *Secret Histories, Novels and Poems,* 4 vols. (London, 1724); the latter of these collections, dated 1725 on its title page, was in its fourth edition by 1742.

11. Earlier, Haywood had dedicated *Lasselia* to Henrietta Howard's kinsman, the eighth earl of Suffolk; upon his death in 1731, Mrs. Howard's husband Charles succeeded him as the ninth earl, and she became countess of Suffolk. There is no record of what happened to cause the kind of bad feeling that would have led Haywood to

attack Henrietta Howard in the *Court of Caramania.* It was no slander, incidentally, to portray her as the prince's mistress; in this respect, Haywood told no more than the truth.

12. Swift to Lady Howard, now countess of Suffolk, 26 October 1731; see *The Correspondence of Jonathan Swift,* ed. Harold Williams (Oxford: Clarendon, 1963), 3:501.

13. Pope based his satiric picture of Haywood on the clumsy portrait by Elisha Kirkall prefixed to the first volume of her 1723-24 collected *Works.* With only minor revision (the elimination of two lines) Pope retained his picture of Haywood in the 1729 *Dunciad Variorum* and in all subsequent editions of the poem through the last he supervised in 1743.

14. This work was a considerable success in the marketplace. It was revised in 1736 and given a new title, *The Companion to the Theatre;* Haywood added a second volume in 1746, and altogether there were seven editions by the time of her death in 1756.

15. This novel was reprinted in 1740 as *The Unfortunate Princess; or, The Ambitious Statesman* (dated 1741).

16. The phrase is from a poem by James Sterling prefixed to Haywood's *Secret Histories, Novels and Poems* in the second (1725) and all subsequent editions.

17. Ballaster, *Seductive Forms: Women's Amatory Fiction from 1684 to 1740* (Oxford: Clarendon, 1992), 170.

18. This is the overriding theme of Schofield's *Quiet Rebellion;* see above, n. 4.

19. Another novel of 1723, *The Rash Resolve; or, The Untimely Discovery,* repeats the strains found in both *Idalia* and *Lasselia.* Its heroine Emanuella defies a tyrannical guardian and is then precipitated into loss of her virtue and her fortune; like Lasselia, however, she is chastened in the end, though she dies of a broken heart instead of finding solace in pious retirement.

20. *Fantomina* was included in vol. 3 of Haywood's *Secret Histories, Novels and Poems,* but it was never separately published.

21. *Idalia* is another, though disguise is less important in this novel than in *Fantomina.* Mary Anne Schofield has collected four of the novels making use of female disguise into a volume titled *The Masquerade Novels of Eliza Haywood* (Delmar, NY: Scholars' Facsimiles and Reprints, 1986). Besides *Fantomina* and *Idalia,* the collection includes *The Masqueraders; or, Fatal Curiosity* (1724) and *The Fatal Secret; or, Constancy in Distress* (1724).

22. See, for example, Ballaster, *Seductive Forms,* 179-92; see also Mary Anne Schofield, *Masking and Unmasking the Female Mind: Disguising Romances in Feminine Fiction, 1713-1799* (Newark: University of Delaware Press, 1990), 44-66, 101-7; and Catherine Craft-Fairchild, *Masquerade and Gender: Disguise and Female Identity in Eighteenth-Century Fictions by Women* (University Park: Pennsylvania State University Press, 1993), chap. 3.

23. The title parodies that of Haywood's earlier play, *A Wife to Be Lett* (1724).

24. See Blouch, "Eliza Haywood: Questions in the Life and Works," 55-57.

25. For full discussion of Fowke's life and career, and of her relations with Hill and Haywood, see the introduction to Phyllis J. Guskin's recent edition of Fowke's autobiography (Newark: University of Delaware Press, 1997), the full title of which is *Clio: or, A Secret History of the Life and Amours of the Late Celebrated Mrs. S——N——M.* Written in the form of an extended letter to Hill, the work was not published until 1752, thirty years after it was completed and long after the death of its author (in 1736) and its intended recipient (in 1750).

26. Blouch, "Eliza Haywood: Questions in the Life and Works," 178, tentatively suggests that Haywood also wrote this play, an adaptation of an anonymous Elizabethan tragedy by the same name dating from 1592. The suggestion is an error, no doubt caused by a mistaken reading of the cast list for the 1736 production. Haywood appears in this list as "Mrs. Haywood, the Author"; the phrase is intended only as a description.

27. See Martin C. Battestin, *Henry Fielding: A Life* (London: Routledge, 1989), 224, 230-31. As Battestin notes, the association between Haywood and Fielding may not always have been a happy one; in *The History of Miss Betsy Thoughtless* (1751), remembering her days at the Little Haymarket, she criticized him as the proprietor of a "scandal-shop."

28. The other novels from these years are *Life's Progress through the Passions; or, The Adventures of Natura,* 1748; *Dalinda; or, The Double Marriage* and *Epistles for the Ladies,* both 1749; *Modern Characters; Illustrated by Histories in Real Life,* 1753; and *The Invisible Spy,* 1754.

29. In January 1756, almost on the eve of her death, Haywood launched yet another periodical, *The Young Lady*, but was so ill that she had to give it up after only seven numbers.

30. See Blouch, "Eliza Haywood and the Romance of Obscurity," 535. Haywood was buried 3 March 1756. There may originally have been a memorial marker at her grave, but in the mid-nineteenth century the churchyard was covered over; it is today beneath the lawn that lies between the Abbey and Saint Margaret's. Saint Margaret's, incidentally, was the church of most frequent choice for fashionable weddings in the eighteenth century. Given the controversy and even scandal that attached to Haywood's name, it is deliciously ironic that she was laid to rest there. One can only hope that she knew in advance where her burial site would be and that she thus had an opportunity to enjoy the irony.

31. James P. Erickson completed a doctoral dissertation, "The Novels of Eliza Haywood" (University of Minnesota), in 1961, but another two decades would elapse before any comparably extensive study would appear in print. Erickson's dissertation has never been published.

32. See Whicher, *Life and Romances*, 12.

33. Chetwood, Browne, Chapman, and then James Roberts, Chetwood's successor in his bookselling business, published most of Haywood's early works.

34. With three of these novels Haywood, or her booksellers, followed a common marketing practice of the early eighteenth century, publishing the books late in one

year but dating them in the subsequent year on their title pages. Thus *The Injur'd Husband* is dated 1723, while *Lasselia* and *The Rash Resolve* are both dated 1724.

35. Ballaster, *Seductive Forms,* 178.

36. Haywood, like most other literate women of her generation, had no doubt read Astell's work, especially *A Serious Proposal to the Ladies* (1694), which strenuously (and elegantly) promotes the idea that a woman ought to brave the difficulties of the female life with dignity, equanimity, and restraint. Astell's ideas were enormously influential, and if she was not always emulated by the women who read her, she was widely admired for the steadiness of her personal resolve. For full discussion of *A Serious Proposal* and related works see Ruth Perry, *The Celebrated Mary Astell: An Early English Feminist* (Chicago: University of Chicago Press, 1986), especially chaps. 4 and 5.

37. The quasi-allegorical French names assigned to most of the characters only underscore the nearly mythic dimensions of the narrative; many of the names are so transparent as to be defining abstractions (Beauclair, for example, but also Tortillée, Du Lache, and numerous others). The meanings of the French names are accounted for below, in the explanatory notes to the text of the novel.

38. The garden is a common setting for scenes of seduction in Haywood's novels. See April London, "Placing the Female: The Metonymic Garden in Amatory and Pious Narrative, 1700-1740," in *Fetter'd or Free? British Women Novelists, 1670-1815,* ed. Mary Anne Schofield and Cecilia Macheski (Athens: Ohio University Press, 1986), 101-23.

39. Richetti, "Voice and Gender in Eighteenth-Century Fiction: Haywood to Burney," *Studies in the Novel* 19 (1987): 265. Richetti notes Haywood's precise awareness of what she was doing by citing (265) her self-deprecating remarks in the dedication (to William Yonge) of *The Fatal Secret.* Writing about love, she says, "requires no aids of learning, no general conversation, no application; a shady grove and purling stream are all . . . that's necessary to give us an idea of the tender passion." What Richetti fails to recognize is that these dedicatory remarks are ironic. Haywood by no means intended to diminish what she did best, but rather to affirm her method's appropriateness to the rendering of experience that no other method (and certainly not an acquired literary language) could, in her judgment, make accessible.

Chronology of Events in Eliza Haywood's Life

For the sake of brevity only short titles are given for most of Haywood's many works; for full titles the reader may consult the listings in Blouch and Whicher (see below, the select bibliography), which are the primary sources for the publication information in this chronology.

?1693 Haywood is born Elizabeth Fowler, probably in January to the Fowlers of Harnage Grange, Shropshire, but possibly as early as January 1689 to Robert and Elizabeth Fowler, London shopkeepers.

1715 Haywood is married by this date (the identity of her husband is unknown), for she appears on stage in Dublin as Eliza Haywood, playing Chloe in Thomas Shadwell's adaptation of Shakespeare's *Timon of Athens.*

1719-20 *Love in Excess* is published in three parts; a translation, *Letters from a Lady of Quality to a Chevalier,* appears in 1720 (dated 1721). Haywood joins Aaron Hill's London literary circle, which includes the poets Richard Savage (later her lover and probably the father of one of her illegitimate children) and John Dyer, the playwright David Mallet, the actress Susanna Centlivre, and the sometime author and literary gadfly Martha Fowke Sansom.

1721 Haywood's tragedy *The Fair Captive* is acted and published.

1722 *The British Recluse* and *The Injur'd Husband* are published, both dated 1723.

1723 *Idalia* and *Lasselia* are published, followed by *The Rash Resolve* (dated 1724), which includes a prefatory poem by Savage; the first three volumes of Haywood's collected *Works* appear, with the fourth volume following in 1724. Her comedy *A Wife to Be Lett* is acted and published.

1724 Haywood begins a twenty-year personal and professional relationship with the playwright William Hatchett, who probably fathers her second illegitimate child. During this same year she quarrels and breaks with Savage. The following new works by her are published: *A Spy upon the Conjuror,* the first of three pamphlets on the celebrated deaf-mute Duncan Campbell (followed by *The Dumb Projector,* 1725, and *Secret Memoirs of the Late Mr. Duncan Campbell,* 1732); *The Masqueraders,* pt. 1 (pt. 2, 1725); *The Fatal Secret; The Surprise; The Arragonian Queen;* a translation, *La Belle Assemblée,* vol. 1 (vol. 2, 1726); *Memoirs of a Certain Island Adjacent to the Kingdom of Utopia,* vol. 1 (dated 1725; vol. 2, 1725); *Bath-Intrigues; Memoirs of the Baron de Brosse* (dated 1725); and a second collection of her writings (in four volumes) titled *Secret Histories, Novels and Poems* (dated 1725; 4th ed., 1742), which includes the previously unpublished *Fantomina* and *The Force of Nature.*

1725 Haywood publishes *The Lady's Philosopher's Stone,* a translation; in this same year she also publishes *The Unequal Conflict;* pt. 1 of *The Tea-Table* (pt. 2, 1726); *Fatal Fondness;* and *Mary Stuart, Queen of Scots,* a biography.

1726 Eight new works by Haywood appear during this year: *The Distress'd Orphan, The Mercenary Lover, Reflections on the Various Effects of Love, The City Jilt, The Double Marriage, Secret History of the Present Intrigues of the Court of Caramania* (dated 1727), *Letters from the Palace of Fame* (dated 1727), and *Cleomelia* (dated 1727).

1727 *The Fruitless Enquiry, The Life of Madam de Villesache, Love in Its Variety* (a translation), *Philidore and Placentia,* and *The Perplex'd Dutchess* (dated 1728) are all published during this year.

1728 Haywood is attacked by Alexander Pope in *The Dunciad,* lines 149-58. The following new works by her appear in print: *The Agreeable Caledonian,* pt. 1 (pt. 2, 1729; reissued in 1768 as *Clementina*); *Irish Artifice* (in *The Female Dunciad,* published by Edmund Curll); a translation, *The Disguised Prince,* pt. 1 (pt. 2, 1729); and *Persecuted Virtue.*

1729 *The Fair Hebrew* appears; Haywood's tragedy *Frederick, Duke of Brunswick-Lunenburgh* is acted and published.

1730 *Love-Letters on All Occasions* appears. Haywood is portrayed as "Mrs. Novel" in Fielding's *Author's Farce,* and possibly acts the part. She takes the role of Briseis in Hatchett's *The Rival Father.*

1732 *Vanelia; or, The Amours of the Great: An Opera* is staged; the work has been attributed to Haywood, but is not certainly hers. She acts the part of Lady Flame in *The Blazing Comet,* by Samuel Johnson of Cheshire.

1733 *The Opera of Operas,* Haywood's greatest theatrical success (written in collaboration with Hatchett), is performed and published.

1734 Haywood translates and publishes *L'Entretien des Beaux Esprits,* a sequel to her translation of *La Belle Assemblée* (1724-26).

1735 *The Dramatic Historiographer,* Haywood's history of the British theater, is published; the work is revised and reissued as *The Companion to the Theatre* in 1736.

1736 Haywood publishes *Adventures of Eovaai,* an attack on Sir Robert Walpole, the prime minister; the work is reprinted in 1740 as *The Unfortunate Princess* (dated 1741). She acts the part of Mrs. Arden in George Lillo's *Arden of Feversham.*

1737 Haywood takes the part of First Queen Incognito in *A Rehearsal of Kings* (author unknown). She also appears in Fielding's *Historical Register for the Year 1736* and *Eurydice Hiss'd;* a benefit night is staged for her on 23 May, after which the Walpole government's Licensing Act ends Fielding's theatrical career, and with it Haywood's.

1741 Haywood's *Anti-Pamela,* a parody of Samuel Richardson's *Pamela* (1740), appears in print, as does a new translation, *The Busy-Body.* She launches a publishing business in Covent Garden, continuing it until 1749 or perhaps longer.

1742 *The Virtuous Villager,* a translation by Haywood, is published.

1743 Haywood publishes *A Present for a Servant-Maid,* her conduct-book guide for girls in service.

1744 *The Fortunate Foundlings,* Haywood's first extended work of fiction since shortly after Pope's attack on her in the 1728 *Dunciad,* is published. Her *Female Spectator,* the first monthly periodical by a woman for women, begins a run that continues from April of this year until May 1746.

1746 Haywood launches a second periodical, *The Parrot,* which runs weekly from 2 August until 4 October.

1747 A new translation by Haywood, *Memoirs of a Man of Honour,* appears in print.

1748 Haywood publishes a new novel, *Life's Progress through the Passions.*

1749	Two new works of fiction by Haywood appear, *Dalinda* and *Epistles for the Ladies.*
1750	Haywood publishes *A Letter from H—— G——g, Esq.*, and is arrested, probably for sedition.
1751	*The History of Miss Betsy Thoughtless* is published.
1752	*The History of Jemmy and Jenny Jessamy* is published (dated 1753).
1753	Haywood publishes *Modern Characters.*
1754	Haywood publishes *The Invisible Spy* (dated 1755).
1755	*The Wife* is published (dated 1756).
1756	*The Husband,* a sequel to *The Wife,* is published. Haywood begins another periodical, *The Young Lady* (weekly, 6 January-17 February), but suspends it because of illness. She dies 25 February, and is buried 3 March in the churchyard of Saint Margaret's, Westminster.
1788	*The History of Leonora Meadowson* is published posthumously.

Note on the Texts

The texts reprinted here are from the Boston Public Library copy of the first edition of *The Injur'd Husband* (December 1722; dated 1723), and from the Yale University Library copy of the first edition of *Lasselia* (October 1723; dated 1724). Haywood made no substantive changes for subsequent editions; indeed, the only changes are in accidentals, and these were almost certainly introduced by her publishers. Only the first editions can safely be regarded as authoritative. In preparing the texts for this edition I have corrected obvious printer's errors and have eliminated the quotation marks that sometimes appear at the beginning of each line of quoted material. The long *s* has been replaced by the modern letter *s*. I have preserved the display capitals that begin each major text segment, but they have not been reproduced exactly. Haywood's frequently idiosyncratic spelling and punctuation have been retained, except that extremely long dashes (a printer's device for filling out lines of text, but sometimes an author's device for indicating emphasis) have been normalized at two-em dashes (——). Some of Haywood's paragraphs are very long, running to two pages or more in the first-edition texts; for the convenience of the modern reader I have introduced breaks in the longer paragraphs wherever it seemed that the interests of clarity might be served by doing so. In *Lasselia,* each paragraph of text begins with a word in all capitals, an occasional eighteenth-century printing convention; capitalization in these words has been normalized to conform to more common eighteenth-century and modern practice.

THE INJUR'D HUSBAND; OR, THE *Miſtaken Reſentment*.

A NOVEL.

Written by Mrs. *Eliza Haywood*.

Short are the Triumphs of the Face *alone:*
Where Conduct *fails, how tott'ring is the Throne!*
Without this Virtue, Woman's weakly crown'd:
Our Minds fix Government, our Eyes but found.
Dryden.

LONDON:
Printed for *D. Brown*, Jun. at the *Black Swan*, without *Temple-Bar*; *W. Chetwood*, and *J. Woodman*, in *Ruſſel-Street Covent-Garden*; and *S. Chapman*, in *Pall-mall*. MDCCXXIII.

[Price Two Shillings.]

Previous page: Title page of first edition, 1722. Courtesy of the Trustees of the Boston Public Library.

To the Right Honourable the LADY *HOW*.[1]

Madam,

Dedications are become so scandalous of late, that, if Modesty were not a Virtue too little fashionable, both the *Patron* and *Writer* wou'd be out of Countenance: The Reason of this is evident; the Press is set to work only to gratifie a mercenary End, and He or She who is look'd on as a Person most likely to serve that Purpose is address'd, and fulsome Praises, and undeserv'd Encomiums generally answer the Design they are given for.

But I, *Madam!* propose to my self a nobler Advantage, by entreating the Protection of a Lady Qualified like *You.* The Subject of the Trifle I presume to offer, is, *the worst of Women;* and while I treat of the Inadvertencies, and indeed Vices, which there is a Possibility that *our* Sex may be guilty of, I wou'd put those of the *other* in Mind, that there is *One* among us, whose *Virtues* may attone for the *Mismanagement* of the rest.

To particularize what they are, or enter into a Detail of those Perfections, which, while they attract the Admiration of *all,* are to be describ'd by *none,* wou'd only prove me guilty of a Self-sufficiency of Thought, and justly render me unworthy of Your Favour: Of two Evils, therefore, I will chuse the least, and rather confess my Inability to speak of You, as You deserve, than by enervate Praises *lessen* the Worth I wou'd *proclaim.* The Sun by his own Rays can only be describ'd, and while the most *Abject* of created Beings receive the Benefit of his Influence, the *Noblest* are at a Loss for Means to represent him. The same Misfortune is the Fate of all who contemplate the Character of Your Ladyship; then why shou'd I lament the Want of that which the most eminently distinguish'd Genius's wou'd find themselves deficient in, tho' not in so far distant a Degree as,

MADAM,
Your Ladyship's
Most Devoted,
Most Faithful, and
Obedient Servant,
ELIZA HAYWOOD.

PREFACE.

Troubling the Reader with any Thing of this Kind, is generally so little to the Purpose, that I have often thought the Authors made Use of such Introductions more to swell the Bulk of their Book, than any other Reason: And how sensible soever I am of the many Faults the following Sheets are full of, I shou'd rather commit my self and them to the Good-nature of the World, than add to them by an impertinent Apology.

It is not, therefore, to excuse my Want of Judgment in the Conduct, or my Deficiency of Expressing the Passions I have endeavour'd to represent, but to clear my self of an Accusation, which I am inform'd is already contriv'd and prepar'd to thunder out against me, as soon as this is publish'd, that I take this Pains.

A Gentleman, who applies the little Ingenuity he is Master of, to no other Study than that of sowing Dissention among those who are so unhappy, and indeed unwise, as to entertain him, either imagines, or pretends *to do so, that tho' I have laid the Scene in* Paris, *I mean that the Adventure shou'd be thought to have happen'd in* London; *and that in the Character of a* French Baroness, *I have attempted to expose the Reputation of an* English *Woman of Quality.*[2] *I shou'd be sorry to think the Actions of any of our Ladies such as cou'd give room for a Conjecture of the Reality of what he wou'd suggest. But, suppose there were indeed an Affinity between the Vices I have describ'd, and those of some Woman he knows (for doubtless if there be, she must be of his Acquaintance) I leave the World to judge to whom she is indebted for becoming the Subject of Ridicule, to* me *for drawing a Picture whose Original is unknown, or to* him *who writes her Name at the Bottom of it.*

However, if I had design'd this as a Satyr on any Person whose Crimes I had thought worthy of it, I shou'd not have thought the Resentment of such a one considerable enough to have oblig'd me to deny it; but as I have only related a Story, which a particular Friend of mine assures me is Matter of Fact, and happen'd at the Time when he was in Paris; *I wou'd not have it made Use of as an Umbrage for the Tongue of Scandal to blast the Character of any one, a Stranger to such detested Guilt. I hope there is not a second* De Tortillée[3] *in the World, but if there be, she certainly is not without a* Du Lache[4] *to advise and assist her; and he, that* Du Lache, *who is most sensible of the Secrets of her Soul, is best able to point her out. For my Part (I thank Heaven) I can solemnly protest, a Wretch so vile never yet reach'd the Observation of*

Eliza Haywood.

THE

Injur'd Husband;

OR, THE

Mistaken Resentment.

A

NOVEL.

The Vicissitude of all human Affairs is so absolutely necessary to give Mankind a true Notion of themselves, that he who *seems* most fix'd in Happiness, and fenc'd from every Blast of adverse Fate, sooner or later, is generally led by some unavoidable Impulse to quit his Haven of Peace, and share the Storm in common with those born under less auspicious Influences. The Baron *De Tortillée,* till he was about the Age of Fifty, had pass'd his Time in a perfect Tranquility; and tho' the Sweetness of his Disposition made him commiserate, and, to the utmost of his Power, assist all who labour'd under any Affliction, yet he himself was wholly insensible what it was to be uneasy: He had from his Infancy been bred at Court, and still continued to frequent it; but as he had preserv'd his Soul untainted with any of those modish Vices, which few of the *gay* part of it are free from; so he also did from that Spirit of Faction, which the *graver* sort, and those who aim at being thought *Politicians,* are so much sway'd by. He was entirely contented with his Lot, had no ambitious Views, and enjoy'd the Goods of Fortune in that Medium, which alone can make Life happy, neither maintaining a Port[5] greater than his Estate wou'd conveniently allow, nor below what was becoming his Quality: this manner of Behaviour made him unenvy'd by his Equals, esteem'd by those of a superior Rank, and infinitely belov'd by his Inferiors; in fine, never was a Man more universally spoke well of.

Thus he *liv'd,* and thus, in all Probability, had he *dyed,* had not his ill Fortune introduc'd him to the Acquaintance of *Madamoiselle la Motte,*[6] in whose Conversation he found Charms sufficient to make him wish to change his Condition, if by it he cou'd obtain her for a Wife. This was a Lady of none of the meanest Families in *France,* and at the Death of her Father was left

Mistress of a considerable Fortune; but tho' she wanted not Wit, she had been extremely deficient in her Conduct, and the Extravagance of her Expences reduced her in a short time to have nothing of the Woman of Fashion remaining but a few rich Cloaths; with these, however, and a tolerable Face and Air, she found Means for a good while to escape that, by the Young and Proud, dreaded Evil; the Show of Poverty. Those on whom before she had bestow'd her Favours *gratis,* were now oblig'd to *purchase;*[7] and as soon as one grew weary of the Bargain, she still had the Address to gain another *Bidder:* Sometimes three or four had an equal Share in the Property, but she had Artifice enough to make each believe himself the sole Possessor. *Don Philip D'Esperanz,*[8] a *Spaniard,* was the last that supported her in this manner; but he being soon to return to his own Country, where he had a Wife and Family, she was beginning to cast about in her Mind where she shou'd find a fresh Supply, at the Time when she first became acquainted with the *Baron.* It is not to be imagin'd, that a Woman in the Circumstances she then was, would refuse an Offer, which in all her Bloom of Youth and Innocence she might have been proud to accept:——No, she knew the World too well; and pretending her speedy Compliance with his Desires was the Effect of a Passion, which Desert, like his, could not but create, deluded the enamour'd *Baron* with a Belief he was the happiest of his Sex; and they contriv'd to huddle up the Wedding[9] in such a manner, that they were marry'd before any of his Friends had the least Notion there was such a thing in Agitation. At the first Discovery of it, 'tis hard to say, whether Pity or Amazement had the greatest Share in the Hearts of those who heard it; but being depriv'd of the Opportunity of informing him what she was, in Time, forbore to let him know the Ruin it was now too late to prevent, and contented themselves with silently commiserating his Condition.

If this Woman had been possest of the smallest Grain of Honour, Gratitude, or even common Good-nature, she wou'd have endeavour'd, by her future manner of Behaviour, to retrieve the Errors of the past.——To be taken from a State of Life, which, if not abandon'd by all Sense of Shame, must have been odious to her——to be reliev'd from all those Terrors which attend Uncertainty——to be deliver'd from the Insults of the judging World, and those, more galling ones, the Man who *keeps* has a Privilege of Inflicting; and rais'd from the lowest and most contemptible Degree of Infamy, to Wealth, to Credit and to Ease, were Blessings, such as one would think she should have been too sensible of not to acknowledge, and wish, at least, to prove they were not ill bestow'd: But she was wholly dead to such Considerations, she look'd on the large Fortune she was now become Mistress of, only as a larger Means to gratify her Inclinations; and as before she had so much Regard to her Reputation, as to endeavour to hinder the World from believing her so vile as she really was, she now gave a Loose to all the Sallies of her ungovern'd Passions, imagining her Quality[10] a sufficient Sanction for her Vices, and that no Body wou'd dare to say of the *Baroness De Tortillée,* what they wou'd have made no Scruple to alledge of *Madamoiselle la Motte.*

The Truth is, the *Baron's* singular good Qualities and affable Behaviour had gain'd him so universal an Esteem, that, in respect to his Character, (since Custom has made the Errors of the *Wife* a Reflection on the *Husband*) People were infinitely more sparing of their Censures than otherwise they wou'd have been, or than her Actions indeed deserv'd. When she was first married, Women of the best Reputation thought it no Scandal to visit her, and be seen abroad with her; and had still continued to do so, if she cou'd have restrain'd her Inclinations within the Bounds of even common Decency; but alas! she had no Sense of Honour or Decorum, but behav'd her self in so wild, so dissolute a manner, that in a little time none who but wish'd to be thought virtuous wou'd take notice of her; the very Men, who glory'd not in Debauchery, shunn'd her Acquaintance, or were asham'd to own it: This, which to a Woman, capable of any solid Reflection, must have made her look back with Horror on the Vices which had so justly rendred her contemptible, did not in the least alarm her, she still had a Set of Company who humour'd her Vanity, and indeed she was easy in no other.

But, oh how blind is Love! the *Baron* still continued to adore her, so much was he deluded by her Artifices, that even her Vices appear'd Virtues; the Profuseness of her Expences seem'd to proceed from a Generosity and noble Magnanimity of Soul, which, however destructive to his Fortune, he cou'd not but applaud; the Liberties she took in her Conversation with Men, pass'd for an innocent Freedom which he cou'd not imagine a Woman really criminal wou'd dare to make use of. In fine, every thing she said, every thing she did was a new Charm to him; and neither the palpable Neglect which he found the whole World treated her with, nor the Remonstrances which some of his Friends, griev'd at his Infatuation, at last, grew free enough to make him, cou'd oblige him to look with a jealous Eye on her Conduct, or in the least abate his Dotage: Indeed, how little soever she seem'd to regard the rest of the World's taking notice of her Faults, she, for the most part, was cautious enough to prevent him from making any Discovery of them; or if at any time she was conscious of an Irregularity which might occasion his Suspicion, she knew how to bring her self off; she had Sighs, Tears, Swoonings, Languishments, at Command; no Woman that ever liv'd was Mistress of more Artifice, nor had less the Appearance of being so: Nature had given her a Countenance extremely favourable for her Purpose; and whenever she was pleas'd to join to those Looks of Sincerity and Innocence any Asseverations that she was so, it was hardly possible to believe her otherwise; her Voice too had a perswasive Softness in it, which it was very difficult to withstand; and one had need to be perfectly acquainted with her *Actions,* before one cou'd distrust her *Words.* And this is all can be said to vindicate the unhappy *Baron* from that Imputation of Stupidity, which the long Series of his Delusions have drawn upon him.

But to return to her History, which alone can give the Reader any just Notion of her Character: There was among the Number of those who now frequented her Drawing-Room, a Fellow call'd *Du Lache;* he was too disagreeable to be receiv'd in the Quality of a Lover, neither did he visit her with any such View; *Fortune* had been less kind to him than *Nature,* for what he wanted in *Beauty* was abundantly made up in *Cunning;* but he was so wretchedly indigent, that, tho' he had been employ'd in the Management of several Intrigues (for which no Body was more fit) he never had met with Persons who thought the Service he did merited the Supply of even the common Necessaries of Life: He was half perish'd for Want, when Chance brought him into the *Baroness's* Acquaintance; they soon found in each other sufficient to create an Intimacy; and she thought her self no less fortunate in engaging to her Interest a Person whose Brain was capable of projecting every thing, and whose Principle was to scruple nothing; than he did in having it in his Power to oblige a Patroness, whose Humour he perceiv'd was not to make scanty Retributions for Service such as his: In a short time his *Tatters* were exchanged for *Embroidery* and *Brocade;* he had Money in his Pocket, went to *Court,* to the *Opera's,* Gaming-Houses, Assemblies, kept Company with Gentlemen, and, to those who knew him not before, appear'd like one himself: His Business was, in all publick Places, to extol the Wit and Beauty of the *Baroness De Tortillée!*——to make all Women appear vile in Competition with *her*——if he heard one fam'd for any Excellence, to form some Story to degrade her——to break off intended Marriages——to render those already wedded the Objects of each other's Hate; and, in fine, where-ever he found a noble Friendship between Persons of different Sexes, to endeavour to *disunite* or make it appear *scandalous. Malice* is seldom barren of Invention, and People that apply themselves to this kind of Mischief, have generally a manner of *insinuating* what they wou'd have believ'd, which *Truth* and *Honesty,* disdaining to make use of, are perfect Strangers to. *Du Lache* was so successful in his Employment, that tho' the *Marquis De Sonville*[11] had long lov'd, and been belov'd by one of the finest Women of the Age; not all her Charms, her Tenderness, her Constancy cou'd maintain the

Place she held in his Affections, when once attack'd by the Artifices of this subtle Villain; he soon was brought to lessen his *Esteem;* and that destroy'd, all that remains of *Love* is scarce worth calling so; *Indifference* immediately succeeds, and the Heart is free to receive the Idea of the first agreeable Object that presents it self. No Body can doubt but that the *Baroness,* for whose sake all this was done, was the Person introduc'd: He was no sooner discover'd to grow cool toward his former Mistress, than he was brought to visit her; and she being extreamly desirous of engaging him, and knowing how to form her Behaviour to all Humours, found it no Difficulty to suit her self to his.

She also found her Account in the Addresses of the young *Chevalier St. Aumar:*[12] he was handsome, gay, gallant, and liberal to an Excess! He profess'd publickly his Admiration of her, waited on her where-ever she went; treated,[13] and made her very rich Presents. One wou'd think, indeed, that this *last* Article shou'd have but little Sway with a Woman of the Station she now was rais'd to; but alas! if the *Baron's* Estate had been twice doubled, it wou'd have been too small for those Expences, which, to indulge a Temper, such as hers, were absolutely necessary: She was now above making Assignations at any of those mean Places of Entertainment she had formerly been accustom'd to; all must now be done with an Air of *Grandeur;* her *Embroiderer,* her *Milliner,* her *Mantua-maker,* her *Tire-Woman,*[14] had all of them Houses of their own handsomely furnish'd at her Charge, and adorn'd fit to receive a *Messalina*[15] equal to the first in Greatness. It must be confess'd that, in *this,* she was politick enough, for whoever had seen her at any of those Peoples Houses, wou'd not have believ'd she came thither out of any other Design than to consult about her *Dress;* but then it requir'd almost a *Prince's* Revenue to supply the Demands of those *Creatures,* and purchase the least tollerable Assurance of their Secrecy. The Jewels, therefore, and other valuable Things, which the Prodigality of *St. Aumar* bestow'd on her, were of great Service; for the poor *Baron,* who was always pleas'd to see her appear magnificent, imagin'd they were bought with that Mony which was really employ'd in Bribery on the Instruments of his Dishonour.

But, tho' she found it very much to the Advantage of her *Interest* as well as *Pleasure,* to converse with *St. Aumar,* her Acquaintance with *La Sourbe*[16] was infinitely more so to the one, tho' far incapable of the other: He was old, deform'd, diseas'd, and had nothing either in his Person or Address which cou'd render his Caresses supportable to a Woman of any Taste; but the Abundance of his *Wealth* counterbalanc'd all other Deficiencies, and this fine Lady receiv'd him in his Turn, with all the Softness and obliging Tenderness that the most lovely of her Admirers thought themselves happy in Possessing; 'twas to them all, indeed, but *feign'd,* and therefore the same Arts she practis'd to impose on others might easily be us'd on him, for in Reality she never knew what 'twas to love sincerely; and, at a Time when, perhaps, there were twenty (tho' *each* believ'd himself the *only* Blest) who possess'd all the Favours she was capable of bestowing, she was over-heard to say, (to one that was Partner in all her Secrets) that that Woman was a Fool that ever gave her self the least *real* Uneasiness on the account of *Love:*—A Topknot tied amiss, said she, would give me greater Pain than the Eternal *Damnation* of all Mankind.——Not to be *Ador'd* indeed, is not to *Live*! and to engage the Assiduity of a Fellow one likes, 'tis necessary to counterfeit a Passion. 'Tis certain she did it with such Success, that the most discerning Eye might have been deceiv'd; How then cou'd *La Sourbe* escape the Snare? He had but little been accustom'd to the Conversation of Women, and was utterly ignorant of the Wiles laid for him.——He thought himself in Heaven, and cou'd scarce contain his Senses amidst that Profusion of Delight, her Wit, her Gaiety, her endearing Softness shower'd upon him. He knew not how, sufficiently, to show the Sense he had of such a Blessing as her Love, and thought of nothing but the Means of returning it to the utmost of his Power!——All his Hours, his Fortune, his very Life, was wholly at her Devotion; and she had so absolute a Command over him, and knew so well her Power, that she even made him the instrument of forwarding her Amours with others. But it was not only to her own Management she was indebted for making this deluded Gentleman subservient to her Ends, *Du Lache,* as in all the rest of her Intrigues, was no inconsiderable Assistant here: He was extremely ready at Invention, had a thousand little Stratagems to prompt decaying Desire, and as many Ways to make the Person whom he found it his Interest to deceive deaf to all Arguments but those he undertook to maintain.

But, notwithstanding all his Cunning, he was extremely put to a stand, when coming one Morning, as was his Custom, to visit the *Baroness,* and receive her Commands, he found her at her *Toilet* uneasie to the last degree; she had two or three Attendants in the Room, whom, as soon as she saw him enter, she dismiss'd, and stepping to him with something of a disorder'd Motion, O *Du Lache,* said she, I have wish'd for you this Hour——I am distracted in my Thoughts, and if your, hitherto successful, Wit should now fail me, I am undone for ever——Forbid it Heaven! answer'd he strangely surpriz'd. Yes, resum'd she, I again repeat it, I am undone, ruin'd for ever, unless you find the Means to help me.——All in my Power, Madam, added he, you know you may command. Talk not of Power, interrupted she impatiently, this must——this shall be in your Power, unless you wish to see me do some desperate Deed——if disappointed here,——in the extremest Wish my Soul e'er knew, I'll murder you,——my self, and all who want the means to ease me: She join'd to these Words so wild a Look and Motion, that *Du Lache* repented he had seem'd to doubt of his Ability to serve her, and endeavour'd to remedy that Fault by swearing that he would bring about whatever she employ'd him in, let the Nature or Consequence be what it wou'd.

She appear'd something more tranquil at this Assurance, and seating her self, and obliging him to do so, I am satisfied, said she, that your Zeal to serve me will carry you to great Lengths; nor do I think, when I have the Power of reflecting, that the Task I now enjoin is at all more difficult than those you have already gone thro', with all the Success I cou'd desire; but, alas! continu'd she, beginning to relapse into her former Disorder, the excessive Eagerness with which my Spirits are agitated in Pursuit of the Blessing I wou'd possess, and the certain, everlasting Misery I must endure, shou'd my Endeavours fail, confuses, drives me mad,——My Soul will never know a Moment's Peace, till sure Enjoyment shall destroy Supense. I cannot rest while there remains a Possibility of being wretched——Wretched, did I say? How poor are Words to express what 'tis I mean!——'Twou'd be a Curse beyond Damnation.—— She uttered many more the like Extravagancies, till *Du Lache,* a little recover'd from the Astonishment her Behaviour had put him in, interrupted her by saying that, if to be *disappointed* of her Aim, wou'd plunge her in such *Horrors,* the *Possession* of it must certainly afford her adequate *Delight,* and begg'd her to think on *that,* and rely on his Industry to compass[17] it, as soon as she shou'd inform him by what Means. Well then, (said the *Baroness* composing her self as much as possible) I will no longer doubt a Management which never yet has fail'd me; nor in the least imagine, that in the Perplexity you see me you will not do your utmost for my Relief. Know then, continu'd she sighing, my present Disorders are occasion'd by a Passion, the Force of which I ne'er before experienc'd.——Oft have I *lik'd,* but never, never *lov'd* till now.——One fatal Moment has inform'd me more, than all the various Amours of many Years cou'd do——Oh! I have seen a Man whose Looks! whose Voice! whose every Motion is Enchantment——At the first View my melting Soul dissolv'd—— but when he talk'd, methought, my very Life flew from me,——the soft Delight was more than Sense cou'd bear.——O, *Du Lache,* thou know'st this Prodigy of Charms——this Wonder of his Sex——this more than Angel——yet, dull, dull as thou art! thou never spok'st him as he is.——Oft have I heard thy Tongue repeat the Name of *Beauclair,*[18] but not with Raptures to enflame Desire.——Why, too ungrateful Friend, wert thou so careless of my Happiness, as not to let me know that there were Joys in Love beyond all I had already tasted?——Cou'dst thou——Tell me, I say, is it owing to thy Stupidity, or the Thanklessness of thy Nature that thou cou'dst converse with *Beauclair*! the adorable *Beauclair*, without a Wish *Tortillée* might be blest in his Possession!

'Tis impossible to represent the Confusion that *Du Lache* was in when he heard the Name *Beauclair* mention'd in that manner: He knew indeed, that he had all the Perfections that the *Baroness* had describ'd, and was not at all surpris'd to find her so much more charm'd with him than ever she had appear'd to be with any other; but he knew also that, all lovely as he was, the *Graces* of his *Mind* were far superiour to the *Beauties* of his *Person*, and was sensible there were some Obstacles which he had good reason to fear wou'd be invincible ones, in her way to the Happiness she aim'd at. In the first Place, the Heart of *Beauclair* had long been devoted to a young Lady fam'd for, and really Mistress of, every Excellence that cou'd adorn a Woman; that he was contracted to her before he went to his Travels (from which he was but lately return'd) and that there wanted nothing to compleat the solemnizing the Nuptials of this accomplish'd Pair, but the Recovery of a darling Brother, who at that time lay ill of a Fever. But tho' this of it self was sufficient to deter *Du Lache* from entertaining any presumptuous Hopes in favour of *Tortillée*, yet the Character of *Beauclair* was infinitely more so, he had Honour, Constancy, Good-nature, and to all these Virtues an excellent Penetration which render'd it almost an Impossibility to impose upon his Judgment: He plac'd not his Affections on *Montamour*[19] (for that was the Name of his intended Bride) without a perfect Knowledge how worthy she was of them: and the Charms of the one, and the Wisdom of the other, was a Bulwark which this insidious Villain fear'd wou'd be impregnable to all the Stratagems his Cunning cou'd invent.

The Vexation this Consideration gave him kept him from making an immediate Answer to what the *Baroness* had said, 'till guessing the true reason of his Silence, she prosecuted her Discourse in this manner. I wonder not, resum'd she, that you appear disorder'd at the Request I make. A Lady who sat by me last Night at the *Opera*, where I beheld this Idol of my Soul, gave me his whole History, and I suppose 'tis his Engagement with *Montamour* makes you doubtful how far you may be able to prevail in behalf of *Tortillée*. You think, perhaps, *her* Charms maintain too forcible a Lustre to be eclips'd by *mine*, and are unwilling to embark in a Design which you imagine cannot easily be accomplish'd; but know (continu'd she with a Frown) that I am resolv'd to triumph over this happy Rival, or die in the Attempt——therefore contrive some Means, and that this Moment too, to make me blest, or be assur'd

I will not brook the Disappointment unreveng'd. *Du Lache,* who knew the natural Obstinacy of her Temper, made much more so by the Violence of her present Desires, found it wou'd be altogether fruitless to set before her Eyes the little Likelihood there was for her to succeed; all he cou'd do, was to entreat her Patience, and protest by all the Oaths he cou'd invent, that he wou'd exert his utmost Abilities to procure the Satisfaction she requir'd: And perceiving nothing but an absolute Dependance cou'd make her less desperate, he was oblig'd to give her Hopes (which himself believ'd were but fallacious) that in a few Days she shou'd be in Possession of all her Soul was bent on.

It was now that he found himself in the greatest Perplexity he had ever been in all his Life; the more he consider'd on the Promise he had made, the less Probability there appear'd of making it good; and to fail, he knew wou'd ruin him with the *Baroness* for ever: his *present Subsistance,* and his Hopes of making his *future Fortune,* depended on her Favour, and he grew almost distracted, when, after a thousand various Projections, he cou'd find none that seem'd feasible to preserve it: He endeavour'd however to delay the Misfortune he dreaded, and by concealing his inward Perturbations, and always, in her Presence, appearing with his former Gaiety, made her indeed believe he really had found the Means of doing what she expected from him. To divert her Thoughts as much as possible from *Beauclair,* he never suffer'd her to be alone; and whenever the *Baron*'s Absence gave them an Opportunity, he contriv'd that either the *Marquess De Sonville,* the *Chevalier St. Aumar,* or *Monsieur La Sourbe,* or some one or other of her *Devotees,* shou'd be perpetually with her; but all this was of but little Efficacy, she was so far of the Humour of *Mankind,* that if *Beauclair* had been less *agreeable,* yet he was *un-enjoy'd,* and, *therefore,* most *desirable.* She was willing, however, to trifle away the Time in these Amusements, till that happy Moment should arrive, which was to give her more ecstatic Joys: And knowing the Subtilty of *Du Lache,* and how much it was his Interest to oblige her, did not greatly doubt but that some way or other he would bring it about.

The Truth is, it ever was uppermost in his Thoughts, but he found so little likelihood that any Efforts he shou'd make wou'd meet with Success, that he was beginning to despair; when on a sudden, his prompting *Fiend,* which seldom left him long unaided, put it into his Head, that *Madamoiselle Sansfoy*[20] might be of Use in the Mischief he endeavour'd: This was a Lady whose extreme Love of hearing herself speak made her often the Instrument of both Good and Ill, without any Intention of her own to serve the End of either; she had a great deal of *Vanity* in her *Nature,* and therefore cou'd not be without an equal Share of *Coquetry* in her *Behaviour,* and as she was excessive fond of being admir'd by the *Men,* cou'd not be capable of any real Regard for the *Women:* She took a vast Pleasure in piquing any one more amiable than herself, and was never so happy as when she had the Power of giving Pain: She dress'd well, was young, gay, and perfectly well shap'd, had very regular Features, and a most delicate Complection——and to all this, an uncommon quickness of Apprehension, a ready Thought, a free and easie Delivery of her Words, and an entertaining Turn in Conversation, which made her Company every where desir'd: She was acquainted both with *Beauclair* and *Montamour,* and had with the latter as great an Intimacy as the Difference of their Humours wou'd permit. It was not difficult for a Person of much less Discernment than *Du Lache* to find out what manner of Address wou'd be most acceptable to this fine Lady; he had several Times happen'd to meet her at a Place where he had visited, and from that took the Liberty of going to see her at her House; he wanted not Words to *excuse,* nor she good Humour to *forgive* the Boldness, and perceiving himself favourably receiv'd, after a thousand Encomiums on her Beauty had usher'd in the Discourse, he told her that nothing had ever so much the Power of giving him Surprize, as that *Beauclair,* who had seen the Wonders of her Charms, cou'd so far wrong his Judgment, and the good Opinion the World had of his Wit, to give *Montamour* the Preference in his Esteem: It must be confess'd indeed, said this subtile Detractor, that she has lovely Eyes, a fine Shape and Air, a vast deal of Wit, and, where *Sansfoy* is absent, is Mistress of a thousand Soul-attracting Graces; but, when you both appear together, I cannot help believing that *Beauclair,* and all (as many such there are) who think like him, are Blind. He very well knew the Effect these Words wou'd produce, and that a Woman of the Temper she was, to whom they were directed, is not so angry with the *Praiser,* as the *Prais'd.*

Sansfoy immediately grew pale with Envy, and imagining that what *Du Lache* had said of the Passion of *Beauclair* for *Montamour,* only express'd a mannerly Commiseration of her Want of Charms who had not Power to engage him, was ready to burst with inward Spite all the time he had been talking; till, able to contain no longer, I know not (said she with a disdainful Toss of her Head) how *many* there may be of *Beauclair*'s Mind in his Admiration of *Montamour,* but I am very sure that *none,* besides himself, take any Pains to be well in her Esteem; and, perhaps, the little Interruption he has to fear in his Addresses there, is the greatest Inducement to his making 'em. *Security,* added she, is a valuable Article in *Marriage,* and as he designs her for a *Wife,* Housewifery, Silence, Meekness, Obedience and Humility are the Accomplishments he thinks most necessary. But Madam! (resum'd *Du Lache,* rejoic'd he had wrought her to a Disposition proper for his Purpose) do you really believe this seeming virtuous Lady is what she appears to be? Is there no favourite Lover who in the dark triumphs over *Beauclair*——I have heard odd Stories, which yet bear a Possibility of Truth—For Heavens sake what? (interrrupted *Sansfoy* eagerly) who is the Man? Pardon me, Madam! answer'd he, I dare not make Reports, which I am not sure may not be fabulous——I would not for the World be guilty of Injustice——Nay, tho' I knew all I have been told were positively True, I am too tender of Ladies Honour to repeat it.

The natural Curiosity which always made her inquisitive into the Affairs of every Body, pointed now with Malice, fill'd her with perfect Agonies; She wou'd have given almost a Limb to be let into this Secret, and the greater Unwillingness he pretended to divulge it, the more she grew impatient to discover it: She entreated him with so much Earnestness, and so many Conjurations,[21] that at last he seem'd won by 'em, and told her a long Story which he had before invented; the Sum of which was, that Monsieur *Galliard*[22] had long been an Admirer, and in secret possess'd all the Favours that *Montamour* cou'd give. The Reason why this artful Villain made this Gentleman a Property to further his Designs was, that he knew *Sansfoy* had a prodigious desire to engage him, and of Consequence wou'd more industriously blaze abroad the Scandal he aim'd at, than if he had mention'd a Person more indifferent to her; he knew also that he had been acquainted with *Montamour* from her Childhood, that he was accounted of an amorous Disposition, and that he profess'd an extraordinary Friendship for that Lady. And tho' there needed not all these Probabilities to make the censorious *Sansfoy* believe all he said, yet he was sensible there was Occasion for many more, and stronger, to oblige the rest of the World to entertain an ill Opinion of a Woman who had ever behav'd with an exemplary Discretion.

This was the first Step *Du Lache* had made toward the disuniting the Affections of these two amiable Persons; the next was to ingratiate himself as much as possible with *Beauclair*. He had a good Voice, and Judgment in Musick, and being told that Gentleman was a great Admirer of it, found means to oblige him to a liking of his Conversation, by presenting him with some fine Compositions which he pretended had been sent him by some of the best Masters in *Italy* whom he kept a Correspondence with. Not all *Beauclair's* Wisdom cou'd defend his Good-nature from being deluded by the Artifice of this common Traytor to all Honour and Virtue, he became extremely pleas'd with him; and far from suspecting his Designs, let him into all his Affairs with a Freedom which some time after he found he had sufficient Reason to repent. One Day as they were alone together, he told him he had been the Night before at *Montamour's*, that *Sansfoy* was with her, and staying till it was late, he had waited on her Home; that as they went, she had given him some Hints he was not so happy in the Affections of his Mistress as she had made him hope, and that *Galliard* was mention'd by her in a manner which, tho' he was not inclinable to Jealousy, had given him much Disquiet. 'Twas with a vast deal of Satisfaction that *Du Lache* found his Plot had so well succeeded on *Sansfoy,* and now began to hope there was a Possibility of deceiving them all, by the same means he had done her; he dissembled his Sentiments however, and seem'd to regard what *Beauclair* had told him, but as a thing in which he had no manner of Concern; tho' all the Time he was in his Company, his Invention was at Work how to make the best Use of what he heard, and having hit on a Thought which seem'd to be a lucky one, disengag'd himself as soon as possible, and went about the Execution of it.

He saw that with Wisdom, Honour, Generosity, Sweetness of Disposition, and a thousand shining Qualities which made up the Character of *Beauclair,* there were certain Frailties mix'd, which prov'd him not absolutely Divine. From their last Conversation he gather'd, that an Impatience of Indignities, and a too great Aptitude to credit all Reports that should be made him, gave Treachery an advantagious Ground to dart her Arrows from; and perceiving that those little Reflections *Sansfoy* had made, had been sufficient to give him Pain, he resolv'd to strengthen what she said, by Proofs which should wear the Appearance of Infallibility.

Toncarr[23] and *Le Songe*[24] were Men that had no other Dependance than on their Wits, and if employ'd in any Design which they found it their Interest to undertake, thought it the least of their Business to enquire whether it were honourable or not. A publick Oath, or private Assassination, were what at any time a Prospect of Advantage wou'd lead them to. *Du Lache* was perfectly acquainted with their Principles, and in his Days of Poverty had been one of their Associates, and therefore made no Doubt but he shou'd find them both willing and able to serve him in his present Affair. The Moment he left *Beauclair* he sent for 'em to his Lodgings, and having communicated the whole matter to them, and receiv'd their Promises of Assistance, they all together agreed on a Stratagem which was accordingly executed the next Morning in the manner following.

Du Lache went pretty early to give the *Bonjour* to *Beauclair* at his Lodgings, and after some little Discourse of ordinary Affairs, ask'd that Gentleman, whom he knew to be a Lover of it, to walk with him, it being a Morning full of Temptation; the Proposition was agreeable, and as soon as he was drest they went together on Foot towards the *Louvre,*[25] designing for the Gardens: But as they turn'd the Corner of a little back Lane, which carried them to the great

Street before the Palace, they heard a sudden Clash of Swords; and immediately saw two Men engag'd in so furious a manner, as if each had vow'd the other's Death: But one of them seem'd less skilful in the use of his Weapon, and was press'd upon by his Adversary with so much Advantage, that in all Appearance he must have fallen or yielded, if *Beauclair* and *Du Lache,* no other Persons happening to be near, had not run in to his Relief: The Moment they advanc'd, the Person that seem'd to be the Foil'd, took to his Heels, and was immediately out of Sight; his Antagonist made an offer of pursuing, yet not so eagerly but that he was easily with-held by *Beauclair,* who asking what had been the Occasion of their Quarrel and how it happen'd that they had made Choice of a Place so unfit for their Purpose, cou'd get no other Answer from him, than that he was undone! and that to have been hinder'd from pursuing the Person with whom he had been fighting, was a more cruel Misfortune than the Loss of his Life would have been, had the other got the better. *Beauclair* was prodigiously amaz'd at these Words; he could not imagine that a Fellow of the Rank he appear'd to be (being dress'd after the manner of a Valet) cou'd have so nice a Sense of Honour as to prefer it to his Life, and had a great Curiosity to know of what Nature this Affair was, which made him extremely pleas'd when *Du Lache* pretending an equal Astonishment, press'd the Man to relate it.

At last, seemingly overcome by the Perswasions of Gentlemen to whom he ow'd his Safety, he told 'em (after he had engag'd their Promises never to reveal the Secret he was about to intrust 'em with) that he was a Dependant of Monsieur *Galliard,* had formerly liv'd with him, and was now employ'd by him in the Conduct of an Amour which, if discover'd, wou'd certainly be of fatal Consequence: The young Lady, said he, with whom my Master (for I still call him so) is enamour'd, is of Quality, and has a Brother whom the least Occasion of Suspicion wou'd set on fire for the Honour of his Family. Every Body knows the Temper of *Madamoiselle*[26] *Galliard,* that she is one of the most jealous Women on Earth, and being fix'd in a Belief that she is not so well in her Husband's Affections as she cou'd wish, makes it her whole Study to find out what Woman is the Cause, for some such one she is sure there is, and if discover'd will not fail to expose her in the most gross and shameful manner imaginable. Now you must know, *Messieurs*! (continu'd he) that this Lady being pretty closely observ'd by the Brother I told you of, and a Gentleman whom she is shortly to be married to, cannot oblige my Master with her Conversation, neither so frequently nor so long as both of 'em desire; but his Impatience had contriv'd a Way to remedy that Misfortune. He provided a little Ladder of Ropes, which she fastening to her Window, he might easily enter, and pass a whole Night with her. This very Ladder, and a Letter appointing the Hour he was to go, I was this Morning to deliver to her; but, Oh unlucky Accident! *Madamoiselle,* whether she over-heard the Orders he was giving me, or whether she only suspected my so often coming to the House and being in private with my Master was on some such Design, I know not, but she immediately sent a Fellow, a Creature entirely at her Devotion, after me, who following me without my taking Notice, or in the least imagining he was behind me, till we came into this bye Lane, where he snatch'd my Bundle from me, which, unsuspecting any such thing, I held carelessly in my Hand, he immediately whipt it into his Pocket,[27] and drawing his Sword to defend his Prize, perceiving I was doing the same to recover it, engag'd me in the manner in which you found us.

There was a visible Alteration in *Beauclair*'s Countenance from the first Moment this Fellow mention'd the Name of *Galliard,* but when he heard him say, the Lady to whom he should have deliver'd the Ladder of Ropes, had a *Brother,* and that she was in a short Time to be *married,* his Face seem'd dy'd in Crimson, his Eyes shot Fire, and wild Impatience distorted every Feature. With what a Pleasure *Du Lache* observ'd it, the Reader will easily imagine, for I believe none will be so stupid as not to see that this was the Contrivance which had been form'd the Night before, and that those Fellows who seem'd such Foes, were no other than *Le Songe* and *Toncarr,* who had confederated with the other, and invented this Story, which was likely enough to confirm the Suspicions *Beauclair* had already, thro' *Sansfoy*'s Suggestions, conceiv'd of the unblameable *Montamour.* This artful Villain, to farther the base Design so successfully begun, immediately cried out in a seeming Astonishment, Oh Heavens! This Lady whom you have been speaking of, is no other than *Montamour,* and this Gentleman, to whom with me you have been discovering her Weakness, the very Man who was design'd to make her happy in a Husband. A thousand Circumstances concur to make me know my Fears are but too true.——What have I done (return'd the other with a well counterfeited Terror) what have I said?—Wretch that I am——has my unwary Tongue let slip ought that may discover what my Master wou'd not for his Soul have known——has any inadvertent Word escap'd me, that may give you reason to imagine 'tis *Montamour* who is enamour'd of *Galliard* to so high a degree, that for his Sake she can consent to suffer Freedoms, such as I have been speaking of——Oh too too sure, (continu'd he tearing his Hair) I am, by some fatal Accident, made guilty, the Secret of my Master is betray'd, the Lady is expos'd, and we are all ruin'd. No, no, (said *Beauclair,* assuming as much as possible his accustom'd Serenity of Countenance) you are so far from being guilty of any thing can be call'd a Crime, that in making this Discovery, tho' undesign'd by you, you have oblig'd a Gentleman who never will be ungrateful. Take this (added he giving him a purse of Gold) and ever be assur'd to find a Friend in *Beauclair.*

The Fellow seem'd to start at the name of *Beauclair,* and after having several Times repeated, Good God! is it possible! fell on his Knees, entreating him, that in what manner soever he express'd his Resentments, that he would take no notice of him in the Affair. I am an unfortunate Gentleman, added he, who have a large Family, and no other Dependance than the Favour of my Master, and as it was not thro' Design but Accident I have made you acquainted with this History (little suspecting, Heav'n knows, how deeply you were interested in it) I beg my unhappy Children may not suffer for the Folly of their Father; for, sure I am, if Monsieur *Galliard* shou'd know it is from me you learn'd the Secret, my Life would be the first Sacrifice he would offer to his Mistress's Reputation. All the Rage of Temper which *Beauclair* had been endeavouring to quell, return'd, at this last Word, with greater Violence than ever; and wholly unable to contain his Fury——His Mistress! interrupted he, Oh Damnation on the Thought! ten thousand Fiends torture her false deceiving Soul——Curse on her treacherous Charms,——her counterfeited Modesty,——her cool Reserve,——the Jilt,——the Hypocrite! was there no Man but me to have made a Property,——am I, of all my Sex, chose out as fittest for the Cover of her secret Lewdness? He wou'd doubtless have vented the o'er-boyling Passions of his Mind in many more such like Exclamations, if *Du Lache* had not reminded him of the Place they were in, and intreated him to conceal his Disorders till he should come into one where Privacy shou'd more conveniently permit him to indulge them. *Beauclair* thank'd him for this friendly Admonition, and turning to *Le Songe* (for it was he who had entertain'd him with this fine Invention) bad him be easie, for what ever he shou'd determine, to revenge the Wrongs *Galliard* had done him, it shou'd never be known by what means he made a Discovery of them. *Du Lache* parted from his confederate Villain with an applauding Smile, for the Success of an Enterprize which they promis'd themselves to be very merry at hereafter, and follow'd *Beauclair,* who, with an Air that spoke his inward Agitations, was walking toward the Palace Gardens: They took two or three Turns there, but the Charms of the Morning having drawn a good deal of Company, it grew troublesome to this distracted Lover; he went Home again, and, giving Orders not to be disturb'd, shut himself into his Closet[28] with *Du Lache.*

It was now this subtle Insinuater had an Opportunity of making every thing appear as he would have it: The prudent and reserv'd Behaviour which render'd *Montamour* an envy'd Example to all the young Ladies of her Time, by his Suggestions now seem'd all Artifice; and the Heart which had so long, and so justly, paid Homage to her as the most truly adorable of her Sex, was now brought to consider her as the vilest. At first his Resolutions were to send a Challenge to *Galliard,* but his mischievous Adviser with reason fearing that if they fought, which ever got the better, such an Encounter might produce an *Eclaircissement*[29] sufficient to detect his Villainy, perswaded him, that as she had render'd herself unworthy of his *Affection,* she also had of his *Regard,* and that it was too much to hazard his Life in a Cause which when known cou'd neither add to his Honour, or restore that of the Person for whom he fought. To what End *Monsieur,* said he, shou'd you engage in a Quarrel of this Nature? *Galliard* is not a Rival whose Addresses *may,* but already *have* obtain'd every thing to the Prejudice of your Passion, and shou'd your Sword have all the Advantages you cou'd desire, what wou'd it avail? *Montamour* wou'd not be less unsully'd; his Blood cou'd never wash her Stains away, nor cou'd his Death give back that Virtue which alone can make her worthy of your Love.

He us'd many more Arguments of this nature; and finding the other inclinable to listen to every thing he said, Methinks, resum'd he, it better wou'd become a Passion injur'd to that Degree yours is, to pay the Injustice with Scorn than Anger,——and since Heav'n, by a Means so unexpected, has given you a perfect Knowledge of her Perfidy, to imagine you will still continue any Professions of Tenderness there, wou'd be to harbour the most despicable Notions of your Understanding; to desist from them, without condescending to give her any Reason for so doing, wou'd be the most galling Revenge you can take.——Let all those who have seen your *Adorations* be Witness of your *Contempt,*——if Chance shou'd bring you into her Presence, behold her with *Indifference,*—speak of her with *Disdain,* and, if possible, think of her as she deserves, with *Hate:* Or, (continu'd he, perceiving *Beauclair* cou'd not forbear sighing at that Word) if that is a Task too difficult to be accomplish'd presently, *feign* at least to do so:——Believe me, who am perfectly well acquainted with the Humour of the Sex, that nothing is so great a Shock as cool Indifference.——*Rage,* tho' exprest in the rudest manner, still discovers there are Remains of Passion in the Heart which harbours it, and only feeds the Pride of her 'tis vented on; but a *sedate,* an *unregarding* Air, stabs the vain *Coquette* in the tenderest Part. You speak my Sense, answer'd *Beauclair,* I do not believe any thing so truly stinging to Womankind, as when they find their Power of creating Inquietudes are past; and yet (cry'd he after a Pause) I ne'er observ'd in *Montamour* that Humour——but, (added he changing his Voice) she is all Artifice——all damn'd Deceit, and knows how to dress the worst of Vices with a Show of Virtue. *Du Lache,* I hate her, by Heav'n I do,——and she shall know I do,——I'll write and tell her so this very Moment. Alas! reply'd he, how little is a Soul, in the Condition yours is, capable of judging of its own Conceptions——to say you *hate,* is to confess you *love,*——for Heaven's sake do not thus unman your self,——if you must write, let it be——What? interrrupted *Beauclair.* I wish, rejoin'd the other, you'd give me leave to dictate. With all my Heart, (answer'd he) write what you think most proper——what you yourself in the like Circumstance wou'd say, but take care be sure, not to let slip one Word may look like Tenderness, and I will copy't over and send it to her strait.

Thus did this unsuspecting Gentleman, blinded by Passion, and sooth'd by the base Arts of the most treacherous of all Villains, join in the Deceit against himself, and aid the Ruin of his own Hopes. *Du Lache* was too assiduous in Mischief to give him Time for Reflection, and taking Pen and Paper immediately writ in this manner.

To Madamoiselle *Montamour.*

Tho' Nothing is more base than for the Tongue or Pen to make Professions of a Passion which the Heart is a Stranger to, yet nothing is more in fashion even among those who pretend to the greatest Honour, of both Sexes; but, as I *resolve to be for ever out of it, so I will not accuse* you, *because I will not give you the Trouble of endeavouring at a Justification, which will be altogether vain.*

This, therefore, comes to bid you an eternal Adieu, *wishing you a long Series of Contentment in those Amusements you are pleas'd, at* present, *to place your Felicity in; and that the Memory of what has pass'd between us, may not* hereafter *afford a more just Occasion of Disquiet to* you, *than to the*

Once Passionate

BEAUCLAIR.

This, being extremely approv'd of by *Beauclair,* was immediately copy'd over by him, and sent to *Montamour:* but notwithstanding the Rage he was in, and the seeming Reason he had to be so, the Respect he had always been accustom'd to pay this Lady, not all his Belief of her Unworthiness cou'd utterly erace; he cou'd not bring himself to treat her in this manner, without giving to his own Soul a Shock the most sensible it cou'd sustain; and tho' he was perswaded to an Assurance that what he did was entirely right, he cou'd not do it without Agonies inexpressible.

But if the *Sender* of these cruel Lines felt such Disquiets, how infinitely more terrible must their Influence be on the unfortunate *Receiver*! the innocent, injur'd *Montamour*! Tho' her Modesty, and the natural Reservedness of her Temper, had kept her from making such violent Declarations of her Passion, as many of her Sex are too apt to do, yet never Woman lov'd to a greater or more sublime Degree; had Life and *Beauclair's* Satisfaction been at Stake, she wou'd have made no Scruple to relinquish the one, if by it she might have purchas'd him the other. With such a Profusion of Tendernesss she regarded him, that her whole Soul was taken up, and render'd incapable of any other Thought; nor had she till this unhappy Moment, thro' the Course of her Affection ever met with the least Cause to make her wish, she could be less devoted to him. How prodigious then, how much beyond what *Words* can represent, or even *Thought,* unfeeling it, conceive, must be her Astonishment, her Grief, her Indignation, at these distracting Lines! It was but two Days since he had parted from her with all the Tokens of a Soul-raptur'd Passion, and what now cou'd move him to abjure it and renounce his Vows, was something so amazing, that it seem'd impossible.——She cou'd not presently believe her Eyes:——She read the fatal Scroll again and again, and being perfectly assured it was his *Hand,* had not the least hold for Hope his *Heart* was untainted with the Vices common to his Sex——She found herself utterly abandon'd, the Letter told her so, in Words too plain to suffer her to make a doubt of it; and what she endur'd in that Reflection, none, but those in the like Circumstance, can guess. The Hints he gave, that she plac'd her Felicity in Amusements in which he had no Part, she consider'd as the common Artifice of Mankind, who when they no longer find it to their Satisfaction to continue their Professions, to veil their own Inconstancy and Levity of Nature, throw the Odium on the Person they forsake: and in this View he appear'd so black, that for some Moments she found Ease in Hate. Stript of those Graces (said she to herself) which distinguish'd him from the rest of Men, and which alone cou'd excuse the Idolatry of my fond Soul, I should deserve the base Contempt he treats me with, shou'd I persist to love,——no, I'll despise him, drive him from my Heart forever—Ungrateful, as he is—unworthy even of my Remembrance.

This Resolution seem'd indeed, most consonant to *Reason;* but alas! how little are the Slaves of *Love* capable of obeying such Dictates? The Weakness of her Sex, or rather the Weakness of her Passion, threw her immediately into soft Complainings. *Beauclair's* ten thousand Charms, his flowing Wit, his sweet enchanting Air, his tender Protestations, Languishments, and Vows, all came fresh into her Mind, and Streams of Tears put out the Fire of Rage. It was about Noon when she receiv'd this surprising Letter; and altogether unfit for Conversation, she was oblig'd to feign herself indispos'd, to avoid dining with her Brother who liv'd in the House with her, and was but just recovering from a long Fit of Sickness: The Necessity she had of shunning his Presence till she had a little overcome her Disorders, was no small Additon to them: The Marriage Ceremony between her and *Beauclair* waited only for this Gentleman's return of Health, and what Pretence she shou'd make for breaking it off, she knew not; for the Thought of telling him in what manner she was us'd by her ungrateful Lover, was insupportable, not out of a Womanish Pride of disdaining to confess she had been forsaken, but because she knew not how far and how fatally his Resentment might transport him, in the Vindication of a Sister affronted in so unpardonable a manner. If her Tenderness for *Beauclair* had, by his late Behaviour, been rendred less prevalent, she had a Generosity in her Soul which made her look upon Revenge as a Passion justly to be abhorr'd; and how to prevent it, her Brother being naturally violent, gave her Disturbances little inferior to her others. She had also a long and an uneasie Debate within herself in what Terms she shou'd answer those Lines which had made so sudden an Alteration in her Fate, or whether she ought to answer them at all; and the Uncertainty in what way it was best for her to proceed in an Affair so every way distracting, took from her the Power of doing any thing for some Time.

Tho' 'tis possible whatever she had writ *Du Lache* might have found means to confute, and by construing her Words turn'd 'em to favour his Design, yet her Silence furnish'd him with an Opportunity of perswading *Beauclair*, that it was not only an Argument of her Guilt, but also, that had she but the least Desire to retain a Place in his Affections, she wou'd have made a Tryal of her Power, and endeavour'd to regain him: Her taking no Notice of your Letter (said he) is a proof that she rejoices in an Occasion to break with you, and thinks to be esteem'd by you is of so little Consequence, that she will not be at the Pains of one Invention (of which her Brain is sufficiently stor'd) to purchase it. With these kind of Suggestions he was always at his Ear, haunted him like his Shadow wheresoever he went, and never suffer'd his Resentments, by a Moment's Cessation, to grow cool, till he thought he had entirely brought about his End, of extirpating all Remembrances which might rise in his Soul in favour of *Montamour*.

Things being in this favourable Position, he thought it now high Time to introduce the *Baroness* into his Acquaintance; he had often mention'd her to him as a Person the most extraordinary of her Sex, and every now and then took Occasion to tell him he had several Times heard her speak the Name of *Beauclair* with a kind of Transport. Were she unmarried (said the cunning Villain) and Mistress of an Empire, the Admiration she pays your Virtues (for she is no Stranger either to your Person or Character) wou'd most certainly intitle you to share it with her. There are very few People, if any, of either Sex, tho' never so free from what we call Vanity, that feel not a secret Pleasure in hearing themselves prais'd, and indeed where such a Desire is not immoderate, it is rather an Argument of a *noble* than a *base* Nature. Ambition is laudable when it extends no farther than to excel in those Qualities which may render us agreeable to Society, serviceable to the World, and pleasing to Heaven; but when disregarding the *Substance* and grasping at the *Shadow,* we aim only at the *Reputation* of a Perfection, without taking any Pains to make us *worthy* of it, 'tis idle *Ostentation,* and often draws the Owner into worse Vices, *Envy* and *Detraction.* Such a Person can hardly endure another to be spoke well of, whereas the other hears his Companion extoll'd with no other Uneasiness than a secret Indignation against *himself,* for either his Inability or want of Application, to attain those Virtues he finds so universally applauded. *Beauclair* cou'd not be possest of ten thousand inimitable Graces, and be ignorant they merited Admiration, and tho' he was so accustom'd to create it, that he cou'd not be much transported at what *Du Lache* told him of the *Baroness,* yet the sweetness of his Disposition made him always think himself oblig'd to the good Opinion of any one, much more to a Lady's of whom he heard such Wonders. He seem'd very well pleas'd to encourage an Acquaintance with her, and the rather because he hop'd the Conversation of a Woman so agreeable and witty, as she had been represented, might be a means more effectual to drive *Montamour* from his Thoughts, than he found all the Efforts he had been able to make.

The Day which was appointed for him to accompany *Du Lache* in his Visit to her being arriv'd, it is not to be doubted but that, having notice of it, she took all imaginable Care to appear amiable in his Eyes; if there be any Charm which Art and Study can acquire, neither was here wanting to procure it; her Dress, her Looks and her Behaviour were all fram'd to please, and having thoroughly inform'd herself by *Du Lache* what best wou'd suit his Humour, she threw the vain *Coquette* entirely off, and wore the Appearance of the Woman of *Honour*——Her Carriage, tho' affable and complaisant, was all on the Reserve, nor did she (so exact was she in Dissimulation) in the least Word or Action, all the Time he stay'd with her, swerve from the most nice Punctilio of Modesty. They parted extremely satisfy'd with each other; he consider'd her as an agreeable Acquaintance, and she him, as a man whom in Time she might be able to subdue.

After this they had frequent Interviews, sometimes at her own House, and sometimes at *Madamoiselle D'ovrier's*[30] where *Du Lache* had also introduc'd him as if it were by Chance, and not with any Design of meeting the *Baroness;* tho' this indeed was one of those Places of Rendezvous before mention'd. But tho' his Carriage was full of Gallantry and Complaisance, yet neither his Words nor Actions had any Simptoms of that Passion she was ambitious of inspiring, and which alone cou'd make her easie: To inform this Dulness of Nature (as she accounted it) she began to lessen her Reserve, and assuming an Air all soft and tender, talk'd to him, and look'd on him with that sort of kind Concern as is usual between the most near and affectionate Relations; and believing it necessary to give some little Hints that there was something yet more endearing in her Soul, wou'd now and then let fall a Word, cast an amorous Glance and vent a Sigh, as if it had escap'd her in spite of her Endeavours to restrain it; in fine, she manag'd with such Artifice, that he must have been as *insensible* as he was really *discerning,* not to have perceiv'd she lov'd him; but the Reluctance with which she seem'd to let any thing slip which might give him Cause to imagine he had made an Impression on her, extremely heightned his Esteem; and tho' he had not been able to drive the Idea of *Montamour* so much out of his Mind as to be capable of entertaining a new Flame, yet he could not help feeling a secret Satisfaction in the Influence he found he had over a Soul so nicely virtuous, and full of noble Sentiments, as he believ'd hers to be.

The good Opinion he had of her, may, perhaps, seem strange, considering in what a vastly different Light her Character appear'd in the Eyes of most People; but till *Du Lache* (who had taken care to prepossess him with Notions all to her Advantage) introduc'd him to her, he was utterly unacquainted either with her Fame or Person. His Travels had taken him up some Years; and since his Return to *Paris,* his Engagement with *Montamour,* and the sincere Tenderness he had for her, entirely engross'd all his Hours, and left him not a Moment to throw away on Enquiries after any other Woman; and as the Sweetness of his Disposition made him always ready to think the best of every Body, it is not to be wonder'd at, that for a Time he was deceiv'd into a Belief of the *Baroness*'s Virtue.

But the Respect which his too favourable Opinion had inspir'd him with, was far from forwarding what her Wishes aim'd at. She easily perceiv'd it, and truly judging, by the Fire she observ'd in his Composition, by the tender Languor which sometimes trembled in his shining Eyes, and by the Air of all his Motions, that he was no Enemy to soft Desires, and that the distant Complaisance with which he treated her, was more owing to the Belief he had, that to offer at a nearer Familiarity wou'd not be receiv'd, than to any Dislike to her, or Coldness in his own Nature, she resolv'd to act in such a manner for the future as should let him see that it was impossible for him to presume beyond a Pardon. She communicated her Intention to *Du Lache,* and order'd him that on all Opportunities he should hint to *Beauclair* something of her Passion, seem to be surpris'd at the Discovery he made of it, and pity the Conflicts he must imagine she endur'd between her Virtue and Desire. He extremely approv'd of what she said, and obey'd her Commands with such Success, that by what he told him, and by what himself had of late gather'd from the *Baroness's* Behaviour, the other was convinc'd it would be no Difficulty to obtain from that Lady the greatest Condescention he cou'd require. If thus encourag'd he had refus'd to take the Advantages were offer'd him, he either must not have been a *Man,* or of a Soul much more refin'd than Man is ordinarily possest of. Tho' *Vanity* and *Curiosity* wear the Name of *Female Foiblesses,*[31] yet they are often (without any other Incitement) the Occasion of making the most deserving Woman lament the Inconstancy of her Husband, or Lover. But to those two Motives, *Beauclair* had, indeed, a third: The Desire of banishing as much as possible all Remembrance of a Person he thought so utterly unworthy as *Montamour,* and as he has since confest, and as by the rest of his Character one may reasonably believe, this last was the most prevailing Argument which induc'd him to imagine an Affair like this cou'd be of any Consequence to his Happiness. But notwithstanding all that his Resentments to *Montamour,* or that Levity of Nature (too incident to his Sex) cou'd suggest, his Inclinations were not so much upon the Wing as to engage him to make any great Haste to prosecute the Consummation of it; and he had, perhaps, delay'd so long till something had happen'd to prevent all Desires of attempting it, if the Lady's Impatience had not made her take such measures as, in a manner, oblig'd him to declare himself.

One Evening as they were alone together at *Madamoiselle D'ovrier's*, (*Du Lache* having excus'd himself from waiting on *Beauclair*) she artfully waving all other Subjects of Conversation, turn'd it in such a manner, that it more wore the Face of *Chance* than *Design,* into an Argument on the Force of *Love:* She pretended to prove that whatever Indecorums were the Consequences of that Passion, they were wholly *unavoidable,* and therefore cou'd not but be *pardonable.* A Man must have been very uncourtly indeed, that, whatever his Thoughts were, wou'd have disputed with a Lady on that Topick; *Beauclair* was more gallant, and believing that, if ever he desir'd any greater Testimonies of the Conquest he had made of her Heart, than what her Eyes declar'd, now was the Time to obtain them; he catch'd her suddenly in his Arms, and strenuously embracing her, cry'd out in a sort of Ecstacy, Oh Madam, how divinely good are you to declare your willingness to forgive Actions which cannot, by him who gazes on your Charms, but with Torments inexpressible be restrain'd: And perceiving she affected a little Astonishment at his Proceeding, Nay,

Madam, continu'd he, by your own Words you stand condemn'd, I own my self a Lover, an Adorer of your Perfections——I am no longer Master of my Passion——I must indulge the burning Wishes of my Soul——and you must pardon 'em——you have said you will,——and sure, you are too Heavenly to retract your Promise.——A thousand melting Kisses, on her Lips, her Eyes, her Breasts, made a delightful Parenthesis between almost every Word he spoke, and took from her the Power of answering, if she had attempted it; but she, who was truly charm'd with him, and had long languish'd for the Blessing she now so unexpectedly possest, was for some Moments too much transported to have Recourse to Artifice: Scarce knowing what she did, she mix'd her Breath with his; and as he held her, press'd him closer still!

But Presence of Mind (which till this Juncture never had been absent from her Breast) resuming its former Place, and reminding her, how cheap, in his Esteem, a too easie yielding wou'd make her appear, oblig'd her to make some faint Efforts to get loose from his Embrace.——Oh unhappy and unguarded Woman that I am (said she, seeming to weep) by my own Inadvertency I am lost——this dangerous Charmer has search'd into my Soul, and found the fatal Secret out, which till this Moment I durst not tell my self—— Oh I am undone for ever (pursu'd she after a Pause, and mustering all her Force to dart one piercing Glance) unless *Beauclair,* the wondrous,——the lovely, dear, destroying *Beauclair* will be kind enough to hate me——to take himself for ever from me——and let me see that all-undoing Form no more. First perish this Form (interrupted he, by this Time fir'd, if not with *Love,* with something which too often bears the Name of it) blind these Eyes! and new, and un-imagin'd Curses light on each Limb and Faculty of *Beauclair,* when he consents even in a Thought to quit the Divine *Tortillée*! Ah then, cry'd she, there is no Power in Heaven or Earth can save me—Fame, Duty, Virtue, are too weak Defence—against those conquering Eyes, that Shape, that Air, that Mein, that Wit, that Voice, those thousand, thousand Worlds of Charms: Death only is a Refuge for *Tortillée.* As she spoke these Words she sunk by degrees, and at last fell quite back, in a counterfeited Swoon, in the Chair she was sitting in; *Beauclair* started immediately from his, and run to the Door, but not to call any Assistance, or bring Water to revive her, (as perhaps some over-aw'd Lovers might have been stupid enough to have done) but to make it fast, and prevent any other Person from sharing with him in the Glory of restoring her to Life; nor was he, at his Return, at a Loss for means to bring her back to Sense: But if he cou'd have had Power to inform that Sense with a just Notion of the Happiness she was Mistress of, she had *indeed* been blest; his extravagant Extent of charming, if not a sufficient *Sanc-*

tion for the Crime, was yet a prodigious *Excuse,* and his unquestion'd Honour a Security for the Concealment of it: But alas! not all the Glories of his Form or Soul, not all the countless Wonders of his Wit and Beauty cou'd work that Miracle, and triumph over the Inconstancy of this universal Dispenser of her Favours: She who, engag'd with a Multiplicity of Lovers, cou'd find no Satisfaction while wanting *Beauclair;* languish'd for others, when possest of him; and this accomplish'd Gentleman in a little time serv'd but to swell the Number of her Admirers, scarce distinguish'd, in her Esteem, from those among 'em of the least Pretence to Merit.

But to go on gradually with her History: She now accounted herself superlatively blest, and perhaps was, for a Time, of the Opinion she never shou'd wish a Joy more elevated than what she had possess'd in *Beauclair;* while he, deluded by his own good Nature, the Insinuations of *Du Lache,* and the Subtilty of this fair Imposture, rioted in Imagination, and grew almost vain on the Influence of his own Charms, which without an Attempt, or even a Wish that way, had vanquish'd a Heart he believ'd impregnable to the united Force of the whole World besides. *Montamour* was now no more remembred, her Beauty, and her reported Falshood were lost, amidst the hurry of his present Transports; but the fallacious Pleasure was hardly more than momentary; an Idea which once has made a true Impression, and which length of Time has rivetted in the Soul, is not with so much Ease eras'd: tho' exil'd for a while, by Cares, by Business, or another Object, a thousand tender Passages, in spite of us, occur, and bring the Charmer back! and he that once has lov'd *sincerely* is in great Danger of *always* loving. This was at least the case of *Beauclair;* he was no sooner at home, and had Leisure for Reflection, than *Montamour,* adorn'd with all her Graces, came fresh into his Mind, and when he endeavour'd to extirpate her by thinking on *Tortillée,* he but gave himself Disorders which he found it impossible to quell——If he compar'd, either the Beauties of their Minds or Persons, how infinitely superior to the *latter,* (setting aside the Belief of her Inconstancy) did the *former* appear! The Raptures he so lately had enjoy'd, already pall'd, and made Desire grow sick. The more he consider'd how much he was belov'd by *Tortillée,* the more he was distracted at the Thoughts that he had been unable to inspire the same Degree of Tenderness in *Montamour:* Glad wou'd he have been to have had it in his Power to return with something more than Gratitude that Vehemence of sincere Affection which the *one* seem'd so profusely to lavish on him, and to have paid the imaginary Contempt and Ingratitude of the *other* with Hatred and Disdain; but both these Wishes were impossible, and he found, in spite of all the Strength of Reason he was master of, that *Love* is not a Passion liable to control.

To add to his Disquiets, and put Reflection more upon the Rack,[32] just as he was going to Bed, a Page from *Montamour* brought him a Letter from her, which hastily opening, he found in it these Lines.

To Monsieur *Beauclair*

That I answer'd Yours no sooner, was only owing to the Uncertainty I was in if I should answer it at all. The Levity of a Mind which cou'd dictate Lines like those you writ, is, indeed, worthy of nothing but Contempt; but I am of a Temper constant to a Fault, and confess my self unable, immediately, to despise, *what I have once, tho' causelessly,* esteem'd!

You need not, however, be under the least Apprehension that after this you shall receive any Persecutions either from my Love *or* Resentment, *and am so far from endeavouring to be justify'd in your Opinion, that I do not so much as ask of what I am* accus'd; *and conscious of no other real Guilt, on your Account, than in putting a too great confidence in your seeming Sincerity and Honour, shall make use of so much Discretion as not to regard whatever imaginary Crime your Baseness may alledge against me, to vindicate your Change of Behaviour.*

I think my self too much indebted to Heaven, for putting so early a Stop to any future *Engagements with you, to look back with Regret on the* past: *much less to languish for a Renewal of those fictitious Protestations with which you once had the Power of Deceiving*

The Unthinking
Montamour.

P.S. *To let you see with how much Tranquility of Mind I bear the eternal Loss of you, I have perswaded my Brother, that our breaking off is owing only to my self; you therefore have nothing to fear either from his or my Resentments: If you never endure more from a too late Repentance, and the Reproaches of your own Conscience, you will be happy—*

Adieu——for Ever.

With what sort of Emotions the Soul of *Beauclair* was agitated at the reading this Letter, wou'd be as impossible to describe, as it was for him to fix on any one Sentiment to give him Ease. The cold Disdain with which it seem'd to be writ, fir'd him, at first, with Indignation; he thought she gloried in her Falsehood, and rejoic'd in an Opportunity to break with him; but when he consider'd it more carefully, he fancy'd he found a certain Stifness in the Stile, which perswaded him her Indifference was but feign'd.——One Moment she appear'd to his Imagination, as she really was, all heavenly Truth, and Innocence, Languishing, Dying with the cruel Alteration of her Fortune, and only *counterfeiting* to despise a Heart which had so ungenerously abandon'd her——the next, he thought he saw her, as her Enemies had represented her, false, perjur'd and inconstant; in *Private,* dissolutely lavish of her Favours, and only hypocritically modest and reserv'd in *Public*—Sometimes, in spite of all Appearances, he was inclin'd to think her virtuous, but then the manner in which he was impos'd on to believe her otherwise, check'd the Suggestions of his Tenderness.——Long did the Fondness of his Passion struggle against all Opposition, till at last, resolving to give the Victory to that which seem'd to be the Result of *Reason*——I will no more debate (said he to himself) nor join to be my *own* Deceiver!——*Heaven* is not more *true* than *Montamour* is *false*——'tis plain, and to have made a Doubt of it, after the Proofs I have had, is most ridiculous and vain:—No Envy, no Malice, no Design cou'd have the least Share in the Discovery of her Perfidy——the very Fellow who betray'd her to me, knew not that he did so;——I 'scap'd the dishonourable Title of her Husband by a very *Miracle,* and to deliberate has made me half unworthy the Deliverance. Oh (continu'd he ready to burst with stifled Love, and madding Jealousy) how wou'd the fair Apostate and her curs'd Minion, the detested *Galliard,* triumph in my Pains, and deride my weak and shameful Irresolution, shou'd any Chance but give them Leave to guess it.

In this Confusion of Thought he pass'd the Night, nor did the Morning bring him any Return of Peace; and *Du Lache* coming pretty early to visit him (as indeed he was seldom from him but in those Hours commmonly allow'd for Repose) was a little startled to find that all he had done, had been unable to fix him in that Disposition of Mind which the *Baroness* requir'd, and being from her perfectly acquainted with the Condescentions she had made him the Day before, had hop'd, till now, that in the possessing her all his Wishes for *Montamour* were utterly extinguish'd; but finding himself deceiv'd, bethought him of another Stratagem, which he had reserv'd as a saving Card, in case there shou'd be any occasion to make use of it, to strengthen the Accusations he had already laid on that unhappy Lady by the means of *Le Songe.* As soon as *Beauclair* had given him an Opportunity, by communicating his Inquietudes to him, he exerted all his Policy in aspersing her, yet in such a manner, as if he did it with Reluctance, and only forc'd to it by the Friendship he had for him. Alas! said he, her Intreague with *Galliard* is not a thing of Yesterday, I long have been acquainted with the Secret, and so have many more, tho' every one knowing the Violence of your Passion forbore to speak of it to you: tho' never Man (continu'd he) had a more great and sincere Esteem for another, than my admiring Soul has ever paid you; yet, to have been Master of an Empire, wou'd not I have been the first to have divulg'd this to you, because I see (with an infinity of Concern I speak it) I see, in spite of all, you still must *Love,* and to know her Crime but racks your Peace, and Reason never can restore you to that Quiet which happy Ignorance bestow'd.

At these Words *Beauclair* flew into the utmost Rage, swore she was hateful to him—that he thought not on her but with Contempt; and to engage the other to a Belief of what he said, protested his whole Soul was now devoted to another. I wish indeed (resum'd this vile Incendiary) that there were a Possibility for you to do so, for I am most sure you cannot any where bestow the Tresure of your Affection more undeservedly.——To convince you of the Truth of what I say, if you please I will wait on you to a Gentleman, a near Relation of mine, who by his Intimacy some time ago with *Galliard,* was privy to the whole Affair; at my Request I know he will inform you of all the Circumstances, which he well knows; and there are some Particulars concerning the Treachery of this *Montamour* to Madamoiselle *Galliard,* to whom she once was dear, which I believe you will confess to be such, as vastly extenuate the Foulness of the Fact. Tho' *Beauclair* thought himself already but too well assur'd, yet the Resolution he had made to hate her, and the Difficulty he found it would be to keep it, made him willing to listen to every Tongue that shou'd repeat her Name in such a manner as might hush the Pleas of *Love,* and drown all soft *Remoras*[33] in the Voice of Scandal. An Appointment was presently made; and in the Afternoon, *Beauclair, Du Lache,* and *Toncarr,* who pass'd for his Kinsman, met at a neighbouring Tavern. It was impossible for *Beauclair* to have any Notion of *Toncarr,* having never seen him but once, and then only in the Struggle with *Le Songe,* when he immediately fled, as was his part; besides, he appear'd now drest *en Cavalier,*[34] and had a Mein and Air agreeable enough to make him be taken for a Man of fashion.

After some few Compliments, *Du Lache* intreated him by their nearness of Blood, and that much nearer Tye of Friendship which was between them, to relate what he had been privy to, of the History of *Galliard* as to his Concern with *Montamour.* He seem'd at first a little scrupulous, but afterwards, artfully pretending to be angry with himself, for denying him so long, Why, said he, shou'd I make any Objections against obliging a Man of Honour and my Friend, when what I have to say can turn only to the Prejudice of a Villain and my Enemy; I have renounc'd all Friendship with *Galliard,* and when I gave him his Life, at his Request, and promis'd Secrecy of all had past, the Conditions on which I made the Promise being broke, to proclaim it now to the whole World can be no Breach of Trust. Know then, Gentlemen, (continu'd he) I owe my Birth to *Naples,* but my Parents dying young, I was sent over, under the Care of some of my Mother's Relations, to *Orleans,* where I had an Uncle; as soon as I arriv'd at the Age of distinguishing Perfections, I became an Admirer of a Lady allow'd to be Mistress of all that Woman can be blest with; but Fortune not then enough my Friend to embolden me to make any Declarations of my Passion with hopes of Success, prompted me to seek Preferment in the Army. *Hungary* was then the Seat of War, and four Campaigns[35] sent me home in a Condition which I thought wou'd not appear despicable in her Eyes, by whom alone I wish'd to be well thought of——But at my Return I found she was remov'd, with her Mother; it was some time before I heard she went to *Paris;* I soon follow'd, but tho' I made all possible Enquiry, was not able to inform my self any thing of her. I went to all publick Places, hoping to see her, knowing she was of a Disposition naturally inclin'd to Gaiety; but all my Search was vain: In this time I became acquainted with *Galliard;* he seem'd extremely pleas'd with my Company, took all Opportunities to oblige me, made me the Confident of his Amours, and among the rest, of his Affair with *Madamoiselle Montamour;* her Brother, as he told me, had forbad him his House, and he found some Difficulty in conveying Letters to her; he form'd a Pretence for me to introduce my self to the Family, which, as it wou'd take up too much time and be of no Consequence to the Story, I shall forbear to repeat: In fine, to repay some Obligations I had receiv'd from him, I took upon me to be his Emmissary, and they had frequent Opportunities of meeting thro' my means.

I cou'd not avoid condemning him indeed, in my private Opinion, because I knew he had a Wife, who I heard by others was a most beautiful and deserving Woman, tho' he spoke of her as the *Reverse;* however, as she was an utter Stranger to me, I thought it would be Imprudence to interfere with any Advice, which 'twas probable wou'd only occasion a Breach of Friendship between us, and be of no Service to the Lady. Thus it pass'd on, till one day he invited me to his House, where I had never been before; but, good God! how shall I express my Astonishment, when in *Madamoiselle Galliard* I found the Charmer I so long had sought. The Confusion with which I beheld her as his Wife, and as a Wife so injur'd by him, must have been visible to him, had he been present; but he was that Moment as she came into the Room retir'd to his Closet to write a Letter which I was to convey to *Montamour.* She blush'd at sight of me, and burst into a Flood of Tears at remembring the Tranquility of her Condition when last she saw me, and perhaps mix'd with a sensibility of the Tenderness my *Eyes* tho' not my *Tongue* had often taken the Liberty of telling her, I felt on her Account. There was then no Opportunity of private Conversation: he soon return'd to us: but after that I had frequent Opportunities of discoursing her, and she made no Scruple of complaining to me of his Unkindness.——I was almost mad at the Inhumanity of my Fate; and tho' I thought my self most wretched in being depriv'd of her, yet I solemnly protest I was not so much troubled that she was *married,* as that she was so *unhappily* married.

I could no longer be passive in the Affair. I told *Galliard,* that now I had seen his Wife, and found her a Woman so infinitely deserving, I cou'd not approve of his Proceedings. At first he laugh'd at my Admonitions, but finding I persisted, seem'd to take it ill, and assur'd me, he should always follow the Dictates of his Inclinations, without any regard to what those who had no Business with it, shou'd think of his Behaviour. Pretty well warm'd before, this Answer set me all on Fire, and I return'd it in a manner he knew not how to brook.——In short, we fought. I had the good Fortune to disarm him, and was about to revenge his Lady's Wrongs, when he intreated me to spare his Life, and swore ten thousand Oaths never to injure her again in the manner he had done.——On this I threw him back his Sword, and went immediately to *Montamour,* told her what I had done, and the Promise I had exacted from her Lover.——She appear'd enrag'd at my Presumption, as she call'd it; but as Women are generally pretty artful in penetrating into those kind of Secrets, she presently guessing my sudden dislike of their Intimacy proceeded from my Friendship to his Wife, soon grew more calm; and changing her Voice, Well *Monsieur,* said she, I see the Charms you have found in *Madamoiselle Galliard* have made you an Enemy to her *Husband;* but suppose I value your Friendship at so high a rate, that to oblige you to my Interest I contrive some way to put you in Possession of the *Wife,* will you refuse me then your Assistance in the Continuance of my Happiness with the *Husband.* So strange a Proposition coming from a Woman, who, bating her criminal Affection for *Galliard,* I always look'd on as Mistress of a good deal of Honour, took from me the Power of making an immediate Answer; and she interpreting my Silence as a Token of Consent, I will not, resum'd she, promise that *Madamoiselle* will yield to your Desires, she is too foolishly fond of her Husband, tho' he despises her, and too great a Bigot[36] to her Matrimonial Vow; but this I will engage, to bring her to a Place where, if you think fit to make use of the Advantage, Denials shall be in vain.

I vow to you, Gentlemen (pursu'd he) that the Shock with which I heard her speak thus, was greater than I am able to represent; the violent Passion I had bore to *Madamoiselle Galliard,* while I believ'd her in a Condition capable of returning it, was now converted to a sincere and noble Friendship; my Affection was too pure to wish to obtain more of her than Honour would permit, tho' with her free Consent; how then cou'd brutal *Force* have any Place in my Intentions? I soon convinc'd this mistaken Lady, that the Person she was speaking to was of a Temper vastly different from what she imagin'd; and endeavour'd, by all the Arguments I could invent, to perswade her to consider the Injustice she was guilty of, to *her self,* as well as to her *Rival:* but all was of no Effect; she seem'd harden'd in her Crime, and pretended to vindicate what she did with so much Haughtiness and so little Shame, that I question if the most common *Fille de Joye*[37] in *Paris* cou'd with such Assurance have behav'd: she call'd me Sot, Fool, and every opprobrious Name her Spite and Anger cou'd put into her Mouth: told me she regarded not what my *Thoughts* were of her Actions, but if I dar'd to report 'em she had a Brother who wou'd not suffer the Abuse to go unpunish'd. *Talking* never was my Talent, and being altogether unaccustom'd to such kind of Encounters, she had very much the Advantage of me, and I was at last glad to leave her unconverted. I heard afterwards that all I had done prov'd ineffectual to break the Correspondence between her and *Galliard;* and I had not fail'd to call that dishonourable Wretch a second time to account, if his Wife had not writ to me, conjuring me to take no farther Notice of the Affair, for it but encreas'd his ill Usage of her in *Private,* and gave occasion for *Publick* Ridicule.

Toncarr here finish'd his monstrous Lye; and *Du Lache,* tho' he had order'd him to form some Story which might seem plausible, to scandalize *Montamour* on the account of *Galliard,* was himself astonish'd at the Power of the Invention which out of nothing cou'd create such a well connected Pile of Falshood: for in reality he knew no more of *Montamour,* or her Brother, *Galliard* or his Wife, than their Names and Places of Abode. How then cou'd *Beauclair,* already prepossess'd (by Proofs, which he thought were undeniable) suspect the Truth of what he heard? He ask'd several Questions, not to entrap him, but to satisfie his own Curiosity; as how they look'd when together, what they said, and in what manner they behav'd; to all which *Toncarr* replied with such an Aptitude and Readiness, as whoever had listned to their Discourse, wou'd have sworn he utter'd nothing but Sincerity.

Tho' such a Story as this, of *Montamour,* some few Weeks past, wou'd have kindled such a Fire of Indignation in the Soul of *Beauclair,* as nothing but the Blood of him that told it cou'd have quench'd; yet now he heard it with no other Disorder than what sprung from the Shame of having been so much deceiv'd in his Opinion. If he had had leisure for Reflection, 'tis probable that in spite of all Opposers, *Love* wou'd still have exerted it self in favour of that Lady; but the Company he was in took care to keep off an Enemy so dangerous to their Designs. *Toncarr* was of a gay facetious Disposition, had a good deal of Wit, and knew how to make himself perfectly entertaining in Conversation; the Subtilty of his Companion furnish'd him with Themes such as he knew wou'd be agreeable to *Beauclair,* and between them both it was no difficult matter to work on that good Nature and Softness of Disposition, the Excess of which was the only Foible of this deluded Gentleman. The Glass went briskly round, and the sprightliness of the Wine gave Life to the Conversation; not a celebrated Beauty in *Paris* but was toasted, and it coming to *Du Lache's* Turn to begin, Come Gentleman, said he, here is all Health and an eternal round of Happiness to Her whose *exterior* Charms (tho' by far surpassing all her Sex besides) are but as Foils, when brought in Comparison with the more shining Graces of her *Mind,* and when I thus describe her, none who boast of a distinguishing Capacity will need be told I mean the Divine *Baroness de Tortillée.* Immediately, *Toncarr,* before instructed, took the hint, and fell into such Encomiums on her, as in reality no Woman ever did, or cou'd, deserve. *Beauclair,* tho' he was far from being of their Opinion, thought himself oblig'd in Gratitude, for the Favours he had so lately receiv'd, to join with them in the Praises they gave her; and as most People are apt to admire what they find the rest of the World do, and having never had the Opportunity of hearing the least tittle[38] to her Disadvantage, began to think on her as a Woman who had more Perfections than he had hitherto found out: he imagin'd it was owing to the Remains of his former Passion, that he had so long been blind, resolv'd to open his whole Soul to receive her Idea, and accus'd himself of Stupidity that he was able to love her no better.

They broke not up till it was late; and *Du Lache* fearing, with good reason, that if *Beauclair* was left too suddenly to himself, some Accident might happen to render all they had done of no Effect, and discover that neither *Montamour* nor *Tortillée* were the Persons they had been represented, was resolv'd to trust nothing to Chance, but he went home with him, and carried him the next Morning to drink Tea with the *Baroness,* in the Afternoon met by Appointment at *Madamoiselle D'Ovrier's,* engag'd him to pass the next Day with *Toncarr,* the ensuing one with the *Baroness* again.——In fine, for a considerable Time he had scarce a Moment which was not taken up by one or other of this Confederacy, and they took care by ten thousand various Artifices to keep his Thoughts in a perpetual Whirl, till they imagin'd all Remembrance of *Montamour* was utterly extinguish'd.

In the mean time, never was a Heart more greatly distress'd than that of this unhappy Lady; to all the Softness of her own Sex, she had that Constancy of Mind, and Steadiness of Resolution, which those of the other *boast,* but rarely *prove* themselves Masters of. Difficult it was to make her entertain a

Passion, but much more difficult to extinguish it. *Beauclair* was the only Man who ever had the Power to inspire her with one tender Wish; but now not *Beauclair's* self cou'd change her Sentiments: The Impression which his *Charms* had made, not all his *Ingratitude* cou'd erace; she lov'd, she worshipp'd, she ador'd him still; within her gentle Soul no Storms of Anger rag'd, no wild Revenge, no Jealousy had Place; and when she reflected how cruelly she was abandon'd, how causelessly affronted, she consider'd it only as a Flaw in his Disposition, a Frailty influenc'd by *Fate,* unavoidable and therefore pardonable. Never Woman bore the *Disappointment* of her Hopes with so little Resentment, nor so strongly defended her self from making any Endeavours to *recover* 'em. In spite of the most ardent Love, the softest languishments, the tenderest secret Meltings of her Soul, cou'd urge, she chose to die away in fruitless Wishes, rather than let the *dear Unkind* be sensible of what she felt. She was so far from desiring to take any Advantage of his ten thousand times repeated Vows, or the solemn Contract that was between them, that her greatest Fear was, lest her Brother (if he knew the Truth of his Behaviour) shou'd take some measures to oblige him to the Performance of it; and for that reason blinded him as much as possible: She told him, that she had discover'd some little Foibles in the Humour of *Beauclair,* which she was afraid might not be very agreeable in a married State,——that she was determin'd to continue as she was for some time, and that she had pretended to be piqu'd at something he had done, on purpose to create a Quarrel to retard the Match.

The Turn she gave to this Affair succeeded well enough, to engage the Belief of a Person who by reason of his great Employments, (being Judge of the criminal Causes, one of the Council, and taken up with many other Concerns of the State[39]) had not too much leisure to consider the Occurrences of his Family; but to the rest of her Acquaintance it was obvious that in *this,* tho' in this alone, she was not free from Dissimulation: her *Eyes,* whenever she attempted to speak of *Beauclair* with Indifference, declar'd her *Heart* was far from consenting to what she said: His very Name but mention'd spread soft Confusion over all her Face; with stifled Sighs her lovely Bosom heav'd! and gentle Tumults trembled in each Limb: she was sensible of it her self, and therefore, tho' her Thoughts were full of nothing else, forbore as much as possible all Discourse of him; but the Violence she did her Inclination was such, as Words wou'd but vainly endeavour to represent: to avoid it, she shunn'd all Conversation as much as she cou'd, without being taken notice of, and pass'd her Hours in Solitude and Silence. Contemplation afforded her widely different Entertainments, unutterable Pleasure! unutterable Pain! when retir'd, shut up within her Closet, no impertinent Interruption near, and *Beauclair's* lov'd Idea only present, his Letters fill'd with ten thousand, thousand tender Vows and soft Professions, lying before her, how did she indulge Imagination! how dwell on each enchanting Syllable! and when read o'er and o'er, Fancy grew warmer still! how did she call the past, blest, Moments of his Presence back! how re-enjoy each Word, each Look, each Touch, and sink in Rapture at the dear Remembrance!——but then! Oh dreadful Change! Imagination tir'd, the visionary Joy dissolv'd! and Sense, *distracting* Sense, return'd, what Racks of Thought, what unmatch'd Horrors sad Despair presented! To be supremely *curst,* one must be first supremely *blest;* never to have been *happy,* is not to be *unhappy;* such only linger out a Life in dull Stupidity, untasting *Pleasure,* and unknowing *Pain;* equally ignorant of *refin'd* Delight, or *exquisite* Disquiet——but, to have *lost*——to have lost, for ever, all the Soul holds dear——to have the Joys, once ours, torn from our bleeding Breasts by the black Hand of separating Fate, no more to be restor'd,—the chearful Land of Hope obscur'd in Shades, and all before our Eyes a barren Prospect, and a Wild of Woe! that, that, indeed, is finish'd Wretchedness! Consummate Misery.

But, if to the being forsaken and affronted by the Man in whose Society she plac'd her whole Felicity, there needed any thing to make her the most unhappy Woman breathing, malicious Fortune found the way to give it. *Madamoiselle Bellfleur,*[40] an Embroiderer, one of those Creatures whose Houses had been at the *Baroness's* Devotion whenever she had occasion for a private *Rendezvous,* had by some Accident discover'd that *Madamoiselle D'Ovrier's* was now the Place that Lady had made Choice of, for the Carrying on her Amour with *Beauclair;* and being excessively piqu'd at it, set her self on being reveng'd some way or other. She was sensible that nothing was more known than the Loves of *Beauclair* and *Montamour,* and that the whole Town was surpris'd at the Delay of a Marriage which so long had been expected; and imagining she had found out the Cause, resolv'd it shou'd no longer be a Secret. She had formerly been employ'd by *Montamour* in the working her some fine Gowns and Petticoats, and making that a Pretence for waiting on her, introduc'd a Story which the Hearer of it had little Reason to thank her for repeating; for tho' it was much more difficult to gain any Credit from this generous Lady to the Prejudice of her ungrateful Lover, than her Enemies had found from him even for the greatest Falshoods; yet the bare Probability that such a thing might be true, was a Shock which cannot well be represented. In Justice to herself, she cou'd not avoid being of Opinion that to be abandon'd for a Woman of the *Baroness's* Character and Humour, was an Indignity such as ought to make the Man that offer'd it, odious to her Memory: But all that Pride or

Reason cou'd suggest, was too too weak to bring her to either Scorn or Hate: Nor, tho' the causeless Change of his Behaviour, the Suddenness of it, and the cold neglectful and indeed affrontive Stile of his last Letter, made it seem likely enough that nothing but a new Passion cou'd occasion it, yet Jealousy was so great a Stranger to her Nature, that she cou'd not but with great Difficulty entertain it: However the little Touches she now began to feel of that eternal Enemy to Tranquility, gave her Perturbations far beyond all she ever knew before.

It was not in this manner the *Baroness* past her Time. Believing her self secure of the Heart she so ardently had wish'd to gain, revell'd in full Delight, and wanton'd in the Assurance of her Happiness, Proud, Vain, and Self-sufficient, she now defy'd all Fears of ever losing what she had acquir'd, despis'd her Rival's Charms, and not only spoke of her, but also really consider'd her as a Creature incapable of giving her any Pain on *Beauclair*'s account; nay, tho' he shou'd discover by what Arts he had been betray'd to treat her in the manner he had lately done. She hated her, however, for the Engagements she had with him, and being naturally of a most malicious Disposition to all amiable Persons of her own Sex, took an inexpressible Pleasure in having it in her Power to mortify 'em. This base Woman thought it not Misery enough to have alienated the Affections of her Lover, but must study to inflict yet more: She cou'd not think herself truly blest in the Possession of *Beauclair,* without triumphing in the Conquest she had made; it was not sufficient for her Pride, that *Montamour* was abandon'd; there wanted, to compleat her Happiness, the making that afflicted Lady sensible for *whom* she had been abandon'd. She was now grown above the Care of her Reputation, and thought it beneath her to regard any thing but the pleasing herself; and, entirely ignorant that *Madamoiselle Bellfleur* had in part perform'd the Work she aim'd at, communicated her Desires to *Du Lache.* He who was always ready to serve her on all occasions, was far from being backward in complying with her in this, and he approv'd of it the more, because he imagin'd, that when *Montamour* shou'd know her Rival, it wou'd encrease her Resentment to *Beauclair,* and render it impossible for them ever to be reconcil'd, and consequently prevent any Discovery of those villainous Impositions which had been made use of to disunite them.

Madamoiselle Sansfoy came immediately into his Head, as the most proper Engine upon Earth to manage this Affair, who wou'd infallibly do all, yet be ignorant herself of the Cause of what she did: And as soon as he had consulted with the *Baroness* after what manner he shou'd set this eternal Clack a going, went to visit her with a Packet of Tidings, which he knew wou'd render him a welcome Guest to a Lady of her inquisitive Temper. He gave her a full Account of all the several Meetings of *Beauclair* and the *Baroness,* the manner of their Conversation, and, because it happen'd to suit best with his Purpose, spoke Truth, in every thing, but when he said the *Passion* was wholly on *his* side, the Desire of coming acquainted *his,* and that all the Assiduity he had paid cou'd engage no other Return than Gratitude, from the cold, inexorable *Tortillée.* But the main Business of his Errand was to tell her, that the *Baron* being out of Town, the *Baroness* had consented to pass the Evening with himself and *Beauclair,* and that they were to meet in the *Tuilleries*[41] at ten a-clock. He told her this, to the end that if *Montamour* shou'd question the Truth of what she shou'd hear from *Sansfoy,* her Curiosity might, perhaps, lead her to satisfie herself by watching at that Place; where he and the *Baroness* had contriv'd to make things appear in such a View as shou'd distract her very Soul.

As he had no other Design in visiting her, than to make her the Instrument of tormenting *Montamour,* so soon as he had said all that he thought wou'd be conducive to his Purpose, he took his Leave: nor did she press him to stay, being as impatient to reveal what she had promis'd to keep Secret, as he was for her to do so; tho' he had artfully engag'd her to the contrary; well knowing that nothing is a greater Incitement to stir up a busie Temper, than to adjure it to be passive. Tho' *Montamour* liv'd but a Street or two off, she thought the Distance was too great; and, as she went the few Steps there was between 'em, had a thousand Dreads that the Person she was going to, might be abroad, or engag'd with Company, or some Accident shou'd happen which wou'd retard the Recital she had to make. But she labour'd not long under these Apprehensions; she found her at Home, and alone; and being receiv'd with the usual Familiarity which that Lady always treated her Intimates with, soon disburthen'd herself of that Load of Secrets she had been so big with; she forgot not the minutest Circumstance she had been told by *Du Lache,* to which her natural Propensity to Scandal made her add a thousand more. *Montamour,* with an aking Heart, listned attentively to all she said, and long'd to hear something improbable enough to make her hope that all the rest was false; but most of the Particulars that *Sansfoy* mention'd, and especially the Place of their Assignation, agreed so exactly with what she had been inform'd by *Madamoiselle Bellfleur,* that she no longer had the Power of doubting. She bore it, however, with a Presence of Mind, which very few, if any Woman, beside herself, cou'd boast of on the like Occasion. She vented no Extravagancies,——she curs'd not,——she revil'd not,——and when *Sansfoy,* surpriz'd, and vex'd to find her of a Humour so different from her Sex, began to testifie her Friendship by some Expressions which sounded like Condolement: Pity not me (interrupted she, turning her Mouth to a half disdainful Smile, while her Eyes trembled to restrain their Tears) Pity not *me*! rather commiserate the unhappy *Beauclair*, whose easie Nature and whose frank Belief makes him the Property of such Wretches as *Du Lache* and his Companions. The Reputation of having an Intrigue with a Woman of the *Baroness*'s Quality, will never balance the disgraceful means by which he has attain'd it. Nor, perhaps (continu'd she with a deep Sigh) will he be always of Opinion that to have possest her is a sufficient Recompence for the eternal Loss of *Montamour*.

It was impossible for *Sansfoy*, who in such a Circumstance wou'd have behav'd in a manner vastly different, to forbear expressing her Sentiments in such Terms as Women commonly make use of——Good God! said she, is this all?——can you sit down so tamely with your Wrongs——I know you love the Villain——and can you bear to lose him——shall a Woman so infamous as *Tortillée* deprive you of him?——will you not be reveng'd?——will you not expose them both——the *one* to the Ridicule of the whole World, the *other* to her Husband's just Resentment.——I am not so ignorant of her Character as to imagine (whatever her Pander *Du Lache* wou'd perswade me) that her Conversation with *Beauclair* is no more than a *Platonick* one—and if you please (continu'd she after a Pause, and finding the other was silent) I will join with you to ruin her: I am acquainted with the whole History of her several Amours,——can prove that *D'Esperanze*, tho' he maintain'd her, was not the only-favour'd Lover;——and that since her Marriage with this foolish *Baron*, she has been had by half the Town,——nay, at this very time, *St. Aumar* and the young amourous Marquis *De Sonville* enjoy an equal Share with the perfidious *Beauclair*.——I know where, and when both of 'em have had Assignations with her.——Count *De la Torre*[42] has also experienc'd how liberal she is of her Favours: when he went out of Town, the other day, his Sister found, among some Papers he had left behind him, Letters which by the Hand we knew to be *Tortillée*'s, and the Contents were such, as are scarce fit for modest Ears:——I'll bring you acquainted with her, she'll furnish you with Stories such as will enable you to revenge your self on this unworthy Rival.

She wou'd doubtless have run on a great deal more, if *Montamour* (whose Soul was incapable of harbouring any mean Notions, and glow'd in her Bosom with a generous Disdain at this Proposition) had not put a stop to the Career of her Revilings. She blush'd to think how justly her Sex was reflected on by the other; and looking on *Sansfoy* with an Air of Scorn, which she was very rarely seen to wear, No madam! no, said she, I never will enter into any such Measures, nor can be pleas'd that others shou'd so far interest themselves in my Quarrel, as to make 'em forget that Decorum, and Mildness of Behaviour, which ought to be the distinguishing Character of Womanhood;—the greatest Proof you can give me of your Friendship, is to let this Story die:——I need not fear my Injuries will go for ever unreveng'd: the Crime it self will bring on Stings far worse than I cou'd wish, much more have Power to inflict. If *Beauclair* after so many Vows of an unalterable Affection can be so basely perfidious to quit me for the *Baroness,* he will also quit her for another——her Empire will be of short Continuance: and to be forsaken, to a Woman of her vain Humour, will be a Punishment, the most adequate of any to her Guilt: or if she be really so vicious as the World believes, her Artifice will not always serve her to conceal it from the discerning *Beauclair,* Remorse will then be sufficiently my Avenger. But if neither of these shou'd happen, shou'd *he* be ever *Blind, she* ever *Cunning,* I am resolv'd, in Justice to my self, to continue entirely passive; for sure a Woman such as she, is as much below my *Hate,* as he by loving her, has rendred himself of my *Esteem*: both equally unworthy of my Thoughts, and only fit for one another.

And is it possible (interrupted *Sansfoy,* more and more confounded) that you really are Mistress of so much Philosophy as you pretend?——will Love, and Pride, and Grief, in such a stabbing Circumstance, be always overpower'd by Prudence? cou'd you endure to *behold* what yet you have but *heard* of?——Cou'd you bear to *see* the Man who has ador'd you——the Man on whom (in spite of your boasted Moderation) I know your Soul still doats, kneel to another, and pay those soft Submissions due only to you!—cou'd you, I say, support a sight like this, and yet contain your Temper?——No, 'tis impossible!——'tis against Nature——and, if I cou'd perswade you to go with me in some Disguise, and be a Witness of their meeting, I believe I shou'd find your Behaviour at such a View far different from what the hearing it occasions. I do not think you wou'd, reply'd *Montamour* coldly: I have already so many Proofs of his Perfidy and Ingratitude, that to see 'em in the most strict Embrace cou'd not give me more. Yet, resum'd *Sansfoy* eager to engage her to an Enterprize in which she promis'd herself so much Diversion, there is something that more nearly touches the Passions in an *Ocular* Demonstration.——It may be so, interrupted *Montamour,* (who knew the other's Humour too well, not to guess at the Cause which made her so pressing) and for that Reason I will not endeavour to convince you, by putting my Temper to any hazardous Tryals, for the vain Glory of surmounting a Difficulty which few of my Sex wou'd have Resolution enough to do. But (cry'd *Sansfoy* vex'd to the Heart to find her still so calm) I advise you to it by all means; it wou'd rather be an Argument of *Stupidity* than *Prudence* to lose such an Opportunity of upbraiding *Him* and detecting your *Rival*: shou'd you but mention the Story now, it might be disbeliev'd,——both might deny it,——and you only be call'd perverse and jealous;——but if you meet them at this shameful Assignation, and face to face confront 'em, you boldly may proclaim him for a Villain, and enjoy that inexpressible Satisfaction of having your Rival in your Power.

She said a great deal more to the same purpose; but all her Reasons had no Effect on *Montamour*: that discreet Lady reflected within herself on the Weakness of Humanity, and how little sufficient *Reason* at some Times, and in some Cases, is to vanquish *Passion*: she knew not how far she might be transported at such a killing Interview; and easily perceiving it was more the Pleasure of having something to talk of, than any Interest she took in her Affairs, which made her Adviser so importunate, resolv'd she shou'd rather want a Theme for the Entertainment of her next Visiting-day, than furnish her with one, which she was not certain might not be to the Disadvantage of the Reputation of that Moderation, she had hitherto taken so much Care to preserve. It was something wonderful indeed, that a Woman who lov'd to that prodigious degree of Tenderness as she did, and had such Appearances how much that Tenderness was abus'd, cou'd so well dissemble the Disorders of her Soul. The whole time that *Sansfoy* staid with her, she continu'd Mistress of the same steddy Resolution she had always profess'd, and that busie Woman had the Mortification, after all the Pains she had taken, to find herself disappointed, and that all she had done was able to draw nothing from her which might be a Subject of Ridicule. But what the unhappy *Montamour* suffer'd while under so cruel a Constraint can hardly be imagin'd. As soon as she was alone, she shut herself into her Chamber, and gave a loose to the long labouring pent-up Passions of her Soul,—her Couch,—her Bed, were now no longer able to sustain the force of her wild Grief,—she grovell'd on the Floor,——she beat her Breast,——she wrung her lovely Hands,——the celebrated Lustre of her shining Eyes was now extinct in Tears; and whoever had seen her in this Condition wou'd have believ'd it impossible she cou'd, but some Moments before, have worn such an Appearance of Serenity.

As it grew nearer to the Hour in which her Rival was to enjoy the Presence of her ador'd *Beauclair*, her Agonies encreas'd. Oh God! cry'd she, now is the happy *Tortillée* preparing to receive a Heaven I have for ever lost,——now, now, she summons all her Charms, adorns her Face with Smiles, and practises a thousand Arts, a thousand Graces, to secure her Conquest——and what, (O torturing Thought) what gives Addition to her Beauty, makes her Eyes sparkle with an unusual Splendor, is the Knowledge that she triumphs over the forsaken *Montamour.* Whenever this Reflexion came across her thoughts, all that she had of Woman in her Soul exerted itself. No, wou'd she say, starting up and wiping away her Tears, with an Air of Derision,—I am not, will not be unhappy——I scorn the Wretch who yields his Heart, where neither Virtue, Wit, nor Beauty claim the Prize, where Novelty is alone the Charm.——He that can love *Tortillée!* the infamous the often abandon'd *Tortillée,* shall henceforth be the Object of my *Mirth,* equally unworthy of my *Love* or *Anger.* But how long she continu'd in this Mind, those who have ever felt the Force of true Affection need not be inform'd; to *them* it may seem superfluous to say, *Tenderness* soon got the better of *Resentment;* but the *Insensibles,*[43] or those who *love* only because they are *belov'd,* will perhaps condemn her when they shall know those Resolutions were no sooner *made* than *broke;* and sinking from that Air of Haughtiness she had assum'd, into one wholly compos'd of Softness, And yet, said she, among the Race of Man, where is there one whose Charms can vie with those, this dear, this false Protestor boasts?——how harsh, and how untunable wou'd sound the Name of Love from any *other* Mouth! and with what Harmony it flows from his!——his Voice,——his Looks,——his soft enchanting Mein, adorn the tender Passion, and make Desire a Virtue.

In this manner was she hurried by the various Agitations of her Mind, till the Clock striking ten put her in Mind that if she did design to be a Witness of this meeting, it was time she shou'd prepare herself. In spite of all the Temperance she had maintain'd in the Presence of *Sansfoy,* the Woman's Curiosity now gain'd the Victory; she cou'd not be assured that the Man who had made so many Vows to *her,* was that Moment about to offer 'em to *another,* without a Desire to know in what manner he wou'd do it: and, perhaps, was not without a secret Hope she shou'd discover a Difference in his Behaviour; and as wretched as she thought herself, found a kind of Pleasure, a sullen Satisfaction in this Thought: enabled by it she got on her Cloaths, and muffling herself up in her Hoods so as it was impossible for her to be known, stole out of the House alone, without letting even her own Woman into the Secret.——What is not *Love,* when instigated by *Jealousy,* capable of performing! She, who at another time, or on any other Occasion, wou'd not have ventur'd where there was the least Appearance of Danger or[44] to her Person or Reputation, now had either *forgot* or had Courage to *despise* the most eminent ones; and led by the Emotions of her tumultuous Passions went, when it was dark, unguarded and unattended to the Place which she was told was destin'd for the Rendezvous of those ungenerous Destroyers of her Peace.

She had not been long in the *Tuilleries* before she discern'd a Man and

Woman coming down a Walk opposite to that she was in; she imagin'd it might be those she sought, and immediately cross'd, making only a little Stand to let them pass, and follow'd at a convenient Distance, so near as to be able to distinguish what was said, but far enough, as she thought, not to have them believe they were observ'd. The *Baroness* (for it was she, indeed, who accompany'd by *Du Lache* had prevented[45] the Hour appointed by *Beauclair* that she might have the Opportunity of executing that Design before concerted with her assisting Villain) presently perceiv'd her, but finding she was alone, cou'd not be assur'd whether it was her *Rival* or *Sansfoy* herself, who she knew had Curiosity enough for such an Enterprize, if she cou'd not prevail on the other: but not doubting, but whatever she shou'd discover wou'd be carried immediately to *Montamour,* began to talk to *Du Lache* in the manner they had contriv'd for the insulting her. I think (said she raising her Voice, that she that follow'd might lose nothing of what was said) I ought no longer to doubt the Sincerity of my charming Friend: he has made no Scruple of revealing to me the dearest Secrets of his Soul; he confest that he formerly had a Tenderness for *Montamour;* which, till he saw me, he took for Love: he acknowledges a *Pity* for the Impression which he finds his Vows of Courtship have made on her too easie yielding Heart, but protests that he has of late desisted from giving her any Proofs of that Affection she once flatter'd herself with, and that since his Acquaintance with me, he never has visited her. I am certain he has not, reply'd *Du Lache,* and in my Opinion you cannot have a greater Testimony of his Passion, than his abondoning a Maid of her Quality and Fortune—one, who in the Judgment of most People is Mistress of a thousand Beauties and Accomplishments; and unto whom, in spite of her Reserve, he knows himself extremely dear. Poor Girl (resum'd the malicious *Baroness*) I pity her: her Condition is truly deplorable: for the engaging *Beauclair* has sworn he ne'er will see her more; and but this very Morn, among a Million of tender Protestations, bound the Promise he before had made me, with so solemn a Vow, that 'tis impossible he should ever dare to speak of her, to write to her, or even to think of her again, with any thing beyond the common Civility of a Stranger.

What pass'd in the Soul of *Montamour* at hearing this Discourse, and what she endur'd in the Struggles of her Passions with her Discretion, can never be represented by Words; the Idea which one ought to conceive of her Sufferings wou'd be lessen'd by Description; therefore, I shall only say that she supported 'em with Life, but that was all; while the *Baroness* went on with her Persecutions in this manner. Another Proof of his Affection, resum'd she, and which I think a prodigious one, is the Uneasiness he expresses at my but speaking to any other Man: he fancies the whole Creation are his Rivals, and envies even the Wind the Blessing of saluting me:——I will tell you a pleasant thing of him, (continu'd she laughing) He came to visit me the other day, and found the *Marquis de Sonville* with me. I knew his Thoughts, and cou'd not forbear smiling, to see how aukwardly he counterfeited a Cheerfulness, till the *Marquis's* Page happening to bring him a Letter, he retir'd to the farther end of the Room to read it, and gave my impatient Lover an Opportunity to vent some part of his *Chagrin.* A Pen and Ink standing upon the Table, he immediately writ, blotting it out as soon as he had done,——O *Tortillée! Tortillée! Divine* as you are in all things else, in the Affairs of *Love* I fear you are but *mortal,* and liable to change: what, O what! must then become of the unfortunate *Beauclair?*

Her Invention, which was seldom at a Loss, when prompted either by her Interest or Ill-nature, wou'd certainly have furnish'd her with many more Stories of this kind, if the coming of *Beauclair* had not put a stop to 'em. Tho' the Curiosity of seeing in what manner he wou'd behave, had been the only Reason which had brought *Montamour* there, she was now hinder'd from the Gratification of it. As subterranean Fires prey on their Mansion,[46] and consume with certain, tho' unseen, Destruction; the various and violent Agitations which rag'd in the Breast of this unhappy Lady, not having Liberty to vent themselves, roll'd stormy for a while, then growing too mighty for Restraint disdain'd all Bounds, and wou'd have burst in Exclamations suited to their Cause, had not her gentle Soul, entirely unaccustom'd to such Struggles, refus'd to obey the Dictates of her Fury; when she was about to shew herself, to speak, and to upbraid, she lost the Power, her Voice forsook her, and her every Sense flew frighted at the Tempest, and left her Body motionless on the Earth. She saw the dear Undoer of her Quiet approach——She saw the detested Pair, whose Discourse had plung'd her into such Agonies, walk hastily from the Place they were in, to meet him; but what their Conversation was after he join'd 'em, her Swoon depriv'd her of the means to observe.

They staid not long in the Walk: the *Baroness* little suspecting what had happen'd to *Montamour* drew 'em immediately out of the *Tuilleries,* for tho' *Beauclair* address'd her with all imaginable Complaisance, and a vast deal of Gallantry, yet he was far from expressing himself with that prodigious Tenderness which she wou'd have her Rival believe.

Poor *Montamour* remain'd for a considerable Time in the Condition they had left her, and for want of Help, join'd to the Coldness of the Earth, might, perhaps, never have recover'd, if an unexpected Accident had not brought *Monsieur Galliard* to her Relief. He had been abroad that Night on an Intrigue, which having met with a Disappointment in, he came thither, thinking to indulge his *Chagrin.* Chance led him to the very Place where she was lying: She had fallen quite cross the Walk; so that dark as it was, it was impossible for him to pass, without perceiving something in his way: the Oddness of the Adventure at first a little surpriz'd him. To find a Person who tho' her Face was hid, by some Jewels which glitter'd on her Breast, he guess'd to be a Woman of fashion, at such an Hour, in such a Place, and in such a Posture, made him begin to imagine that Fortune had design'd him a Reparation for the Disappointment he had lately met with; but he soon lost that Hope, tho' to the Encrease of his Amazement, when kneeling down by her, and pulling back her Hoods, he discover'd who she was. The fresh Air immediately restor'd her to Life, but it was a good while before she regain'd her Senses; she knew not where she was, nor who was present, and remembring nothing but the Cause which had thrown her into this Disorder, frequently repeated the Names of *Beauclair, Tortillée,* and *Du Lache,* but in so wild and incoherent a manner, that if *Galliard* had not been pretty well acquainted with the Reasons she had for Jealousy, he cou'd not have been able to guess 'em by her Words. The Respect he always paid her, and which, indeed, her Conduct exacted from every Body, made him behave himself to her in a manner very different to what he wou'd have us'd to any other Woman in the like Circumstance; and as he had a great deal of good Sense, whenever he pleas'd to exert it, he made Use of a great many fine Reasonings to dissuade her from giving way to the Suggestions of her Passions. She stood very little in need of his Advice, whenever she had the Liberty of Thought; and now beginning to resume it, was more angry with herself for the Indiscretion her Curiosity had made her guilty of, than with those who had occasion'd it. She knew *Galliard* to be of a Temper not much different from *Sansfoy,* and cou'd not hope that this Adventure wou'd be kept a Secret; she did not fail however to conjure him to it, and 'tis possible his extraordinary Esteem for her might have oblig'd him to put a Constraint on his Inclinations, if an unexpected Accident had not discover'd the whole Transaction without his Help.

During the Time that *Montamour* was in her Swoon, and that she pass'd in Discourse with *Galliard,* which was several Hours (for tho' she stole out of the House without being taken notice of, she knew not how to get into it, in the same manner, and therefore was not over-hasty to be gone) *Beauclair* was entertain'd by the *Baroness* in the most splendid manner, that her Love and the natural Profuseness of her Temper cou'd invent; and knowing that Wine is no small Provocative to Desire, she had provided a vast Variety of the most choice ones; but not all she cou'd do was able to drive the Idea of *Montamour* from his Remembrance: In the Height of all the Gaiety with which *Tortillée* endeavour'd to divert him, he cou'd not forbear reflecting with how much more solid Felicity he had pass'd his Hours with the other; the more he saw of her Behaviour, the less careful she grew of disguising it, and the more he found in it to disesteem. In spite of her well-acted Tenderness, and in spite of all her Instrument *Du Lache* had told him of her Sincerity, he cou'd not consider with what Facility she had granted him the greatest Favours, without a Suspicion that others might also have the same Freedom. To enhance his Admiration, she was perpetually telling him how many had sought her Affection; and by what he knew of her Humour, had little Reason to believe their Labour had been in vain:——In fine, all her Actions, all her Words, serv'd only to show him the prodigious Disproportion which was between those Charms she wou'd be thought to have, and those *Montamour* was really possest of. Tho' these kind of Reflections came frequently into his Mind, yet they had greater Force this Night than ever; he grew excessive melancholy on the sudden; and tho' both the *Baroness* and *Du Lache* took all imaginable Pains to exhilerate his Temper, their Endeavours were in vain: and finding it impossible for him to be any Company, begg'd Leave to retire. The Reader will easily imagine how much the Lady was alarm'd at a Behaviour so distant from her Expectations: She made use of all her Artifice, she wept, entreated, counterfeited Swoonings, but all fail'd of the Effect she aim'd at; and tho' *Du Lache* reminded him how uncourtly it was to leave a Lady who had receiv'd him in so generous a fashion, he persisted in his Resolution, and only making a slight Excuse, took leave of her, accompany'd by *Du Lache,* who wou'd not part from him till he had found out the meaning of this Alteration.

It seem'd as if the unusual Sadness which seiz'd the Soul of *Beauclair,* and oblig'd him to quit the *Baroness*'s House so much sooner than he intended, was influenced by *Fate,* on purpose to bring him to a Place, where he shou'd have a View of what wou'd give him Torments pretty near equal to those his late Deportment had inflicted on the disconsolate *Montamour.* He pass'd by the *Tuilleries* the very Moment that *Galliard* was conducting her out: She had too much Distraction in her Thoughts to have remember'd to pull down her Hoods, and it being now just Day-break, her whole Face appear'd to the Eyes of her impatient Lover. In spite of all that *Du Lache, Toncarr,* and *Le Songe* had told him of her Perfidiousness, he never cou'd bring himself to a thorough Assurance of it: and there were some Moments in which he cou'd not help believing all he had heard was false: but what Excuses now cou'd his Passion alledge against so positive an Appearance? To see her in a loose *Dishabillée*[47] at so irregular an Hour,—in such a Place, and so accompany'd, was sufficient to justify whatever her worst Enemies cou'd suggest to her Prejudice.

Du Lache, tho' he was infinitely rejoic'd at an Encounter which so unexpectedly favour'd his Designs, was unwilling that *Beauclair* shou'd take notice of her, with reason, fearing if they shou'd enter into a Conversation it might produce something which might ruin all, and perswaded him to pass without speaking; but the other was too full of Rage to listen to the Arguments this artful Villain was preparing to prevent him, and stepping hastily to her, 'Tis an early Hour, Madam! said he, (with a Look and Gesture which sufficiently testify'd his Disorders) for Ladies, such as *Montamour,* to be abroad;——but I perceive you are not without a Guard, else shou'd make Offer of my Service to attend you. You have infinitely more agreeable Engagements on your Hands, answer'd she, (counterfeiting an Air of Gaiety) and I think my self extremely happy in the Knowledge of your Humour, because it gives me the Liberty of indulging my own. She spoke no more, nor indeed had she the Power: the Pain she suffer'd in restraining the struggling Passions of her Soul, was very near throwing her again into that Condition from which *Galliard* had so lately recover'd her. These few Words, however, had the effect she aim'd at, to sting *Beauclair* to the Quick; and wholly unable to contain himself, If there be any thing like a Change in my Humour, (resum'd he impatiently) *Montamour* ought, indeed, to approve it, since I but follow'd an Example she gave me. If she had heard this, it might perhaps have made her reply in a manner, which wou'd have given him some Light into the Arts by which they both had been impos'd on; but her Agitations were too violent to permit her to stay; she was remov'd several Paces from him, and he thought it wou'd look like Mean-spiritedness to follow her, after what he had *seen,* which seem'd to be so great a Confirmation of all he had been *told*: in short, both believing themselves injur'd, each disdain'd to do any thing which might appear like a Desire of Reconciliation: and this little Pride, fatal alike to the Repose of both, gave the common Deceivers all the Opportunity they cou'd wish to compass their pernicious Ends, of separating two Hearts which by all the Ties of Gratitude and Tenderness were thought to be cemented.

When *Montamour* was come home, and the first Emotions of her Passions a little abated, she began to consider with more Sedateness on this Adventure; and being unable to find any reasonable Excuse for *Beauclair's* Behaviour, resolv'd to tear him from her Heart: She foresaw it wou'd cost her most terrible Pangs, but yet it must be done, and therefore the sooner she endeavour'd it, the better. But tho' she found no great Difficulty in the forming this Resolution, she did in fixing on what means she shou'd make choice of for the Execution of it. To think to displace him by entertaining the Idea of any other Man, was vain: there was none who in the Perfections of either

Mind or Body cou'd *vie* with the charming *Beauclair,* much less *exceed* him: neither cou'd she hope that Variety of Company, or Diversions, wou'd so far amuse her, as to make her forget him, but on the contrary more remind her, how little, in Competition with the soft Hours of mutual Love, are those past in that Hurry which the Mistaken World calls Pleasure. Such an Alteration in her Behaviour, she consider'd, might endanger her *Reputation,* but ne'er restore her *Quiet.* Therefore, after many disturb'd Reflections, a *Cloister*[48] seem'd the only *Asylum* where she cou'd hope for Peace: the Duties of Religion so strictly practis'd in those Places, the pious Examples and heavenly Conversation of the holy *Sisterhood,* she doubted not wou'd set her Mind at Ease, and raise her Wishes beyond worldly Views. When she consider'd with what a Sublimity of Tenderness she had regarded *Beauclair,* she look'd upon it as a *Sin,* for which she was justly punish'd in his *Inconstancy*: she accus'd herself of Sacrilege, in paying to a *Mortal* that Adoration *Heaven* alone had Claim to, and vow'd to devote the remaining Part of her Life to Penitence for that Transgression. She was extremely strengthen'd in this Design by her *Confessor.* She had a large Fortune in her own Possession, which, on her embracing a Monastick Life, wou'd be wholly employ'd in the Service of Mother *Church,* of which he was too true a *Son* to let slip so fair an Opportunity of Advantage. He magnify'd the Comforts of Retirement, and the innate Contentment which flows from an entire abandoning the World, in so florid and perswasive a Stile, that in spite of all that her Brother and other Relations and Acquaintance cou'd do, to disswade her she went into a Nunnery about four Leagues[49] distant from *Paris,* fully determin'd to take Orders as soon as her Year of Probation shou'd be expir'd.[50]

While *Montamour* was thus employ'd in endeavouring to vanquish an Inclination she thought so ill plac'd, *Beauclair* was using his utmost Efforts for a Conquest of the same Nature. Her Behaviour, when he met her with *Galliard,* made her appear more vile than even *Du Lache* and his Adherents had represented her: He cou'd not think he had ever lov'd her, without being asham'd of his Affection.—*Tortillée* seem'd now less faulty in his Opinion,——he believ'd her guilty of no other Failings than what were incident to her Sex, for if *Montamour* was false, he imagin'd all Women must be so. An honourable Passion was what, for the future, he resolv'd to avoid, and being enter'd in an Amour with the *Baroness,* fancied he might pass his Hours in her Company with as much Felicity as in any others. To make the Favours he receiv'd from her as great a Blessing as possible, he took abundance of Pains to establish a Tenderness in his Soul on her Account, like what he formerly had felt for *Montamour,* but how much did he deceive himself in such an Attempt! the lovely Maid, all Guilty as she seem'd, maintain'd her Empire still! the more he struggl'd with his Chains, the more he found the Impossibility of breaking them: and what he endur'd in the Conflict between *Passion* and *Resentment* was almost insupportable. But, despising himself for what he thought so great a Weakness, he resolv'd to do nothing that shou'd give the World occasion to suspect what pass'd within his Soul; and to that end, paid his Devoirs[51] to the *Baroness* in a more assiduous manner than he wou'd have done, perhaps, had Inclination only prompted him.

This mischievous woman now exulted with a malicious Joy at the Knowledge of her *Rival's* Grief, for in spite of all that Lady's Caution it was soon blaz'd abroad, that she was miserable in the Loss of *Beauclair.* The Condition in which *Galliard* had found her in the *Tuilleries* was no Secret; for tho' the Esteem he had for her oblig'd him to conceal her Name, it cou'd not restrain him from diverting himself and Companions with the Relation of such an Adventure; and *Du Lache* being with *Beauclair* when he was conducting her out, made him know it was she her self, and not *Sansfoy,* who had come thither to observe the *Baroness;* so that between them the whole Affair soon grew the common Chat[52] of every Tea Table: and it was the Knowledge of being thus expos'd, which doubtless, more than any thing, made *Montamour* deaf to all the Perswasions of her Friends from a Monastick Life. *Beauclair* was soon inform'd of her Resolution, but whatever he felt within himself seem'd little to regard it, and was in reality not sorry she had taken Measures which wou'd render it impossible for him ever to let her know the Power she had over him; and being allowed, and indeed *courted* to take all imaginable Freedom with the *Baroness,* whoever had seen him with her wou'd have believ'd his Soul was wholly hers; but, in spite of all the Pleasure this wicked Woman conceiv'd in the Opinion she was Mistress of a Heart, the united Beauties of the whole Sex without an equal Proportion of Wit and Virtue was insufficient to deserve, in spite of the unequall'd, unexpressible Graces he was possest of, she cou'd not resolve to be his alone: *Sonville, St. Aumar, Le Sourbe* and others had the same Liberties with her as before; but, as I have already taken Notice, she had her particular Places of Assignation with them all, and *Beauclair* had not the least Suspicion of any Rivals in his Happiness, and was pretty near an Infatuation equal to that her Artifices had wrought on the unhappy *Baron.*

Thus all things for a while went smoothly on, till one unhappy Day had like to have made a total Discovery of her Falshood to him whom it was most her Interest to deceive. *Beauclair* as well as others of her Admirers frequently visited her at Home: and happening to come one Afternoon, and finding her in her Bedchamber, no Company with her, the *Baron* abroad, and she in a loose Undress (in which indeed she look'd most amiable) he cou'd not resist a sudden Inclination to make use of so favourable an Opportunity, and taking her in his Arms and throwing her on the Bed, was about to repeat at *Home* what many times she had condescended to *Abroad*: The Violence of his present Desire, and the Ecstacy she was in to find him so much more than ordinarily transported, depriv'd them both of that Caution they were accustom'd to make use of. The Chamber Door was only carelessly put to, and the *Baron* chancing to return, and come into that very Room, was struck with a sight, which no other Witnesses but his own Eyes cou'd have convinc'd him had been true. He wou'd have drawn his Sword, and wash'd the Stain they cast upon his Honour with the Blood of both, but Astonishment took from him the Power: She was in a Posture such as cou'd have left no other Woman a Possibility of Excuse; but so ready was she at Invention, and so cunning in deceiving, that even in this, the greatest Tryal she cou'd meet, she brought herself off with a Dexterity which prov'd how much she was Mistress of the Art of Jilting.[53]

Her Face lying toward that side of the Room where her Husband enter'd, she had an Opportunity of seeing him immediately, and before *Beauclair* cou'd have any Imagination of the Truth, the Person who in his Arms that Moment was uttering Raptures, amaz'd him, on a sudden, with struggling to get loose, and crying out, *Help! Oh Help!—a Rape!*——where are my Servants——will none come to my Assistance——for Heaven's sake *Monsieur* desist——I'll rather die than live to wrong the best of Men and Husbands. Then disengaging herself from his Embrace, and running to the *Baron* (pretending not to have seen him before) Oh my dear Lord! said she, how opportunely are you come to save me from Dishonour, from Ruin, from *Death,* for sure I wou'd have flown for Refuge to the *latter* rather than have endur'd the *former.* That barbarous Man (added she, bursting into well-dissembled Tears) wou'd have depriv'd me of all I value Life for——he wou'd have violated my Innocence——corrupted my Duty——made me utterly unworthy of my dear Lord's Affection——and finding his impious Perswasions were in vain, he wou'd have *forc'd* me to the horrid Deed——a Deed my Soul abhors——a Deed which must have made me hateful to both Heaven and Earth.——Oh had I not been inspir'd for some Moments with an unusual Strength, and had not my Heart's Treasure, my dear dear *Baron,* come to my Assistance just when that Strength began to fail, how wretched had I been!——Oh be ever prais'd ye Saints and Angels! ye ministring Spirits! the Guardians of my Honour, for your Protection in this dreadful Hour!——Oh still continue watchful o'er your Charge! and save me ever from Infamy and Guilt. She fell on her Knees, and pronounc'd these last Words in so exotic[54] a manner, and with a Countenance so exactly suited to every thing she said, that *Beauclair* was much more startled at her Impiety and Dissimulation than he had been when rising from the Bed he perceiv'd what it was that occasion'd it.

The Scene must certainly have been pleasant enough to observe, if any disinterested Person had been Witness of it: to behold a couple of Men stand gazing on each other without Power of Speech or Motion, while a Woman was acting over a thousand various Passions in Gestures and Grimaces suited to them all——sometimes rejoicing at the *Deliverance* she pretended to have had——sometimes feigning to look back with Horrour on her past *Danger*——now *weeping,* as it were thro' Tenderness,——then *exclaiming* against the Baseness of Mankind——with one Breath *Cursing* her own Charms for being the occasion of inspiring loose Desires,——and with the next, *Blessing* Heaven for giving her the Means of resisting them. The Surprize which both the Husband and Lover were in, gave her sufficient Opportunity to exercise her Talent; but as *Beauclair* was Master of a much greater Presence of Mind than the *Baron,* so he recollected himself much sooner, and perceiving the Lady was very capable of making her Party good with her believing Husband, thought, in such a Circumstance, the most prudent Action he cou'd do was to retire. The first thing he had done after he started from the Bed was to snatch up his Sword, not doubting but he shou'd have occasion to make use of it: but finding he was not immediately call'd to the Account he expected, took the Advantage of the *Baron*'s Confusion, and left him to adjust matters with his Spouse, as they shou'd agree it between 'em: only telling him, as he went out of the Room, that if he imagin'd himself injur'd, he knew where to demand Satisfaction; he staid not for an Answer, nor had the other recover'd himself enough, as yet, to make one; he continued, for some Moments after *Beauclair* was gone, fix'd in the same stupid Posture he had been in ever since he came into the Room; till, at last, the hurried Spirits beginning by little and little to resume their proper Stations, he fetch'd a deep sigh, and breaking from his Wife, who had all this while been holding him in her Arms, walk'd hastily to and fro, by that Action only discovering the inward Disorders that oppress'd him: But what is it that is not in the Power of a Person belov'd to accomplish? What a commanding Force there dwells in Tears, when flowing from the Eyes we worship! they give the lye to Reason, and make our very Senses but unavailing Witnesses, when oppos'd to any thing they wou'd insinuate.

The tender-hearted *Baron* at first testify'd the secret Yieldings of his Soul but by a Look; but she, who perfectly understood the Language of the Eyes, immediately knew her Work was more than half compleated, and assuming an Air all full of Languishment and Softness, I have liv'd too long, said she, (in a dying, trembling Accent) I have liv'd too long, since my dear Lord, the only Man, Heav'n knows, I ever wish'd to please, regards me with Indifference—is this dumb Coldness, or this distant Posture a Proof of that Passion you have sworn shou'd be unchangeable, or a fit Welcome for a Wife, rescued by Providence from threatned Ruin? O my only Dear, my Love, my Life, my Husband, continu'd she (seizing his Hand and clapping it to her Mouth with a well counterfeited Transport) Take, Take me to your Breast, or kill me. There needed no more to make the poor *Baron* quite beside himself; his Soul, before overcome by soft Emotions, now quite dissolv'd and melted in a Sea of Tenderness: He clasp'd the Syren in his faithful Arms! kiss'd her dissembling Lips! and while he spoke the fondest, most endearing Words that Tongue e'er utter'd, or Heart e'er conceiv'd, a Flood of honest Tears stream'd from his Eyes, and bath'd her treacherous Bosom! Oh thou art all Divine, cry'd he, in a Rapture, all Angel! thy *Mind* like thy bright *Body,* charming! Pure and untainted with any of the Frailties of thy Sex! Dear to *Reason,* and ravishing to *Sense!* and then again, let me no longer live than I adore thee (pursued the affectionate Deluded) Thou Excellence——Thou lovely Abstract of all that's good in Woman!

'Tis not to be doubted but that she answered these tender Expressions, and return'd the Caresses he gave her, in a manner which seem'd to him, to proceed from, at least, an equal Ardency: and this Accident was so far from lessening her in his Esteem, that it made her, if possible, dearer than before; he was too little acquainted with Artifice himself, to imagine there was a Possibility for the Woman he ador'd to be Mistress of so much; the entire Confidence he always had of her Love and Virtue was now in as full force as ever, and all those Notions which had crowded into his Soul at his first coming into the Chamber, and beholding so unexpected, and indeed, so distracting a Sight, now vanished and were no more remembred! *Love,* now, triumphant Love! unmix'd with Fears, with Jealousies or Doubts, blaz'd with Almighty Lustre, and struck all other Remonstrances dead. He thought he look'd into her very Soul and found it all Perfection, nothing that he cou'd wish were alter'd, excepting a little too much Freedom and Condescention in her Behaviour, which tho' he believ'd altogether innocent and undesign'd, he thought might have encourag'd *Beauclair* to hope greater Favours. He did not fail to acquaint her what his Sentiments were on that score, and conjur'd her for the sake of his eternal Quiet, and her own Honour and Reputation, to endeavour to wear a more distant and reserv'd Air in her Conversation with those Men whose Principles she was not perfectly assured of.

This Advice, tho' accompany'd with ten thousand soft Professions, and given with the greatest Complaisance, relish'd but ill with her 'twas apply'd to;

but she had Policy enough to conceal her Chagrin, pretended to think as he did, and assur'd him in all the seeming good Humour imaginable that for the future she wou'd be more wary: but from that Moment she conceiv'd an inexpressible Hatred for him; if he had Eyes to see a Failing in her Conduct, she knew not but in Time he might gather Courage to condemn, or to controll it; and the bare Thoughts that there was a possibility she might one Day be debarr'd from taking the Liberties she now enjoy'd, made her almost distracted: if this medling Husband was to be no longer *blinded* he must be *remov'd; Murder* was now the Employment of her Thoughts, and seem'd so absolutely necessary for the Security of her Pleasures, that she found no Shock, or such as she could easily pass over, in resolving to undertake it: and she wou'd most certainly have found some means to perpetrate her horrid Intentions, if her Agent in all mischievous Enterprises, *Du Lache,* had not advis'd her to another, tho' almost as *execrable,* yet a less *dangerous* Method of getting rid of him. He procur'd a Potion compos'd of such pernicious Drugs, that tho' it wou'd not absolutely destroy Life, and drive the Soul from her tormented Habitation; yet it had that unhappy Effect on all the sensitive Faculties as to reduce the Person who shou'd swallow it, to a Condition little preferable to that of an Ideot.

This cursed Mixture did that Monster of a Woman give to her unsuspecting Husband, and while his tender, truly generous Soul was wholly taken up with the Study how to please her, himself was sinking into the most miserable State that Hell-bred Mischief could invent: At first he was seiz'd with a Lethargy of Thought, a kind of lazy Stupefaction hung on his Spirits, which every day encreasing, at last over-whelm'd the Throne of Reason! Reflection was unhing'd! the noble Seat of Memory fill'd with Chimeras[55] and disjointed Notions! wild and confus'd Ideas whirl'd in his distracted Brain! and all the Man, except the Form, was chang'd.

The *Baroness*'s shameful Conduct was too visible to the World, for any Body to wonder at her Husband's Frenzy; and tho' every one pitied the Condition they saw him in, yet there was none that had the least Suspicion she had made use of any other means to bring him into it, than what was public. She suffer'd him to continue a few Days in Town after his *Delirium;* but then, under the Pretence that change of Air might be of Service, sent him down to a little Village about forty Miles from *Paris* where she had him boarded at a cheap rate, out of his large Estate scarce affording him the common Necessaries of Life.

Now all the gay, loose, Part of her Acquaintance of both Sexes, which to pleasure him for a little time she had pretended to discard, return'd with usual

Freedom to her House; her Drawing-Room was every Day fill'd with Visitants, her Antichamber with Musicians, and her Hall with Attendants: the whole Dwelling became a Seat of Luxury——Dancing, Singing, Playing, Drinking, Feasting, all that cou'd charm the Sense might here be found in full Profuseness of Satiety: but tho' these Entertainments were ravishing to most of the Company they were prepar'd for, *Beauclair* had no Relish for 'em, his Morals were too excellent, and his Soul too much refin'd and delicate to be pleas'd with those gross Debaucheries he daily saw acted there. The *Baroness,* whom a long time he had but little esteem'd, especially since that monstrous Dissimulation with which he was Witness she treated her Husband, now appear'd odious in his Eyes: his good Manners wou'd not permit him to desist wholly from visiting her, but he never staid long, and went not so often as he had been accustom'd. He made no Scruple of letting *Du Lache* know his Sentiments, when he was ask'd by him, the reason of estranging himself; but the other took not now the Pains he had done to conceal the *Baroness*'s Vices; he knew that *Beauclair* was now grown as indifferent to her as any of his Predecessors or Cotemporaries, and that to preserve his good Opinion was a thing she gave herself not the least Concern about.

All the Thoughts of this inconstant Woman were at present taken up with young *La Branche,*[56] one of the most vain, conceited Coxcombs in the Town, one who had no other Merit, no other Charm, than his being a new Conquest, to engage her: tho' worthless as he was, there was a Girl, to whom he formerly had made court, that valued his Conversation at a very high rate, and endeavour'd by Letters, Messages, and all the Stratagems that her Passion cou'd invent, to retrieve the fickle Heart of this ungrateful Lover. The Knowledge that there was a Rival in the way, always made the *Baroness*'s Desires more eager; to give *Disquiet* to her *own* Sex heightned her Satisfaction in the Enjoyment of the *other*: She was of that *malicious,* one may justly say, indeed, *devilish* Disposition, that her chief *Pleasure* consisted in the inflicting Pain: wanting the Poignancy of *Revenge,* not all the Joys that *Love* affords (warm as her Inclinations were) had any Relish. The Embraces of a God, *unenvy'd,* wou'd have been tasteless and insipid: No longer than his Engagement with another kept her in Suspence was the *Marquis de Sonville* the Object of her Affection. When the Continuance of *St. Aumar*'s Addresses to her render'd him despis'd by all the other Women of his Acquaintance, he became immediately so by her; and her Apprehensions of *Montamour* no sooner were remov'd, than *Beauclair* was disregarded; a kind Look from that insignificant Trifler, *La Branche,* was now of greater Value with her, than all the Caresses of these accomplish'd Gentlemen. The unfortunate young Creature that lov'd him was now the Sacrifice which her insatiate Pride requir'd, and the whole Time and Invention of *Du Lache* was now employ'd in means to compass it.

But how fond soever the *Baroness* was of a *new* Intrigue, Heav'n never form'd a Man whose Charms cou'd oblige her to discontinue any of her *former* ones, nor was she ever so much over-whelm'd in Passion as not to know how to conceal it, whenever she found occasion; whenever any *one* of her Admirers took notice that she regarded *another* with more Tenderness than he approv'd of, she had a method of silencing his Doubts as *artful* as it was *base;* she pretended that the Person suspected was only indulg'd by her in some little Freedoms to take off all Imagination of a real Amour between him and a *certain Lady* of her Acquaintance; and then, if press'd to it, wou'd frame a long Story of some Woman, no matter who, but any body that came into her Head at that Time was made the Property to bear her Shame: the truth is, indeed, she kept no Company whom any thing she said cou'd make appear much worse than in reality they were. By this means she prevented any Quarrels from arising between her Lovers, and preserv'd to herself a Reputation with them which she was very far from deserving. She was also extremely indebted to her good Fortune, that all this while among so many she had, hitherto, to do only with Men whose Honour wou'd not permit them to boast of a Lady's Favours: and something too, I think, she owed to their want of Penetration, as well as her own Artifice, that she cou'd so long and so easily impose on their Judgments.

If *La Branche* had been of the same Disposition and Principles with the others, she might, perhaps, have retain'd the good Opinion of them all something longer than she did; but that Wretch was too much elevated with his good Fortune, in being belov'd by a Woman of the *Baroness*'s Quality, to conceal it: He talk'd of her wherever he came, toasted her as a Mistress, read her Letters publickly, and was so careless in putting them up, as to lose two of 'em, which happening to fall into the Hands of an Intimate of the *Marquis de Sonville,* were immediately brought to him. Never was any Surprise superior to that of this Gentleman, when he found what they contain'd; nor Rage equal to that he flew into, at reflecting on the Indignity she offer'd to his Merit; for in the whole Course of his Amour with her, never had she made a more passionate Declaration of Love to him, than he now found she had done to *La Branche*: the more he consider'd on the Worthlessness of the Fellow, the more he grew enrag'd, and resolving to be reveng'd on her Meanness of Spirit, on her Perfidy and Ingratitude, set himself to study what measures he shou'd take to expose her, and make her appear as vile and as detestable to the whole World as she was grown to him: his Resentment soon inspir'd him with a

Thought lucky enough for his Purpose; He knew that the next Day was that on which she kept her Assembly, and had generally a greater Affluence[57] of Company on that than any other Day: He went not till it was pretty late, that he believ'd they were all met, because he was desirous to have as many Witnesses as possible of what he did. He came into the Room with his usual Gaiety of Air, entirely dissembling his Chagrin, and stepping up to the *Baroness,* who was at a little Table busily engag'd at *Ombre*[58] with *St. Aumar* and the young *Count de la Torre,* I thought Madam! (said he to her, after having look'd round the Room and seen he was not there) to have found *Monsieur La Branche* among this good Company; by Accident some Letters directed for him have fallen into my Possession, and I wou'd willingly have restor'd 'em. For Heav'ns sake let me see them, cry'd the jealous *Baroness,* presently imagining they had been sent to him by her Rival. No, Madam! reply'd the *Marquis,* since your Curiosity wou'd lead you to examine the Contents, I will save you the Trouble, and read them my self, aloud, that all here may partake of the Diversion they will afford: He had no sooner spoke than all the Gentlemen and Ladies in the Room, among whom were *Monsieur Beauclair* and old *Le Sourbe,* flock'd to the Place where he was standing, and prepar'd to give Attention, while he pull'd one of the Letters out of his Pocket, and began to read as follows.

To the dearest of Mankind, the lovely and accomplish'd
La Branche.

How can you pretend to love, and yet deny me the only Joy I have in Life! what Excuse can you make for not coming as you promis'd? The *Day,* indeed, that curs'd detested thing call'd *Business* may engross, but *Love* and *I* might surely claim the *Night*——

He was not permitted to proceed: the *Baroness,* who from the first Word had discover'd a strange Uneasiness and Confusion in her Behaviour, now started from her Chair, and running to him and endeavouring to snatch the Paper out of his Hand, Hold, my Lord! said she, trembling with the inward Disorders of her Soul, I conjure you by all you fear *above* or love *below,* not to expose the Contents of that Letter. Your Ladyship is unkind, (interrupted *de la Torre* who knew her well enough to guess the reason of her Concern) we all have cause to complain of your want of good Nature, in endeavouring to deprive us of an Entertainment which the *Marquis* promises so much Diversion in. I cannot (resum'd she recollecting herself as much as possible) suffer the Secret of my Friend to be divulg'd——that Letter is from a Woman I entirely love, and tho' I writ it for her to prevent any Discovery, yet 'tis possible some here by the Contents may guess the Person.——I doubt not, madam, (answer'd the *Marquis*) but that every body will: but, (pursu'd he ironically) I have so vast a Regard for the *Baroness de Tortillée* that I cannot consent to bury in Obscurity so uncommon a Proof of her good Nature as the signing her *own Name* to a Complaint such as this. How! cry'd all the Company with one Voice, her *own Name*! and immediately a loud Laughter ensu'd among the *Women,* and Signs of an universal Consternation among the *Men.* The revengeful *Marquis* observ'd it with Pleasure, and was about to go on with the Letter, but the *Baroness* quite beside her self with Passion, still struggling to get it from him, for some Moments retarded his Design, till finding her continue obstinate he thought fit to show that he was resolv'd to be so too, and holding it above her reach, and gently putting her off, 'Twere too much, Madam, (resum'd he, with a malicious Smile) to do so much for the Service of a Friend, yet be deny'd the Praises due to so elevated a Sincerity!—You must and shall receive the Glory which your Actions merit, and if you *now* prevent me, the publick News-papers *tomorrow* shall proclaim your Virtues.

'Twould be impossible to represent the Violence of her Rage, when she found that neither Entreaties nor Commands were of force to oblige him to stifle this Testimony of her Infamy; she rav'd like one distracted, call'd him ten thousand Villains, and perceiving her self on the very brink of being exposed in the most shameful manner imaginable, no hope from Artifice! no Relief from Dissimulation! she threw the Mask of Softness off! unheard-of Curses issued from her Mouth! her Eyes shot Fire! in all her Air the Fury stood confest! and quitting the *Marquis,* and looking wildly round on the rest of the Company (who waited with Impatience for the End of this Adventure) and seeing none offer to assist her in wresting this fatal Paper from the Hand that held it, she flew out of the Room, wishing Eternal Damnation on 'em all. The Indignation and Confusion she express'd was so great a Gratification of the *Marquis's* Spleen, that he had certainly follow'd her to prosecute the Raillery he had so tormentingly began, but that to fully satiate his Revenge it was necessary he shou'd stay where he was, since he cou'd never meet with a fitter Opportunity than what offer'd at present for the making her appear what she really was before so many Persons, some of which he knew wou'd not fail to blaze it; and every Body crowding about him, he immediately proceeded with the Letter, which continued to declare the Passion it began with, in these Words;

Languishing for your Approach, and all dissolving in the pleasing Expectation of those Joys your dear-lov'd Presence brings, some Hours slid soft away; but when the Time was past, what Horror! what inconceivable Inquietudes ensu'd! my Heart, so lately the Seat of Rapture, was now fill'd with racking Doubts, and torturing Jealousy——What shall I do?——I am wild with Apprehension——the Memory of *past Delights* but heightens *present Woes*——O, *La Branche!* shou'd you, indeed, forsake me, not *Hell* contains a Wretch more curst than I——but sure it cannot be!——that lovely Form can harbour no Deceit—'twas my ill Fortune, but not thy Fault, that all the Night my longing Arms were stretch'd, in vain, to grasp thee; thy Soul, I know, thy Wishes all were mine—make haste my Love, my Life! my Angel, make haste to give and take such Joys as but in *Idea* to the vulgar World are known, tho' real and *substantial* to the charming *La Branche* and his

Passionately fond

Tortillée.

Methinks, said the *Marquis,* here is neither want of Passion or Softness in this Billet, to make the Author asham'd of its being read; but this is nothing to what this Prodigy of her Sex can do——here is (continued he) a Testimony of her Abilities, in which several of this Company have some Concern.——In speaking these Words he took out the other Letter, and without staying to hear what Reply any Body wou'd make, added to the Surprize they were already in, by reading these Lines.

To my Soul's Treasure, the most Adorable La Branche.

If Jealousy betokens Love, how happy should I think my self in receiving so many Proofs of yours? But say, thou dear Destroyer of my Peace! charming Unbeliever! say, what must I do to convince thee that I *am*——that I *can* be only Thine—O, didst thou know thy self, thy own Unequal'd Charms were a sufficient Security for my Truth——what is there in Man desirable that my *La Branche* does not possess in so eminently distinguish'd a Degree, that the whole Sex besides are worthless Nothings when compar'd with him!——You seem to make it an Occasion of Complaint, that I admit of so much Company; but tell me, how can I avoid it?——How can a Woman of my Quality, without becoming the Subject of Ridicule, refuse the Visits of Persons of her own Rank, and who call themselves her Husband's Friends; that Hated Fatal Tie, alas! obliges me to many things contrary to my Inclination. Besides, as he is now from Home, and under that unhappy Indisposition which all, but me, lament, shou'd I deny the Conversation of those he esteem'd, and those whom I can find no plausible Pretence for breaking with, wou'd it not be evident enough to the judging World 'twas for the sake of some dear unknown Favourite I did so? By a promiscuous Acquaintance I shun the Infamy of being too fond of *one,* and 'tis by this Method alone that I can secure my *Love* and my *Reputation.* It is for thee——for thee! Lovely, Cruel Suspector as thou art, for one Dear, Undisturb'd, Untalk'd-of Hour with thee I undergo the uneasie Task of dissembling in Publick; and to conceal my real Tenderness for *thee,* wear a pretended one to *all*——Methinks you shou'd approve an Act of Prudence so convenient for us both, and ought to know me better than to imagine I am so lost to Honour, or have a Soul so little delicate, as to stoop to a *plurality* of Amours——No, no, I am for nothing less than the most excellent of his Sex——to vanquish a Heart, till now, a Foe profest to Love and all its tender Follies, and triumph over a Virtue established like mine, it was necessary there should be a *La Branche!* Those whom your groundless Fears point out as *Rivals,* either because their *Quality* obliges me to treat them with a greater Share of Civility than I do others, or because you consider them as Men of more *Merit* than the generality of those you have seen with me, are in Reality the Objects of my Aversion and Disdain; if there be any thing like Perfection in any of them, 'tis hid amidst a Crowd of Faults: The *Count de la Torre* has indeed some Wit and Spirit, but then he is insufferably Insolent, Robust[59] and Vain——most People allow that the *Chevalier St. Aumar* has Nature and an agreeable Person, but at the same time make a Jest of his Understanding—those who are pleas'd with the *bon mein*[60] and Air of the *Marquis de Sonville* despise him for his Pride and Ostentation——*Beauclair*'s refin'd manner of Conversation, good Address, and Sublimity of Genius can never make Amends for his Want of Sincerity, and Affectation of a Passion for *all* Women, which he has not Stability of Temper enough to make him truly feel for *one;* any more than old *le Sourbe*'s Wealth can counterbalance his other Deficiencies——Wretches! Wretches! all, unworthy of *your Fears* as they are of *my Regard,* and with my *Husband* equally *odious* to my Soul's fond Wishes—Name them no more, unless you'd have all Desire in me grow sick, and at your next Embrace receive into your Arms a Senseless Log instead of

Your most Transported,
Melting, Longing, Dying,
Tortillée.

The *Marquis* had no sooner concluded the Reading this Epistle, than every Mouth in the Company was opening to express the various Sentiments which the Hearing it inspir'd in each of them: But *Count de la Torre,* whose Soul had burn'd with fierce Impatience from the Mention made of him, got the start of all the rest, in revenging on her Character the Reflection she had made on his; and as he was naturally passionate, and little regardless of the

Reputation of those Women that put themselves in his Power, now thinking there was not the least Obligation for Secrecy, said enough to let every body know, that she once took as much Pains to convince *him* of her Sincerity, as now she did *La Branche*. The *Marquis de Sonville* was not more generous; but *Monsieur le Sourbe* and the *Chevalier* spoke not a Word: both these Gentlemen had bore a true Affection to the *Baroness*, and were too much confounded at these strange and unexpected Discoveries of her Perfidy to be able to reply to any thing that was said: *Beauclair* observ'd it, and tho' he never knew what 'twas to feel a serious Passion for her, was as much nettled as the others, but he dissembled his Chagrin, and putting on a Countenance which had more in it of Disdain than Anger, For my part, said he, I find no Cause of Wonder but the Sight of yours: My Acquaintance with this Lady has been of a much shorter date than most of yours, yet in the little Time I have convers'd with her, I have seen enough not to be surpriz'd at this Testimony of the Levity of her Temper: those two Gentlemen (continu'd he, pointing to *St. Aumar* and *le Sourbe*) have, perhaps, been ignorant of each others Happiness: each believ'd himself the only favour'd, and gloried in a Self-sufficiency of being able to please the *Constant*, the *Distinguishing Tortillée*.

The *Constant*, the *Distinguishing Tortillée*, as your self once thought her, good *Monsieur*, interrupted a pert Lady (who stood near him, and who from *Sansfoy* had learn'd the whole Secret) do not imagine that your Intrigue with her has been invisible to all Eyes but your own; the whole Town knows she has had Arts to blind even the discerning *Beauclair*, or he wou'd not, for her sake, have abandon'd so deserving a Woman as *Montamour*. True Madam! true, said a Gentleman that was by; that unhappy Lady you mention'd had not been reduc'd to so sad a Condition as *Monsieur Galliard* found her in, in the *Tuilleries*, if the *Baroness* had never seem'd more worthy of regard, nor had she forsook the World for a Cloyster if *Monsieur Beauclair* had always profess'd the same Indifferency as now. That is an Affair of which no body is ignorant, added another. Yet, resum'd the Lady that spoke first, he has been as much deceiv'd in believing it a Secret, as he was in the Fidelity of his Mistress. There were several in the Room of both Sexes that seconded the Raillery she had begun on this score; and *Beauclair*, who from the first mention of *Montamour* had been struck with Remorse, and a kind of Self-Condemnation, cou'd not presently recover his Presence of Mind so far as to be able to answer them, and it was but with an half assur'd Accent that he at last brought forth these Words——I know not well what 'tis you mean (said he): *Madamoiselle Montamour*, by all I ever saw of her Behaviour, was never ambitious of becoming a publick Chat; she is a Woman I ever *did*, and ever *shall* esteem; the

Town is sensible I shou'd have married her, had she been so dispos'd; but whatever Accident has happen'd to occasion our eternal Separation, I shou'd be sorry to think any one shou'd imagine a Bar so weak as the *Baroness de Tortillée's* Artifices shou'd have Power to do it.

Notwithstanding his Belief to the contrary, there were too many present that were acquainted with the Story to have let it rest so, if the *Marquis de Sonville,* willing in this grand Assembly of the best part of her Acquaintance, to expose the *Baroness* as much as possible, had not turn'd the Conversation on the two silent Gentlemen, *St. Aumar* and *Le Sourbe.* It was a good while before one Word cou'd be got from them; but when they spoke, it was in a fashion which convinc'd the whole Company of what they before had Cause enough to suspect, that the Gratitude for Favours she had conferr'd, and the Astonishment at the Discovery of any others being Partakers in that Happiness each of them had the Vanity to believe he had engross'd, had, till now, depriv'd them of the Power of Utterance. If the *Marquis's* Desire of Revenge had been rais'd by something more injurious than the petty Misfortune of a Mistress's Falshood, he found enough to gratifie it: every body now took the Liberty of speaking what they knew; and there being scarce one Person in the Room that was not privy to one, or more, of her Intrigues, each now contributed their Part, and the whole Scene of all her monstrous Actions was laid open to them all: Never was Woman so expos'd and ridicul'd——so despis'd and hated.

Some took so great a Pleasure in affronting her, and the rest so little regarded her Resentment, that the being within her House, and probably within her Hearing, did not in the least hinder them from saying all that so ample a Field of Scandal to indulge in, cou'd give room to: till *Harriot* the *Baroness's* chief Woman coming in, told them her Lady was very much indispos'd, and not being able to return to the Company desir'd they would dismiss. We'll send *La Branche* to comfort her, said the *Marquis* tartly. Ay my Lord! pursu'd the *Count,* he has an Art of pleasing, to which, it seems, we are Strangers. However, let us not add to the Schedule[61] of our Faults, that of Ingratitude: Be sure you tell the Lady, continu'd he, turning to *Harriot,* That *De la Torre* and the other Gentlemen, she so handsomely gave a Description of, are infinitely obligated to her for the Pains she has taken to clear them of an Affair, of which none of them wou'd be proud. No, no, cry'd *Beauclair,* let *La Branche* possess alone the unenvy'd Happiness. *Tortillée* and *La Branche* (resum'd the *Marquis*) are only capable of pleasing each other, and indeed are only fit for one another; as this Fellow (continu'd he taking hold of *Du Lache,* who that Instant came into the Room, and giving him a scornful Turn) this

Pimp! this wretched Pander! is only fit for the vile Offices he is employ'd in——O forbear, my Lord! interrupted *De la Torre* (with an Air and Voice full of Derision) this ingenious Gentleman but wears the Livery of the munificent *Baroness,* and must obey the Hand which feeds him——if he has made use of any Stratagems to deceive you, or me, or any here, 'twas to serve a Mistress who liberally rewarded the Procurer of her Pleasures: for my part, I confess, tho' he has favour'd me sometimes with a Summons, not much unlike what just now your Lordship read, I never had Gratitude enough to make him any other Retribution than barren Thanks: nor, perhaps, have any of you, *Messieurs!* been more bountiful. I think the least we can do, to recompence the Obligations he has confer'd on us, is to recommend him to the Service of some *Italian Courtezan,* in whose Amours he would stand in admirable stead, and 'tis probable pick up for himself a more lasting Subsistance, than he can hope for from the precarious Dependance of his present Benefactress, whose *Charms* begin now to grow out of Date, and almost of as little Reputation as her *Virtue.*

As crafty as this Villain was in making almost any Appearances subservient to his Ends, when he had Time for Deliberation, these sudden and unexpected Salutations entirely bereft him of all Artifice; he was now as harmless, as undesigning as a Fool; he was, indeed, two or three times about to speak, tho' he knew not what to say; he found that the Secret of the *Baroness*'s Temper, and the Hand he had in her Conduct, were discover'd; but had neither Time to guess by what means, nor to contrive any Expedient which might evade the Obloquy such a Discovery must bring on; 'tis possible he might, at last, have muster'd Courage enough to ask what 'twas they meant, but the *Chevalier St. Aumar,* who by the Reasons already mentioned had all this while been prevented from making any outward show of his inward Disorders, having now got the better of his Surprize and Confusion of Thought, Rage took the whole Possession of his Soul, the Sight of *Du Lache* and the Reflection how much he had suffer'd himself to be deceiv'd by the Artifices of that Villain, put him beyond all Patience. He drew his Sword, and running furiously at him as he was about to speak, had certainly silenc'd him for ever, if *Beauclair* who happen'd to be next him had not been quick enough to lay hold of his Arm. Hinder not, *Monsieur,* said he! the Hand of Justice; that Wretch is unworthy of Life, and since our Laws are but too deficient in punishing Crimes such as his, those who like me he has wrong'd, have a Title to revenge themselves.

It was with all the Difficulty in the World that *Beauclair,* the *Marquis,* and all the Company persuaded him to sheath his Sword; and perhaps all they cou'd say, to represent how much so despicable a Creature, both by his Birth and Principles, was below the Resentment of a Man of Honour, had been ineffectual, if *Count de la Torre* had not catch'd hold of the cowardly Wretch, who all this time stood hanging down his Head and trembling, and bringing him to the *inrag'd Chevalier* whose Arm he found *Beauclair* had still possession of, See here, *Monsieur,* said he, when once *Reflection* gets the Mastery of Passion, how wou'd you blush to think you must be question'd in the *King's* Name why you depriv'd him of so worthless a *Subject!* 'Tis thus, and thus, pursu'd he, giving him two or three Kicks,[62] we shou'd chastize the Insolence of such Wretches. In speaking these last Words he turn'd him, who was glad of an Opportunity to make use of his Heels, out of the Room. No body staid long after; all had been said and done that cou'd convince the *Baroness* her Reign was at an End, and now the Company separated, every one to think or talk of this Adventure as their several Sentiments of it prompted them: to the Ladies it was matter enough of Diversion; nothing can be more pleasing to those Women who set up for being admir'd, of which sort were most of this Assembly, than to see the downfall of a reigning *Toast*: The prodigious Power the *Baroness* had, till now, maintain'd over so many Hearts, had long been the Envy of each pretending Fair; and to behold it sunk in a Moment—her Charms depriv'd of all their wonted Force—her Arts, her Blandishments no more Effectual——Contempt in the place of Esteem, and Detestation in the room of Love, gave a Joy too exquisite to be describ'd by any thing but it self: their Looks! the chearful Accent of their Voices! whenever any Occasion offer'd to speak of this Affair, cou'd only demonstrate the secret Satisfaction glowing in their enliven'd Souls.

Of all the Men interested in this Discovery, only *Le Sourbe* was inconsolable; the Weakness of his Intellects together with the Meanness of his Spirit, made him the most unfortunate Creature on Earth: he had fancied himself superlatively blest! distinguish'd from all the rest of Mankind! belov'd! admir'd! ador'd! caress'd by the most Lovely, most Ingenuous, most Faithful of her Sex; and now, at once, to find his Happiness imaginary! the Woman he had idoliz'd, he had worshipp'd as a *Goddess,* but meer *Mortal,* with all her Sex's Failings, truly eminent in nothing but Hypocrisie! the Favours he had receiv'd only the Overflowings of a *Luxurious* Appetite, or condescended to, to gratifie a *Mercenary* one! made him almost distracted. He seem'd either never to have known, or to have forgot his own Imperfections, which if he had duly weighed, he cou'd never have been deceiv'd into an Opinion that a Woman neither old nor unlovely cou'd have been blind to 'em, and consequently scap'd a Disappointment so grievous: Not a Person of his Acquaintance but he told the Story to, making most pitiful Lamentations, saying how dearly he had lov'd the *Baron-*

ess, how much he had studied to oblige her, what Presents he had made her, the Pleasure with which she had seem'd to accept of his Services, describ'd the a thousand times repeated Endearments which had pass'd between them, and then (bursting into a Flood of Tears) Yet she is false, wou'd he cry, she is false! *forsworn to all the Gods and me!*[63] The poor Wretch, to his other Fopperies, had also a passionate Affection for Rhiming, a Vanity almost as unbecoming to one of his *Age,* as *Love;* and now having two such Themes as Despair and the Perfidy of a Mistress, *Melpomene*[64] was every Day invok'd, the whole Town was persecuted with his Complaints in *Metre,* and 'tis hard to say, which suffer'd most in his publishing 'em, the *Baroness*'s Reputation of *Honour,* or his own of *Understanding.*

Not in this manner behav'd the *Marquis de Sonville,* the *Count de la Torre,* the *Chevalier St. Aumar,* and *Monsieur Beauclair;* the *three former* immediately enter'd into new Attachments, in the Pleasures of which the Memory of the old one was easily forgot: and the Condition of the *Latter* was such as wou'd neither permit him to complain, to rail, or to condemn: He was not perhaps in so great a Surprize at the late Discovery of the *Baroness*'s Humour as some others appeared to be, but the Treatment which he was witness *Du Lache* had receiv'd, and the Character he heard of him, was what involv'd him in the greatest Perplexity: he now began to imagine that there was more than a Probability that all he had been told of *Montamour* was false, and the Horror he conceiv'd at having suffer'd himself to be impos'd on to the Prejudice of that Lady's Reputation and his own Inclinations, was such as Language is too weak to represent. Once he believ'd nothing cou'd be a greater Misfortune than the Assurance she was unworthy his Affection; now he dreaded that he shou'd one Day be convinc'd she was but too meritorious. If she be innocent, said he to himself, what a Villain, what a Monster, must I have all this while appear'd?——Ignorant of the Arts by which I have been deluded, she must despise and hate me——What shall I do to acquire a Knowledge of the Truth?——how find out the fatal Certainty of her Virtue! a Certainty which must for ever damn me to Despair, since Devil like, I have renounc'd my Heaven; yet frightful as the Precipice appears, I must plunge in—must fathom the wild Abyss!—must drag up *Confirmation,* tho' she comes waited on by all the Terrors of *Remorse,* Self-condemnation, and the ever-during[65] Sting of Conscience—Hell, Hell it self affords no Torture like *Suspence,* cruel distracting Sense-destroying *Suspence!*——Give, give me, Fate! some Means to ease the present Anguish, and order all hereafter as thou pleasest.

In this manner whenever he was alone did he torment himself, and when in Company no more appear'd the Man he was! a sullen Cloud hung ever on his Brow! his once enlivening Conversation was now exchang'd for Peevishness! his Gallantry for cold Neglect! his gay Address for silent Churlishness! perpetual Ill-nature and an incessant Gloom diffus'd it self thro' all his Air, and darkned every Grace! Whenever he heard the Name of *Tortillée* (as the prodigious Eclat[66] the Adventure of the Letter to *La Branche* had made in Town gave him frequent Occasions) it fill'd him with mortal Disquiets; if that of *Montamour,* he was unable to contain himself. In this Confusion of Thought he sought *Du Lache,* resolving to force from him a Clue[67] to guide him thro' a Labyrinth which at present seem'd so intricate; but that Villain was no where to be found, and to hope for any from the *Baroness* was ridiculous; besides the Sight of her was now grown insupportable, and 'tis possible he wou'd rather have remain'd for ever as he was, than have been oblig'd to her for an Eclaircissment, had there been any Probability she wou'd have been prevail'd on to make one. In these Perturbations let us leave him for a while, and see what became of those who had occasion'd them.

Du Lache, after receiving that contemptuous Usage from the *Marquis,* quitted not the *Baroness's* House; but being retir'd into an inner Room, a little to recollect himself and consider what it shou'd be that occasion'd it, was seen by *Harriot,* and immediately directed to her Lady, whom he found in a Disorder scarce possible to conceive; yet wild, and incoherent as her tempestuous Passion was, he soon discover'd what had happen'd, and join'd with her in exclaiming on the Vanity and Neglect of *La Branche,* who had so little regard of a Lady's Reputation as to suffer her Letters to be expos'd. He had also another Account to give of this unworthy Lover, which, if any thing cou'd have heighten'd the Fury she was already in, the Knowledge of wou'd have done. Not all those Artifices which had triumph'd over the Judgment of so many Men of Sense, had been able to work the desir'd Effect on *La Branche.* Stupid as he was in every thing else, in this he had the Advantage of those of the best Understanding, and in spite of all that *Du Lache* and his politic Instructress cou'd do, the young woman, whose Engagements with him had perhaps been the greatest Motive which intitled him to be lov'd by the *Baroness,* was now going to take him from her for ever; they were to be married in a few days, and this vile Woman had the just Mortification to be told, that to make Reparation for his former Transgression, he had bound himself in an Obligation never to see her more.

To represent in what manner she receiv'd this News, one had need be acquainted with the Inhabitants of *Bethlem;*[68]her Words, her Looks, her Air, were all Distraction—she saw she was utterly undone with the *Marquis de Sonville,* the *Count de la Torre,* the *Chevalier St. Aumar, Beauclair,* and *Le*

Sourbe; and to be abandon'd by the Man for whose sake she had lost the Esteem and good Opinion of them all, was such a killing Stroke, as nothing cou'd enable her to support. Wanting the means of Vengeance on those who had occasion'd it, her unavailing Rage, recoil'd upon it self; she tore her Hair and Face, and bit her very Flesh in the Extremity of her Passion: it was not now in the Power of her Emissary *Du Lache* to say or do any thing that cou'd give her Consolation; the Case was now too desperate to admit Relief from any of those Stratagems he had formerly so well succeeded in; his Artifices were discover'd, and therefore no more effectual! He was now a known Deceiver! a Villain proclaim'd, as his Patroness was a Jilt! and all that either of 'em cou'd do, was to vent some Part of their enervate[69] Malice in Curses: After having rail'd themselves almost out of Breath against *La Branche,* the *Marquis,* and all who had seem'd to approve of his Proceeding, they began, as 'tis the Custom of all base People when their Designs miscarry, to reflect one on another; You might have prevented all this, Madam, said he, but your ungovern'd Passion for *La Branche* wou'd suffer you to listen to no Reasons.——Villain! cry'd she, to what end have I heap'd unnumbred Obligations on thee, but to engage thy subtil working Brain to procure my Pleasures, and protect my Fame! but stupid, or ungrateful! thou now hast ruin'd both—my Reputation's lost, my Love undone! the Earth contains not so forlorn a Wretch——yet thou canst calmly tell me, *this might have been prevented*——Yes, it might, had thy Management been equal to thy boasting. Madam! what cou'd I do? resum'd he, I never approv'd of your entring into an Engagement with *La Branche,* I knew he was unfit, and therefore advis'd you.—Thou Fool! interrupted the impatient *Baroness,* what Lover ever took Advice? His Humour or his Principles being unsuited to my Purpose made not his Form less pleasing to my Eyes——'twas thy Business to have wound thy self into his Soul, chang'd every Movement there! created all a-new, and fashion'd it to my Design. Thus did each endeavour to lay the Blame of this Misfortune on the other, and the Dispute growing higher, at last it came to a down right Quarrel, and they parted almost as ill satisfied with one another as both were with the World.

Some Days past before they met again: the *Baroness* shut herself into her Chamber, and wou'd see no Company; and *Du Lache* was beginning to think what Course of Life he must now take up, believing there was no more Profit to be expected from that he had lately profess'd. But he was too skilful an Engineer[70] to be discarded so; when he had given over all hope of ever being employed by her again, a Messenger came from the *Baroness* to let him know she desir'd to speak with him immediately: The Summons was too welcome not to be readily obey'd: he went, but found not the Business what he imagin'd, to endeavour to reinstate her in the Affections of any of her *former* Lovers, or to contrive some plausible Pretence for the introducing her to a *new* one, but to assist her once more to get rid of a Husband, who was coming to call her to a dreadful Account for her Behaviour. She had just received News, that the *Baron's* Distemper having reach'd the Ear of a skilful Physician, who happen'd to be at that Time in the Country where she had dispos'd him, he attempted to cure it, which he had accomplish'd to the Wonder of every body who had been Witness of his Frenzy; That this much-wrong'd Gentleman was preparing for *Paris;* and that the Person who had restor'd him to Reason, had also made him know it was but by some supernatural[71] Means that he so long had languished in the Want of it. This was a terrible Shock, a Blow indeed, which all the Artifice of this guilty Pair was at a Loss for Means to parry: They spent some time in bewailing their common Misfortune; she upbraided *Du Lache* for his ill-tim'd Mercy, as she call'd it. I wou'd have put an end to my Fears, said she, by taking away the Life of this Troubler of my Repose; had your Advice not interpos'd, I had not now been so curs'd in the Apprehension that I must be obliged to answer for my past Conduct, and regulate the future——But for you, continu'd she, I might have been blest as my utmost Wish cou'd make me, Mistress of my self! entire Possessor of the whole Fortune of this foolish *Baron!* and independant of the World's Opinion! Now I must flatter, sooth, cajole, and all, perhaps, in vain, for a precarious Subsistance——wretched, wretched Fool (cry'd she out, stamping and biting her Nails) to be thus persuaded contrary to my Interest, to my Inclinations, to my Eternal Peace.——Hold, Madam, hold (interrupted he) have Patience, 'tis not yet too late to prevent the Ills you dread; the Instruments of Death are still at Hand, and when, like Fate, you give the Word, shall rush to Execution.

The horrid Deed being thus resolv'd on, all they had to do was to contrive the Means to bring it about. After several Inventions form'd and rejected because they were either Unsafe or Unsure, it was at last pitch'd on, that she shou'd write a most tender and passionate Letter, congratulating his Return of Health, and pressing his coming Home; that it shou'd be convey'd to him by *Le Songe* and *Toncarr,* who were to pass as Servants she had lately taken into her Family, and recommended to attend him to *Paris.* This way, said he, will certainly be the most effectual, for it will prevent him from hiring any Servants, who perhaps might be resolute enough to defend their Master, if our Friends should attack him on the Road; but being receiv'd by him in this manner, he will be entirely in their Power, and they may have an easie Opportunity of dispatching him in the Journey, whenever they find a Place convenient. The *Baroness* approv'd of it extreamly, and thinking every Moment an Age till her wicked Designs were brought about, immediately set down to write, while *Du Lache* went to prepare his assisting Villains for the Enterprize they were to undertake.

Enough has been said of the Character of these two Wretches, to make the Reader know they were capable of any Mischief which had a Prospect of Advantage: they readily agreed, and being equipt in Habits proper for their Design, took Horse the same Night, promising they would bring back a satisfactory Account of what they had done. An Accident happen'd immediately after, which convinc'd the *Baroness* how necessary what she had contriv'd was to the Conservation of her Fortune. *Du Lache* was under an Arrest on the Account of some Riot he had lately been guilty of, to redeem him from which there must be a good sum of Money deposited; she sent to the Banker in whose Hands lay the best part of the *Baron*'s ready Cash, but he refus'd to pay her any, saying he had a Letter of Advice to the contrary, and that he wou'd disburse no more, till he either saw her Lord, or had Orders from him to do it. This was enough to let her know the Power she once had over him was at an End, and that if he liv'd to return, she must expect another sort of Treatment than she had been accustom'd, or cou'd endure to receive. Money however must be rais'd, her Instrument must not remain in Confinement; but having now no Credit even with a Lover, she procur'd some on her Jewels, and releas'd him without giving herself much Trouble about the Matter, believing she shou'd soon be in a Condition to redeem them, having a Will by her which the *Baron* in the Time of his too abundant Fondness had made, wherein she was left sole Executrix and full Mistress of every thing he had in the World. This she design'd to produce as soon as the wish'd-for News of his Death shou'd arrive, to the Disappointment of all his Relations, who were utterly ignorant of his having been guilty of so much Injustice. Some Debts also, which the Extravagance of this Fellow had contracted, now threatning to come upon him, and the Impossibility there was at present for the *Baroness* to discharge them, oblig'd him, as soon as he was releas'd from his Confinement, to take shelter in her House, till the happy Hour was come in which they were to have all things in their Power.

It was in this Time of his absconding that *Monsieur Beauclair* was in Search of him every where, but in the Place in which he really was; but tho' it was highly probable he might have been heard of at the *Baroness*'s, yet so great was his Aversion to that House, that he cou'd not think of going to it on any Account whatsoever; and to send any other Person to make an Enquiry, he knew wou'd be in vain, since he was told the Reasons of his concealing himself: But notwithstanding the Impossibility he found there was of coming to any Knowledge of the Truth thro' his means, he was inform'd of enough to make him but too sensible for his Repose, that he had been betray'd into a wrong Belief: He sometimes visited *Madamoiselle Sansfoy;* and that Lady, who had not the Gift of concealing any thing she knew, soon made him acquainted that it was only from *Du Lache* she had been told any thing to the Disadvantage of *Montamour*'s Reputation, and that as to the Story of *Galliard,* she was now fully convinc'd it was entirely false. The Pangs which at this Discourse seiz'd the Soul of the too late repenting *Beauclair* were such as were very near driving him to Distraction: The Reflection how by the *worst* of Women, and her cursed Agents, he had been led to injure the *Best;* one who lov'd him, one for whose sake, while he believed her true, he wou'd have forgone all that this World calls dear, was so dreadful a Shock to his Honour! good Nature! every generous Principle of Humanity! that all the Strength of Reason and Discretion he was Master of, cou'd hardly enable him to sustain: Cou'd his whole Fortune, nay his very Life, have called back Time, and cancell'd the Actions of a few past Months, how gladly wou'd he have resign'd it! but such a Wish was both ridiculous and vain; nor cou'd he hope the sincere Remorse and Grief he felt for what he had done, cou'd expiate his Guilt; the Person he had injur'd was insensible of his Repentance; she was ignorant how much he suffer'd in a self-Conviction; or if by any Means he could acquaint her with it, he cou'd not assure himself she wou'd think it a sufficient Inducement to engage her to forgive: Yet all the Consolation his Sorrows wou'd admit, was to make Tryal of her Goodness. Perhaps, thought he, if I cou'd once more have the Happiness to throw my self beneath her Feet, to confess my Fault, to implore her Pity, she may yet have some Remains of Tenderness, which my Complaints may waken! Ungrateful as I seem, she still may love me, and nothing is unpardonable to *Love!*

With these and the like Suggestions, which the natural Chearfulness of his Temper, and the Experience he had of the Sweetness of her Disposition inspir'd him with, did he repel Despair, whenever he found it attempted to assail him. But a true Passion cannot for any long Time content it self with an *Ideal* Bliss: it was not sufficient that he imagin'd a Possibility of being forgiven, of being blest as he had been in the Affections of his, now more than ever, adorable and belov'd *Montamour,* without an Assurance that he was so. And tho' Hope is the best Cordial to preserve Desire, those who sit down with that, and delay the Prosecution of a farther Satisfaction, are like those who build Castles in the Air, pleasing themselves with an imaginary Happiness, which, whenever they gather Courage enough to endeavour to lay hold on, flies from the Embrace, and cheats the vain Attempter. *Beauclair* was for no such Unsubstantial Blessings, the Comfort he found in entertaining an Opinion that he might one Day be happy, hinder'd him not from an Impatience to be so.

Love, ever fertile in Invention, and aiding to the Wishes of a zealous Votary, soon furnish'd him with a Stratagem, which promis'd him Success, at least so far as to give him once more an Opportunity of seeing and speaking to *Montamour.* He was acquainted with a Fryar of the Order of St. *Dominic,*[72] one who was not the most strict of his Profession, one who had himself experienc'd the Force of Love, and knew how to commiserate the Woes it very often was the Cause of. To him did the restless *Beauclair* apply for Relief; he made no Secret of the whole History of his Passion, and the Delusions he had been ensnar'd by, and entreated his Assistance in the Design he had form'd. He so far prevail'd on him, as to engage him to procure a Fryar's Habit for him, and got his Instructions in what manner to behave, that he might pass for such to the *Abbess* of the Monastery where *Montamour* had enter'd herself. Every thing being ready, he soon set out for the Land of Love, not greatly despairing but that at his Arrival he shou'd find himself not an unwelcome Guest.

He follow'd so exactly the Directions had been given him by the good-natur'd Fryar, that whoever had seen him in that Garb wou'd have suspected him for no other than what he seem'd.

Being come to the Monastery, the Sanctity of his Appearance gave him an easie Admittance, and telling the Abbess that he had taken that Journey at the Entreaty of the Brother of *Montamour,* who had inform'd him that he was under an Apprehension that there was more of *Pique* than true *Devotion* in her abandoning the World, and desir'd him to discourse her on that Affair: When he told me this, said the Counterfeit Venerable,[73] I thought the Duty of my Function obliged me to search into the Truth, and use the best of my Endeavours to prepare her, if she is not so already, for the Happiness which a Religious Life affords! With this and some other Expressions of the same nature, the Reverend Matron was wholly won to his Purpose: she left him alone, while she went to acquaint *Montamour* of his being there, and the reasons which had brought him; but when she return'd leading her in, and had presented her to him, how impossible would it be to set forth the Confusion he was in: the sudden Rush of painful Ecstasie! the darting, throbbing, tingling Mixture of Delight and Terror, which every Vein confess'd! and shook the alarm'd Heart with almost mortal Tremblings: not all the natural Boldness of his Sex, not all that Presence of Mind which us'd to be his inseparable Companion, not all the Resolutions he had form'd, not all the Care he had taken to arm himself for this Encounter, were sufficient to defend him when once the lovely injur'd *Montamour* appear'd! He thought she look'd more fair, more beautiful than ever! and tho' her Eyes had lost nothing of their wonted Sweetness, yet a long Habitude of Melancholy had abated a little of the Gaiety of their Rays, and the Austerity of the Life she was about to embrace had given her a greater Composedness in her Countenance; conscious of Guilt, and too too sensible of his own Unworthiness to find Mercy, she seem'd to him such as Imagination figures a destroying Angel, adorn'd in shining Ruin! all gloriously Cruel! and severely Just!

It was not in the least owing to his own Conduct that his Disorders were not visible to the *Abbess,* but that good Lady believing that on the Account he came it was improper to have a third Person Witness of what he had to deliver, took her Leave, only telling him, that when their Conference was ended, she shou'd entreat his Company to take part of what their Cloyster afforded: but he neither heard nor had Power to make any Answer to this Compliment; every Sense was absent, and Thought dissolv'd in the vast Hurry of his various Emotions; but when *Montamour,* who little suspected the reason of the *Fryar's* Silence and distant Behaviour, desir'd him to sit, and was beginning to enquire after her Brother, the Sound of her dear, well-remembred Voice, the graceful, charming manner in which she express'd herself, and that engaging undiscribable, inimitable Something which is not to be acquir'd, and which is only to be found in the Air and Mein of those whom *Nature* and not *Art* embellishes, putting him more strongly in Remembrance of the felicitous Moments her Conversation formerly had bless'd him with, and revolving in an Instant ten thousand little nameless Softnesses,——the thrilling, melting, rapturous Amusements,——the Consequences of mutual Passion,——and comparing the *present* with the *past,* what he endur'd was not to be conceal'd!——a sudden burst of wild impetuous Passion broke thro' all Disguise! blaz'd in his Eyes! and shew'd the burning Lover plain! Forgetful of what his cooler Thoughts had form'd, he threw himself on her Bosom, grasping her with a Violence scarce supportable, and fixing close to hers his glowing Lips, had Power no other way to express the Ecstasie he now again began to re-enjoy——a thousand fond endearing things crowded at once into his Soul, and press'd for Utterance——he wou'd have spoke 'em all, but the tumultuous Meanings were too great, too many, and overthrew each other in the Throng, and all he cou'd bring forth was *Montamour!*—Angelick *Montamour!*—Divine, Adorable *Montamour!*

This was indeed sufficient to make her sensible who it was she entertain'd, and nothing can be more amazing than that in the Surprize of such an Interview, she acted not the least Extravagance.——Neither the Shock which the Remembrance of his late ill Usage gave her Pride, vented itself in Fury and Revilings; nor the secret Pleasure, which in spite of her Resentment, her continued Tenderness felt at his Repentance and Return, was discoverable by either Word or Look; but doubtful that she might not retain this Command of her Temper, if she trusted herself to listen to the Charms of his Persuasion, wou'd not put it to the Venture; but getting loose from his Embrace, and giving a sudden Spring to a little Bell which hung in the Room, rung it with such a Force, that the *Abbess* and several of the *Nuns* came running in before this disappointed Lover cou'd say or do any thing to prevent her. What this holy Man (said she turning to the *Abbess*) has to offer, may, perhaps, be very good! but as my Resolution to become a *Devotée* is fix'd, I think it needless to hear any thing which is designed as an Endeavour to alter it; if my Brother is possess'd of any Scruples, or wou'd infuse any into you, of my Unworthiness of the Profession, he may communicate them by Letters either to you or me, for I am fully determin'd to enter into no Conversation with any Stranger, till my having taken the Orders has put a Stop to all the Arguments which may possibly be prepar'd to hinder me. In speaking these last Words, which she pronounc'd with the most resolute Air, she flew out of the Room, leaving him to make his Excuse as he cou'd to the *Abbess,* and those of the Sisterhood who had accompanied her. The Consternation they were in at her Behaviour was very favourable to *Beauclair;* for while they were looking on one another, wondering what it should be that had occasion'd it, he gain'd a little Time for the Recovery of his scatter'd Spirits, but not enough to enable him to speak of this Adventure as a Person so unconcern'd as that which he represented wou'd have done. The Confusion, however, and Hesitation of the few Words he spoke, were look'd on only as occasion'd by his Chagrin for the indifferent Reception he had met with; and he left them as full of Trouble for the Disrespect they imagin'd had been paid to a Man of his Reverence, as they wou'd have been of Anger had they suspected the Imposture.

But when he was return'd to the Inn where he had taken up Lodgings for this Affair, how infinitely short of what he felt wou'd all Description be! For some Hours he was utterly incapable of Reflection, and its Return serv'd but to torture him with redoubled Agonies! All the Horrors, all the Woes that can be imagined to attend disappointed Passion work'd up to the most elevated Degree that Human Nature can sustain, rag'd in his Soul, and tore him with Variety of Anguish. It was the least of his Vexations that he owed them only to himself; if *Montamour* was incens'd it was his own ill Conduct was the Cause; and if she never shou'd be brought to a Reconciliation, what but his own Unworthiness cou'd he accuse! In fine, he was quite Soul-sick and mad at the thoughts of what he had done, and the forgetfulness he had suffered himself to fall into, in losing an opportunity so hard to be found, of endeavouring once to move her in his favour. But as impossible as at present it seem'd of getting any means of seeing or speaking to her again, he cou'd not think of returning to *Paris* thus unsatisfied: Her Year of Probation was now almost expired—the fatal Time drew near in which she was to take an Eternal farewel of the World, and then not all his Tears, his Vows, Entreaties, or Repentance, not even her own Desires had power to make him happy——Some Contrivance therefore must be form'd, and speedily, and he resolv'd, let the Course be never so desperate, to hazard all for one more Interview.

Invention charg'd with the Commands of Passion brought forth a numerous Issue of unjoynted Projects—but abortive all, disown'd by Reason and unnerv'd for Action——to think of entring the Monastery as a *Fryar,* tho' by never so different a Pretence from that he lately went on, was ridiculous and vain; he had been detected in that Habit by the Person from whom, till she was a little softned, he found it was most his Interest to be conceal'd; and she being under the same Roof would afford him slender Consolation, if denied the Privilege of entertaining her——Sometimes he was thinking to disguise himself as a Criple, pretend he had fallen from his Horse, and being unable to travel, implore the Charity and Assistance of the Sisterhood; but the remembrance that there was a College of Jesuits within a Bowshot from the Monastery, to which they would probably send him, as a Place more proper and convenient, put an End to that design——Another Stratagem was to dress himself as a Woman, whom some unexpected ill Turn of Fortune had driven from her Parents, and beg an Asylum there; but this his Stature forbid——It was a considerable Time before any thing which seem'd feasible offer'd it self to his Fancy; but what is it that a Lover cannot at last get the better of, when Resolution is on his side! As he was walking one Day by the Walls which encompass'd the *Nunnery* Gardens, he perceiv'd a piece of it had lately fallen and was now repairing by the Workmen, he presently bethought him of becoming a Labourer, and by that means having free egress and regress to carry Mortar, Stone and other things for the Work, he might easily hide himself among the Bushes, and watch an opportunity of *Montamour*'s coming out to walk.

This Enterprize was no sooner conceived than put in Execution, his Fryar's Vest was now exchanged for a ragged Coat, his Cowl for a Linsy

Woolsey[74] Cap, and his Beads for a Hod;[75] by offering himself for a low Hire he was immediately entertain'd by the Master; his business being only to fetch and carry, he was not at all found fault with, but perform'd what he had undertaken with more diligence than those who had all their life been accustomed to it; so much more is it for the truly well-bred to descend to the meanest Offices, than for those born to Beggery to bear Prosperity and an affluence of Fortune superior to their hopes. Nor did his Toil in the Day make him forgetful of what he had design'd in the Night, but as soon as he saw they were about to leave work he took his opportunity to slide down from the Wall and conceal him in the most remote part of the Garden. The *first* Night of his watching he had no other Reward than a distant sight of *Montamour* as she was at Prayers among the rest of the *Nuns,* for the Chappel had a Window into the Garden, and was low enough for him to look in as he stood a Tip-toe. The *Second* indeed paid his Pains much better; she walked above an Hour close by the place where he was hid, and tho' he cou'd not speak to her, because there were two of the *Nuns* with her, yet he had the satisfaction to observe she was extremely pensive, and that all her Companions cou'd do was ineffectual to remove a Melancholly which he had leave to hope was influenced by her secret Thoughts of him.

But the *Third* gave him an Opportunity full as his Soul cou'd wish. It chanc'd to be an extream fine Evening, and the fragrancy of the Air had drawn a great Number of the young *Devotees* out to refresh themselves; *Montamour* was among them, and he still found she was as thoughtful as before. They past some Hours there, some walking——some sitting on the grassy Banks,——some sporting with the various colour'd Flowers which grew on the Borders, and seem'd to court the Gatherer's Hand,—some cooling their Fingers in the Fountain, and wantonly throwing the Water on their Companions——every one diverting herself as her innocent and undisturbed Fancy led her—but *Montamour,* whose Mind was more perplexed, and who in the late Adventure with the lovely *Fryar* had found that Self-denial was the hardest of all Virtues, affected to walk alone; she either not observed or had no relish of the little Recreations they enjoy'd, but singling her self from the rest, he saw her strike down an Alley which led to a fine *Grotto* at the lower end of the Garden: The Place he had that very Night fortunately made Choice of for his Concealment was a long narrow Walk of *Camomile,*[76] the end of which came almost to the *Grotto,* and was shelter'd all the way with a thick Row of Palms,[77] on this he cou'd walk without being in the least heard or seen by any body in the Garden; and as soon as he saw which way she went he immediately follow'd. He was at the end of the Walk almost as soon as she was in the *Grotto,* but he durst not enter, while there was Company so near, fearing the strength of her Resolution and the Prejudice she had conceiv'd against him, and which he but too justly had deserv'd, shou'd influence her to treat the *Labourer* in the same manner as she had done the *Fryar.*

These Suggestions were indeed most consonant to Reason, but they were presently oppos'd by others of a very different Nature; he began to think that if she left the Garden before the others he might never have so good an opportunity as now, that there was scarce a probability he shou'd ever find her entirely alone, and that it was better to hazard her Good-nature if she wou'd suffer him to speak to her now, than run the risque of not speaking to her at all; while he was thus debating, and irresolute what to do, he heard the Charmer who had occasioned this Conflict in his Soul, tune her Guittare;[78] in Expectation of that Melody, he for a while suspended his Cogitation, and heard her sing in a soft, low, but sweet and harmonious Accent these Words, which 'tis probable were of her own Composing.[79]

I.

No more, fond Maid! direct thy fruitless Aims
To Bliss thou canst but in Idea *know;*
A Love so Pure as thine Heaven only claims,
Nor will be rival'd by the Toys below!

II.

Fly! Fly! Oh Fly! the Sense-alluring Bait
Of gay Deceit, in tender Raptures drest!
Remorse and Shame do on Believing wait,
And late Repentance rends th' unwary Breast.

III.

From Damon's[80] *Air! his Shape! his flowing Wit!*
His thousand, thousand Worlds of countless Charms!
Fate *weak Defence from* Virtue *does permit,*
Unfurnish'd by Devotion's[81] *stronger Arms.*

IV.

Nor can Resentment, or thy Sex's Pride
For Injuries receiv'd, set free thy Mind:
Before Love's Fire those meaner Flames subside,
And shrink away like Vapours in the Wind!

V.

In Piety, alone, a Refuge dwells
To shield thy Soul from Passion's pleasing Pain:
The base Efforts of faithless Man repels,
And renders all their soft Enchantments vain.

With trembling Limbs and aking Heart the repenting *Beauclair* heard her sing these Lines, which gave him so much Cause to fear all his Endeavours to bring her to a Reconciliation wou'd be in vain. What hope to conquer, when with Heaven we contend! Yet tho' despairing, he wou'd not thus give over, and was moving softly towards the *Grotto,* resolving, let the Consequence be what it wou'd, to know his Doom at once, and end the Tortures of Suspence: But as he was just at the Entrance, the late ceas'd Harmony of her melodious Voice began a-new to charm his listening Ears, and oblig'd him to delay the Prosecution of his Design, that he might not lose the Pleasure of hearing her sing, which she immediately did these Stanza's.[82]

I.

The Heart that once has Power to change,
And with a second Passion burn,
Tho' to the First it shou'd return,
Will ever be inclin'd to Range.

II.

Then Charming, Faithless, Swain give o'er!
Nor think by Prayers, or Sighs, to move!
A Rebel, once, to me, and Love,
I may Forgive, but Trust no more.

III.

No more will I deluded be;
Tho' with secret Wishes lying
All dissolving, melting, dying;
To Death I'll yield, but not to Thee!

Tho' the Musick to which these Words were set gave them an Air infinitely more gay than the former, yet she cou'd not conclude them without a mixture of Sighs, which occasioning a Hesitation in her Speech made a perceivable Variation in the Tune, and seem'd to mitigate their rigid Meaning:

The Sense, indeed, was cruel, but the manner of Pronunciation was such as renewed in the attentive List'ner some of those Hopes with which he had formerly been enliven'd. The Gardens were by this time wholly free from Company, no Interruption near, every thing favour'd his Design, and now he thought he boldly might advance; but still the Terrors occasion'd by a Consciousness of his Unworthiness, and ever the Companions of Guilt, made him enter the *Grotto* but with Tremblings, and kept him for some Moments at an awful Distance: She was fallen into so deep a *Resverie*[83] that she discern'd not that any Person was near, tho' the Moon, which was then at the Height, glitter'd thro' the Trees, and shone directly on him. Gladly wou'd he have indulg'd Contemplation, and fed Reflection with gazing on her Beauties, while thus unseen, and uncontrolled by the Severity of her Glances: but the remembrance how he had been disappointed by his late giving a Loose to the Ardors of his Passion, made him resolve to proceed with Art and Circumspection: He moved with gently-treading Steps to the Bank on which she sat, and was close by her, before she in the least perceiv'd him; but when, lifting up her Eyes, she saw a Man, and felt his Touch, (for he had seiz'd fast hold of her to prevent her stirring) she sent forth a great Shriek, loud enough to have alarm'd the *Convent,* had they had any Notion that any belonging to it was abroad. But to hinder her from repeating it, and unwilling to suffer her to continue longer in the Fright she was in, he threw himself on his Knees, and bathing the Hand he grasp'd with a Stream of Tears, Hold Madam! hold! said he, this is not the Posture of a Ruffian——I come not to alarm your Breast with Fears, but to move Pity there——'tis Pity only the adoring *Beauclair* asks, and that is what indeed his Miseries may claim. *Beauclair!* said she, surpriz'd beyond Expression, but perhaps not altogether so much displeas'd as afterwards she feign'd to be. Yes Madam! resum'd he, the Despairing, Dying, but still Adoring, *Beauclair* entreats you but to hear what vast Appearances of Reason urg'd him to seem so careless of his Happiness, and rashly trespass against Heaven and you——and, if you *hear,* you will I hope *forgive.*——By what has already been said of the Passion of *Montamour,* the Reader may be better able to judge the Conflict she endured, than I am to describe it; but resolving to keep up her Resentment, and give no room for him to imagine there was a Possibility of renewing in her again those soft Emotions he once had the Power of inspiring her with; I am sorry *Monsieur,* answered she, (with an Accent which had nothing in it of Tender) that you shou'd have given your self a Trouble wholly unnecessary: Where there's no Wrong there needs no Justification——I have profited too much by your Change of Humour, to be offended at it——Those Vows which your Inconstancy releas'd me from, will soon be paid to a

Sublimer Object: what you despis'd, Heaven will I hope accept, and by your Ingratitude I arrive at the only perfect Happiness here. How ought I then to bless the early Knowledge of your wavering Nature——to Thank you for your quick discover'd Baseness, that I in time might fly, and scorn your Faithless Sex.

It was not so much the Words, as the Manner in which they were spoke, which seiz'd the Soul of him they were address'd to with Horrors he had never known before. Not the past Torturing Pangs of her imagin'd Falshood, nor the ensuing Terrors of Remorse for his own Guilt, were half so dreadful as the *present* Racks. Amidst the doubtful Gloom some intermingling Beams of Hope had still dawn'd o'er his Wishes, chearing Expectance with promises of a future Day! But all was Darkness now,—all black Despair! The fix'd Coldness, the unmov'd Constancy which every Word and Look, and the whole Air of *Montamour* denoted, now made him but too sure she was inevitably lost—Nor did the remembrance of the Fault he had been guilty of, permit him even the poor Comfort of complaining of her Severity. A while he gaz'd upon her with such Inward, Tumultuous, Emotions as depriv'd him of the Power of Speech, till perceiving she was about to go out of the *Grotto,* and leave him in the same manner she had done before, he threw himself on his Knees, by Force retaining her, till he had recover'd himself enough to endeavour to persuade. All that the tenderest Love, the fiercest Wishes, the most bleeding, burning, Passion, made desperate, and raging, can inflict, was to the Life demonstrated in all his Words and Actions; his trembling Limbs, his wild distracted Looks, his faultering Speech, his unconnnected Expressions, display'd the Deity[84] in his full genuine Force. Unshadow'd, Undisguis'd, with any of those Pageant Arts of Pompous Eloquence, which oft adorn a Counterfeited Flame; but are forgot and lost amidst the Ardors of a true Affection. Oh wou'd the unwary Fair, when thus address'd, but give her Reason scope to Judge, how easily might she discern the real *Lover,* from the flattering *Courtier;* admire the *Wit,* but scorn the *Affected Passion* of him who comes but to seduce, and ruin her. But indeed, there are so few of either Sex sincerely touch'd with a noble and generous Desire, that 'tis no wonder they mistake it in another: Deceit meets with Deceit, and both are unconcern'd alike.

But *Montamour* was vastly different, as was her *Beauclair,* from those fashionable Enamorato's: with Truth, with Tenderness, with Zeal, she lov'd; and tho' she had all the Reason in the World for keeping up her Resentment, and had Strength enough of Resolution to restrain the Fondness of her Passion from showing it self to one who had so greatly injur'd her, and whose Repentance she thought too small a Recompence; yet did her Soul pity the

Agonies she, by her own, was too—too sensible were Unfeigned, and must her self of Consequence suffer far greater. Passions of all kinds find Ease in the discovery, but smother'd Anguish preys on the very Vitals, the stifled Sighs recoil on the tormented Heart, and crack the Strings of Life. Yet persisting in her Coldness, and resolving rather to dye than recede from that Indifference she had vow'd to wear for ever in her Behaviour to him, all that his Tears, Entreaties, agonizing Groans cou'd move her to, was to sit down and listen to all he had to say in Vindication of his late Proceedings; which was to relate, in as brief a manner as he cou'd, the Delusions of *Du Lache,* and the Artifices by which he had been brought to a Belief of her Inconstancy: he kept back nothing of the Truth, but that which Honour forbad him to reveal, the Favours he had received from the *Baroness.*

But *Montamour,* who was no Stranger to that part of the Story, having patiently heard the rest, and perceiving he had done, wou'd not omit this Opportunity of letting him know, not the most secret Transactions of his Guilt had been hid from her. You do well *Mounsieur,* said she, to make a Repetition of every thing which may seem to excuse the ill Treatment you have given me, artfully concealing, while you relate the Accusations laid on me, the Charms of my Rival, without which all the Suggestions of a Villain like *Du Lache* had been ineffectual. Oh too severely judg'd! interrupted the Soul-tortur'd *Beauclair;* be witness for me Heaven, and send down instant Punishments on my Devoted Head, if I swerve in the least Tittle from the Truth——if e'er my Soul conceived one tender Thought, once form'd a Wish, or knew one soft Desire, which centred not in *Montamour*——if still she was not, even at the time when most I fear'd she scorn'd me, the only dearest Object of my Thoughts by Day, and Dreams by Night,——if even her Anger, killing as it is, wears not more Charms to me, than all the Endearing Smiles of her whole Sex besides——if in this Dreadful Moment, this Cruel Now, when all my Tears, my Prayers, my Sorrow and Repentance, my inward Agonies, the speechless Torments of my poor rending, bleeding, breaking Heart cannot obtain one pitying Glance, one kind commiserating Word, she be not dearer to me than Life, and all the gay Delights this World can give——and if it be not greater Pleasure here to expire before her, than live whole Ages in a Queen's Embraces, may all the Curses due to Perfidy fall heavy on me.

He would have proceeded, but she prevented him. Hold! said she, forbear these Imprecations. I believe, you once did Love me, nay, I am of Opinion you have resum'd that Tenderness you had for a Time thrown off; but (continued she with a Smile which had in it more of Disdain than Satisfaction) while you imagin'd me false, it was but reasonable you should seek some

Consolation, and where so probable to find it as in the Arms of a Woman so every way qualified, and so desirous to please, as the *Baroness De Tortille?* The disorder'd Lover hung down his Head, utterly unable to make any Reply to these cutting Words: He was too open and sincere in his Nature to be guilty of denying that it was really his Desire of forgetting *Montamour,* which had induc'd him to visit the *Baroness,* and to confess it he thought wou'd be an Aggravation of his Crime. At last, Oh Madam! resum'd he, the Opinion I was ensnar'd into of your Unkindness drove me Mad, I knew not what I did——but of this one thing I am sure, and of that alone, that I have never ceas'd to Love you—and whatever Appearances may be against me, my Heart cou'd never be but yours. Notwithstanding all that prodigious Presence of Mind which *Montamour* was Mistress of, and the Resentment with which she had arm'd her self as soon as she saw *Beauclair* was near her, she began to find it now impossible much longer to preserve it in his Presence; and looking on the secret Pleasure which, in spite of her Indignation, she felt in entertaining him, as a Sin to Prudence, and the Resolution she had made of forgetting him, muster'd up all the remains of Anger in her Heart, to inspire her with all means of Banishing him for ever; and taking the Advantage of his last Words, One wou'd, indeed, (said she, with a Voice full of Austerity) believe that you knew not what you did, or sure he who has so publickly avowed himself the Lover of the *Baroness De Tortille,* wou'd never after that imagine his Pretensions were capable of creating in *Montamour* any other Passion than Disdain and Hatred——I shou'd have an Aversion to my self (added she, after a little Pause) if I cou'd think any Action of mine has ever given you leave to judge so meanly of me, as to make you hope there cou'd be an Atonement for Injuries like those you've offer'd me——No, *Beauclair!* No; I am not twice to be deceived——nor, had I the most undeniable Assurances that you lov'd even more than you wou'd persuade me that you do; nay, were I weak enough to feel for your return of Passion the same soft Emotions which heav'd my credulous Heart when first I listned to your Vows, not to preserve *your* Life—my *own*—or the Eternal Peace of both, wou'd I forgive, or e'er consent to see you more.

As soon as she had done speaking she turn'd away, resolving to give him no farther opportunity of Conversation; and it was but for a very few Moments that he had Power either by Persuasion or Force to detain her, for perceiving his Despair made him have recourse to the latter, she darted from his Arms with an uncounterfeited Fury, vowing that if he presum'd to hold, or follow her, she wou'd alarm the Convent with her Cries, and expose him to all the Punishments of the Ecclesiastick Justice. This last Threat wou'd have avail'd but little, if the fierceness of the fair Menacer had not disarm'd him of all that Boldness, which is in some cases a necessary Qualification to make a Lover Master of his Wishes. He had not Courage to offend her more——All that Vivacity of Thought——that Energy of Soul, which despises Opposition, and triumphs over the most strict Reservedness of the denying Charmer, was now utterly extinguish'd in him——he suffer'd her to depart——he saw her go——and while his straining Eyes pursu'd her till the exclusive Walls depriv'd him of that Blessing, his enervate Limbs refus'd to bear him after her——senseless and motionless he stood——chill Horror invaded every Faculty, and even Desire was froze: Had he regarded her with less Purity and Respect, he had perhaps succeeded better; but *Love* has ever this Incongruity in its Effects, that the more violent it is, the less it is capable of serving itself.

It must be a Pen infinitely more capable of Description than mine, which cou'd represent the true State of his Condition: when left alone, all that Despair, and Rage, and Grief, heighten'd by a Consciousness of Guilt, and justly meriting every thing he suffer'd, cou'd inflict, was his. He thought it now altogether vain, ever to attempt her more; he gave himself up wholly to Distraction, and Life or Death were become Things indifferent to him——The Morning found him in this wretched Circumstance——the Sun, whose chearing Beams drive all the Mists and Vapours far away, dispell'd not his; odious and hateful to himself, he curs'd the Day, and wish'd eternal Darkness.——In this wild Hurry of confus'd Emotions, he neither consider'd where he was, nor the Danger of being discover'd to have been there all Night; he attempted not to escape, nor so much as once thought of it; and instead of concealing himself among the Bushes till the Workmen coming might give him an Opportunity of mingling with them, as twice before he had done; he now lay flat on his Face in an open Alley of the Garden, where he was not only visible to his Fellow-Labourers, but also wou'd have been so to the whole Convent, if by chance any of them had look'd thro' the Windows. It must certainly have been pleasant enough to have seen (tho' the Repetition would afford but little matter of Diversion) the Astonishment and various Conjectures these Fellows put, on their finding him in that Place and Posture: some wou'd have it that he was a Thief, and had lain there with an Intent to rob the Monastery; others, that having been guilty of some notorious Crime, he had been ordered to run so great a Danger by way of Penance; but the most good-natur'd among them, observing the Disorder of his Looks and Words (for he was little prepared for Excuses) imagin'd he had been seiz'd with a sudden Fit of the falling Sickness, or Apoplexy; the Master himself was of this Opinion, and happening to be of a Disposition less inclining to create Disturbances than the generality of his Station, who are for the most part greatly delighted with Noise and Confusion of what kind soever, contented himself with discharging him from his Service, without giving any Notice of what had happen'd to the *Abbess* or any of the *Nuns.*

One thing in this Passage I cannot let slip without observing, which is, that among the many different Conjectures which had been form'd, on the Discovery that a Man had dared to conceal himself all Night in that forbidden Ground, there was not one who imputed it to the true Cause; which proves how little People of such low Capacities are able to entertain any Just Notions of that tender Passion, and how impossible it is for any but a Lover to conceive the Force of Love, and to what Lengths it will transport the Votary inspir'd with an unfeign'd Ardour. But setting aside Reflections, which the sensible Reader need not be put in mind of, tho' our unfortunate Lover came off much better from this Adventure than he cou'd have expected, had he consider'd it all; yet the losing his Employ was the utter Loss of all Opportunity ever to try his Fortune there again, if it had been possible for him to have recovered Courage sufficient to attempt it: He was now oblig'd to leave her to the Performance of her Vow; but with what a Tempest of Mind, and how accompany'd, he return'd to *Paris,* those only who have ever been acquainted with the Furies of Despair, Remorse and a too late Repentance, can imagine.

While Affairs were in this melancholy Position between the Lovers, those who had been the Occasion of their Misfortunes were in a Condition much worse, tho' infinitely less deserving Compassion. The Hour was now come in which the wicked *Baroness,* and her Instruments of Mischief, were to prove, that Crimes, like theirs, howe'er triumphant for a while, will not always escape the Cognizance of avenging Heaven. One Evening as she was sitting in her Closet, accompany'd only by *Du Lache,* who for the Reasons before-mention'd was still in her House, they heard a loud knocking at the Gate, and immediately after, the Noise of several Persons coming hastily up Stairs: the impatient Expectation they both were in for the Return of *Toncarr* and *Le Songe,* made them presently believe it was they, whose Haste to report the joyful Tidings they had brought, had made them stand on so little Ceremony; but what was their Astonishment and Horror, when *Harriot,* who knew pretty well her Lady's Disposition, tho' perhaps not let into the depth of her Designs, came runnning into the Room, breathless and frighted out of her Wits, crying, O Madam! my Lord——She had time for no more: the *Baron,* followed by several Gentlemen, was close behind her, imagining by her Hurry his Wife might be there, and probably not without a Thought he shou'd find some with her whom his Presence wou'd alarm; but he was deceiv'd in this last

Conjecture, for *Du Lache,* on the first Appearance of *Harriot,* the Terror he saw in her Countenance, and the Words she spoke, was apprehensive of the Truth, concluded himself betray'd, tho' he had no leisure to reflect by what Means; and agitated at once with Guilt, and Shame, and Fear, the Villain's Curse, he flew backward to the Protection of a Screen which happen'd to be there, behind which there was a Door that open'd to a little Gallery, whence, in the present Confusion, he easily escap'd without being seen, at least by any who wou'd offer to detain him.

But not the prodigious Surprize the *Baroness* must be in at seeing before her the Person she believed had been destroyed; not all the Terrors which seiz'd her guilty Soul at the sight of him she had so highly injur'd, and in whose Eyes she read her Doom, had Power to deprive her of that Artifice which had so often secured her from Discovery, and might even now have stood her Friend, had the Proofs against her been such as wou'd have admitted of the smallest Scruple: With Tears of Joy she seem'd to welcome her long absent Husband——She flew into his Arms, hung on his Neck, and fainted on his Breast with an admirably acted Transport of extravagant Affection——with such strenuous Embraces did she press him, that it was as much as he cou'd do to disengage himself; but when he had, Spare your self, Madam! said he, turning his Head from her, spare *your self* the Pains, and *me* the Shock of remembring there can be such monstrous Dissimulation in the World—You see I have escap'd the Daggers you employ'd against me, and might, methinks, imagine I now know too much to be subjected to your Arts as heretofore. What means my Lord? interrupted she, I employ Daggers! Oh Heaven! what *Feind* hast thou permitted to accuse me? and turn the once fond Heart of my dear Lord to such unheard, unthought of Cruelty.—'Tis all——'tis all in vain, resumed the disordered *Baron,* and 'twou'd become you better of the two to avow your Hate, and say I was unworthy of your Bed, than poorly thus to counterfeit a Tenderness and deny a Guilt which all these here (continued he pointing to the Gentlemen who were with him) know as well as I——but to leave you no Shadow of an Excuse, I will inform you that it is by your own Emissaries you are betrayed——and when I repeat the Names of *Toncarr* and *Le Songe,* those design'd Murderers——those pretended Servants, sent by your self, and recommended by you, Shame, sure, will stop your Mouth!

The Amazement she put on at these Words, and the Asseverations she made use of, that she was entirely ignorant of what he meant, and that she knew those Men he mentioned for no other than what she sent them for, honest and diligent Attendants, was to no purpose to make her appear less vile; and the Disturbance of Soul which the *Baron* was in, damping the Power of expressing himself in as clear Terms as he wou'd have done, one of his Friends took upon him to address the Lady in this Manner. Madam, said he, I fear that all you can say, or do, will be ineffectual to wipe off the Odium of an Accusation which so many Circumstances concur to make appear but too just——The unhappy *Delirium* which this much wrong'd Gentleman long labour'd under, is evident, from the manner in which he was seiz'd, the Testimony of the Physician who restor'd him, and several others of the Learned that have been consulted in it, that it proceeded from something that had been given him, and not from any natural Disorder;——then your Behaviour, while he languish'd under that Misfortune, has been, I'm sorry to say it, so contrary to what that of a Wife shou'd be, that it gives foul Suspicions 'twas by your Means he swallow'd the Occasion of his Distemper——but for this last, this yet more monstrous Contrivance, to murder him, both *Toncarr* and *Le Songe* have confest it was from the *Baroness* they were to receive that vast Reward *Du Lache* had promis'd them. 'Tis impossible to represent the Rage she flew into at these Words, or the Imprecations she made that every Article of this Accusation was false; but the *Baron,* now, too well convinc'd, growing impatient at her Obstinacy, wou'd not suffer her to speak much; and the Gentleman who had began to discourse her on this Occasion, resum'd it in these or the like Words: Where Proofs are plain, said he, Denial but adds to the Crime, and justly aggravates the Person injur'd. Your Case wou'd be infinitely more worthy Commiseration, if touch'd with a due Sense of the Wrongs you have done the best of Husbands, you freely did acknowledge it, and in that Acknowledgement make known for whose sake, and by whose Artifices, you had been ensnared to forget all the Ties of Virtue, Honour and Gratitude, that we might take Revenge on the Deceiver, such as his generous Heart, which burns with unextinguishable Love, can ne'er inflict on you.

The *Baroness* was not more distracted at what she had seen and heard, than perplex'd by what Means it came about that her Designs were discover'd; she cou'd not think that either *Toncarr* or *Le Songe,* staunch and experienc'd Villains, shou'd, all of a sudden, feel Remorse, much less believe that they shou'd, from any imagin'd Interest to themselves, betray her, since from obliging *her,* a thousand Advantages were likely to accrue, which Men of their Principles cou'd never hope for from the Baron's Virtue; and being desirous to know the Certainty——Oh! 'tis I alone am wrong'd, said she; those Wretches have been set on by some secret Enemy of the *Baron*'s, whom to screen from Justice, they throw the black Aspersion of his Crimes on me!——unhappy guiltless me! No Madam! answer'd he, they were but too faithful to the Trust repos'd in them——Your noble Husband escap'd the horrid Assassination by an Accident almost miraculous, in which, thank Heaven, 'twas my good Fortune to be instrumental. Chancing to ride that Way, I saw those Wretches with detested Hands about to plunge their cruel Swords in his defenceless Breast, I rush'd between, with timely Aid preserv'd him from their Treachery, and with the Assistance of my Servants, bound and pinion'd them; having first, by Threats of instant Death, extorted from their Mouths an Account of what they were, and how encourag'd to this vile Attempt.——They are now in *Paris,* in Custody of the Officers of Justice, in whose Presence they have been oblig'd to make Oath of what before they had declared——they still stick firm to what they alledg'd at first, and I lament there is no room to hope my Friend is less unhappy than he thinks himself in his fair Wife's Unkindness.

All the Courage which this unexpected Turn of Fortune had left the *Baroness,* forsook her at these Words; she cou'd not be assur'd she was convicted, without being as certain she shou'd meet with the Punishment which her Crime deserv'd: all her Policy forsook her, she no longer had the Power of dissembling, nor durst lift up her Eyes to him she knew wrong'd beyond a Possibility of Forgiveness——Streams of unfeigned Tears now trickled down her Cheeks——real Sighs heav'd her disorder'd Breast, and if she felt not a true *Repentance* for her Guilt, she did a severe *Regret* for the Condition it had reduc'd her to. The *Baron,* fully acquainted with her Unworthiness, and sensible of his own too great Good-nature, dared not trust himself to look upon her long, lest his relenting Heart shou'd pardon all, and be again deluded; but turning to the Gentlemen who had accompany'd him, Come worthy Friends, said he, we trifle time with this ungrateful Woman; it yet remains to bring to Justice the chief Agent of her Crimes——for her, if Conscience, by repeated Crimes, be not quite lost and stifled in her Soul, 'twill find a Voice to speak and to upbraid, open the monstrous Legend of her Actions, and with the black Remora's[85] drive her mad. He went out of the Chamber with these Words, which were the last she ever heard him speak; for tho' when she had a little recover'd herself, she sent a thousand times to beg a Moment's Audience, he never cou'd be prevail'd upon to grant it, or to see her more.

After they had left her, *Du Lache* was sought thro' every Room in the House, for the *Baron* was presently inform'd by some of the Servants, that he had been there conceal'd: but that Villain was, by this time, past their reach; and tho' there was all imaginable Diligence made use of to discover where he was, yet many Days pass'd over without being able to give the least Account of him. By this Means the Tryals of *Le Songe* and *Toncarr* were delay'd, the *Baron* thinking it necessary to have both the Accusers and Impeach'd Face to Face.——They were kept in close Prison however, and the *Baroness* confined to her Chamber, without so much as *Harriot,* or any Servant she had ever seen before, to attend her.

If in the *Baron's* Soul there was the least Spark of Tenderness remaining for his perfidious Wife, he soon met with what was sufficient to extinguish it, when looking over the Accounts of his Estate, and seeing under her own Hand to his Banker and Steward the exorbitant Demands she had made on them, he found that in three Years, the Term of their being together, she had consum'd more ready Money (for he was immensely rich) than wou'd have supported the Retinue of the first Prince of the Blood for twice as long: Bills, also, for Debts she had contracted, were hourly brought him for Expences of so superfluous and luxurious a sort, that his *Amazement* at an Extravagance so unbounded, so unexampled, was almost equal to his *Chagrin* at being oblig'd to discharge them. Besides, as it is the way of the World to expose in their worst Colours the Vices of a Person in Disgrace, his Ears were continually teiz'd with some new Account of her ill Conduct; and tho' it was scarce possible to report her more vile than she really was, 'tis certain there was nothing of the Truth omitted.

The dejected *Beauclair* was, perhaps, the only Person in Town whom this Adventure had not reach'd; his Soul was too much taken up in the Contemplation of his own Misfortunes to listen to those of another. As soon as he return'd to *Paris,* and had got to his Lodgings, he threw himself into Bed, from which none of his Servants (who were entirely ignorant what it was that disordered him, or where he had been) cou'd prevail on him to rise, or to admit the Visits of any of his Acquaintance. A young *Chevalier* coming to lodge in the same House, express'd a prodigious Concern when he was told his Neighbour's melancholy Condition. He sent to entreat the Liberty of visiting him, but was refus'd, till one Day, happening to see a Servant going in with something his Master wanted, he took that Opportunity (which probably he had watched for) to beg that Favour himself. It was not in the Power of any Misfortune to make *Beauclair* forget that Gentleman-like, complaisant Behaviour which render'd his Conversation as charming to the *Women,* as the Soundness of his Judgment, and almost an universal Knowledge of every beneficial Study, made it esteem'd and coveted by the *Men,* and cou'd not avoid doing the Civility of his Chamber, when one who appear'd so much a Gentleman desir'd in Person to be admitted: besides, there was something so extremely engaging in the Air and Mein of this young *Chevalier,* which, whether he wou'd or no, attracted his Admiration; he grew immediately charm'd with him without knowing that he was so, and began to find a Pleasure in conversing with him, such as had been a Stranger to his Soul, since his breaking off with *Montamour.* He fancy'd, indeed, he found something in his Features, and the Accent of his Voice, so much resembling that Lady's, that had it seem'd possible, he shou'd have believ'd it her; but that was a vain and soon-rejected Thought,—she was far off—shut up within a Monastery,——tho' had she been near, and at Liberty, there was little likelyhood that she, who wou'd not by all his Entreaties be won to grant him one Moment's willing Audience, when he had risqu'd such imminent Dangers to obtain it, shou'd come, of her own accord, to seek him, at his own Lodgings, and in a Garb so much unsuitable to her Nicety and Reserve. Besides, the *Chevalier* had darker Hair, a far less delicate Complection, and a certain Boldness in his Look, becoming enough in one of his Sex, but vastly different from that modest Mildness he had always seen in hers. The bare Imagination, however, that there was a Likeness, tho' never so small a one, was sufficient to make him valuable.[86] He was so far from being chagrin'd at the Intrusion, that he became a Petitioner for the same Favour the next Day, and the other was too well satisfied in entertaining him not to comply with his Request; there soon grew an Intimacy between them, which seem'd rather the Consequence of many *Years* Acquaintance, than a few *Days.*

'Tis very difficult for the Tongue to forbear speaking something of what the Soul is full of: the despairing *Beauclair,* wholly taken up with his Passion, cou'd not sit so many Hours with his new Friend without revealing the whole History of it to him,——he let him into every Particular of his Transgression, and Repentance for it, complain'd of the uncommon Severity of *Montamour,* and entreated his Advice: Nor was he, while making this Recital, agitated with more violent Emotions than the Hearer of it appear'd to be. The Young *Vrayment*[87] (for so he call'd himself) discover'd he had a Heart, tender, and susceptible of Love's soft Impression: He cou'd not listen to some Passages, and restrain his Tears, nor suffer a Sigh from *Beauclair* to pass unanswer'd by one of his own. But when he found he was beginning to accuse the Cruelty and unforgiving Temper of his Mistress, he cou'd not forbear taking her Part.

Ah *Monsieur Beauclair!* said he, in spite of the Pity due to what I see you suffer, and the Inclination I have to be of your side, Justice now obliges me to engage in the Defence of one I know not, against him whose Friendship I profess an Ambition to become worthy of. I cannot think the Proceedings of that Lady are in the least to be condemn'd; had she acted otherwise, you might indeed have applauded the Effects of a Passion which made you Master of your Wishes, but what must the disinterested part of the World have thought of her Behaviour? Wou'd not the Meanness of her Spirit, and her easie Fondness, have been the Subject of Ridicule? by what your self has said, I find she loves you—loves you with a Tenderness, at least, equal to your own—and, doubtless, when she pronounc'd the Sentence of your eternal Banishment, felt Torments greater than she gave:—But, there are some sorts of Injuries which Honour cannot pardon; among which, I think those are she has receiv'd from you! Yet Heaven, cry'd the half distracted *Beauclair,* forgives the *Penitent* Offender. Yes, resum'd the other, but *here* the Case is widely different: the Heavenly Mercy is accountable to nothing but it self; but we poor Mortals, whose Actions are censur'd by each other, and scarce the best can scape Reflection, must be cautious, ever watchful, how we tread that slippery Road, the World's Opinion; for Reputation is so nice a thing, so finely wrought! so liable to break! the least false Step disjoints the beauteous Frame, and down we sink in endless Infamy——Consider, added he, the Reasons why Women are, by our *Salique* Law, debarr'd from reigning?[88] Why, in all Nations of the Earth, excluded from publick Management? us'd but as Toys, little immaterial Amusements to trifle away an Hour of idle Time with! is it not because their Levity of Nature, their weak Irresolution, pleas'd and displeas'd oft at they know not what, and always in Extreams, makes them unfit for Counsel, for Secrecy, or Action?——if one among them can tow'r above the Follies of her Sex, and awe her encroaching Passions with superior Reason, we should admire a Virtue so uncommon,——and tho' the Freedom of my Speech shou'd lose me the Honour of your Friendship, the Love I bear to Truth obliges me to say that, in my Opinion, had *Montamour* granted to your Inconstancy that kind Reward its contrary had merited, she had proved the *Lover,* but not the Woman of *Discretion,* and had been guilty of an Injustice to herself, which I know not how she wou'd have been able to account for.

This manner of arguing wou'd not, perhaps, have been very agreeable to *Monsieur Beauclair,* had it come from any other Mouth, but nothing was unpardonable from this young Favourite; he had already gain'd so great an Ascendant over him, that it was in his Power to persuade him almost to any thing. Hurried by the Violence of his Despair, he had certainly had recourse to some desperate Remedy, to ease the present Anguish, had not the other's prudent Advice, and philosophical Reasonings (which seem'd far above his Age) interposed to stay him: Whenever he found him more than ordinarily sad he wou'd endeavour to divert his Griefs, or when he found him (as sometimes he did) transported with Excess of Passion, and appearing like one totally depriv'd of Reason, he wou'd for a while give way to the Tempest of his Despair, then gently parly with the Fury, till by degrees he sooth'd it to a Calm.——Never man, overwhelm'd like him in Sorrows, met a Comforter so kind, so industrious, and so artful in allaying them; he look'd on him as his Guardian Angel, sent down from Heaven to soften his impetuous Passions, and restore his Peace. It was seldom they were asunder, but whenever it happen'd so, each seem'd to want the better half of himself:——they eat together—drank together, and *Beauclair* wou'd very fain have persuaded him to take part of his Bed; but the other excus'd himself from that; he told him, that having been guilty of some youthful Follies, the Church had forbad him, by way of Mortification, the Ease of reposing in a Bed, for a certain Time; when Morning comes, said he, I throw my self upon it, and tumble the Cloaths, to prevent the People of the House from taking notice, but for many Nights past have rested on the Floor. *Beauclair* was himself too strict an Observer of the Orders of the Church, to press him farther, and these were the only Hours in which they were separated.

Neither of them had been abroad[89] since they came to *Paris;* and *Beauclair,* something more easie than he had been, began to think it a piece of Ingratitude that he had not yet paid a Visit to the friendly *Friar,* by whose Instructions he had first gain'd Admittance to *Montamour*: He told *Vrayment* of it, and that he wou'd that Day pass some Hours with him; the other offer'd to accompany him if he approv'd of it, which not being thought at all improper, they both went to the *Convent,* where they were told, the Person they enquir'd for was extremely ill, and unfit for Conversation; but *Beauclair,* whose Intimacy with him authoriz'd his Freedom, ran immediately to his *Cell,* leaving the *Chevalier* to divert himself in the *Cloyster* Walks, till his Return. But how great was his Astonishment, when after having paid his Civilities to the *Friar,* and turning his Eyes a little on one side, he saw a Person sitting on the Bed by him, whom, in spite of the Darkness of the Place, he presently knew to be *Du Lache!* All the Rage and Violence of Passion, which by the Artifices of his agreeable Companion were a little hush'd to Peace, return'd at the Sight of this Villain: scarce cou'd he restrain himself from sacrificing him that Moment to his Resentment. Villain! detested Monster, cry'd he, have I found thee!——Comest thou to scatter thy abhorr'd Practices among the Saints——He took him by the Throat, with these Words, and dragging him from the Bed, had his Sword half out; when the timorous Wretch, fearful to die, tho' unable to live, fell on his Knees, and begg'd him to forgive him; and the poor sick *Friar,* strangely alarm'd at what he saw and heard, cry'd out to him to forbear, and whatever his Injuries were, not to prophane that holy Place with Blood.——This Remonstrance a little brought *Beauclair* to himself, and having begg'd his Pardon for giving him this Disturbance, he turn'd to *Du Lache,* Rise, said he, thou unworthy of the Name of Man!——Oh *Monsieur!* interrupted he, (by this time a little more assur'd) for the Love of Heav'n do not quite undo me——I am already as miserable as your Wish can make me——do not betray me here, and my whole *future* Life shall be spent in an Endeavour to expiate the *past.* What new Deceit, resum'd *Beauclair,* thou execrable Lyar! woud'st thou now impose upon me?——Permit me but a Moment's patient hearing, answer'd the other, and I will confess all I have done,—you shall be let into the whole Secret, which as yet it is impossible you can know without me.

Tho' there was little of Truth to be expected from this Villain, yet *Beauclair* was willing to listen to what he had to say, and perceiving he wou'd not declare himself before the *Fryar,* went with him out of the Room: The Cloyster Walks were pretty full of Company, and they walk'd together into a little Field behind the Convent, where *Du Lache,* as he had promis'd, related to *Beauclair* every Particular of the Treasons he had been guilty of both to him and *Montamour;* he told him also, that the *Baron de Tortillée,* being perfectly recover'd of his Frenzy was return'd to *Paris,* and incens'd against his Lady had taken care to deprive her of all those Gallantries she formerly had so freely indulg'd in, by confining her to her Chamber; and that himself, look'd on as a Person instrumental in her Amours, was prosecuted with his severest Resentment, and that, on that Account, and the misfortune of some Debts, he had been oblig'd to abscond, and concealing his Name in that of another, take shelter in this *Convent,* where the Charity of the Fathers was all his Dependance. Tho' *Beauclair* had been before wholly assur'd of the Innocence of *Montamour,* yet he cou'd not be inform'd of the Truth of those Artifices by which he had been ensnar'd into a contrary Opinion, without lifting up his Eyes and Hands in token of Amazement; and tho' he knew nothing of the distracting Potion which had been given to the *Baron,* his intended Murder, nor a thousand other hellish Practices, yet he stood struck dumb with Wonder that there cou'd be three such prodigious Villains in the World, as *Du Lache,* and his Confederates *Toncar* and *Le Songe.* But while he was thus employ'd, an Accident hapned, which more than ever inform'd him, how dangerous it was for a Man of Honour to be of the Acquaintance of such Wretches.

Full of troubled Cogitations, the unhappy *Baron* avoided as much as possible all Society; his Misfortunes were publick, and he cou'd not imagine any body look'd on him without Pitying, or despising that Weakness which had suffer'd him to fall into them; Chance, or his ill Genius, led him into that Field, at the very Hour, at the very Moment, that these two were in Conference. He immediately knew the Villain he so long had sought, but the sight of *Beauclair* fill'd him with more Violent Agitations: ever since the knowledge of his Wrongs, he had imagin'd this Gentleman was the prime Cause of them; nor was this Thought altogether opposite to Reason, considering the Manner in which he once had found him with his Wife, and now beholding him thus accompany'd was sufficient to confirm those Conjectures——Now all the Injuries he had sustain'd, his violated Honour——his ruin'd Fortune——his Madness——his intended Murder! all at once presented themselves to his Remembrance——and fatally transported with Excess of Rage, he drew his Sword, and flew on the astonish'd *Beauclair,* giving him no other warning of the Danger which he threatned, than that Action: It was indeed sufficient to make him stand upon his Guard, but being desirous to know on what Account or by whom he was so Challeng'd (for in his present Surprize he saw not that it was the *Baron*) he stept two or three Steps back, and was opening his Mouth to enquire the Cause of so unexpected a Salutation, when the other, still advancing, cry'd out to him to stay; Recoyl not, base unworthy Man! dishonourable *Beauclair!* said he; but if you are not Coward too as well as Villain, defend the Wrongs you have done me with the same Boldness as you acted them. Ha! replyed *Beauclair,* equally provok'd, and who art thou who dar'st to joyn such Language with the Name of *Beauclair?*——Is it possible (continu'd he, looking more earnestly on him) that the *Baron de Tortillée* should so forget himself? 'Tis thou, resum'd the impatient *Baron,* that hast forgot thy Virtue——debased the Honour of thy noble Family——and rendred thy self a Companion of Panders, Vagabonds, and Ruffians——but we trifle time,——this Woman's War of Words is not for Men, who ought to hate, like us!

As much addicted to Passion as *Beauclair* naturally was, he wou'd if possible have avoided this Combat, but the other resolving to afford no longer Parly, press'd on him so hard, that he was oblig'd to make use of his best Skill for his Defence. *Du Lache* had all this while his Sword out too, not with a Design to prevent them from doing each other a Mischief, but to take part with which ever was like to be the Conqueror. The *Baron,* whether it was that he was less expert, or that Transported by his Fury he rush'd too eagerly on his Antagonist, is uncertain; but *Beauclair* had the good Fortune to disarm him at the third Pass. Sufficiently satisfied with this Advantage, and rejoyc'd this Adventure had terminated in no worse Catastrophe, he was preparing to re-deliver him his Sword, with all complaisant, and sincere Inclinations imaginable for a thorough Reconciliation, when the mischievous Stander-by stab'd him in the Back with so accurst a Force, that the unhappy Gentleman fell with the Wound, and spoke, nor breath'd, no more. Thus ended a Life, which, if not blemish'd by a too great Affection for the most Vile of Women, might have been long and happy. *Beauclair,* struck motionless with sudden Horror at a Deed so monstrous, seem'd like one transfix'd with Thunder, and before he cou'd recollect himself enough for Speech, or the Murderer cou'd determine what Way wou'd afford most Security for his Escape, they were encompassed by a Crowd of People which the Cries of the *Chevalier Vrayment* had drawn together. That young Spark having seen *Beauclair* and *Du Lache* (whom he very well knew) go hastily cross the Walks, he follow'd them into the Field, apprehensive that they were gone thither on no friendly purpose. He observ'd their Behaviour at a distance, till the approach of the *Baron,* and the manner in which he accosted *Beauclair,* made him resolve to trust nothing to Fortune, but timely endeavour to hinder whatever Consequences either Rage or Treachery might attempt; yet fearful to leave 'em while he ran for Help, he bethought him of calling to some Men whom he saw cleaning the way on the other side of the Wall which encompass'd the Field he was in: They presently resounded the cry of Murder, which ecchoing from one to the other, gather'd Numbers immediately, which tho' they had a good way to come round, were at the Heels of *Vrayment* when he got to the fatal Scene.

Du Lache, when they came near, was looking wildly round as tho' distracted with the Horrors of his Guilt, his Sword lying on the Grass dyed to the Hilt with Blood. *Beauclair* with both the Swords still in his Hand, his Head a little reclin'd, was stooping over the dead Body, which was fallen just at his Feet. The sight of *Vrayment,* and the Noise of those that follow'd rous'd him from his Lethargy, and he presently cry'd Oh my Friend! behold this dreadful Object——then turn your Eyes on that Consummate Fiend, (whom yet you know not, but by my Description) the curs'd *Du Lache.* Before the Person to whom these Words were address'd cou'd make any Reply, a robust Fellow, bawl'd out, A dreadful Murder indeed, my Masters, but 'tis hard to know which of these two, or whether both are not guilty of it: 'Tis true, said another, therefore let us carry 'em both away to the Officers of Justice: Ay, ay, hollow'd out the whole Crowd, away with them both. It wou'd have been but to little purpose to have argued with the Multitude, had they endeavour'd it; but *Beauclair* was willing to go, that the murd'rous *Du Lache* might receive the due Reward of all his Crimes; nor did that Wretch seem now so timorous as might have been expected from his Cowardly Disposition, he fed himself with a secret Hope, that he might be able by his Insinuations to make *Beauclair* appear at least a Party concerned, if not a chief Instrument of the *Baron*'s Death; which if he cou'd once bring to be believ'd, the Sentence must be the same on both, and then he doubted not but that Gentleman had Interest enough to procure a Pardon, which must, where the Guilt was equal, extend to one as well as the other. The *Chevalier* was not at all dissatisfied, as not doubting but the bloody Sword of *Du Lache,* and his own Evidence, who saw the murder, wou'd be sufficient to clear *Beauclair* immediately; but he found himself mistaken. The known Amour which he had had with the Wife of the deceas'd, and the Intimacy which had been taken notice of between him and the Murderer, went a great way to make him appear guilty of consenting to his Death: but nothing cou'd be determin'd till the Tryal, which was order'd shou'd be in a few Days, and in the mean time both were sent to Prison, neither being allow'd the Privilege of Bail.

Vrayment appeared much more concerned than *Beauclair* was for himself, and omitted nothing, during the time of his Confinement, which cou'd be expected from the most zealous Friendship: He went to all his Acquaintance, to engage them to appear in his behalf on the Day prefix'd for the Tryal. But tho' many did, and his Character was such, as cou'd give no one leave to imagine he cou'd be guilty of a Baseness such as he was call'd in Question for; yet the *Baron*'s Relations were so vigorous in their Prosecution, that in spite of all *Vrayment* (who saw the whole Transaction) cou'd say, the Court began to think it wou'd be very difficult to acquit him. The *Baroness* having, by *Toncarr* and *Le Songe,* been accused of a Design to murder her Husband, was also summon'd to appear; and *Du Lache* having found means to send to her while he was in Prison, let her know the only way for their common Safety was to accuse *Beauclair*: She did it, to his Face, with an Assurance such as sure no Woman but her self cou'd ever boast; and to make her Evidence bear the greater appearance of Truth, with counterfeited Blushes, and Streams of Tears, she confest her Criminal Affection for him had won her Consent to the *Baron*'s Death, that she might give her self wholly to him.

Never was any Soul Alarm'd, Confus'd, Enrag'd, like *Beauclair,* when he heard this monstrous Allegation; scarce cou'd he contain himself in the presence of the Judge (who hapned to be the Brother of *Montamour*) from speaking to that bad Woman, when he denied what he was charg'd with, in terms such as her Impudence deserv'd; but all that he cou'd say without being guilty of an Indecorum to Modesty, or Irreverence to the Presence he was in, he did. This Accusation however had a very great Influence on the *Judge,* who imagin'd presently that this Amour was the occasion of his Sister's breaking with him; and the Indignity which he thought was offer'd to his Family, by preferring a Woman of the *Baroness's* Character to a Maid whose Reputation had ever been Unblemish'd, heighten'd his Displeasure against the Prisoner to so great a Degree, that he was just going to pronounce him deserving the same Fate with *Du Lache;* when *Vrayment,* easily guessing what his Thoughts were, and distracted to find all he cou'd do to save him was in vain, And is then my Evidence, my Lord, said he, no more to be regarded? I, who was Witness to every part of the whole Action, and know *Beauclair* as free from any share in this Guilt as Heaven is from Falshood; or Hell, or these his vile Accusers, from Truth——You speak with Passion, young *Monsieur!* reply'd the Judge, which in a case like this savours too much of Partiality, to be regarded——You are his Friend——and Friendship may be byass'd. I scorn the Thought (interrupted fiercely the enrag'd *Vrayment*) I love *Beauclair* 'tis true, but 'tis because his Virtues challenge my Esteem——did I but think he cou'd forgo his Honour, and become an Accomplice with these horrid Wretches, I wou'd be the first shou'd urge your Justice to condemn him: But as I know him clear——clear as my own Soul——as yours my Lord, or any here, from such detested Crimes, I must, I will stand up in his Vindication, tho' the whole World should censure and hate me for it.

While he was uttering these Words the Judge look'd on him with an Eye which spoke Amazement; and not replying presently, a Friend of the dead *Baron*'s, one who had appeared the most zealous of any of them in his Revenge, took this opportunity to endeavour to weaken what this young Champion had offer'd in defence of *Beauclair.* I hope my Lord! said he, the Testimony of one, bold tho' he seems, so much unknown, and doubtless bought, will be of little weight, when Circumstances so plain make void his Evidence. Injurious Man (resum'd the little Heroe) know I was bred to hate a Lie——Nor shall I be unknown when he by whose Sentence I, in my Friend, must stand or fall, shall see this Token. With these Words he pluck'd a Ring off his Finger and presented it to the Judge, who after he had taken it, look'd carefully on it, then on him that gave it, and rising from his Seat, I am enough convinc'd said he, and here pronounce the Witness most substantial, and *Beauclair* innocent.——Let the Court adjourn; To-morrow the other Prisoners must attend their Doom. It was to little effect that the Friends of the Deceas'd petition'd, for a further hearing. The universal Joy which appear'd in the Faces of all the disinterested Part of the Assembly, and the loud Clap which they gave when *Beauclair* was acquitted, hush'd the feeble Murmurs of the contrary Party. As the Judge pass'd by the Bar where *Beauclair* was standing, he took him by the Hand, and speaking to him in a low Voice; Dine with me To-day, said he, and be sure to bring your young Advocate with you.

The other had no time to make any other Answer to this obliging Invitation, than a low Bow; but the Surprize he was in at this sudden Change of his Affairs was such, as it wou'd be very difficult to represent; he cou'd not however, in this publick Place, have leisure for Reflection; he was immediately surrounded by a great Number of his Friends and Acquaintance, who came to congratulate him on being clear'd; when the Press was a little over, *Vrayment* came up to him, and with a Countenance much more grave than he had ever seen him wear, You are now safe, *Monsieur!* said he; but beware how you hereafter enter into Engagements with Persons of the *Baroness*'s Humour. *Beauclair,* unwilling to hold any Discourse on an Affair which he wou'd have been glad to bury in Oblivion, answered these Words only with a Sigh and a little shaking of his Head; but, after he had embrac'd and thank'd him for the Service he had done him, owning it was to him (as indeed it was) that he was indebted for his Life, he entreated him to inform him, by what Means he came to know the *Judge,* and what the Mystery of the Ring was, which, like some Enchantment, had the Power in a Moment to unlock his Fetters and reverse his Doom: Of that, reply'd *Vrayment,* you shall be told hereafter; but you must pardon me if I say it is a Secret, which at present you must not be inform'd of. I will not press it then, resum'd *Beauclair,* but perhaps, at the *Judge*'s House, to which he has engag'd me to bring you To-day, you will be good-natur'd enough to ease my Curiosity. 'Tis highly possible indeed, answer'd the *Chevalier,* that there the Riddle may be solv'd. They passed from this to several other Subjects of Conversation relating to the Tryal; 'till the Hour drawing near in which they were to wait on the Judge, *Vrayment* excus'd himself from going with him, saying he had some Business another Way which he was obliged to dispatch, but when that was ended, he might expect to see him; the other entreating him not to fail, took his Leave for a much longer Time than he imagin'd.

The Judge, who waited with Impatience for their coming, receiv'd *Beauclair* with all imaginable Civility and Kindness, till finding he was alone, he a little alter'd his Countenance, and with a Voice which expressed his Discontent, What *Monsieur!* said he, wou'd she not come?——or did you fear to trust her in a Brother's House? What means my Lord? cry'd the other, (more surpriz'd, if possible, at these Words, than at all his late Adventures.) You counterfeit a Consternation well, resum'd the former, tho' I know not for what Cause——My Meaning needs, I think, no Explanation——you were not, as I take it, the only invited Guest!——Most true, my Lord! answered *Beauclair,* and cou'd my Persuasions have prevail'd on the *Chevalier Vrayment,* to put off to another Day a Business he had appointed on this, I had not singly waited on you. The Judge thinking himself trifled with, began to lose great Part of his Patience: You do ill, *Monsieur!* said he, to reward the kind Intentions I had for you, in this Manner,——Why do you pretend to keep me in Ignorance of what by this Time you must be sensible I know full well?——Why, when I demand to see my Sister, do you make an Excuse for the Absence of the *Chevalier Vrayment?* Ha! (interrupted the transported Lover, half wild 'twixt Ecstacy and Wonder) what said your Lordship?——your Sister!——Oh bless my exulting Soul, and tell me all!——Is it possible (rejoin'd her Brother) that you shou'd need be told by any but herself, that *Montamour* and *Vrayment* are the same? Oh Heavens! cry'd *Beauclair,* now quite o'ercome with Rapture, Oh all ye gracious Powers! is it possible?

All that he cou'd say was scarce sufficient to make the Judge believe his Sister cou'd be in *Paris,* and so intimate with her Lover, and remain unknown to him, till he recounted to him, his Progress to the Monastery, the Severity of her Usage to him there, and the Improbability there was that she shou'd have altered her Resolution. Neither of them knew what to think,——that it was she was evident, though her Hair and Complection were alter'd, which might easily be perform'd by Art. The Features of her Face, her Voice, were perfectly known to her Brother; and more than all, the Ring she gave him, which was one he had put on her Finger at parting, left no room to doubt it was any other than herself: but how so wonderful a Change had happen'd, or for what Reason she had left the Monastery so disguis'd, and come in Search of the Man she had so industriously strove to avoid, was what puzled the Capacities of them both. After some little Time of Expectation, *Beauclair* began to fear, that it was in vain to hope she wou'd make good her Promise of meeting him there, and ran Home, believing he might probably find her; but how great was his Disappointment, when he was told the *Chevalier* had discharged his Lodgings, and had not given any Intimation where he design'd to go. Full of a thousand perplex'd Reflections for this second Ruin of his Hopes, he return'd to her Brother with the melancholy Account, and found him reading a Letter he had just receiv'd from her.

As soon as the Brother of *Montamour* saw him enter, You need not, *Monsieur!* said he, give your self the Trouble of repeating our common Misfortune; the Person we both, tho' prompted by different Emotions, are so impatient to Embrace, resolves we shall not, at least for a while, enjoy the Happiness we aim at. See here (continued he, giving him the Letter) the Intelligence I have just now received. *Beauclair* had no sooner cast his Eye upon it, than he knew the Character to be *Montamour*'s, and with a Mixture of Hope and Fear, as tho' about to unravel the Mystery of his future Fate, read o'er these Lines.

I am sensible it is now too late to entreat my dearest Brother to keep from *Monsieur Beauclair* the Knowledge who the Person was that endeavoured to do him Service at his Tryal. But that I did not satisfie yours, and my own Desire, in seeing you at your House, was because I cou'd not bear to appear in my own Shape before a Man who had affronted me in the manner you are now no Stranger to: However, my late Behaviour may inform you I am not desirous of Revenge,——his Repentance since has, perhaps, been Punishment sufficient, and I would not have you less willing to forgive——I have also a Pardon to beg for my self, for making use of your Name to countenance my Elopement from the Monastery, and conceal the Pity I had for an unworthy Lover, in the Pretence of Tenderness for the best of Brothers.——Yes, I confess, that disturb'd at some Testimonies I had of his Despair, I told the *Abbess* that I cou'd not profess till I had once more bid Adieu to you, and by that Means gain'd her Consent to come to *Paris.* Judge not too unkindly of this Deceit, but believe you are, and ever shall be, most Dear to the Soul of

Your Affectionate Sister, and
Obliged Humble Servant
MONTAMOUR.

Beauclair had scarce finished the reading this, when his Servant brought him another, which he told him was given him by the *Chevalier Vrayment,* with a strict Charge to deliver it to his Hands. The hearing that Name, and the Sight of this second Mandate, increas'd the Tumults of his Soul to such a Height, that the Disorder he was in was what nothing but it self can represent: to comprehend in any measure what it was he felt, 'tis necessary to be possest of all those burning Passions!——those distracting Whirls of tortur'd Thought, which scarce afforded Patience till he could unfold the dear, and at once welcome and unwelcome Paper, which contain'd these Words.

To Monsieur Beauclair.

Think not, because I have given you Proofs of an unextinguish'd Tenderness, that I think your Penitence a sufficient Expiation for your Crimes, nor that my Pity for your Sufferings can influence me so far as to make me forget what I owe to my own Honour——No, *Beauclair!* there is a Justice to be done ones self, which if I shou'd dispence with, you might perhaps, and indeed with much more Reason than hitherto you have had, be perswaded to believe, I might hereafter fail in it towards you——What though you swear your Heart was ever mine——what though your late Repentance and Despair induces me to think that Protestation real; the World! the judging World will never be of my Opinion——My easy Nature, and my fond Belief, wou'd be the Jest of every Table——All I can do for you, therefore, and I know not if by the Grave and Wise that wou'd not be thought too much, is to wish it were as much in my Power to reward that Tenderness you now have for me, as it is to pardon those past Actions which have made us both unhappy. I cannot, without deviating from that Sincerity which has been ever the Dictator of all my Words, deny that my Love for you has ever been unshaken—that it was not even in your own Power to lessen one Grain of that exhaustless Store of Passion you inspir'd me with——that it still blazes with a Flame so pure, so true, so lasting, as nor Time, nor Absence, nor Unkindness can put a damp to——that my whole Soul is full of you—and that in putting in Execution that cruel, but necessary Resolution of flying from your Sight for ever, I suffer Pangs more terrible than Death it self cou'd be. But entertain no Hope from this Confession, nor attempt to alter a Determination which is fix'd as Fate—Write not to me, unless you can restrain your Sentiments to such Bounds as may be fitly read by one of that Order I am going to profess my self——But above all Things, I conjure you, not to make use of any Stratagems for the future to distract me with the Sight of your Despair——The Thought of it is more than I can bear——Heaven! Heaven only can enable me to support the coming, killing Certainty, which takes from me all Possibility of ever being

Yours,

MONTAMOUR.

Who that has been present when Death's Icy Hand has on the sudden seiz'd on the Faculties of some one in Company, may figure to themselves what *Beauclair* was at reading this: Just so the Blood flew from his Lips and Cheeks, his Eyes grew dim, the Life and Vigour of his Air chang'd to cold Trembling, all his Limbs enervate, and down at once he sunk into the Chair he was sitting on. The Brother of *Montamour* guessing the Cause of this Disorder, took the Letter from his shaking Hand, and inform'd himself at full of what he before suspected. Come *Monsieur,* said he, recall your Courage, I see nothing in this Letter that can give you Cause of Chagrin, but rather the contrary——My Sister makes a Declaration here of Tenderness, much greater than I cou'd have imagin'd from her Reserve——and since she Loves, take my Word for it, neither of you shall Despair. The dejected Lover cou'd not recover himself enough to make any other Answer to these obliging Expressions than a Sigh: But the other, continuing to assure him, in the Manner he had begun, that he wou'd not rest till he had procur'd his Happiness, made a visible Alteration in his Countenance, and by little and little, he became again the Man he was.

Nor was the Judge forgetful of what he had promis'd; but, because it was impossible to prosecute the Design he had form'd till the Affair of the Prisoners was dispatch'd, he commanded their Appearance the very next Day. The

Crime of *Du Lache,* as being the immediate Murderer of the unhappy *Baron,* was too evident for any thing to be offer'd in Opposition to his Sentence, which was to be broke upon the Wheel:[90] *Toncarr* and *Le Songe,* having been prov'd by the Witness of the Gentleman and the Servants who rescued the *Baron,* to have assassinated and design'd his Death, receiv'd the same Doom: But the *Baroness,* though the known Contriver and Abetter of the horrid Deed, was remanded back to Prison, till he had more Leisure to consult in what Manner he shou'd decree her Punishment.

This being over, he immediately set forward with Monsieur *Beauclair* to the Monastery where *Montamour* had resolv'd to pass the Remainder of her Life. They arriv'd there the very Day before that in which she was design'd to take the Order: Her Brother found an easy Admittance to her; but not all the Arguments he cou'd alledge were of Force to engage her Consent to see *Beauclair,* till he, who had waited in an outer Room expecting to be call'd in, as the Judge had made him hope, growing Impatient at this long Delay, and resolving to hear once more from *Montamour*'s own Mouth his Doom, ran hastily in to them, and throwing himself at her Feet, pleaded his own Cause with such Success, that though she did not absolutely promise to grant all he ask'd, yet there appear'd a sort of Consenting in her Eyes; which her Brother observing, back'd the Intercessions of the other with Arguments so strenuous, that she was wholly at a Loss for Words to form Denials, if the Relentings of her swelling Heart wou'd have dictated them, to what her Lover and her Brother urg'd. The Abbess, whose Company on this extraordinary Occasion was desir'd, join'd her Perswasions; and had *Montamour* been less prompted from within, it had been hardly possible to have held out against such united Forces: In fine, she was at last prevail'd on to give her *Hand* to him from whom nothing cou'd estrange her *Heart.* They were Married that Evening, and it wou'd be needless to endeavour, as well as impossible to set forth, as it deserv'd, the Raptures, of the o'erjoy'd *Beauclair* at so unhop'd a Condescension.

It was not many Days between their going and coming back to *Paris;* yet at their Return, they met the Tidings of an Act of Horror which they little expected. The wicked *Baroness,* impatient of her Fate, desperate, and as some say struck with Remorse, and terrified in Conscience, hopeless of Mercy here or hereafter, had swallow'd Poison, and ended her shameful Life by as ignominious a Death: The three Wretches who had been the Instruments of her vile Actions, suffer'd the Sentence which had been given by the Judge, and with their last Breaths allow'd the Justice of it, and confess'd their Crimes. Thus was not only the *Baron*'s Death reveng'd at full, but also the Disquiet which the Contrivers of it had brought on the Innocent *Montamour,* and her belov'd *Beauclair.* The Manner of their Living together since their Marriage, is such as might be expected from that unalterable Affection which each felt for the other before, and full of that sincere Tenderness, which might furnish many more Examples, were Love and Virtue the chief Inducements to *Hymen.*[91]

FINIS.

LASSELIA:

OR, THE

SELF-ABANDON'D.

A

NOVEL.

Written by Mrs. ELIZA HAYWOOD.

Love various Minds does variously inspire;
He stirs in gentle Natures gentle Fire,
Like that of Incense on the Altars laid;
But raging Flames tempestuous Souls invade:
A Fire which ev'ry windy Passion blows,
With Pride it mounts, and with Revenge it glows.

DRYDEN.

LONDON;
Printed for D. BROWNE *jun*r. at the *Black-Swan* with-out *Temple-Bar*; and S. CHAPMAN, at the *Angel* in *Pall-Mall.* M.DCC.XXIV.

Previous page: Title page of the first edition, 1723. Beinecke Rare Book and Manuscript Library, Yale University.

To the

RIGHT HONOURABLE THE
EARL OF SUFFOLK AND

Bindon.[1]

My Lord,

When I presume to entreat your Protection of a Trifle such as this, I do more to express my Sense of your unbounded Goodness, than if I were to publish Folio's in your Praise. A Great and learned Work honours the Patron who accepts it, but little Performances stand in need of all that Sweetness of Disposition so conspicuous in the Behaviour and Character of your Lordship, to engage a Pardon. 'Tis to be something of a piece with Heaven, to regard the will more than the Merit of the Offering; and my Knowledge how zealous an Imitator you are in all Things else of that, gives me an almost assur'd Hope you will not swerve in this, *only to punish my Presumption.*

My Design in writing this little Novel *(as well as those I have formerly publish'd) being only to remind the unthinking Part of the World, how dangerous it is to give way to Passion, will, I hope, excuse the too great Warmth, which may perhaps, appear in some particular Pages; for without the* Expression *being invigorated in some measure proportionate to the* Subject, *'twou'd be impossible for a Reader to be sensible how far it touches him, or how probable it is that he is falling into those Inadvertencies which the Examples I relate wou'd caution him to avoid.*

I take the Liberty of mentioning this to your Lordship, to clear my self of that Aspersion which some of my own Sex have been unkind enough to throw upon me, that "I seem to endeavour to divert *more than* improve *the Minds of my Readers."*[2] *Now, as I take it, the Aim of every Person, who pretends to write (tho' in the most insignificant and ludicrous*[3] *way) ought to tend at least to a good* Moral *Use; I shou'd be sorry to have my Intentions judg'd to be the very reverse of what they are in Reality. How far I have been able to* succeed *in my Desires of infusing those Cautions, too necessary to Number, I will not pretend to determine: but where I have had the Misfortune to* fail, *must impute it either to the* Obstinacy *of those I wou'd persuade, or to my own Deficiency in that very Thing which They are pleased to say I too much abound in——a true description of Nature.*

But I will give your Lordship no farther trouble than what proceeds from

Gratitude; and with entreating you to accept my humble Acknowledgments for all the unmerited favours I have received,[4] *conclude,*

My LORD,
Your Lordship's most Oblig'd,
Most Faithful, and
Obedient Servant,
ELIZA HAYWOOD.

LASSELIA:

OR,

The Self-Abandon'd.

A

NOVEL.

Never was a Court more resplendent with Beautys, than that of *France,* in the Reign of their late Monarch *Lewis* XIV.[5] That Prince, in spite of his Ambition, found room for Love, nor could the incessant Hurry of his other Affairs deprive him of the Pleasures of Gallantry. He was for ever engag'd in some Amour: one Desire no sooner sicken'd, than another kindled in his Soul. But of all that had the power to charm him, none ever maintain'd a more absolute Dominion, than Madam *de Montespan;*[6] and if it was not so lasting as that of the celebrated *Maintenon,*[7] yet for the time it held, it was as strong. In the House, and under the care of this great Lady, did the lovely *Lasselia* receive her Education; who being her Neice, and extreamly belov'd by her, 'tis not to be doubted but that she had all those Advantages and Improvements, which are necessary to accomplish a Maid of Quality for Conversations such as were suitable to her Character.

The Mistresses of Kings are not consider'd in the same view with those of private Men: the Interest every one had in making their Court to Madam *de Montespan,* and the perpetual resort of the best Company to her House, gave our *Lasselia,* as she grew up, Opportunities of improving herself, which she could have found in no other place: and those Advantages, join'd to a natural Genius of her own, much more sublime than is ordinarily observed in Persons of her Sex, especially at such an Age, made her Behaviour surprizing to those of riper Years; grey Hairs would listen to her Talk with pleasure, the Delicacy of her Notions was such, that the Wisest would acknowledge themselves edify'd by her Conversation——But if the grave Part of the World were charm'd with her Wit and Discretion, the Young and Gay were infinitely more so with her Beauty; which tho it was not of that dazling kind which strikes the Eye at first looking on it with Desire and Wonder, yet it was such as seldom fail'd of captivating Hearts the most averse to Love. Her Features were perfectly regular, her Eyes had an uncommon Vivacity in them, mix'd with a

Sweetness, which spoke the Temper of her Soul; her Mein was gracefully easy, and her Shape the most exquisite that could be: in fine, her Charms encreas'd by being often seen, every View discover'd something new to be admir'd; and tho they were of that sort which more properly may be said to persuade, than command Adoration, yet they persuaded it in such a manner, that no Mortal was able to resist their Force——And, indeed, when Passion enters the Soul by such gentle and unperceiv'd Degrees, it generally takes a surer hold, and is with much less ease extirpated, than when it rushes all at once upon us, and boldly tells us that we must obey.

Lasselia being such, and infinitely more agreeable than I have power to represent her, 'tis easy to believe she was not without a very great Number of Adorers: Both her Parents being dead, Madam *de Montespan* was never at rest for the Sollicitations of those whom the Perfections of her beautiful Neice had attracted to desire her in Marriage: but that Lady having Affairs enough of her own to manage, troubled not herself much about it; and had *Lasselia* been inclinable to alter her Condition, whether to her Advantage or not, 'tis probable the other, in spite of the Kindness she had for her, would not have taken much pains either to have forwarded or prevented it.

The young, and as yet insensible[8] Subject of this little History, thought herself happy in this Disposition of her Aunt, which gave her so much the liberty of acting as she pleas'd; for finding in herself rather an Aversion to Marriage, than any Inclination to it, nothing could have been so shocking to the Humility and Sweetness of her Disposition, as to have found herself oblig'd, either to have yielded to enter into a State, which, in the Humour she was at present, must have made her wretched; or, by refusing, incur the Displeasure of a Lady, who she consider'd as a Parent, and for whom she had the greatest Esteem, and tenderest Regard.

Thus charming, and uncharm'd, did she pass her Days in the most perfect Tranquillity that cou'd be; no austere Parent, or Guardian, to over-awe Aversion, and force her to receive with Smiles the Man she hated——No Hopes, no Fears, Suspence, Perplexity, nor racking Jealousies, disturb'd her Peace of Mind——she knew no Wish beyond what she enjoy'd——and if she thought of Love at all, it was but to wonder at the Influence she saw it have on others. Among the Numbers that address'd her, there was not one whose *Absence* cou'd give her a moment's Pain, tho' several whose *Presence* pleas'd; but then it was only such a kind of Pleasure as might have flow'd from the Conversation of one of her own Sex, equally qualified with good Sense and Complaisance——a cold Respect, or, at most, a bare liking of their Company, was all that the most favour'd could boast of from her; nor did she once imagine she should ever be brought to entertain any other Notions of that uneasy Passion, than what she was at present possest of——that it was all *Chimera;*[9] and that those who seem'd most fatally sway'd by it, had only so long *affected* to be mad, that at last they grew so in *Reality.*

'Tis possible, indeed, she never might have chang'd her Sentiments, had she continued in *Paris,* where she had already seen every body worthy her Consideration, without confessing herself the least susceptible of what so many had endeavoured to inspire: But an unexpected Turn happening in her Affairs, brought her to a different Scene of Observation, and convinc'd her how little, in spite of her fine Sense, she knew the true Disposition of her own Heart.

The King coming one day to visit Madam *de Montespan,* and hearing she was laid down to Repose, contented himself with passing an Hour or two in Talk with her fair Neice, designing no more than to divert himself till the other shou'd awake; but he was so infinitely pleas'd and surpriz'd with the Charms of her Conversation, having never till that time had the Opportunity of entertaining her alone, that he cou'd have wish'd a longer Continuance of it.

He was but just beginning to let her know the Satisfaction this Interview had given him, when he was prevented from saying more by the coming of Madam *de Montespan.* 'Tis probable her Presence never had been so unwelcome before, and he testified the Chagrin he conceiv'd at it, by a tender Pressure of the young *Lasselia*'s Hand, as she withdrew, telling him she left his Majesty to a Conversation more worthy of entertaining him. As artless as she was, and as indifferent an Opinion as she had of Love, she easily perceiv'd she had inspir'd him with that Desire which bears the Name of it, and was so far from being proud of her Power, that it gave her a very great Uneasiness; she foresaw a world of Difficulties would attend the Conquest of this Royal Slave, and heartily wish'd that what he had said to her, might prove to be only the Effect of an unmeaning Gallantry, and forgot as soon as spoke. But, alas! her Charms had made a much deeper Impression on the Heart of this amorous Monarch, than she desired they should; the very next Day confirm'd her Knowledge of it—Happening to meet her in a Gallery as she was passing thro' to visit some Ladies in the Palace, he stopp'd her, and made so passionate a Declaration to her, that she stood in need of all her Wit to answer him in Terms which shou'd neither affront the Offers he made, nor encourage him to repeat them: But tho' her Replies to all he said, were full of Respect and Gratitude for the Consideration he seem'd to have of her, yet she maintain'd that cool Reserve, that Majesty of Modesty, which all Women, tho' in the lowest Rank of Life, owe so much to themselves to wear even to the highest, when their Virtue is assaulted; that it might have dash'd a Lover less accustomed to Success. But he was so well acquainted with the Ambition that most Women have of being the Favourite of a King, that he consider'd her Refusals only as the Result of what she might fear from the Indignation of her Aunt Madam *de Montespan,* and therefore sent *Monsieur le Brosse,*[10] one who at that time was Gentleman of his Bed-Chamber, to let her know, That, if she pleased, she had it in her power to be greater than the Person she at present had a Dependance on, and to make her an Offer of a very fine Castle near the River *Sein* for her residence. *Lasselia* was more concern'd than can be well express'd when this Message was deliver'd to her, and conjur'd him that brought it to return some Answer, in what manner she did not care, so it were such as would cut off all room to believe she ever could be prevail'd on to do any thing which might deserve such Bounties——Let the King, *said she,* think me imprudent, or unwise, his Opinion, nay, his Indignation, cannot give me more Chagrin, than does his Affection. It was in vain that the *Confidante* represented to her the Advantages there were in being Mistress to a King, she was not to be mov'd, nor had Grandeur any Charms when it was to be purchas'd at a Rate so dear as loss of Virtue: and he found himself oblig'd to return without being able to gain any thing from her, which might make his Master satisfy'd with his Negotiation.

But all this could not pass without the Observation of Madam *de Montespan;* she had taken notice in what manner the King had look'd, when he took leave of her Neice that Day she had entertain'd him in her Absence——She had her Spies which had inform'd her of his talking to her in the Gallery——and the coming of *le Brosse* to her House, and the private Conversation they had together, sufficiently confirm'd her, she had a Rival in her Neice, and fir'd her jealous Soul with an inexpressible Indignation——She upbraided the innocent *Lasselia* with Falshood and Ingratitude, and vow'd a Vengeance suitable to the Cause; and it was to no purpose for a long time, that the other endeavour'd to clear herself from these Aspersions. Rage is always deaf. This Misfortune, as it was unforeseen, was the more terrible to be borne; nor is it to be wonder'd at, that she should be prodigiously alarm'd at what so nearly touch'd her Interest, and was so shocking to her Pride, to find the Power she had so long maintain'd over the Heart of one of the greatest Monarchs in the World, in such an imminent danger of being near an end; and to owe her Downfall to one of her own House, of her own Blood, and one who she herself had taken care to adorn with all those Accomplishments which had attracted Admiration, was such an Aggravation to her Discontent, as Words would but poorly represent.

All the Assurances that *Lasselia* gave her, that she would die rather than yield to injure her in the least, and the Detestation she express'd at the thoughts of such an Action, was not sufficient to pacify her——She could scarce believe there was a Possibility of for ever resisting the Addresses of a Monarch so every way agreeable, as all that knew him confess'd him to be——But if there were, the *Attempt* was enough; her haughty Soul could ill endure the sight of one who was thought more lovely than herself, and who had it in her Power to make her unhappy, if she pleas'd——But how to get rid of her, she could not tell; if she put her out of her House, she consider'd, that it would but give her the more opportunity of being seen by the King, and receiving Proofs of his Passion; which, while she continu'd with her, he had still too much Respect publickly to avow. While she was in this Dilemma, the generous *Lasselia* perceiving her Discontent, and very much disquieted herself at the continued Sollicitations of a Monarch, whose Passion for many Reasons was no way pleasing to her, thought of a way to ease at once both her own and her Aunt's Uneasiness: And, desiring leave to wait on her in her Chamber, (for the other, of late, not well able to brook her Presence, had deny'd her that Privilege) approach'd her with these Words: Madam, *said she,* as I am the innocent Cause of your Chagrin, I come now to implore your Permission, to ease you of the sight of a Person who I am very sensible you no longer can behold with Satisfaction——The many Favours I have receiv'd in your House, would make me quit it with the utmost Concern: but when I consider, that your Goodness in suffering my continuance in it, renders you uneasy, I can do no less, in Gratitude, than remove——I entreat therefore, *added she, after a little Pause,* that I may depart: and since I have offended, though against my Will, the only thing I can do to contribute to your Peace, is, to take away the Cause; and by this *voluntary* Doom I pass on myself, may have hope you will pardon a Crime which is *involuntary.* And where, *cry'd Madam* de Montespan *hastily, (imagining perhaps her Intentions were very different from what they were)* where would you go? Far enough, *reply'd the other,* from any Place that may give you Apprehensions that I mean any otherwise than to make you easy——You know I had a very great Intimacy with Madamoiselle *Valier,*[11] she is now retir'd into the Country with her Husband, and I only stay for your Permission to go to her; she will be glad of my Company, and I can tarry there till those slight Impressions I have made on a Heart which ought only to be yours, are erased—I will not return till your Commands shall call me—or, if you please, my Banishment from you, and *Paris,* shall be eternal.

How! *Lasselia, interrupted her Aunt, (with an Air which at once express'd Astonishment and Joy)* are you in earnest? Can you for no other Motive than my Repose, be content to bury any part of your Time in a Solitude so remote from all those Gaieties your Youth has been accustom'd to? Not only Part, *resum'd she,* but All—Nay, my very Life, to do you Service; and to convince you how little Share I have had in contributing to disturb you. 'Tis kind indeed, *said Madam* de Montespan, and I must confess you generous and grateful, beyond my Expectations; but I should give you but small reason to have the same Opinion of me, should I suffer you to do what you have offer'd——No, *pursued she with a Sigh,* I never will be outdone in Good-nature, you shall still stay with me; tho your fatal Beauty, like a Basilisk,[12] murders my Quiet, and destroys my Hopes, we will not part——I am now convinc'd of your Sincerity; and till some Change in your Affairs makes it your Interest to leave me, I will run all Hazards rather than turn you hence. The Voice with which she pronounc'd these Words, made the discerning *Lasselia* easily perceive she wish'd not as she said; and repeating her Request, and assuring her with a great deal of Truth, that she desir'd nothing more than to be remov'd from the Persecutions she was every Day liable to from those Emissaries the King had employ'd, won her to afford a well-pleas'd Assent. After having concluded on her going, they began to think that Distance would be so far from a Protection from those Disturbances she would avoid, that being in any other House than that of Madam *de Montespan,* would rather give an Opportunity for them; they both determin'd that the Place of her Retirement should be kept a Secret, and to that end a Coach, and only one Servant to attend it, was order'd to be got ready at Midnight; and when all the Family were drown'd in Sleep, the willing Exile began her Journey, with this Satisfaction in her own Mind, that she eas'd another's of a Load of Care.

It was but to *Collumiers,* a small Village about seven Leagues from *Paris,*[13] that she went, and she reached there a little after Day-break. Madamoiselle *de Valier,* and her Husband, receiv'd her with all the Demonstrations of Joy imaginable, tho' infinitely surpriz'd at so unexpected a Visit: She was perfectly well acquainted with their Secrecy and Discretion, and therefore made no Scruple of revealing the Cause which had induc'd her to come in that manner: and if before they had a very tender regard for her, it was now prodigiously encreased by their Admiration of her Virtue.

She liv'd with them for some time in all the Contentments imaginable——She partook in all the rural Diversions of the Place; and having her mind once more at ease, made one in all the little Assemblies that were form'd by the Gentry thereabouts. In spite of the distance from any great City, she found no want of Company; the Conversation of Madamoiselle *de Valier* was very engaging at home; and whenever she had an Inclination to go abroad, the House of *Monsieur de l'Amye*[14] was not above a Bow-shot off; there she was always certain to meet good Company: for that Gentleman having been gone some time to *Paris,* in order to settle some Affairs, and take possession of an Estate lately left him by his Father; his Wife endeavour'd to compensate for his Absence, by making Entertainments for all those who had any pretence to Wit, of which she was a great Admirer——This Lady grew exceeding fond of *Lasselia* in a short time, nor was the other behind-hand in Acknowledgments for the Kindness she receiv'd from her—Thus every thing was easy, every thing was gay at *Collumiers,* while the still discontented *Montespan* languish'd at *Paris* in continual Disquiets, and restless Perplexities; she found the Absence of her Neice had added but little to her Endeavours of retrieving the estrang'd Affections of the inconstant King—He was all Fury when first the News was brought him that *Lasselia* had left the Town, and appear'd dissatisfied that her Aunt pretended Ignorance of the Cause—This Disgust, by little and little, encreasing, and heighten'd by her Jealousies, which she had not always Prudence enough to conceal, at last converted into a mortal Hatred; and this great Favourite saw herself reduc'd to a Condition pityable by those who envy'd her before: so uncertain is a Happiness founded on Passion, and depending on the still wavering, ever-changing Vows of faithless Man!

The Felicity that *Lasselia* all this while enjoy'd, was of another, and more durable Nature than that which Love, even at the best, affords; her Pleasures were unmix'd and pure, nor did she so much as dream there was a Day of Woe in store, which shou'd make her in vain look back, and wish for past Tranquillity: But now the time was come, when her Indifference and boasted Peace of Mind, were to be no more: Happening to be at Madam *de l'Amye*'s at *Ombre*[15] one Evening, accompany'd by Monsieur *de Valier,* and his Lady, their Diversion was on a sudden interrupted by a Servant running hastily into the Room, telling them his Master and two other Gentlemen were alited at the Gate. 'Tis not to be doubted but that the Cards were immediately thrown aside, and every body rose to receive them. The Welcome which Madam *de l'Amye* gave her long absent Husband, was such as was suitable to his great Merit, and long Absence; and the Returns he made, apologiz'd[16] for the most violent Transport she cou'd have express'd: but these mutual Tendernesses were but of a short Continuance; the Husband after having saluted all those whom he found in Company with his Wife, with all the Complaisance and Gaiety imaginable, just as he came to *Lasselia,* three Drops of Blood[17] fell from his Nose, which stain'd a white Handkerchief she happen'd to have in her Hand.

This Accident occasion'd a good deal of pleasant Raillery; Monsieur *de*

Valier told him, that had he been unmarried, this would have pass'd for an Omen of a future Union between him and the young Lady. Madamoiselle his Wife, and the two Gentlemen who had accompanied *de l'Amye,* made themselves merry for a good while on this occasion; but the Jest was not so agreeable to Madamoiselle *de l'Amye* as they, perhaps, imagined; being naturally pretty much addicted to Jealousy, these kind of Discourses gave her an Uneasiness which she was not able to disguise. Her Looks confess'd it, and her whole Behaviour was in a moment so alter'd, that not a Person in the Company but perceiv'd it, and guess'd at the Cause. *De Valier* having been but a late Acquaintance, and till now entirely ignorant of her Temper, was heartily vexed at what he had said, and endeavour'd, by a thousand Compliments, to restore her to her former Good-Humour; but the Poison had too great an Influence to be easily expell'd, she knew her Husband to be of a Disposition amorous enough, and the Charms of *Lasselia* were too prevailing, not to make her think there was a Probability, that what had been spoke in *Raillery,* might one Day prove too true in *Earnest,* she fell into so deep a *Resvery,*[18] and appear'd so much dissatisfy'd when any thing was offer'd to rouze her from it, that Monsieur and Madamoiselle *de Valier* thought it high time to take leave of her. *Lasselia* being only introduc'd by them, cou'd not do it without the Proposal being first made by them, but was extreamly glad of the Motion, and from that moment resolv'd never to make a Visit there again.

When they came home, nothing was talk'd of but the *Foibless*[19] of Madam, who had expos'd her Ill-humour for so trivial a Cause. Madamoiselle *de Valier* laugh'd heartily at it, but *Lasselia* had Reflections more grave; she was a little inclin'd to Superstition, and cou'd not forbear thinking the bleeding of *de l'Amye,* just as he approach'd her, was a Presage of something extraordinary: Besides, she imagin'd something within her bade her beware, nor trust her Eyes to gaze on this dangerous Charmer. The Disorder she was in when he first enter'd the Room, wou'd have been visible to the Company, had any of them been at leisure to regard it; and the Flutter which still continued on her Spirits, confirm'd her, that the sight of him had wrought an Effect on her she had never felt before: But as she was Mistress of a vast deal of fine Reasoning, she exerted it all in examining from what Source these Disorders proceeded; loth she was to think she was falling into a Passion she had so long ridicul'd——and lother to imagine it was for a Man for whom it was neither consistent with Virtue, nor Discretion, to indulge it——Is it impossible, *said she to herself,* that the seeing a Person so every way agreeable as *de l'Amye* cou'd give me Shocks such as, one wou'd think, cou'd only be inflicted by the Appearance of some horrid Spectre, some frightful Enemy to Nature!—

—What is there either in his Person or Behaviour to terrify?——Is not all about him lovely and engaging?——Oh! yes (*cry'd she after a little Pause*) I ne'er before beheld a Form so perfectly compleat, a Shape so exquisite, Eyes so bewitching, an Air so soft, so charming, and, I too well remember, the fond Endearments he paid to Madam, first struck my Soul with that chill Horror, which ever since remains. Had he been in the same Circumstances with his two Companions, and receiv'd no other Welcome from that happy Woman, it would have been with Satisfaction alone I shou'd have regarded him——But, oh! (*continu'd she, bursting into Tears, which it was impossible for her to restrain*) he is marry'd, and 'tis Madam *de l'Amye* only who can look on him without Confusion, such as I endure.

By these kind of Arguments she was at last convinc'd, how fatal an Enemy to Repose, the sight of an Object too amiable may prove; but tho she resolv'd not to give way to an Impression so pernicious, she found it impossible to erase it; she was still thinking how happy she might have been if *de l'Amye* were unmarried, and how willingly she cou'd submit to be a Wife, if just such another Man were to be found. In this manner would she sooth Imagination for a while; but then a sudden return of those uneasy Tremblings which, at first sight of him, possess'd her, would put an end to those pleasing Amusements, and she wou'd start like one in a Frenzy, and cry out, Oh! it was not for nothing that those ominous Drops of Blood fell from him on my Handkerchief!——It was not for nothing I was seiz'd with such an unusual Horror!——Nor is it in vain that my Soul shrinks, and seems to dread a second Interview!——They are all, I fear, too sure Predictions of some fatal Consequence. Then, when she had a little yielded to these disturb'd Emotions, as if asham'd of the Weakness she had been guilty of, wou'd she summon up all her Resolution, and endeavour to overcome those Terrors. Yet what, (*resum'd she*) what can happen worthy of my Fears!——What Power has one, so much a Stranger as *de l'Amye,* to injure me?——Perhaps I ne'er may see him more; or if I shou'd, where wou'd be the Danger? Thus did she torment herself when ever she was alone; and, in Company, appear'd the most alter'd in her Behaviour that ever was: all Diversions grew tasteless to her, and those Gaieties of Conversation which, in her Days of Indifference, she had the greatest Relish for, were now stripp'd of all their *Agreeable,* and became rather *teazing,*[20] than any way *delightful.* Nor is this at all to be wonder'd at; whoever has known any thing of Love, will easily confess, that that Passion brings with it a consequential Train of Images, sufficient to fill the most extensive Soul, and too strong to suffer any Intermixture of Opposers.

This Change of Humour was too visible, not to be taken notice of by all that knew her: Madamoiselle *de Valier* was extremely troubled at it, and, imagining it proceeded from her living in a Retirement she had not been accustom'd to, was fearful she was falling into a Melancholy, which might be dangerous; and therefore endeavour'd to divert her by all the Means her Good-humour and Friendship cou'd invent. The other, tho Company was grown painful, and Solitude the only thing she coveted, yet cou'd not be so rude and disobliging as to refuse the kind Invitations made her, on purpose to drive away those Vapours with which she seem'd to be overwhelm'd.

One of those Scenes of Gaiety, to which the Wife of *Valier* wou'd needs oblige *Lasselia* to go, was to a Wedding which was to be solemniz'd at the House of a Relation of her's, some Miles distant from that in which they liv'd——The Nuptials were celebrated with a great deal of Magnificence, all the Nobility and Gentry of the Country, for many Leagues round, being invited: Amongst the Number were Monsieur and Madam *de l'Amye.* This was the second Time *Lasselia* had ever seen him; but if she was not altogether so painfully alarm'd as at the first, she felt enough to make her know she was agitated with Emotions, the Catastrophe of which she had good cause to dread. She cou'd not forbear, however, indulging the sweet Anxiety his *Presence* gave, tho certain to condemn herself for it in his *Absence:* She examin'd each particular Charm which shone about his Form—She listen'd to every Word he spoke—Stretch'd wide each Faculty of her Soul, to take the whole of his Perfections in, till she became quite ravish'd in Contemplation——

They happen'd to dance together; and the easy and graceful Manner in which he entreated her to be his Partner, his fine Address, and the Sprightliness of Conversation with which he entertain'd her, added to that Admiration she before had been but too sensibly touch'd with for him.

After this she had frequent Opportunities of seeing him; Madam *de l'Amye* and *de Valier* having, at this Wedding, renew'd that Intimacy which they formerly had together, and which that little Pique Monsieur *de Valier*'s Words occasion'd, had for a time suspended, the two Families were seldom asunder—*Lasselia* was always one among them, nor did she any longer seem desirous of Solitude: The Pleasure she took in the Company of *de l'Amye* was too great to be resisted, nor did she any more make herself uneasy at those Shocks which, every now and then, endeavour'd to check the Transports she indulg'd—She thought it enough that she restrain'd her Wishes within the Bounds of Modesty; and perceiving not the least reason to imagine, by his Behaviour, that he would ever tempt her to transgress them, believ'd she might, without a Crime, indulge herself in those Felicities which at present appear'd so innocent——Thus borne away with a Tide of Delight, which still encreas'd from a nearer Conversation with him, all the Warnings of her good Genius were hush'd, and her whole Soul was overwhelm'd with Passion——Hence follow'd wild Desires!——Tumultuous Emotions!——The God of Love exerted his utmost Force, and prov'd how impossible it is, when once a Heart has given him Entrance, ever to expel him thence——But this she was not yet acquainted with, nor knew the Danger she was in; and tho the greatest Security she cou'd have for her Honour, was the Insensibility *de l'Amye* seem'd to have of her Charms, yet she cou'd not forbear wishing he were otherwise—And would frequently sooth Imagination with a Belief he lov'd her: and in giving way to these destructive Tendernesses, *Fancy* took the Part of *Passion,* and in Dreams, wou'd represent him to her, dissolving, melting in amorous Languishments—Nor were her *sleeping* Thoughts the only ones that err'd this way; *waking,* the Charmer was ever in her View; she talk'd to him, form'd Answers such as 'twas probable he might in reality have made, had he been present——Nay, wrap'd in the extatick Contemplation, went so far sometimes (as she afterwards confess'd) as to kiss, embrace, and possess, in *Idea,* a thousand nameless Joys, which Love too soon inspires a Notion of: but these Excesses we'll suppose she permitted only, when she found there was a Necessity by chearing her languid Spirits with an *imaginary Bliss,* to preserve her from falling into a *real Despair:* 'tis certain that at her guarded Hours, Honour was her chiefest Aim; nor wou'd she have wish'd to have been belov'd by *de l'Amye,* had she not thought herself sure of continuing Mistress of her Resolution——But, alas! how little do they know the Hazard they run, who depend on their own Strength alone for Protection. Love is a subtle, and a watchful Deceiver, and directs the Votary he designs to bless, to make the Attack when the *Fair* is least capable of Resistance.

It was in one of those longing, wishing Moments, already mentioned, when the amorous *Lasselia* extended at her length on a fine grassy Bank, canopy'd o'er with shading Jessamins, and spreading Vines, was told a Messenger waited with a Letter, which, by no means, he wou'd deliver into any hand but her own: She was unwilling to quit the sweet Retirement she was in, and carelessly order'd the Person shou'd come to her, imagining it was some body sent from Madam *de Montespan,* and gave herself but little Concern what the Mandate might contain: But when she received it from the Messenger, who seem'd to be a Country-Fellow, and knew the Hand to be *de l'Amye*'s, which she had often seen before in Songs and little Pieces of Poetry; what Tongue can express the Surprize she was in!—She could not imagine on what occasion he shou'd write to her, and was once or twice about to return it unopened to the Hand that brought it; but her ill Fate repell'd those

Dictates of her Guardian Angel, and confus'd and trembling, now blushing with Shame, then pale with Fear, she broke the fatal Seal, and read these Lines.

To the Divine *LASSELIA.*

Heaven, Love, and the more powerful Charms of the adorable Lasselia, *are not to be withstood! long have I struggled with a Passion which is not the less unvanquishable, because it is hopeless; but, like Oil pour'd on Flames, all my Endeavours serve but to make the aspiring Blaze more violent, and now 'tis grown as impossible to be conceal'd, as it is to be overcome——I burn, consume, and die, in inward Agonies——Pardon this Declaration——the World, alas!——the prying, judging World——will soon discover the Secret in my alter'd Looks; but a Day more, perhaps, and I shou'd have been reported* Lasselia*'s Slave, before* Lasselia*'s self had known it——and I wou'd not, methinks, have you, who caus'd, the* last *to pity what I feel——I am persuaded there is a Stock of Mercy in your Soul, that, whether you will or no, will induce you to* compassionate *a Despair which the wretched Circumstance I am in forbids me to hope you will relieve——But whatever Sentence you are pleased to inflict on me, let me from your own Mouth receive it, and I shall never repent that I am ordain'd,* Your Everlasting Adorer,

De l'Amye.

It wou'd have been impossible for *Lasselia,* had she endeavoured it, to conceal the swift Vicissitudes of her rolling Thoughts while reading; alternate Joy and Shame, Surprize and Fear, and sometimes a Start of virtuous Pride and Indignation, sparkled in her Eyes——a thousand different Passions succeeded one another in their turns—all too fierce to be restrain'd, and too sudden to admit Disguise. But, alas! she took no care to do it; she suspected not that she had a dangerous Observer in the Person who deliver'd her the Letter; nor 'tis possible, in the Confusion she was in, remember'd any body was near her——Again she attempted to read over the dear surprizing Lines, but had not power; the strange Disorder of her fluttering Heart, depriving the Blood of its usual Circulation, all her Limbs forgot their Function, and she sunk fainting on the Bank, in much the same Posture she was in before she had rais'd herself a little to take the Letter. How much wou'd such a Sight have transported *de l'Amye!*—How much did it transport him! for it was no other than himself, who, disguis'd in the Habit of a *Rustick,* had been his own Messenger, and was Witness of all the different Agitations his Declaration had occasion'd——Encourag'd by them, and 'tis probable by some Glances he had before observed—and prompted by his own violent Desires, which, from the first Moment he beheld her, had taken possession of his Soul; all those little Fears, and distant Awe, which generally accompany *Love* in its beginning, were no more. He threw off his upper Garment, and a black Peruke[21] which had serv'd him as a Disguise, and flinging himself down by her, with a thousand Kisses and Embraces, at once restor'd her to that Sense she had so lately lost, and shew'd her the Deceit he had been guilty of—It was in vain she struggled to rise—in vain that she endeavour'd to repel the soft Endearments of his Lips and Arms; her Eyes confess'd the unwilling Transport of her Soul, and told him all he wish'd to ask: nor was he scrupulous of letting her know how well he was acquainted with his Happiness——he made her sensible of it by a thousand Liberties, which a Man who had not been certain of Forgiveness, wou'd not have dared to take——She had too much Frankness in her Nature, and had been too little accustomed to Artifice, to be able to disguise her Sentiments in a Juncture like this——*Surprize* at first had depriv'd her of all those necessary Cautions she wou'd else have made use of; and now *Love!* transported, raptur'd *Love!* wou'd not suffer her to have recourse to them——Trembling and panting, 'twixt Desire and Fear, at last she lay resistless in his Arms, with faultering Accents confess'd a mutual Ardour; and if he did not obtain the highest Favour she cou'd grant, he had too much to boast of, to fear she cou'd deny him any thing; and 'tis probable that he had not left her without the utmost Gratification of his Wishes, had he not been apprehensive of a Discovery either from Madam *de Valier,* or some of the Family, whom the Coolness of the Evening might invite to that Place, and which was not a great distance from the House——He wou'd not part, however, till he had engag'd a Promise from her to make him fully blest the next Opportunity should offer; which, as he told her, was his Fault, if not contriv'd with a Speed suitable to the Impatience of the Love he profess'd.

I doubt not but this early Condescension in *Lasselia,* will be of so great Prejudice to her Character, that it will take off the Pity which is really due to the Misfortunes it brought on her; and I have nothing to alledge in her Behalf, but that the long Suppression of a Passion which she had always consider'd as fruitless, now on a sudden let loose, was beyond the Power of Reason to restrain——To add to this, tho' both, I am afraid, will seem too weak to excuse her, never was Man so form'd to charm as *de l'Amye.* I have heard several of his own Sex who know him, aver they never saw any thing so lovely, an Air so noble, so majestick, and withal so soft and tender—Eyes so bewitching——a Shape so excellent——such a Harmony of Parts—such an agreeable Regularity thoughout the whole—Then for his Wit and Conversation, it was not to be equall'd——he was so perfect a Master in the Art of Persuasion, that whoever would resolve on any thing, must be sure not to hear him plead against it; so impossible was it to dissent from him in Argument, or continue in any Opinion he seem'd to disapprove——One of the many Letters which pass'd between him and *Lasselia,* being found among some other Papers since both their Deaths, may give some little *Idea* of what he was; which, tho it was writ by a Woman in Love to Madness, and one who had abandon'd all things for her Passion, has been acknowledged by those of cooler Sentiments, and consequently better capable of judging, to be no more than what Perfections, such as his, might justify.

LASSELIA to her most Dear, most
Lov'd, and most Ador'd *de l'Amye.*

You command me to tell you, my Dear, my first, my only, my everlasting Love! in what manner I pass my Hours in your Absence—'tis a Question I know not how to answer——for, methinks, I am never absent from you—I have your Image ever in my View——your Voice always in my Ears——so strongly does Imagination bless me, that believing you indeed are present, I stretch my Arms to clasp the dear Illusion, and only then am undeceived, when back they come, and miss the warm Embrace——O! to what an elevated Height does Love, like mine, transport the Soul! a thousand times I have ask'd myself which of your Charms had most the Power to move me——which of my Senses receiv'd the noblest Pleasure——and in Idea *travelled through all the mazy Wonders of your Mind and Person, but never cou'd decide the mighty Contest——all were alike enchanting!—all equally transporting—Last Night employing my fond Thoughts in their usual Contempation, a Standish*[22] *happening to be on the Table, I took up the Pen, which, without the Aid of any Muse to guide it, run into these Lines,*[23] *which I have ventur'd to call*

The Impossibility; or, the Combat
of the SENSES.

When on thy Form *I feast my ravish'd Eye!*
I think no *Bliss cou'd Want of Sight supply;*
Or, when the Musick of thy Voice *I hear,*
My soul is all collected in my Ear!
What envious Darkness wou'd in vain deny,
Th' attentive *Faculty does well supply:*
Thy Charms are such, each can make known the rest,
And all *by* one *is to the Sense exprest;*
Whither thou speak'st *in* Looks, *or* smil'st *in* Words,

The present *Joy no higher Wish affords;*
But when——O! who Infinity can speak!
Imagination *owns itself too weak,*
When with fond circling Grasp my straining Arms
Press, to my Bosom, thy whole Heav'n of Charms!
When all! at once! *the thousand Ways I prove,*
Which make, indeed, Divinity *in* Love!
My ravish'd Heart tumultuous Pleasure swells,
Nor Fear, nor Shame, th' unruly Rapture quells;
With wild Delight each hurry'd Sense alarm'd,
'Tis Insolence to say which most *is charm'd:*
Each Look, each Word, each Touch, each melting Kiss,
Gives raging Extasy!——distracting Bliss!
Amidst that Sea of Wonders Thought *is lost,*
My Soul no more can nice Distinction *boast;*
Excess of Transport does itself destroy,
And Life flies trembling from th' o'erpouring Joy.

Let the kind Meaning excuse the bad Poetry and Deficiency of Expression: For, O! I own no Words can reach thy Worth—there are two Things in Nature *which never can be described by* Art; *and they are, that Profusion of Perfections thou art stor'd with, and my Adoration of them——but if thou woud'st guess at the latter, hasten to my Arms, for 'tis only there thou canst have any just Notion how much——how truly thou art Master of the Soul of thy*

Ever-Passionate, Ever-Tender, Ever-Faithful
LASSELIA.

But, to return: The unthinking Fair was no sooner left alone, and had leisure to reflect on what the Hurry of her Spirits had before prevented her from doing, than she reproach'd herself for suffering the Secret of her Soul to be so easily discover'd by him from whom she ought most to have conceal'd it——But, alas! she now had gone too far in the fatal Labyrinth of heedless Passion, to know how to retreat; and the Arguments he had made use of to persuade her it was no Crime to bless a Love so perfect as his, had the same Effect they ordinarily work'd on all whom he endeavoured to bring to his Opinion; to make her think as he did—and the greatest Matter of Concern to her, was that she so *soon* had condescended—She fear'd the easy Attainment of his Wishes, wou'd, in a little time make her seem cheap in his Esteem—and such an Apprehension was a Dagger to her Soul; she resolv'd, therefore, that in spite of the Promise she had made him, to *delay* the Performance of it, and put him off till Time, Assiduity, and some further Proofs of his Sincerity, should render her yielding more the Effect of Gratitude than Inclination— This, 'tis possible, she might have *endeavoured;* tho', if we consider the little Government she had of her Passion, 'tis scarce to be believ'd she wou'd have been able to accomplish, if an unexpected Summons to *Paris* had not broke all her Measures, and left her no Choice but either to run immediately into the Arms of *de l'Amye,* or quit all Thoughts of him for ever——The very next Morning, after the Evening she had past some part of in the manner already described, she received a Letter from her Aunt, Madam *de Montespan;* the Contents of which were these.

TO *LASSELIA.*

If you left Paris, *as you pretend*[24] *you did, merely for the sake of my Repose, you will make no Difficulty in returning to it, when you shall know it is my Interest calls you——the unjust* King *has treated me in a manner I should disdain to acknowledge, were there not an absolute Necessity you shou'd know it—— I have either been betray'd by some I have put Confidence in, or my ill Genius has whisper'd him, that I have but deceived him in feigning an Ignorance to what Part of the Country you are retir'd——Since you left me, I have never receiv'd any Mark of his former Favour; and of late (what will not arbitrary Authority dare!) he has, even to my Face, avow'd his Passion——Last night he left me with Menaces, such as I too well know him not to dread, that I shou'd dearly repent my Attempt of eluding him by an Artifice too shallow not to be seen through—In fine, I perceive every day my Court decrease—I am no longer sollicited——no longer hurry'd with the Attendance of petitioning Courtiers——sure Marks of a declining Favourite——all that can re-establish me in my former Interest with him, is your Return——I can boldly demand a Support for my Ambition, when I consent to the Destruction of my Love, and to the death of my own Hopes bring a belov'd Rival to his Arms—Make haste, therefore, thou fatal Beauty! to* Paris, *to the sight of an adoring, impatient* Monarch; *a Monarch, who wants but Constancy to make him equal with the Angels——Haste, I say, to bless his Eyes——and by making him happy, in part retrieve the Injury you have, tho unwillingly, done the*

Unfortunate
MONTESPAN.

P. S. *Come, if possible, with the same Expedition as you went——I have sent this Moment to your Royal Lover, to acquaint him I have discover'd where you are, and that I expect you to-morrow——Delay it not, unless you wish to see my Ruin.*

Such a Command as this was as vexatious, as it was surprizing to the Person who receiv'd it—Had her Inclinations been in the very same Position as when she left *Paris,* she wou'd have been far from consenting to return to it, on the Terms propos'd; but as her Heart was now entirely taken up with the Thoughts of *de l'Amye,* to endure the Addresses of another, was detestable to her——*Love* gave this happy Favourite infinitely the Preference in her Esteem, over the greatest and most agreeable Monarch in the World—To be the Mistress of *de l'Amye,* tho in a Cottage, she look'd on as a Blessing superior to all the ambitious Views which tempted her in the Embraces of a *King;* but resolved, if possible, not only to find some Expedient utterly to escape what was her *Aversion,* but also to delay the Gratification of her *Wishes* till Time shou'd render them more excusable—To this end, she communicated Madam *de Montespan*'s Letter to Monsieur *de Valier* and his Wife, entreating their Advice, how she shou'd avoid a Danger which so imminently threaten'd her Virtue. The noble-minded Pair, little imagining that she had any other Reasons for refusing to return to *Paris,* than those which had oblig'd her to quit it, and altogether ignorant of what had pass'd between her and *de l'Amye,* applauded her Resolution; and told her, that they cou'd not enough extol her Bravery of Soul, who, to preserve her Honour, cou'd be blind and deaf to all the enchanting Charms of Power and Grandeur, and chuse rather to be bury'd in an *innocent Obscurity,* than shine the Envy of the World in *guilty Greatness.* These Encomiums were not perhaps so pleasing to *Lasselia* as they imagin'd; a Consciousness of not meriting what they said, embitter'd all the Sweets such Praises, if deserv'd, wou'd have bestow'd: therefore waving all that might remind her how really *Criminal* she was, while she appear'd all *Virtue,* she begg'd them to think of some Method by which she might evade the Commands of Madam *de Montespan,* and the Sollicitations of the *King.*

This was no small Difficulty to bring to pass, it was not to be doubted, since that Lady had been prevail'd upon to sacrifice her Love to her Ambition, so far as to become an Intercessor; but she wou'd proceed to compass what she aim'd at, by all imaginable Measures——It seem'd therefore an Impossibility that *Lasselia* cou'd be any more safe at *Collumiers,* than at *Paris;* but where she shou'd retire, or on whose Fidelity she cou'd depend for Concealment, was the Question: Neither Madamoiselle *de Valier,* nor Monsieur knew of any body on whom they dared depend in any Affair of so much Consequence, which, if divulg'd, or by any Accident discover'd, might involve the Persons concerned in it, in the Displeasure of a King, who was not of a Humour to pardon Indignities of this nature. *Lasselia* perceiving they were in a Pause, and uncertain what to advise her to, and knowing very well she must immediately resolve on something, spoke to them in this manner: Since (*said she*) the only Person on Earth, from whom I cou'd have expected Shelter from the King's Addresses, has been drawn to a Resolution to betray me to him, it will be in vain to hope that, by tarrying here, I can escape the Snares laid for me; Arbitrary Power can easily find Means to force me hence: I will therefore go where, I believe, I may promise myself an unknown, and therefore safe Retreat; and because I will not oblige either of you to the Constraint of an Untruth, for, doubtless, you will not pass unexamin'd, I will not acquaint you with the Place of my Retirement, till the Noise of my having left you is entirely over. These Words gave a good deal of Satisfaction to the Persons they were address'd to, being unwilling to be brought under the Displeasure of the King by detaining her, and more unwilling to yield her up a Victim to his unwarrantable Passion——They presently imagin'd it was to some *Monastery* she wou'd fly for Refuge, and commended her Discretion in concealing the Name of it; well knowing, that if it were discover'd, not even that holy Sanction would avail against the united Commands of the *King* and Madam *de Montespan,* and the very *Religious* themselves be scrupulous of entertaining a Person in opposition to their Power.

But I doubt not but the Reader will easily guess it was not to be a *Recluse* that *Lasselia* intended: however, she was willing enough to let Monsieur and Madamoiselle *de Valier* continue in their Opinion that it was so, and they all concluded that she should leave their House the next Night. She told them she would depart in the Habit of a *Pilgrim,* and for the first Night take up her Lodging at a common Inn, from which she knew how to get conveniency to be carry'd to the Place she design'd to go to; and for the better deceiving Madam *de Montespan,* Madamoiselle should write to her, taking no notice that she knew any thing of her having order'd *Lasselia*'s Return; but to acquaint her, that that young Lady had left *Collumiers* unknown to any body; and that both herself and Husband were in the greatest Consternation imaginable what was become of her, and for what Cause she had, in such a manner, quitted a Family, whose Care it had been to use her with all possible Respect. This Contrivance was applauded by all concern'd in it; and Madamoiselle immediately went about providing a *Pilgrim*'s Habit with the utmost Secrecy, and Caution, for not one of the Servants were to be trusted with it.

In the mean time, *Lasselia* had her Thoughts full of Confusion; it was to *de l'Amye* she had determin'd to go; his Arms were her intended Sanctuary, and his Love her Asylum; but how to let him know what had befallen her, was a Perplexity she knew not how to remove: To write to him, was an Impossibility, without having the Affair known to the whole Country; and, as if Fortune had a Design to contradict her Inclinations, he happen'd not to come to *de Valier's*. All Things being ready, and the Evening appointed for her Departure arriv'd, she grew almost distracted what Course she should take; her going was unavoidable, unless renouncing all she had said, and blasting her own secret Wishes, she could have contented herself to remain there till a second Mandate, back'd with Force, should have oblig'd her to return to *Paris.* And where to go she knew not, nor could think of any plausible Pretence whereby she might advertise *de l'Amye* of her Proceedings: The Distraction of her Mind show'd itself in her Countenance, she was ready to sink with Apprehension what might happen to her, wandring alone, a Stranger, and uncertain where she should find Shelter, even from the Weather——While Madamoiselle *de Valier* was helping to dress her like a *Pilgrim,* she trembled, and had scarce Strength to suffer any thing to be done; but this pass'd for the Trouble she was in, at being oblig'd to depart from them in a manner so odd; and, with much ado, she was at last equipt. The Care of Monsieur and his Lady had dispatch'd all the Servants, some one way, some another, that when the fair *Pilgrim* was to make her *Exit,* there was nobody in the House but them three. The Parting was extremely moving; Madamoiselle held her in her Arms for some time, without being able to let her go, while the other seem'd as unwilling to get loose, till Monsieur reminding them, that probably some of the Family might return, and disappoint all the Measures they had taken, they broke with mutual Tears from one another's Embrace. The Lady retir'd to her Closet, to pray for a good Event of this, as she thought, pious Fraud; and her Husband conducted the disguis'd Fair-One to the Road where she desir'd him to leave her, assuring him, she would write by the first Opportunity, to give notice *how* she was, tho not *where* she was.

The Reader's Imagination here must help me out, for Words wou'd be insufficient to represent what 'twas *Lasselia* endur'd, when left alone; all that one can think of Dread!—of Anxiety, was short of her enduring——She was naturally timorous; and having never been expos'd to any Dangers, now all at once to brave so many, was more than all the Resolution she had muster'd up could enable her. She accused *de l'Amye* of Ingratitude and Coldness, that he had not been at *de Valier's* these two Days——Oh! (*said she to herself*) had he lov'd with that Ardency as he pretended, a Sympathy of Souls would have brought him—By Intuition he would have known I was about to do something that requir'd his Aid——Is Love a Divinity, and does any Spark of it inform his breast, and not by some secret Impulse warn him, that his *Lasselia* has, for his sake, abandon'd herself to all that can be thought of Misery, and Horror? Thus did she upbraid the Passion that possess'd her, while wandring up and down the *Fields,* for the Fears she was in, wou'd not suffer her to keep the *Road*——The sight of any Passengers, though at a distance, terrify'd her beyond expression; she imagin'd that, if seen, she shou'd be known in spite of her Disguise, and her distracted Apprehension form'd a thousand Ideas of Dangers all frightful, and hideous to Nature!——The Darkness coming on, encreased them, and she would now have given all the World to have been in some Place of Shelter; but she was wholly unacquainted with the way to any Inn, and being stray'd a good distance from the Road, was hopeless of finding it. 'Tis probable, in her present Fears, she would have return'd to *de Valier*'s, had she known her way back: but that was also impossible; and as she had run herself into this Misfortune, there was nothing for her to do, but patiently to bear whatever might be the Consequence. It would be too tedious to repeat the Lamentations she made, or the various Turns of Anguish which the different Passions created in her Soul. So I shall only say, that when it grew quite dark, she withdrew to a little *Copse,* which she found in the middle of the Field; and there covering herself as well as she cou'd with her *Pilgrim*'s Weed, lay all Night on the Earth, no other Bed than a few fallen Leaves, nor Canopy, than the Skies. Hard Lodging for a young Lady bred in all the Delicacies of the most pompous and magnificent Court of *Europe!*

'Tis easy to believe she rested not much, her Griefs and Uneasinesses were of a nature too violent to admit the Influence of the God of Sleep, nor did the Dawn afford her any Consolation, she was still in the same wretched State; and after casting in her Mind a thousand various Projections, which all seem'd impossible to accomplish, she laid herself down again, quite stupid with her Griefs; resolving, as much as she had power of resolving on any thing, to rise no more.

But she had not continued long in this Lethargy of Thought, before she was rouz'd from it by a sudden and loud Noise of Horses, Hunting-Horns, and a great Cry of Dogs; they rush'd just by the Place she was in, and had not the Gentlemen been too eager on their Game to regard any thing else, she must needs have been discover'd by them, as they pass'd, in spite of her leafy Covert. The unexpected Sound made her start at first hearing; but lifting up her Head a little, as much as she had Courage, and perceiving what it was that had occasion'd it, she slunk down again, trembling for fear she shou'd be seen, and continu'd in that Posture for some time: at last, hearing nothing but the rustling of the Leaves blown to and fro by the Winds, she once more ventur'd to rise, and walk; not that she had any hope of mending her Condition, but to seek a Place more remote to die in. She had not gone many Paces from the *Copse,* which had been her Habitation that Night, before she saw a Man on Horseback, riding leisurely cross the Field just opposite to her——All the Terrors her confus'd Imagination had created, return'd with double Force at this Sight; and endeavouring to avoid him with too much Precipitation, her Feet happen'd to be entangled with some bushy Twigs that lay in the way, and down she fell. She wou'd have rose nimbly enough, but the same spriggy Substance which had thrown her, still hung about her, and all she cou'd do was insufficient to disengage herself, till the Gentleman, perceiving the Accident, alited from his Horse, and ran to her Assistance: But how shall I set forth, as it deserves, that vast Excess of insupportable, unutterable Joy! which rush'd at once into her Soul, when looking up, she saw in the Person she had *fled,* him whom to *meet* she had run so many Dangers; her dear, her ador'd *de l'Amye*— The swift Vicissitude from the Extreme of one Passion to another was too violent for her Weakness to sustain——it took away all power of Utterance, or of Motion.

Madamoiselle *de Valier* had so artificially disguis'd her, that till finding she was fainting away, he began to pull the things from her Face, in order to give her Air; he knew not to whom it was that Pity and Good-nature had engag'd him to do that good Office: But when the Face of *Lasselia* was discover'd, the same, or if possible, a greater degree of Transports than she had felt, were now his Turn to experience——both were too much lost in Rapture to express it by any other way than Kisses, Embraces, and all the fond Endearments of mutual Extasy——Words were too poor, too mean Acknowledgments of the unbounded Bliss of such a Meeting——nor cou'd they, for some Minutes, be able to relate to each other the means by which it came to pass, till Curiosity claiming a Share in his other Emotions, he contented himself to give a little Truce to the tumultuous Pleasure he enjoy'd in her Embraces, to ease his Wonder at seeing her in that Garb and Place; which she, endeavouring to recollect herself, as much as possible, oblig'd him in, by shewing him Madam *de Montespan*'s Letter, and acquainting him with the Reasons why she had left *Paris;* and since the House of *de Valier*—Such a discovery must have been an addition, if it cou'd have admitted of any, to the Passion he profest for her——to fly from the Embraces of a *King,* to lose for ever all the Advantages she might have expected from the Favour of so great a Lady as Madam *de Montespan;* and to endure such Terrors, such certain Hardships as had been her Portion the Night before, and might have continued on her till Death had put an end to them, had not Chance directed him that way, only for the uncertain Hopes of finding a safe Harbour in his Arms at last, was such a Proof of condescending Tenderness, of Love the most sublime, the most violent that ever was, that he confess'd it far surpass'd all possibility of a return, and grew even painful to a grateful, generous Heart, which, he said, had not the means to thank, as it deserv'd, such a profusive Waste of lavish Kindness——But *Lasselia* soon remov'd that Discontent, by assuring him she shou'd think herself more happy in the Conquest of his Heart, than in that of the whole World; and that all she entreated of him, shou'd be Constancy.

This little amorous Contest being over, she began gently to reproach him for the want of that Impatience, which, by herself, she knew was incident to Love. How cou'd you, (*said she*) after so many tender Declarations on your Side, and Condescensions on mine, have the Inhumanity to keep two long Days from the only Place where you cou'd expect to see me?—Had you been kind enough to have sought me at *de Valier*'s, what thousand Afflictions had you sav'd me——all the Terrors of this last cruel Night had been unfelt, and in their room I had been possest of Joys inconceivable—Bliss without a Name, and which is no where to be found but in the Presence of my ador'd *de l'Amye*. You do well, (*reply'd he, tenderly embracing her*) you do well, my Angel! by the divine Softness of your *last* Words, to make me Reparation for the injustice of your *former* ones.—O! did you know on what a Rack of high-rais'd Expectation I was kept, you would not blame, but pity me—to a Man in my Circumstances, Opportunities are scarce; nor cou'd I, in all that Age of Hours, which you call but two Days, find one which I cou'd hope wou'd bless me, till, mad with the Delay, I contriv'd a Hunting-Match, and invited *de Valier* to be Partaker of it, and at the same time entreated his Wife wou'd bear mine company at our House, till the Chase shou'd be over. I flatter'd myself with a Belief you wou'd discern my Meaning, and make some Pretence to stay at home, while I wou'd, unperceiv'd, have drop'd my Company, and stole unsuspected to that dear Bower where first I had the glorious Discovery of your tender Sentiments; but all these Hopes were dash'd, and I wonder how I surviv'd the killing News, or that at least my Countenance did not discover how nearly I was interested, when *de Valier*, at his coming this Morning, told me you had last Night left his House, unknown to all the Family; and that it was the greatest Mystery in Nature, on what Occasion, or to what Place, you were retir'd—The Force[25] I have done myself, since this Information, in putting on a constrain'd Good-Humour to him and the rest of the Company, can by nothing be made known to you, but by your own dear extensive Imagination: and I shall only tell you, that not able to endure it longer, I took the Advantage of their Eagerness to pursue a Stag just rouzed, and turn'd from them to indulge a Melancholy I believ'd I had but too just a ground for—I was resolving, under the pretence of travelling for Improvement, to put myself into some Disguise, and search the Country round, till I had found you—when Chance!—bless'd Chance! which from henceforward shall be my Deity, brought you to my Sight, and in a Moment chang'd the Hell of my Despair, to all the Heaven my Soul is capable of possessing.

A thousand Kisses, and strenuous Embraces, clos'd this Discourse; nor wou'd they ever have known when to have given over so delightful an Employment, but that a repeating Watch, which he happened to have in his Pocket, striking Eleven, reminded him that 'twas possible the Hunters might return, and that this was no fit Place to continue their amorous Entertainment; therefore, remounting his Horse, and taking her up behind him, who joyfully put herself into his Protection, he rid a quite contrary way to that he expected them to come, and stopping at an Inn, where he had some little Acquaintance, he recommended her to the People of the House, and charging them to take particular Care of her, without asking any Questions who, or what she was, forc'd himself to leave her, having first obtain'd a solemn Promise from her, that she would endeavour by Repose, to recover the Fatigue she had undergone, assuring her that he wou'd return before Night. She doubted not the Performance of his Promise, both in this and every thing else: *Love* is ever credulous, and inspires so good an Opinion of the darling Object, that it is not without great Difficulty the Heart which harbours it, can be brought to believe any thing to the prejudice of what it wishes, even where there is the greatest ground for Suspicion; and, indeed, there was here occasion sufficient for an implicite Faith; the little Knowledge she had of the Principles of *de l'Amye,* was but a too reasonable Cause for Doubt, that when he had nothing more to obtain, he might retain as little Regard for the Person who so generously gave him all, as his Sex ordinarily do—it was but a Chance whether by putting herself under his Protection, she shou'd not fall into the most miserable Circumstance to which a fond believing Woman can possibly be subjected; and in such a Venture there were ten thousand Blanks to one Prize.[26]

But *Fortune,* in this Particular was on her Side, *de l'Amye* had a Stock of Good-nature, Honour, and Sincerity; which had it been divided among his whole Sex, might have bless'd the Race of Womankind—he never *promis'd* more than he *perform'd*——his *Professions* never outsoar'd his *Meaning*—and tho no Man that ever liv'd, had a greater Command of Language, he chose rather by *Deeds* than *Words,* to express his Passion—In the whole Course of his long Amour with her, she had it not in her power to accuse him of having told her one Untruth—To the End of his Life he lov'd her with an undiminish'd

Ardour—was strictly careful of her Reputation, while there was a Possibility of preserving it—zealous for her Interest, and ever eager for her Love—Such a Ruin (as by the nicely Virtuous, the Sacrifice she made him of her Honour could be call'd no other) was too pleasing to permit her to repent it——Fame, Reputation, Grandure, all that the Generality of Souls are sway'd by, seem'd little in competition with his Love; and whenever the Reflection, that by the Laws of the Nation their Pleasures were no other than criminal, came a-cross her Thoughts, he had taught her to absolve herself, by arguing with her Conscience in this manner: Why (*said she*) should I condemn that as a Fault which *Heaven* ne'er made one? 'tis Custom only and Priestcraft make me guilty——What Right had those imperious Dictators to impose Laws on their Fellow-Creatures? Not any of their Legends can boast a Divine Mission to authorize their Insolence.——In former times, Plurality of Wives and Concubines was allow'd of, and to this Day are forbidden but by a small Part of the World——So far were the Suggestions of him who made it his chief Care to reconcile her to what she had done; but *Love,* and her extreme Admiration of him, furnish'd her with more——But suppose (*would she say*) it were indeed a Crime with any other man, the Case is widely different with him I love; the charming, the unequall'd *de l'Amye,* that Pride of Nature! that Boast of the Creation! cannot sure be thought to *err* while he obeys the first, great, undisputable Command——*Go forth and multiply*[27]——A thousand Wives, were there so many Women worthy of his Love, should rather spread his glorious Image round the peopled Earth! adorn Humanity! and bless the Age to come!—With these, and the like wild Notions, did the Violence of her Passion transport her, and stifle all Remorse; which however really condemnable in themselves, serv'd to make her entirely easy in a Life which else must have been full of Disquiets.

But I forget that by these Digressions I shall become tiresome to my Reader: To go on therefore with the History of this (whom I may justly call) *Self-Abandon'd Fair.* Some Hours before she expected him, did the impatient *de l'Amye,* pretending sudden Business, get rid of the Company he had invited, and returned to the Inn where he had left her; the Joy of their Meeting was proportion'd to that Excess of Passion they were mutually transported with, and he, having order'd his Affairs so as to be absent from Home, stay'd with her all Night, and without any more Resistance than such as but heighten'd Desire, enjoy'd those Charms a King had vainly languish'd to obtain. When a little Cessation from Rapture would give leave for cooler Conversation, they began to consult where, and in what manner, she shou'd be conceal'd; and after many various Proposals on his side, and Refusals on hers, as being either dangerous, or improper; at last it was concluded she shou'd stay where she was, not only because the People being of a mercenary nature, Gold might make them entirely at his Devotion, but also that it being very near his House, he might with the more Convenience be often with her: to add to this, her Face was utterly unknown to them, and whatever Rewards might be offered by the *King,* or Madam *de Montespan,* for the discovery of *Lasselia;* their Ignorance that they had the Charge of such a Person, wou'd be her Security.

She lived for some Months in all the Felicity that Love, in the most elevated Degree, can afford to those who devote themselves entirely to that Passion; but, alas! how transient is a Happiness built on this Foundation? If the darling Object of our Tenderness, by some uncommon Principle of Honour, or a Constancy seldom incident to the Nature of Mankind, returns not, with Ingratitude or Falshood, the Condescensions we have made; the Hand of Fate, by some unforeseen, some unimagin'd Blow, dashes the short-liv'd Bliss, hurls us to lasting Wretchedness, and forces us to own, tho' late, the sad Effects of our mistaken Zeal, Madam *de l'Amye,* who, as I have before observ'd, was not without a good deal of womanish Pride and Jealousy in her Nature, either by finding a difference in her Husband's Behaviour, or some other Reason, began to grow prodigiously disquieted, and resolv'd to know the Truth of what that Business was which he pretended oblig'd him to be so often from home, and where it was that he, of late, had past so many Days and Nights; in order for this discovery she sent a Servant, whom she cou'd confide in, to watch at a distance where his Master went: but the Caution of *de l'Amye* rendred these Endeavours fruitless for a long time; for he never went directly to the Inn where *Lasselia* was lodg'd, but made short Visits at several Houses which happened to be not far distant from his own: And 'tis probable that by this means she wou'd never have had it in her power to have made herself wretched, by a Discovery of that, which for her own Peace, as well as that of the other Persons concern'd in it, had much better have been eternally conceal'd, if an Accident had not happened, that when she had almost given over all Hope of it, brought every thing to light.

The History of the two Madamoiselle Douxmouries.[28]

A friendship of a very ancient standing having been between the Families of *de l'Amye* and *Douxmourie,* it was mutually desir'd, that the former having but one Son, and the other no more Children than two Daughters, the Amity between them might be preserv'd by his Marriage with one of them.—

—The eldest of them, being most favour'd by her Father, was the Person propos'd, and old *de l'Amye* agreeing to it, every thing was concluded on before the Inclinations of the Parties themselves were consulted: The young Gentleman, who had been on his Travels, tho' he was every day expected home, did not return till some Months after this Affair was settled; so that his intended Bride had much the advantage of him, in knowing to whom she was ordain'd.——The Expectations that she would be a very considerable Match, being Coheiress with her Sister of a vast Estate, join'd to her other Accomplishments, had attracted a great number of Admirers, all which her Father oblig'd her to dismiss, and told her he had provided a Husband for her, whose Quality and Fortune were what he approved of, and whose personal Merits were not to be equalled by any of those who pretended a Passion for her: Nor was it from her Father alone she received this Character of him, several Gentlemen, who had accompanied him to some of those Courts, which he had visited for Improvement, being returned before him, reported him to be grown a perfect Master of all those Accomplishments which can render a Man truly valuable. The thing was publickly talk'd of, all her Acquaintance wish'd her Joy of a Happiness which was look'd upon as good as compleated, and among them there were not a few who wou'd have rejoyced to have had a possibility of putting themselves in her place, and envy'd her more for the good Fortune she was to enjoy in the possession of so charming a Husband, than for the Dowry she received from her Father. She, who had a Heart intirely unprepossess'd with any other Object, was perfectly satisfied with the Choice had been made for her; and tho' it cou'd not be said she was in love with one whose Person she had never seen, yet 'tis certain that from the prodigious Character she had heard of him, she had form'd so great an Idea of Happiness in being his Wife, that she obey'd the Commands of her Father in resolving to become so with an *Inclination,* at least, equal to her *Duty.*

At length, the long-expected Charmer was arriv'd; and as soon as the first Demonstrations of Joy for his Return were over, was inform'd by his Father of what he had concluded on for him: the old Gentleman did not fail to represent the Advantages of such a Match in Colours the most agreeable, and extoll'd the Merits of the Lady he design'd for him to so high a Degree, that a youthful Heart, naturally amorous, was easily inflam'd by so elegant a Description——The Fatigue of his Journey had not taken from him that Impatience, and Curiosity, which such an Occasion commonly inspires: he was eager to see her, and desir'd he might be introduc'd immediately. His Father, overjoy'd to find him in a Humour so much dispos'd to Obedience, comply'd with his Request, and they went together to the House of Monsieur

Douxmourie. Old *de l'Amye* being told he was gone to take a Walk in his Garden, went to seek him there, leaving his Son in the Parlour till his Return, little imagining what Event that short Time of his Absence would bring forth. The youngest of the *Douxmourie's* having heard the Congratulations which had been paid to her Sister on the account of her intended Marrige, and the Admiration every one that knew him had express'd of the graceful Person, and Behaviour of him who was to be the Husband, had a Desire, which indeed had something more in it than Curiosity, to see him: and being told by some of the Servants that he was below, resolv'd to be a Witness of what so many had alledg'd in his favour: She had the better Opportunity of doing it, because her Sister was that Afternoon gone out to make some Visits: Therefore coming into the Room where he was, with a Gaiety and Freedom which is pretty common among the *French* Ladies, struck his Fancy, at first sight, with something to her Advantage, which she was far from expecting. He no sooner saw her, than he wish'd she might be the Person his Father had made choice of for him; and his Travels having furnish'd him with a good Quantity of Assurance, tho no more than what is agreeable, provided the Person possess'd of it knows how to temper it with Good-Manners, he presently made her sensible how happy he should think himself if she were the Daughter of Monsieur *Douxmourie.*

Young as she was, she was not so dull of Apprehension as not to understand him; but perceiving he either had not been made acquainted, or had forgot that there were two of them, forbore to remind him, prompted thereto by some secret Dictates, to which as yet she was herself a Stranger to the meaning of; and only answering him in the Affirmative, that she had the Honour to call that Gentleman Father, prevented him from giving any Check to the Passion which was just then kindling in his Soul: and thinking himself the happiest Man on Earth, to find in one Person all that cou'd indulge his Love, and at the same time gratify his Interest, and his Duty, was too much transported to restrain his Joy, or wait the dull Formality of her being presented to him: but telling her who he was (which she knew well enough before) and asking her if she had never heard of such a Man, who had been flatter'd with the hope that he should, one day, be blest in the possession of the Daughter of *Douxmourie:* Yes, Monsieur, (*answer'd she, blushing; and with an Air which still confirm'd him she was the Person he wish'd, and also that the sight of him had given her Emotions, in some measure, proportion'd to those he felt for her*) I am, indeed (*said she*) the Daughter of *Douxmourie,* nor are you deceiv'd in your Conjecture, if you imagine I have heard enough of *de l'Amye* to make me impatient for his coming. He was about to reply to these obliging Words, in Terms full of Tenderness, when the coming in of both their Fathers prevented either of them from proceeding. After the first Civilities were over, Monsieur *Douxmourie* began to speak of the Happiness he propos'd in uniting their Families; and young *de l'Amye* assur'd him, that, in providing for him in this manner, he thought himself under greater Obligations to his Father, than for all he ever did, or wou'd do for him besides. You are infinitely gallant, *reply'd Monsieur;* and I hope, if what you tell me be your real Sentiments, you will have no occasion to alter them when you see my Daughter, who, not appriz'd of the Honour of a Visit from you, happens to be abroad; but I have sent for her, and I know she will be here immediately. What mean you Sir? (*interrupted* de l'Amye, *strangely surpriz'd*) is not this Lady your Daughter! One of them (*resum'd the other;*) but she that the discerning Eyes of your rightly-judging Father has pointed out for you, as much exceeds her in all the Perfections of Mind and Body, as this might seem to do an untaught, tawny *Ethiope.*[29]

It is not to be imagin'd what an Alarm these Words gave the Person they were address'd to——He was hardly able to recover himself so far as to be able to make any Answer, and when he did, it was in this manner: I doubt not (*said he coldly*) but that all your Family have Excellencies peculiar to themselves——but I should never wish a nobler Satisfaction, than what is in the power of this young Lady to bestow. Had a disinterested Person been present, it would have been pleasant enough to have observ'd the Surprize and Vexation which appear'd in the Faces of the two old Gentlemen——They stood for some time looking on one another in a fix'd Posture, as if some supernatural Event had happen'd, which had depriv'd them of the Power of Speech, till the Father of him, who had been the Occasion of it, first broke silence in these or the like Expressions——You must pardon (*said he*) the Deference which my Son has Gallantry enough to pay to the *present* Fair——He has travell'd, you know, and that sort of Education generally inspires a Desire of becoming pleasing to all——I hope he is better acquainted with my Intentions, than to prefer in reality any to her I have appointed for him——Aye, aye, *cry'd the other,* it is all owing to this forward Girl——Leave the Room! (*continu'd he, turning to his daughter, who had been all this while trembling with Confusion and Uncertainty how to behave in this Affair*) be gone!——You are too young for Conversations such as we are upon.

Tho, by what after ensu'd, one may believe she wou'd have given her Soul almost to have staid; she was kept in too much Awe by the Severity of her Father, to dare to disobey him, and she went away in Tears: which so sensibly touch'd *de l'Amye,* that not all the Respect he ow'd to the Presence of his Father wou'd have been able to have restrain'd him from uttering a much greater Part of his Sentiments, than yet he had done, if the immediate Entrance of that Lady, for whose sake the other had been treated in this manner, had not made it improper: She no sooner appear'd, than, after having paid a civil Respect to the two Strangers, she ask'd her Father what had occasion'd his Commands for her Return home. That, *reply'd he,* which I doubt not but all here will at last think themselves happy in. In speaking these Words, he presented her to *de l'Amye;* and for form sake, told her who he was, tho the Servant who was sent for her had before related the News.

Nothing could be more dazling than the Appearance of this Lady; her Person was every way agreeable, she had the finest Hair and Complection in the World, her Features were perfectly regular; nor could the nicest Eye find a Defect either in her Face or Shape, unless that she were something too tall; but then there was an Air of Majesty about her, which little People very rarely can boast, and which made her appear extremely charming——To all that *Nature* had bestow'd, *Art* had done its utmost to embellish her: she was dress'd in so *rich* as well as *becoming* a manner, as might easily inform those that saw her, there was nothing wanting from her *own Care* for the *one,* or *Indulgence* of her *Father* for the *other.* But not all the attractions she was Mistress of, were sufficient to make her appear half so amiable in the Eyes of *de l'Amye,* as did her Sister: there was an easy Freedom in the Behaviour, a winning Softness in the Air and Face of that young Creature, tho dress'd in a more plain Apparel, and not set off with any Illustration,[30] which took more with him, and he continu'd to think her infinitely more lovely in her native Charms, than this, adorn'd in all the gawdy Pomp of Finery, and Blaze of Jewels. The Passion he was possess'd of for the other, and the Reflection how indifferently she had been used on the account of this, work'd so strongly in his Soul, that he had scarce power enough over himself to pay her even those common Compliments, which cou'd not be omitted without Ill-Manners——In fine, the little he said to her appear'd so forc'd, so different from what is dictated by the Heart, that a Person, far less capable of judging than she was, might easily perceive he was little influenc'd in the manner she expected.

By the Description I have given of her, I believe my Reader will not imagine her to be the humblest of her Sex; tho, had she been such, a Disappointment like this was sufficient to rouze the smallest Sparks of Pride, and kindle up Resentment; but as she really was of a Humour perhaps the least inclinable to pardon an Indignity of this kind, of all others, she grew all Fury, and her tumultuous Thoughts meditated nothing but Revenge: but if his not loving her had power to raise such a Tempest of Rage in her Soul, to what an infinite Degree did the Knowledge (which she soon after receiv'd) that it was to the more prevailing Charms of her Sister she ow'd this Mortification, transport her! All that can be conceiv'd of Violent, was mean to that with which her haughty Temper was agitated. The poor young Lady felt the Effects of it; her Father was so much inrag'd, that by her showing herself the Match might probably be broken off between *de l'Amye* and his favourite Daughter, that he wou'd not suffer her to come in his sight; but order'd she should stay in her Chamber, whence he vow'd she should never come out, unless it were to be dispos'd in a Monastery, without *de l'Amye,* repenting the Declarations he had made in her favour, consented to the Consummation of what his Father had agreed upon for him——Nor was this all the Hardship she endur'd; she was deny'd Ease in her Confinement, her Sister was perpetually coming in to insult her, and whenever any Company or Business gave her a small Cessation from this Vexation, her own disturb'd Thoughts were sufficiently her Tormentors——She lov'd the charming *de l'Amye,* tho she had seen him but once, with a Passion as fierce, as violent, as her Soul naturally mild and gentle was capable of admitting. And the Impossibility there was, that her Father ever shou'd be brought to consent she shou'd be his, to the prejudice of her Sister, even tho he should really like her well enough, to continue giving her the Preference in his Inclinations, I believe, by all who have experienc'd that Passion, will be allow'd to be a Torture poynant enough to break a Heart more resolute than her's.

While the Family of *Douxmourie* were in these Perplexities, that of *de l'Amye* was not much better: the young Gentleman plainly told his Father, he never would marry the Person propos'd, and obstinately refus'd making any more Visits to that House, unless he might be admitted to pay his Addresses to the youngest Daughter. This created many Arguments between them; and neither of them being able to overcome the Resolution of the other, the whole Affair, for some time, continu'd in suspence.

Old *de l'Amye* at length having, for many Reasons, a prodigious Desire his Son should marry into that Family, endeavour'd to persuade Monsieur *Douxmourie* to give his Consent that he should have her he seem'd most to approve; but he was too partially fond of his other Daughter, to listen to such a Proposal: and since he had no other way to revenge the Contempt she had been treated with, encreas'd his ill Usage of her Rival Sister in such a manner, that she would not have been able to have supported it with Life, had Heaven not sent her a Relief, by taking him away, in whose power alone she was. He was taken suddenly ill of a violent Fever, and died in three days: but the approach of Death made but little Alteration in his Sentiments, he did not indeed wholly cut off his younger Daughter of a Child's Part in his Estate, but left her far inferior to her Sister, and that too to be forfeited if she marry'd *de l'Amye.*

She was now, however, her own Mistress; and 'tis not to be imagin'd that when she was so, she wou'd continue in the same House with a Sister, whose unforgiving Temper had cost her so much Uneasiness: She took Lodgings in the Town, and being still possess'd of her former Passion, tho as hopeless as ever of gratifying it, sent to let *de l'Amye* know she shou'd take it as a favour if she saw him among the number of those who came to console an unhappy Orphan.——This Summons was too kind a one for a Man of his Gallantry to refuse, had he been less in Love; but still retaining the same Desire which the first Sight of her had inspired him with, tho' now degenerated to a less noble Aim, he obeyed with a speed which testified the Pleasure he took in it: The former Tenderness with which they had regarded each other, encreasing by a nearer Conversation, both became at length too much overcome by it, to have the Government any longer of their Actions.——And, to what Extremes will mutual Love transport its Votaries?——They yielded to the all-commanding Force——gave up their Souls as Victims to his Sway—and prov'd that it was not in the power of the inexorable *Douxmourie* to deprive them of any other part of the Joys of Marriage than the Ceremony. The Consequence of this was, what might naturally be expected, the Censure of the World, and a living Proof[31] that those Censures were not undeserv'd; but in spite of those two, which must be reckon'd stabbing Afflictions to a Woman who has any Pretence to Honour or Reputation, the generous Fair had too great a Tenderness for her lovely Undoer, to press him to take off the Reproach she suffer'd by making her his Wife.——A noble Friendship went hand in hand with the Passion she had for him, which would not suffer her to wish he should take to his Arms a Bride unportion'd; nor indeed, as his Affairs stood, great part of his Father's Estate being involv'd, could he have done it, without bringing manifest Destruction on himself, and her he married.

But the Case stood not in this manner with the Sieur *Le Blessang.*[32] He, tho' infinitely superior to her in Fortune, wou'd have thought himself happy, would she have yielded to be his Wife; and when he heard the Rumour that every one's mouth was full of, of her Intimacy with *de l'Amye,* he was the last that believ'd it; nor, perhaps, never would have done so, if her Sister, who hated her more deadly, since she knew the continued Tenderness *de l'Amye* still had for her, and was ever watchful to expose her, had not contriv'd a Stratagem, to give him ocular Demonstration. She persuaded him to dress like a Footman, and under the Pretence of bringing a Letter from that happy

Lover, he easily got Admittance into the House, where the unfortunate Lady was in her Child-Bed.——That Secret being also discovered by the Spies of that assiduous Contriver of Dissension.——Having gain'd Entrance, Love, Curiosity, Jealousy, and a Resolution of being satisfied of the Truth, emboldened him to follow the Maid that carried up the Letter; and found her, indeed, as he had been inform'd; and the undeniable Testimony of what she had been guilty of, lying on the Bed by her. The Surprize he was in, in spite of all had been told him, to see her really in that Condition, was so great, that he had power to utter no more than, O! cou'd I have thought it!—Cou'd I have thought it!——and then ran down Stairs immediately——the Confusion she was in, at seeing a Fellow at her Bedside, and the Oddness of his Behaviour, hindred her from ordering he shou'd be stay'd——but when she open'd the Letter, and found it only a Blank, she perceiv'd she had been betray'd, and was immediately seiz'd with so violent a Disorder, that it threw her into Fits which had like to have been fatal to her.

There let us leave her for a while, and return to the enrag'd Lover, Monsieur *Blessang*—He had no means of venting his Indignation on her who had so ungratefully repaid his generous Affection, but he cou'd not bear the Man who deprived him of her Affections shou'd live; he, therefore, writes a Challenge immediately to Monsieur *de l'Amye,* who, though he cou'd not guess by what way he had affronted a Gentleman who was altogether a Stranger to him, had too much Bravery to refuse meeting him, and went to the Place, and at the Hour appointed——It was natural enough, before they encounter'd, to enquire the Cause which had provok'd him to send a Billet of that nature; which the other answer'd with all the Frankness imaginable, telling him the whole Secret by which he had discovered the Amour——But, *said he, not yet able to vanquish the Tenderness he had for her;* tho' she is for ever lost to me, and with her all my Soul holds dear, so precious is her Fame, and Peace of Mind to me, that if you will swear to recompence the Injury you have done her, by an honourable Marriage, I am willing to pass over my own Misfortune in Consideration of her Happiness, and will here change Vows with you, never to molest your Peace—*De l'Amye,* tho' 'tis possible he might, after Possession, have had Gratitude enough to have done every thing in his power for her Ease, knew very well his Circumstances would not admit of his marrying in that manner; but either not willing to let the other into that Secret, or believing all he cou'd say on that score would seem but as a Pretence to avoid fighting, thought it better absolutely to refuse it——This threw off all the Goodwill Monsieur *Blessang* before had to an Accommodation; and, drawing his Sword——Now, *said he,* nothing shall protect thee from me; I fight not now to satiate my Revenge on a Rival, but to punish a Villain, a base Violater of Innocence——Have-at-thee, then, *continued he, making a Pass at him*—Defend thyself, if thou canst, against the Cause of Justice, and of injur'd Virtue. He made his first Push with so much Fury and Skill, that *de l'Amye* stood in need of all his Dexterity to parry it; but having foil'd him once or twice, and by this time equally enrag'd, gave a home Thrust, with these Words—This, *cry'd he,* to show how little I deserve the Contumely, thy rash mistaken Rage has branded me with——The unhappy *Blessang* cou'd answer to these Upbraidings no otherwise than with a Groan, which was indeed his last; for that Moment put a Period at once to his Love, Life, and Indignation.

Monsieur *de l'Amye* was exceedingly troubled at this Accident, not only because he had robb'd the World of a Gentleman whose Life might have been of Service to it, but also that he knew he had too many powerful Friends for him to hope to obtain a Pardon for the Misfortune he had been the Cause of to them——As he was reflecting a little on the Vexations which frequently arise from giving way to that Bane of Quiet, Love, he saw three or four People cross hastily over an adjacent Field, and seem to be coming directly to the Place where he was standing by the dead Body of him who so unluckily had fallen by his hand. Self-preservation put him in mind that this was no fit Place for Contemplation; and turning another way into a Road, the Entrance of which he knew very well, he made the best of his way to the Lady for whose sake all this had happen'd: he found her very ill, and not in a Condition to be acquainted with what he had to deliver, therefore was obliged to leave her; zealously entreating the Care of all about her, designing, if she recover'd, to write an account of all to her, as soon as he shou'd be in a Place of Safety; which, not believing was to be found in *France,*[33] he took Shipping immediately, and embarked for *Flanders.* Where when he had landed, he sent Letters to his Father, and some others whom he cou'd confide in, desiring they would let him know, by Post, every thing that pass'd concerning the Death of Monsieur *Blessang.* The first Answers he receiv'd, were little to his Consolation, tho' no less than he expected: The Persons whom he saw in the Field, were brought by the Servant who was employ'd in carrying the Challenge; who, imagining what it might contain, had come in hope to have prevented the Mischief; and finding they were too late, went that moment to a Magistrate, and gave in an Information——he also was informed that great Search had been made for him, and that he must never expect to see *France* again, unless he meant the Visit should be fatal to him——But in the midst of all these sad Accounts, he had this to comfort him, that his Father was very busy with all those who were accounted Favourites at Court; that he spar'd no Cost nor

Trouble to procure a Pardon; and that there were some among them, who had given him hope of succeeding.

This Misfortune was very terrible to old Monsieur *de l'Amye,* not only because it depriv'd him of the pleasure of his dear Son's Company, but also that it was the tearing to pieces of his already broken Estate: and the Trouble and Fatigue it occasion'd him, was such, as was very near bringing him to his Grave.

But what Tongue is able to express the Grief, the Distraction of the unfortunate Cause of all this Woe, when first she heard the fatal News: Had it not been prevented by the watchful Care of those about her, she wou'd not have liv'd a Moment to endure the Obloquy of the World, and those severer Stings of Conscience which she now began to feel, for having, by her ill Conduct, occasion'd such Scenes of Death and Ruin—The *Idea* of the unhappy *Blessang* was ever in her mind; and at some times Imagination work'd so strongly on her perplex'd Thoughts, as to make her think she saw him. She continued for some time in a Condition little different from Madness; but when Reason had a little recovered its usual Sway, a deadly Melancholy succeeded Passion; and tho' she had frequent Letters from *de l'Amye,* in which he press'd her to come to *Flanders,* she cou'd not be prevail'd on, to repeat that Folly which had caus'd such Misfortunes in the World, and which she now accounted as a Crime unpardonable: But to do all she cou'd to expiate it, after putting her Child, which happen'd to be a Boy, under the Care of a *Fryar,* of whose Goodness and Piety she was well assured, she retir'd into a *Convent,* where she resolv'd to pass the Remainder of her Days in Penitence.

Her haughty Sister all this while exulted in triumphant Vengeance; but aiming still at the Life of *de l'Amye,* she join'd her interest, which was pretty considerable, with the Relations of the Sieur *Blessang,* the better to render fruitless all the Endeavours the unhappy Father cou'd make in his Son's behalf——But, at last, notwithstanding all the Efforts of Malice, he succeeded, a Pardon was sign'd, and he call'd home: It would be needless to repeat the mutual Transports of the overjoy'd Father and Son at meeting; whoever will give themselves leisure to think what they would feel in such a Circumstance, need not be inform'd——It had however been more pure, if not mix'd by the melancholly Reflection how much this Accident had impoverish'd their Fortune; and by making so many Enemies, took from the young Gentleman all Hope of repairing it, as he once designed by getting a place at Court: but being inform'd of the Particulars of all that had been done in his Absence, he resolv'd at least to gratify one Passion; and putting on a Countenance as full of Gaiety as he cou'd, went to make a Visit to her whom his Indifference had made his implacable Enemy, Madamoiselle *Douxmourie.* The Surprize which appear'd in the Face of the Servant who open'd the Door to him, gave him a sort of gloomy Satisfaction, not doubting but he shou'd create a much greater in the Lady he serv'd. He was not mistaken in his Sentiments; she no sooner was told he enquir'd for her, than a cold Sweat came all o'er her Limbs; she trembled like one in a Palsy, and not able to imagine what shou'd have occasion'd his coming, was not without a Thought, that repenting his Contempt of her, he meant to entreat her Pardon, and perhaps endeavour to expiate his former Coldness by a Declaration of Love. This was too agreeable a Belief for her to oppose it: For *de l'Amye* having had the same Charms for her, as for almost all her Sex besides; and her Hatred having only been occasion'd by his not loving her, such a Suggestion gratified more than one Passion in her: therefore, looking in her Glass, and setting herself in that Air which she thought would be most engaging, she went down to receive him with a Pleasure, which those who knew the Violence with which she had express'd herself against him, would scarcely have believed.

But how was she mortified, how much more insupportable was this second Disappointment, than the first he had given her; when instead of accosting her with humble Looks, and Words all compos'd of Sweetness and Persuasion, as she expected, he offered her nothing but Insults, and reproach'd her for her Inhumanity to a Sister, who he told her was infinitely more deserving than herself, in Terms so bitter, and so severely just, that tho' she cou'd ill endure to hear them, her secret Soul avowed what he alledg'd, and join'd to torture her. This Self-Condemnation abated great part of the Fury his first Salutation had put her in, and at length, she either was, or fancy'd herself to be, truly sorry for what she had done, and opening all her Bosom, made no Scruple of confessing the Source of all the Mischief. She confess'd it was not *Pride* for the Preference he gave her Sister, which had alone stirr'd up her Resentment, but that Love, jealous, disappointed *Love!* had at least an equal Share in driving her to those Extremes she had been guilty of.——And at last fell so low as to tell him, that if he yet cou'd bring himself to return the Passion she felt for him, she would repair the Losses she had occasioned in his Fortune by giving him her own, and by publickly marrying him, testify to the whole World from what Original the Hatred she had shewed to him had sprung: 'Tis impossible to describe with what a Look *de l'Amye* list'ned to this unexpected Offer; all that can be conceived of Scorn, Contempt, and Detestation, were to the Life display'd in his expressive Eyes——but, as if they were not intelligible enough—Weak, vile Woman! (*said he*) as mean-spirited as base! Can you believe that I, who, when unknowing the foulness of your *Mind,* could find no Charm about your *Person* worthy my Regard, can now descend to take a Wretch who wants but Opportunity and the Temptation of the Devil to be a Witch?——No——did but one Thought agree——should I forgo my Principles, renounce my Honour, and debase my Nature but even so far——cou'd I but hesitate, if for a sordid Consideration I shou'd take to my Arms so loathed a Creature, I shou'd indeed be only fit for thee——but I too much despise thee to think whatever thou canst offer worth a Moment's serious Consideration——thou art now grown as much beneath my *Resentment,* as thou art unworthy of my *Pity.* I cannot have the same Sentiments for you (*reply'd she, fiercely, and running at him with a Penknife which she happened to have in her Pocket*) nor shalt thou live to triumph over both the Daughters of *Douxmourie.*

She was very near plunging it into his Body, before he saw what it was she had in her Hand; and had not a Chair, by catching hold of her Sleeve, a little retarded the Speed with which she flew to him, he had inevitably fallen a Victim to her Fury; but easily disarming her, when he perceived what she was about, Wretch! (*cry'd he, if possible with an added Scorn to that with which he had before look'd on her*) Fortune will no longer assist the Mischiefs thou art form'd to execute.——Thou hast already done all to me thou ever can'st have power to do, by depriving me of thy Sister, and forcing my unwilling Arm to rob the World of so accomplish'd a Gentleman as the Sieur *Blessang.*—I now despise whatever Efforts thy future Malice may make against me——and leave thee an Object at once meanly *despicable,* and transcendently *wicked.* With these Words he flung out of her House, resolved to hear no more, had she attempted to speak; but the o'er-boiling Passions of her Soul suffer'd not themselves to be discharg'd in Words, but rising all at once, suffocated her, and she was found by her Servants in a Swoon.

To repeat the many Stratagems she afterwards form'd for his Destruction, would be as tiresome as impertinent, since none of them for a long time met with Success; and she had the inexpressible Mortification to see him in a small time married to a young Widow vastly rich, part of whose Wealth paid off the Mortgages of the Estate which was to descend to him, and they lived together on the Remainder in a manner more grand than ever he had done before.

But now the Time was come at once to prove how dangerous it is to have a watchful Enemy, though ne'er so known a one, and to make *Lasselia* sensible how much she had deceiv'd herself by false Reasoning when she concluded that Errors, such as she was guilty of, were little taken notice of by Heaven. The implacable *Douxmourie,* out of humour with the World, which afforded her a Gratification neither of her Love nor Resentment, was going into the Country to indulge a Discontent she cou'd not have so much leisure to do at *Paris.* In the Road to the Place she was going to, was that Inn in which *de l'Amye* had placed his belov'd *Lasselia.* It was the Effect of the other's Ill-fortune, that she happened to bait[34] there, and a little more fatigued than ordinary, resolved to go no farther that Day. *Lasselia,* who while the Sun was up, ne'er dared to peep abroad, used commonly to take the benefit of the Air in an adjacent Field every Evening: She was in one of those nocturnal Refreshments when Madamoiselle *Douxmourie,* who in leaving *Paris,* had not left her Disquiets, weary of sitting alone in her Chamber, and it being too early to go to Bed, went to take a little Walk: accompany'd only by her Woman, whom she had taken along with her. It was their Chance to go into that very Field; which being very near the House, made it not unsafe for them to venture without any other Guard than their own Voices; which, if they were assaulted, might easily bring People to their Assistance. They had walk'd but a little way in it, before they fancy'd they stood in need of Protection; they heard a rustling among the Leaves on the other side of the Hedge, and presently after a muttering of Voices; they immediately imagined there were Robbers near them, and presently began to run back, crying all the way, Thieves, Thieves!—— Help! Help! or we shall be murder'd in a Moment. There were immediately 20 People about them from the Inn, and some little Cottages which stood near it—What's the matter? where are the Thieves? bawl'd they all out with one Voice—O! just in that Thicket (*reply'd* Douxmourie, *pointing toward the Place where she had heard the Sound*)——'Tis not to be doubted but they ran in hope of a certain Reward which had been allow'd to all who had the good Fortune to take any of these lawless Adventurers.

Douxmourie was so much out of breath with her Fright, that she was obliged to rest on her Woman's Arm, before she cou'd go any farther; and she was not got into the House, when the Mob her Outcrys had rais'd, were returned: she stopp'd a little to know their Success——for Fear had magnify'd the Noise she heard to such a degree, that she thought there were at least a hundred of them that made it——See, Madam, (*cry'd one of the Fellows*) for what Cause you have been alarm'd——there was no Thieves; you have only made us interrupt a loving Couple——but, however, since we have been at the pains of taking them, we'll e'en carry them before their Betters——they shall give an account who they are, and what Business they had there, before we part with them. It was to no purpose that the Gentleman endeavour'd, by mild Arguments (for to have made use of Force, would have been Madness) to prevail on this rude Multitude, to let him, and the Person he had with him, who was dying with her Fears, go about their business. They were obstinately bent, and all his Eloquence was thrown away on them. *Douxmourie* was all the while they were talking, in the greatest Consternation imaginable; she fancy'd she knew the Voice of him who had fallen into this Misfortune, but cou'd not recollect where, or when she had heard it before; and the Moon being pretty obscure, and the Press of People who encompass'd him round, would not give her leave to see his Face, till being all come near the Inn, the People themselves running out with Lights, she immediately saw, to her inexpressible Surprize, as well as Joy, that it was the Object of her Hatred, Monsieur *de l'Amye,* and with him a Woman of a very good Appearance, (for *Lasselia* had long ago thrown off her *Pilgrim's* Habit) but that distracted Lady, willing to conceal herself as long as she cou'd, holding a Handkerchief to her Eyes, took from the other the means of knowing her, which else she must infallibly have done, having often seen her at Madam *de Montespan*'s; but this she was certain of, that it was not his Wife, by the difference of her Shape and Stature; *Lasselia* being a great deal taller, and something more slender than Madamoiselle *de l'Amye,* whom before her Marriage she had been intimately acquainted with.

The Master and Mistress of the House were very much vex'd at this Accident, not expecting any other, than that by this Discovery Monsieur *de l'Amye* would be oblig'd to carry his Mistress and Generosity to some other Place: but to bring them off as well as they cou'd, they told the Rabble that they might disperse themselves, for they wou'd be answerable for the Character of those Persons, that the Lady was a near Relation of their own, and the Gentleman an Acquaintance who sometimes call'd to see them——Thus, with much ado, the Lovers at last had their Liberty; but were extremely perplex'd, lest this Affair should get Air. *De l'Amye* could not be certain that, among such a Number of People, there were not some who might know him; but that was the smallest of their Vexations, *Lasselia* had till then been conceal'd with that caution, that not a Servant in the House, but one, whose Fidelity the Mistress of it was secure of, knew there was any Woman lodg'd there, a Passage being made for her on purpose out of her Chamber into the Fields; and she never stirring but when it was dark, prevented her from being seen by any body.

But it was now natural to suppose, that being found with him, and afterwards own'd as a Relation by the Inn-keeper, would create Suspicion enough in those sort of People, therefore they concluded that it would be wholly improper for her to continue there. But whither to remove her, he could not for his Soul contrive; tho, had he known how dangerous an Enemy he had in the House, and who had been both the Occasion and Witness of the Bustle which had happen'd, 'tis certain they would rather have chose to have shelter'd themselves that Night under the Boughs of some spreading Oak, than tarry'd under the same Roof with her. But the malicious *Douxmourie,* to have the better Opportunity of compleating the Mischief she intended, withdrew the moment she had seen his Face; which, by the Advantage of the Lights being brought behind her to the Place where they were, she cou'd easily do, before he cou'd, if the Distraction he was in would have given him leave, have perceiv'd her.

She went presently to her Chamber; but having several Servants with her, she order'd them to watch about the House, and bring her word of all the Motions of those two Persons: and being inform'd by the most diligent among them, that, for a certainty, that Gentleman and Woman lay both of them there, she pretended on a sudden to be taken extremely ill, and that not expecting to live an Hour, she must send for some Friends she had in that Country; so ordering a Horse to be got ready, that Footman who had brought her this Intelligence, having his Message given him privately, was dispatch'd to the House of Madam *de l'Amye,* where he was to tell her, that he belong'd to a Gentleman who had the greatest Concern imaginable for her ill Usage; and had sent to inform her, that her Husband having an Intention wholly to abandon her in a short time, of late had been very busy in disposing of some Lands, which Money he had made a Present to a young Girl, whom he was excessive fond of, that he design'd to live with her as his Wife; and as a Proof of the Truth of all this, she might that Night find them together at such an Inn——But that, if she requir'd this Testimony, she must not lose this Oppportunity, which probably might never offer again——Madamoiselle *Douxmourie* charg'd him, if possible, to fire her with a desire of coming immediately, because she was not sure how long they might stay.

It was scarce a quarter of an Hour's riding to the House of *de l'Amye;* and telling the Servants he had Business of greater Consequence than Life to impart to their Lady, she order'd he should be admitted, tho she had on her Night-dress, and was preparing for bed——The Fellow perform'd the Business he was sent about with so much Art, that she presently assented to the Proposal of going that moment to detect her Husband, on whose Ingratitude and Perfidiousness she bestow'd ten thousand Curses; but not thinking it proper to go alone, especially with this Man, who was altogether a Stranger to her, she sent to Monsieur *de Valier,* and rouz'd him and his Lady, desiring they would come to her on an extraordinary Occasion——They obey'd her Summons, and were there by the time her Coach was got ready, which they all went into, accompany'd on each side by Madamoiselle *Douxmourie*'s Man, two of *Valier*'s, and one of her own, all on Horseback——As they went along, she told them on what account she had entreated the favour of their Company: and they both took the liberty of assuring her, that had they been of her Counsel beforehand, they should have persuaded her against it; because in such Cases, Extremes are often fatal to the Peace of both, and that it was better sometimes to appear blind, than too quick-sighted: But Jealousy is not of a nature to endure Controul, she was resolv'd to have the pleasure of upbraiding, and bid the Coachman drive as fast as possible. They got to the Inn about three in the Morning, when all the Family were drown'd in Sleep, except Madamoiselle *Douxmourie,* and those that sat up to attend her, and open the Door to those Friends she told them she had sent for.

Her Servant, who had the Conduct of the whole Affair, brought them up into his Lady's Chamber, where Madam *de l'Amye* was not a little surpriz'd to find to whom it was she ow'd the Discovery she was about to make; and possibly, in spite of her own jealous Rage, wou'd rather have seem'd to have disbeliev'd all she heard, than gratify the Malice of this Woman, who she knew had the greatest Hatred imaginable to her Husband. *Douxmourie,* perhaps, guessing at her Sentiments, as soon as she had put every body out of the Room belonging to the House, Madam, *said she,* I forbore to let you know I was the Person who, by the greatest Chance in the World, have this Opportunity of convincing you of the Perfidy of your Husband; because the open Enmity I have always profess'd for him, might have made you suspect there was more of Spleen, than Justice in what I had told you: but as you are now in the same House, and on the same Floor with him, and the Person he prefers to you, I doubt not but before you leave it, you will satisfy yourself what 'tis he merits from you——All, and more, *cry'd she,* than my Resentment can inflict, and if it be as your Messenger inform'd me, by all that's sacred I'll——She was going to make some rash Protestation, when Monsieur *de Valier* stopp'd her Mouth; Hold, Madam! *interrupted he,* I must not suffer you to give way to Passion, till you are ascertain'd you have cause for it——*Anger* sometimes blinds the *Reason;* and as this Lady avows her Hate to Monsieur *de l'Amye* 'tis not impossible but that she may have been mistaken, and has been led to credit something more than the Truth of him she is willing should be found guilty.

This hinder'd the enrag'd Wife from saying any more, till Madamoiselle *Douxmourie* recounting the manner by which she had made the Discovery, which she illustrated with abundance of aggravating Circumstances, made her relapse into her former Fury——She was then for breaking open the Door upon them; tearing them to pieces, exposing them to the whole World, seem'd too little to satisfy the Wrong——She vented the Passion she was in with so much Vehemence, that she who had rais'd it, endeavour'd to abate it——Madam, *said she,* 'tis not impossible, but in such a House as this, there may be Back-ways; which, if there be, this shameful Pair are, doubtless, but too well acquainted with: and should your Voice discover you are here, or any force be used to get Entrance, before that can be done, they may perhaps escape, and disappoint our Aim——I, therefore, wou'd advise you to be patient till the Morning, which now is near at hand; and when either of them opens the Door, which one of my Servants shall diligently guard, we will all be ready to rush in upon them——This Method of proceeding receiv'd a general Approbation; and Madam *de l'Amye* did all she cou'd to suppress the Violence of her Indignation at present, that it might fall more heavy on the Persons who had caus'd it; for she resolv'd in her own Mind never to forgive, or live with her Husband more.

The Lovers, who had pass'd their Time in as great, tho' different Anxieties, having at last fix'd on a Place to go to, thought it most proper to leave that they were in, before Day-break; and accordingly Monsieur *de l'Amye* rose, and opening the Door to call the Hostler to get his Horse ready, was surpriz'd to find himself, as he was stepping back into the Chamber, push'd violently in by a rush of People who follow'd him: The Candles they had in their Hands, immediately inform'd him who they were. As confus'd as he was, he had Presence enough of Mind to run towards the Bed, where he thought to defend his dear *Lasselia* from their View, or die to expiate the Disgrace she must suffer for his sake; but that unfortunate Lady, hearing a Noise, had rais'd herself in her bed to see what 'twas: which when she did, Surprize, and Shame, and Fear, took away her Senses so far, as to deprive her of any Thought in what manner she shou'd conceal herself; and sat still, stupid and motionless, expos'd to every body in the Room—'Tis hard to say whether the Fury of Madam *de l'Amye,* or the Wonder that she and all her Companions were in, was greatest, when they found it was *Lasselia* with whom he had transgress'd—nor cou'd either of them surpass that which *de l'Amye* felt, to see *Douxmourie* with them: He no longer doubted by whom he had been betray'd, and not answering the Invectives which his Wife pour'd out upon him, he utter'd as many against that *She-Devil,* for that was the only Name he vouchsafed to call her by.

While all were in this Confusion, Madamoiselle *de Valier,* having a little recover'd that Confusion the Sight of *Lasselia* had occasion'd, having a tender Friendship for her, went towards the Bed with a design to have spoke to her, when the undone Fair, just then waking, as it were, from that Absence of Mind she had been in, into a Sense of the Shame to which she was expos'd, starting suddenly from the Posture she had been in, and catching Monsieur *de l'Amye*'s Sword, which lay on a Table by the bed-side, was about to end her Life, and the Infamy that attended it: it was the good fortune of that sincere Friend to prevent this Act of Desperation from being accomplished; but the *Attempt* put the whole Company into so great a Consternation, as was of excellent Service to the silencing their Clamours. *De l'Amye,* though he was ready to fly into his Charmer's Arms, and chase away her Despair by a thousand soft Endearments, yet he ow'd too much to his Wife, to give her so provoking an Instance before her Face, that she was but the second in his Esteem—but the Pain he endured in this Restraint, took from him all Inclination to continue his Reproaches to Madamoiselle *Douxmourie;* and he stood speechless, and seem'd lost in Thought, as did his wife; who, tho' extremely fiery and passionate, had a great deal of Good-Nature, and so manifest a Proof of her Rival's Penitence and Despair, wrought on her so far, as to engage her Pity—and she thought, if that wou'd make her easy, she could forgive the Wrong she had done her, provided she wou'd never more repeat it.

Monsieur *de Valier,* who had watch'd the Abatement of her Rage, perceiving her Looks were very much soften'd, beg'd her to withdraw with him a Moment into another Room; to which she having consented, he laid so many Arguments before her, how infinitely better it would be to hush up this Affair, than to make herself and Husband, as well as the Person who had injur'd her, the Chat[35] of the whole Country; that she at last consented, on condition she would immediately retire into a Monastery, thereby to put it out even of her own power to wrong her more—Having obtain'd thus much from her, he endeavour'd to bring *de l'Amye* to consent; and was labouring a long time before he cou'd prevail on him but to promise an eternal Separation: but the Remonstrance the other made him, how he was indebted to his Wife for almost every thing he was possess'd of; her Love, her Faithfulness to him, her Good-nature, her condescending Temper, making an Allowance for that one Foible, Jealousy, won so far on his Gratitude, join'd to the Reflection, how impossible it wou'd be for him to keep the possession of *Lasselia;* believing, not without Reason, that if the Discovery of what had happen'd, shou'd reach the Ear of Madam *de Montespan,* as in all probability it wou'd, she wou'd take effectual Measures to prevent his coming near her: all this put together, oblig'd him to an unwilling yielding to what was propos'd.

While Monsieur *de Valier* was thus employ'd with the Wife and Husband, his Lady, who had taken the Hint privately from him, was no less busy with *Lasselia;* she had a double Task to reconcile that distress'd Lady at once to the Thoughts of Life, and quitting the Conversation of her beloved *de l'Amye;* but the Power her experienc'd Friendship had given her over her, enforcing the strong Reasons she made use of, in a little time work'd their desired Effect, and this Affair ended vastly different from what the beginning promis'd. The malicious *Douxmourie* was the only Person vex'd at it—as for *de l'Amye,* tho' he never ceas'd to think of *Lasselia* with a Tenderness which cou'd not but be attended with some melancholy Reflections; yet the Temper of his Wife, who, after this, took double Care to make herself agreeable to him, by degrees, made him grow more chearful. *Lasselia,* who, as she had promis'd, went directly to a Convent, strengthen'd by the good Advice of Madamoiselle *de Valier,* who frequently visited her, and the religious Conversation of the holy Maids she was among, in time was weaned from those sensual Delights she had before too much indulg'd herself in, and became an Example of Piety even to those who never had swerv'd from it.

FINIS.

Notes to the Novels

The Injur'd Husband

Title Page. The epigraph is not from Dryden, and it has not been found in the work of any other poet. Possibly Haywood made up the lines (she was not above doing such a thing), attributing them to Dryden and thus dignifying her new novel by appropriating his name for its rhetorical value.

1. Mary Sophia Charlotte, Lady Howe (1695-1782), the wife of Emanuel Scrope (Howe), Viscount Howe, was born in Hanover and was once thought to have been the illegitimate daughter of George I. A powerful and influential woman, she was Lady of the Bedchamber to the Princess of Wales. No particular connection with Haywood has been traced, and it is likely that the dedication was written in the hope of some small monetary token of recognition; such a practice was common among early writers.

2. In this and the next paragraph Haywood adapts a standard ruse of early novelists, affirming the authenticity of her work by a kind of double gesture: she protests that the story is not about an English woman, thus planting the suggestion that it may indeed be about just such a person; she further protests that the account of the French baroness is true, that it is the record of her character and history as described by a trusted friend who knew her. The whole is, of course, a fiction disguised as a scandal chronicle. But the baroness does indeed appear to have been based on a real person, Martha Fowke Sansom, a former friend of Haywood and, with her, a member of Aaron Hill's literary circle in the early 1720s. The "Gentleman" referred to in the first line of this paragraph is probably the poet Richard Savage, also a member of Hill's circle and Haywood's former lover. See above, the introduction, xix-xx.

3. Fr. *tortiller:* to wiggle, wriggle, writhe. The nominative form of the word, *tortillage,* means underhand intrigue—shuffling, hedging, hanky-panky.

4. Fr. *lâche:* loose, slack, cowardly.

5. Carriage, equipage.

6. The baroness's maiden name (Fr. *motte*) means clod or sod; earthy, of the earth, a mound. A motte was also the central fortified place in a castle.

7. That is, she now obliged her lovers to keep her as a mistress.

8. Fr. *espérance:* hope, expectation, trust.

9. That is, they hurried the occasion while hushing all talk of it.

10. That is, her rank.

11. This name has no clear significance, but the combination of Fr. *son* (sound) and *ville* (town or city) suggests that the marquis has the voice and manner of an urbane gentleman.

12. Fr. *chevalier:* knight, soldier; a gentleman of high rank but without title. There is no French *aumar,* but the spelling is phonetically equivalent to the *Omer* of St. Omer, a town southeast of Calais. Haywood may actually be punning on the name of the Roman god of war (Mars) to hint at the chevalier's manner as a warlike figure. This possibility is underscored by St. Aumar's later martial reaction to the exposure of Du Lache's part in the baroness's deceptions.

13. Entertained, regaled.

14. Mantua-maker: dressmaker, seamstress; tire-woman: hairdresser, maker of head-dresses. All of the shopkeepers mentioned here are letting out their places of business to the baroness for her assignations.

15. Valeria Messalina (d. A.D. 48), third wife of Claudius, emperor of Rome. Notorious for her lasciviousness and infidelity, she was put to death by her husband.

16. Not French; the name (sour-be) is no more than a bit of word-play hinting at this character's disposition.

17. To accomplish a purpose, to encompass; an archaic usage in Haywood's time, but still occasionally repeated for some years afterward.

18. Fr. *beau* (handsome), *clair* (clear). The name is obviously intended to idealize its owner, and the character himself is very probably a representation of Aaron Hill. See above, the introduction, xx.

19. Fr. *mont* (mount, hill), *amour* (love). Again, as with Beauclair, Haywood uses a name to idealize its owner. In this instance there are multiple meanings. The name can be read to mean "lover of Hill" (almost certainly in reference to Haywood herself), but it also suggests the erotic appeal of the chaste female body, since it refers explicitly to the genital area, or *mons veneris.* See above, the introduction, xx.

20. Fr. *sans* (without), *foi* (faith); thus, faithless. Haywood may have been echoing Spenser's use of the same name, in Book 2 of *The Faerie Queene,* for one of the three brothers (the other two are Sansjoy, "joyless," and Sansloy, "lawless") figuring in an episode concerning the suppression of the Protestant religion during the reign of Queen Mary.

21. Oaths; sworn promises to absolute secrecy.

22. Fr. *gaillard:* a vigorous, robust, strapping fellow. The same French word is also the name given to a spirited dance in triple time that remained popular well into the eighteenth century.

23. Fr. *ton* (tone, sound), *carré* (blunt, plain). The name does not seem to fit the character in his role as Du Lache's accomplice; but in the later (feigned) history he tells of himself, he is a soldier and thus aptly named.

24. Fr. *songe:* dream, fancy. The name is appropriate for one who lives by his wits or invention.

25. Until the French Revolution still a royal palace, originally built for Francis I

in 1546. Later French monarchs enlarged the palace and began the process of acquisition by which the Louvre came into possession of one of the world's great art collections. The Grande Galerie was opened to the public in 1793.

26. In Haywood's time the term *mademoiselle* (here in a common alternate spelling) was used in reference both to a single girl of marriageable age and a young woman already married.

27. A pocket was a bag or pouch either carried freely or (more likely in the present instance) sewn to the inside of a coat and large enough for a purse, letters, memorandum book, and other incidental items.

28. In this eighteenth-century usage a closet is not a storage space but a small private room for retirement or writing, usually located adjacent to a bedroom.

29. Clarification.

30. Fr. *ouvrier:* skilled worker. This woman is probably a milliner, dressmaker, or hairdresser; in any case, as the text goes on to make clear, she is one of those shopwomen whose places of business the baroness had earlier used for meeting her lovers.

31. Modern Fr. *faiblesses;* weaknesses, frailties. In the early eighteenth century, French still used "oi" instead of the later form "ai"; thus English *foibles* and French *foiblesses* have the same root and are exactly parallel.

32. That is, to increase his emotional anguish. "Upon the rack" was a conventional expression deriving from an early form of torture by which a victim's body was fastened to a frame and, with the wrists and ankles attached to rollers at each end, painfully stretched.

33. Obstacles, hindrances; an archaism in the early eighteenth century. Haywood here seems to use the word to mean regrets or remorse.

34. Gallantly, as a chevalier, a soldier.

35. Toncarr seems to refer to the two-year war (1716-18) between the Austrian and Ottoman empires, during which the French were allies of the former. Among other achievements, the victorious Austrians excluded the Turks from Hungary, which they had occupied for more than 160 years.

36. Obstinately attached to a creed, belief, or ritual, in this instance the marriage vows.

37. Courtesan, prostitute.

38. Whisper, as in tattle or gossip.

39. Haywood here seems to refer to a feature of the English legal system at the time. Montamour's brother is clearly a magistrate, specially commissioned to preside over criminal trials and to serve as an advisor to the state in legal and other matters. If Haywood was indeed of the Shropshire family of Fowler, the reference is most probably to her own brother, Sir Richard; see above, the introduction, x-xi.

40. Fr. *belle* (beautiful), *fleur* (flower). Given the character of this woman as one of the hosts to the baroness's illicit assignations, the name (although suitable for an embroiderer) is clearly ironic.

41. Or Tuileries, the palace built for Catherine Medici in the sixteenth century. The gardens, where Beauclair, the baroness, and Du Lache are to meet, were laid out

by the famous landscape architect André Le Nôtre in the seventeenth century; they are all that now remains of the palace, which was destroyed by fire in 1871.

42. In this character's name Haywood seems to conflate Fr. *tort* (wrong, injustice) and *tour* (turn, trick); the name is intended to suggest the cruelty of the baroness's dalliance with the count, whom she has duped into a belief that she loves him.

43. A common eighteenth-century noun form used to describe a person who lacks perception and consciousness or is incapable of deep feeling.

44. An archaism still common in eighteenth-century usage as an alternative to *either.*

45. Preceded, arrived before; an archaism still occurring in eighteenth-century usage.

46. In this usage the term *mansion* means a room or rooms of a house; the image, then, is of a fire in a basement or cellar.

47. Literally, a state of undress; but in the eighteenth century the term was used to refer to a negligence of dress, or dishevelment.

48. A convent or nunnery.

49. About twelve miles. A league was a European measure of distance, varying from country to country but usually estimated at approximately three English miles.

50. That is, Montamour has decided to become a nun, and to take her vows at the end of the mandatory year of probation.

51. Compliments, but here meaning the duties of a lover.

52. Topic of familiar conversation or gossip.

53. The word is employed broadly here (in a common eighteenth-century usage) to mean deception, though the familiar sense of casting off a lover is at issue too, as the baroness is prepared to do just that to Beauclair in order to save herself from her husband's wrath.

54. Unusual, surprising; here, in the sense of being alien to or inconsistent with her previous behavior. This usage is an archaism, rare in Haywood's time.

55. Foolish fancies, the products of an overactive imagination. The chimera was, in Greek mythology, a fantastic fire-breathing she-monster.

56. The name is intended to diminish the character: a (small) branch, a sprig; a child. Fr. *branché* means fashionable, trendy; Haywood's La Branche is an effeminate little fop (note the feminine *la*).

57. Abundance, profusion.

58. A card game popular in the eighteenth century, played by three persons with forty cards.

59. Crude, clumsy.

60. Good appearance, bearing.

61. Record, list.

62. The gentleman's code of honor required that one draw and fight if challenged. But Du Lache is a coward, and the count, by kicking him, inflicts the ultimate punishment of shame and humiliation.

63. This appears from the italics to be a quotation, but its source has not been traced.

64. In Greek mythology, the muse of tragedy.

65. Here *during* is used in an archaic sense as the present participle of the verb *dure,* to last or endure.

66. Public scandal.

67. A string or bit of thread. The allusion here is to the Greek myth of Theseus and the Minotaur, but the idea was so conventional that Haywood may have appropriated it without intending any reference to a particular source.

68. The Hospital of Saint Mary of Bethlehem, at the time London's largest asylum for the insane. The hospital dated originally from the thirteenth century, and since being rebuilt in 1674-75 had stood in Moorfields. The word *bedlam,* a corruption of "Bethlehem" (frequently shortened to "Bethlem," as here), became the common term to describe such scenes of chaos and frenzy as might be witnessed at this asylum, which was notorious for its squalor and its inhumane treatment of inmates.

69. Weakened, debilitated.

70. Here the term is used in a common eighteenth-century sense to mean plotter or contriver.

71. Unnatural, abnormal, extraordinary; a common eighteenth-century usage.

72. The preaching order of Saint Dominic, founded by its Spanish namesake (c. 1170-1221), was approved by Pope Honorius in 1216 and quickly spread throughout Europe and into England. From their dress the Dominican monks were called Black Friars.

73. *Venerable* is an epithet for ecclesiastics.

74. A coarse textile of inferior wool, woven upon a cotton warp, sometimes in a mixture of wool and flax.

75. A hod is a builder's device for carrying mortar, stones, or bricks.

76. A creeping herbal plant frequently grown at the borders of gardens or along walkways; its yellow and white flowers, apple-like in their scent, were (and still are) used in medicine for their tonic value. The plant has been traditionally associated with the experience of suffering women, as the more it is trodden the better it grows. Two works by twentieth-century feminists call up this association in their titles: *The Camomile: An Invention,* by Catherine MacFarlane Casswell (London: Chatto and Windus, 1922); *The Camomile Lawn,* by Mary Wesley (London: Macmillan, 1984).

77. Either Haywood is mistaken about the climate in and around Paris, which seems unlikely, or she means willows, the branches of which were traditionally cut for use on Palm Sunday.

78. In earlier times, *guitar* was frequently used as a generic term for the entire class of strummed instruments. Possibly Montamour plays a lute, or perhaps an early version of the modern guitar, with four or five "courses" (*i.e.,* one or more strings tuned to a single pitch) instead of the six found on instruments after the eighteenth century.

79. The verses that follow appear to be of Haywood's own original composition. They are not separately printed in her *Poems on Several Occasions* (included in vol. 4 of her *Works,* 1724), so it seems likely that they were written for this novel.

80. Damon was the generic name for a rustic swain, taken from the shepherd singer in Virgil's eighth *Eclogue.*

81. Here *devotion* means religious feeling.

82. Again, the verses that follow seem to have been composed by Haywood specifically for this novel; see above, n. 79.

83. Alternate form of Fr. *rêverie,* from which the English *reverie* was adapted in the seventeenth century; an archaism in Haywood's time.

84. That is, the god of love.

85. See above, n. 33.

86. Estimable.

87. Fr. *vraiment:* truly.

88. The Salic law, derived from the early code of the Salian Franks established in the sixth century, was a rule of succession to the throne that excluded women and men whose line of royal descent was only through women; the rule prevailed in France from 1316, when it was first given full legal force.

89. That is, out of the house.

90. The wheel was a Medieval instrument of torture, still used for punishment in France during Haywood's time, especially for treason. Du Lache, as the murderer of the baron (technically his master), would have been guilty of the crime of petty treason. The wheel's effect was excruciatingly painful and usually fatal, as the joints were dislocated and the bones broken.

91. The ancient god of marriage.

Lasselia

Title Page. The epigraph is from John Dryden's heroic play, *Tyrannick Love, or the Royal Martyr* (1669), 2.1.299-304. The name Lasselia, clearly an echo of the kinds of names associated with heroines of romance, seems also to combine Fr. *lascive* (lascivious, lewd) and *lasser* (to tire, weary, exhaust); it is thus perfectly appropriate for Haywood's passionate but troubled young girl. It is possible that the character of Lasselia, like the baroness of *The Injur'd Husband,* is based on an actual person; but if so, no model has ever been identified.

1. Edward Howard (1672-1731), eighth earl of Suffolk, a prominent Whig and sometime patron of writers. Haywood seems not to have known that the earldom of Bindon became extinct with the death (in February 1721/22, long before her dedication was written) of Howard's nephew and predecessor, Charles William.

2. Haywood may be quoting here from some contemporary, but no source has been traced. This complaint against her novels was in any case a common one, and her reference may be general rather than specific.

3. Sportive, playful.

4. An obscure reference. Haywood was entirely capable of merely hoping (as she seems to have done when dedicating *The Injur'd Husband* to Lady Howe) that a dedication might actually bring a favor or two (or a guinea or two), and so she may be

referring to some anticipated response. There is no surviving evidence of favors conferred by the earl, either before or after the publication of *Lasselia.* Indeed, for some unknown reason an enmity would later develop between Haywood and the Howard family, leading her to attack Mrs. Henrietta Howard as the licentious Ismonda in her *Secret History of the Present Intrigues of the Court of Caramania* (1726). Mrs. Howard was a friend of Alexander Pope, whose outrage at this attack was among the reasons for his savage treatment of Haywood in *The Dunciad.* See above, the introduction, xii.

5. Louis XIV, the "Sun King" (1638-1715). His long reign (from 1643 until his death) was marked by the great flourishing of French culture and, simultaneously, by ambitious national expansionism. His court was the scene of sexual promiscuity as well as glitter and glory, and Louis himself kept many mistresses—among them Mme De Montespan (see below, n. 6).

6. Françoise Athenaïs de Rochechouart, Marquise de Montespan (1641-1707). She became mistress to Louis XIV in 1667; thereafter, she had her marriage to the Marquis de Montespan annulled, and for a time she enjoyed significant influence in the court, as the king insisted on official recognition of her position. She bore Louis seven children before being displaced by other favorites. By giving the historical Mme de Montespan a prominent place in her story Haywood carries out the pretense that it is authentic; there is no evidence, however, that Montespan had such a niece as Lasselia.

7. Françoise d'Aubigné, Marquise de Maintenon (1635-1719). Originally married to the writer Paul Scarron, she became the king's mistress (one of the successors to Mme de Montespan) and then, in a secret ceremony, his second wife following the queen's death in 1683.

8. Lacking self-awareness, but also lacking sexual desire and emotional need.

9. See above, *The Injur'd Husband,* n. 55.

10. Fr. *brosse:* brush. The name is generic for a groomsman. It occurs again in Haywood's fictionalized scandal chronicle of the French court titled *Memoirs of the Baron de Brosse, Who was Broke on the Wheel in the Reign of Lewis XIV* (1724). In this narrative the title character is a rogue who meets his just reward at the hands of the beautiful Larissa, a resilient young woman who resists him, along with the courtly glitter he represents, and winds up her story happily as the wife of a count. It is hard to avoid the suspicion that this work and *Lasselia,* with their similarly named heroines, were intended as companion pieces.

11. The name is related to Fr. *valoir:* to be valued, considered meritorious. The lady is married; see above, *The Injur'd Husband,* n. 26.

12. The mythical serpent whose glance had the power to kill.

13. The name of the town is Coulommiers, and it is located about thirty-five miles east of Paris; in Haywood's time it was a small market center already becoming known for its cheese. Haywood miscalculates the distance; seven leagues are approximately twenty-one miles. See above, *The Injur'd Husband,* n. 49.

14. Haywood here appears to combine Fr. *ami* (friend) and *âme* (soul, feeling). The name is appropriate for this early embodiment of the type of the passionate, sentimental male.

15. See above, *The Injur'd Husband,* n. 58.

16. Excused, explained.

17. A familiar portent of doom, though the blood is also a sign of love or passion.

18. See above, *The Injur'd Husband,* n. 83.

19. See above, *The Injur'd Husband,* n. 31.

20. Annoying, vexing.

21. Wig.

22. A stand designed to hold pen, ink, and (sometimes) other writing accessories.

23. The verses that follow appear to be from Haywood's own pen; as they are not separately printed in her *Poems on Several Occasions* (see above, *The Injur'd Husband,* n. 79), they were no doubt written for inclusion in *Lasselia.*

24. An obsolete usage; though it hints at the modern connotation of feigning or deceit, the word here literally means to explain, profess, declare. This double sense was common in the early eighteenth century; Defoe, for example, employed it in the editor's preface to *Moll Flanders* (1722).

25. Violence; an archaism.

26. A reference to lotteries, still relatively new in England during Haywood's time but increasingly popular. Established first in sixteenth-century Venice, they were all the rage in France throughout the years in which *Lasselia* is set.

27. "And God blessed them, and God said unto them, Be fruitful, and multiply, and replenish the earth" (Genesis 1:28).

28. The name combines Fr. *doux* (soft, sweet) with an Anglicized form of Fr. *mourir* (to fade or die); thus, sweet death, which suggests the effects of love. But the name seems ironic for both of the daughters in the interpolated story that follows: the youngest degenerates from a lovely innocence into ruin and retreat; the eldest, embittered by her rejection, turns from an appealing beauty into a vengeful monster.

29. Ethiopian; in the eighteenth century, a generic term for a black person.

30. Adornment.

31. A child; the young woman is pregnant.

32. Fr. *sieur* (sir, monsieur), *blessé* (hurt, wounded). The title *sieur* makes it clear that this character is a gentleman of some standing; his surname almost exactly coincides with his eventual fate.

33. Duelling was a serious crime in France; royal edicts against it, with accompanying legislation, had become increasingly severe since the early seventeenth century, and during the reign of Louis XIV enforcement of anti-duelling laws was more vigorous than ever. If a duel was fatal, the penalty for the survivor might range from confiscation of property, to banishment, to death. See François Billacois, *The Duel: Its Rise and Fall in Early Modern France,* ed. and trans. Trista Selous (New Haven: Yale University Press, 1990), especially chap. 15.

34. To pause for rest and refreshment during a journey.

35. See above, *The Injur'd Husband,* n. 52.

Select Bibliography

Editions of *The Injur'd Husband* and *Lasselia*

The Injur'd Husband: or, The Mistaken Resentment. A Novel. London: For D. Browne, Jr., W. Chetwood and J. Woodman, and S. Chapman, 1723. (Published December 1722.)

Second Edition. London: For D. Browne, Jr., W. Chetwood and J. Woodman, and S. Chapman, 1723. This edition subsequently included in vol. 2 of Haywood's collected *Works* (1723-24).

Third Edition. Bound with *The British Recluse.* Dublin: For J. Watts, 1724; London: For D. Browne, Jr., and Sam. Chapman, 1725. This edition subsequently included in vol. 2 of Haywood's collected *Secret Histories, Novels and Poems* (1724; 4th ed., 1742). Reprinted in *Four Novels of Eliza Haywood,* ed. Mary Anne Schofield (Delmar, N.Y.: Scholars' Facsimiles and Reprints, 1983).

Lasselia: or, The Self-Abandon'd. A Novel. London: For D. Browne, Jr., and S. Chapman, 1724. (Published October 1723.) Reprinted in *Four Novels of Eliza Haywood,* ed. Schofield.

Second Edition. For D. Browne, Jr., and S. Chapman, 1724. This edition subsequently included in vol. 4 of Haywood's *Works* and in vol. 4 of her *Secret Histories, Novels and Poems.*

Other Works by Haywood in Select Modern Editions

Anti-Pamela; or, Feign'd Innocence Detected. In *Richardsoniana.* New York: Garland, 1975. A facsimile, part of a series devoted to reproduction of works prompted by or otherwise connected with the novels of Samuel Richardson.

Bath-Intrigues: In Four Letters to a Friend. Intro. Simon Varey. Augustan Reprint Society No. 236. Los Angeles: William Andrews Clark Memorial Library, 1986. Facsimile, with brief introduction.

The British Recluse; or, The Secret History of Cleomira. In *Popular Fiction by Women: An Anthology,* ed. Paula Backscheider and John J. Richetti. Oxford: Clarendon, 1996. Helpful introductory discussion of Haywood, some annotation.

Fantomina; or, Love in a Maze. In *Popular Fiction by Women,* ed. Backscheider and Richetti.

The Female Spectator: Being Selections from Mrs. Eliza Haywood's Periodical. Ed. Gabrielle M. Firmager. Bristol, U.K.: Bristol Classical Press, 1993. Reprinted excerpts from the first collected edition, 1746.

Four Novels of Eliza Haywood. Ed. Schofield. Includes, besides *The Injur'd Husband* and *Lasselia, The Force of Nature* and *The Perplex'd Dutchess.* Facsimiles, with a brief general introduction.

The History of Miss Betsy Thoughtless. Ed. Beth Fowkes Tobin. Oxford: Oxford Univ. Press, 1997. A critical reading edition, with introduction and explanatory notes.

The History of Miss Betsy Thoughtless. Ed. Christine Blouch. Petersborough, Ont.: Broadview Press, 1998. A critical reading edition, with introduction and explanatory notes.

The History of Jemmy and Jenny Jessamy. Ed. John Richetti. Eighteenth-Century Novels by Women. Lexington: Univ. Press of Kentucky, forthcoming. A critical reading edition, with introduction and explanatory notes.

Love in Excess; or, The Fatal Enquiry. Ed. David Oakleaf. Peterborough, Ont.: Broadview Press, 1994; rpt. 1996. A critical reading edition, with introduction and explanatory notes.

The Masquerade Novels of Eliza Haywood. Ed. Mary Anne Schofield. Delmar, N.Y.: Scholars' Facsimiles and Reprints, 1986. Includes *Fantomina, The Fatal Secret, Idalia,* and *The Masqueraders.* Facsimiles, with a brief general introduction.

Philidore and Placentia; or, L'Amour trop Delicat. In *Four before Richardson: Select English Novels, 1720-27,* ed. William H. McBurney. Lincoln: Univ. of Nebraska Press, 1963. Modernized text, with explanatory notes.

The Plays of Eliza Haywood. Ed. Valerie G. Rudolph. New York: Garland, 1983. Includes *The Fair Captive; Frederick, Duke of Brunswick-Lunenburgh;*

The Opera of Operas; and *A Wife to Be Lett.* Facsimile reprints, with brief introductions.

Three Novellas: The Distress'd Orphan, The City Jilt, The Double Marriage. Ed. Earla A. Wilputte. East Lansing, Mich.: Colleagues Press, 1995. Brief biographical and critical introduction, some annotation.

The Foundations of the Novel. Gen. ed., Michael F. Shugrue. New York: Garland, 1972-73. This facsimile series includes the following works by Haywood, all with brief introductions by Josephine Grieder: *Adventures of Eovaai, The Agreeable Caledonian, Memoirs of a Certain Island Adjacent to the Kingdom of Utopia, The Mercenary Lover, The Rash Resolve,* and *The Secret History of the Present Intrigues of the Court of Caramania.*

The Flowering of the Novel. Gen. ed., Michael F. Shugrue. New York: Garland, 1974-75. This facsimile series includes the following works by Haywood (there are no introductions): *The Fortunate Foundlings, Life's Progress through the Passions, The History of Jemmy and Jenny Jessamy,* and *The Virtuous Villager.*

Secondary Works

Ballaster, Ros. *Seductive Forms: Women's Amatory Fiction from 1684 to 1740.* Oxford: Clarendon, 1992.

Beasley, Jerry C. "Eliza Haywood." In *The Dictionary of Literary Biography: British Novelists, 1660-1800,* ed. Martin C. Battestin, vol. 39, pt. 1. Detroit: Gale, 1985.

Blouch, Christine. "Eliza Haywood: An Annotated Critical Bibliography." In *Eighteenth-Century Anglo-American Women Novelists: A Critical Reference Guide,* ed. Doreen Saar and Mary Anne Schofield (New York: Prentice-Hall, 1997), 263-300. The most complete and current listing available.

———. "Eliza Haywood: Questions in the Life and Works." Ph.D. diss., Univ. of Michigan, 1991.

———. "Eliza Haywood and the Romance of Obscurity." *Studies in English Literature* 31 (1991): 535-51.

Bowers, Toni O'Shaughnessy. "Sex, Lies, and Invisibility: Amatory Fiction from the Restoration to Mid-Century." In *The Columbia History of the British Novel,* ed. John Richetti et al. (New York: Columbia Univ. Press, 1994), 50-72.

Craft-Fairchild, Catherine. *Masquerade and Gender: Disguise and Female Iden-*

tity in Eighteenth-Century Fictions by Women. University Park: Pennsylvania State Univ. Press, 1993.

Guskin, Phyllis J. Introduction to *Clio: The Autobiography of Martha Fowke Sansom (1689-1736).* Newark: Univ. of Delaware Press, 1997.

London, April. "Placing the Female: The Metonymic Garden in Amatory and Pious Narrative, 1700-1740." In *Fetter'd or Free? British Women Novelists, 1670-1815,* ed. Mary Anne Schofield and Cecilia Macheski (Athens: Ohio Univ. Press, 1986), 101-23.

Pettit, Alexander. "Our Fictions and Eliza Haywood's Fictions." In *Talking Forward, Talking Back: Critical Dialogues with the Enlightenment,* ed Rüdiger Ahrens and Kevin L. Cope. New York: AMS, 1997.

Richetti, John J. *Popular Fiction before Richardson: Narrative Patterns 1700-1739.* Oxford: Clarendon, 1969.

———. "Voice and Gender in Eighteenth-Century Fiction: Haywood to Burney." *Studies in the Novel* 19 (1987): 263-72.

Schofield, Mary Anne. *Eliza Haywood.* Boston: Twayne, 1985.

———. *Masking and Unmasking the Female Mind: Disguising Romances in Feminine Fiction, 1713-1799.* Newark: Univ. of Delaware Press, 1990.

———. *Quiet Rebellion: The Fictional Heroines of Eliza Fowler Haywood.* Washington, D.C.: Univ. Press of America, 1982.

Schulz, Dieter. "'Novel,' 'Romance,' and Popular Fiction in the First Half of the Eighteenth Century." *Studies in Philology* 70 (1973): 77-91.

Spacks, Patricia Meyer. "Ev'ry Woman Is at Heart a Rake." *Eighteenth-Century Studies* 8 (1974): 27-46.

Spencer, Jane. *The Rise of the Woman Novelist: From Aphra Behn to Jane Austen.* London: Basil Blackwell, 1986.

Spender, Dale. *Mothers of the Novel.* London: Pandora, 1986.

Todd, Janet. *The Sign of Angellica: Women, Writing, and Fiction 1660-1800.* London: Virago, 1989.

Whicher, George Frisbie. *The Life and Romances of Mrs. Eliza Haywood.* New York: Columbia Univ. Press, 1915. Includes a nearly exhaustive listing of Haywood's works.

Williamson, Marilyn. *Raising Their Voices: British Women Writers, 1650-1750.* Detroit: Wayne State Univ. Press, 1990.

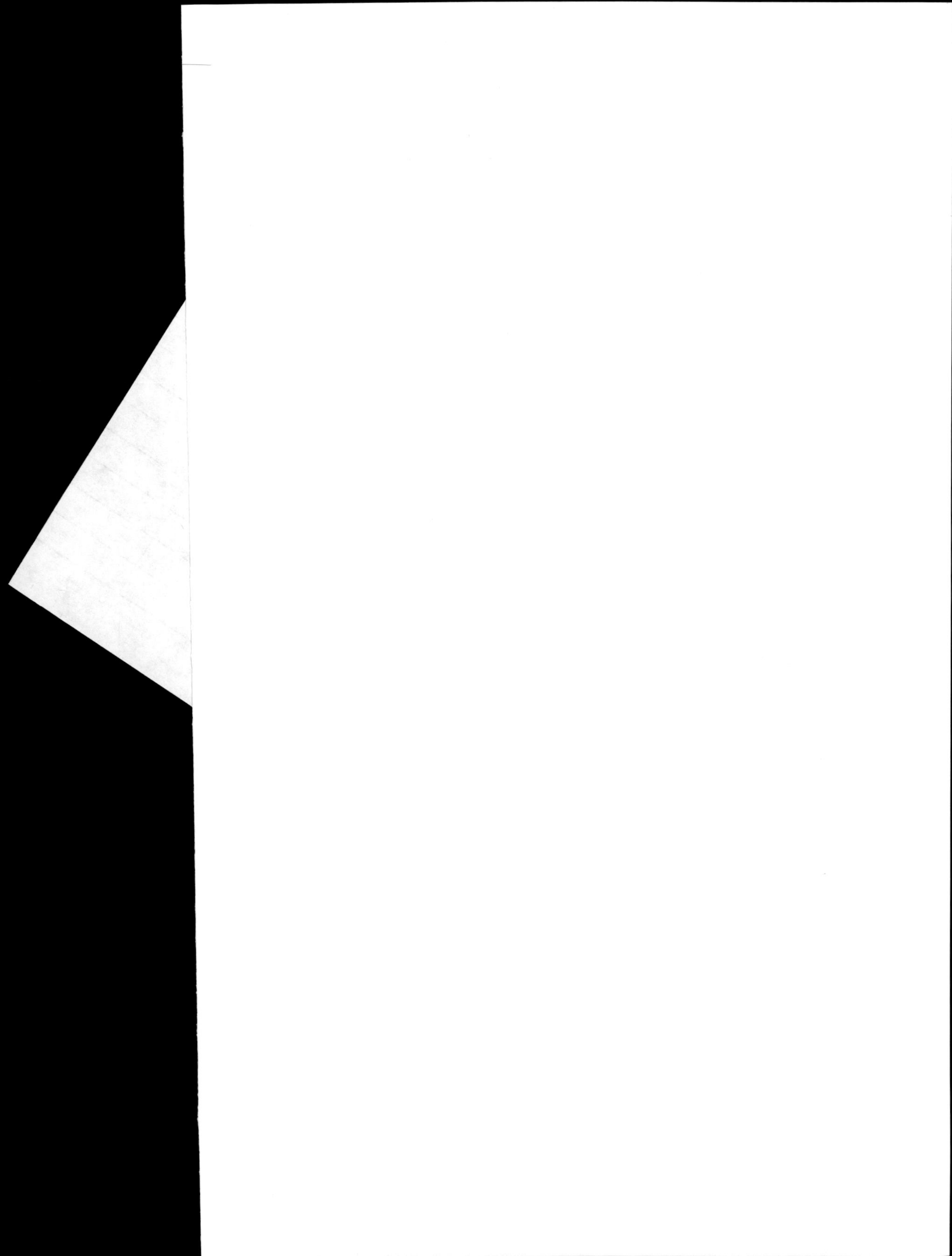

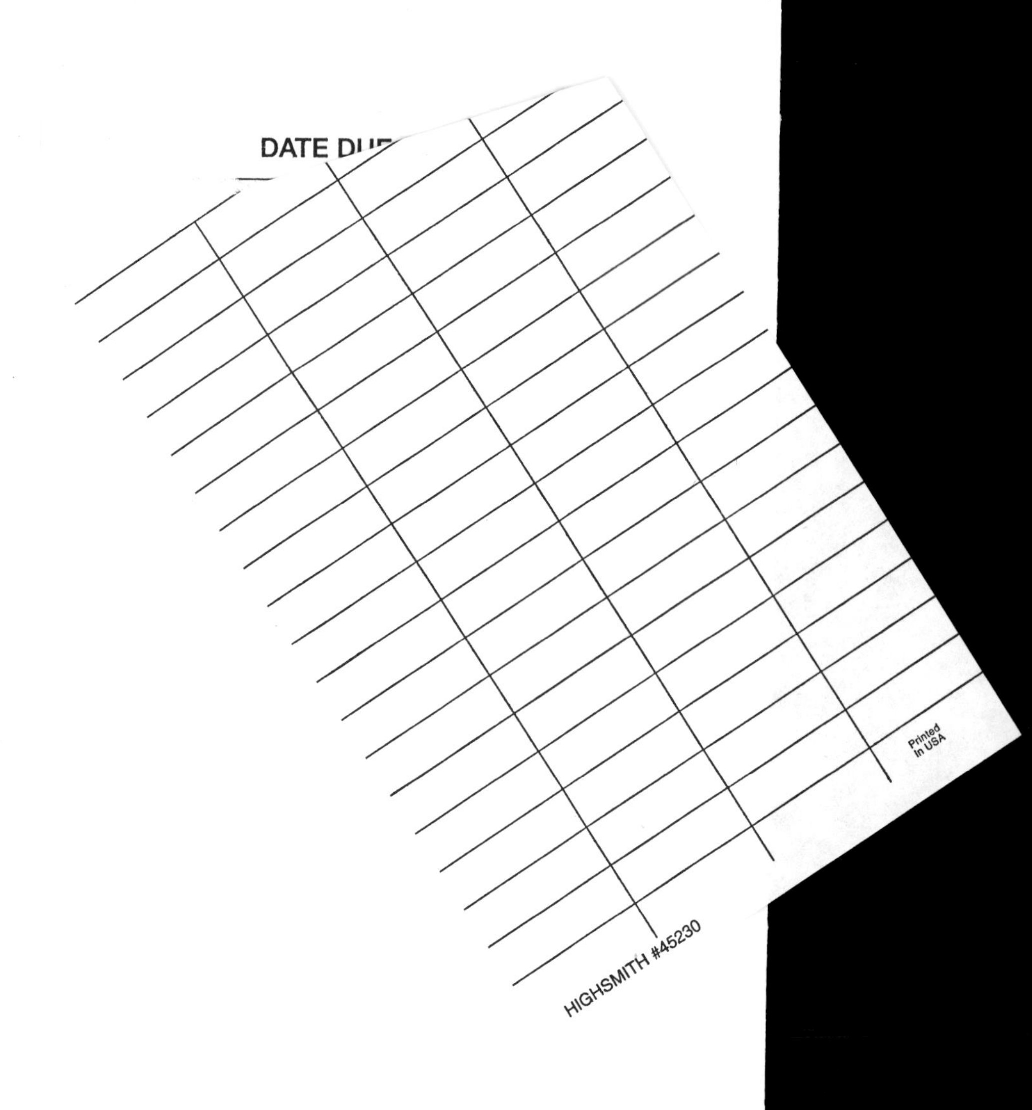